PASSIONATE BARGAIN

She gasped as his tongue teased hers, then ventured over the velvet curve of her lip. Her fingers crept up his muscled forearm and rested lightly on his broad shoulders. As the kiss deepened, Sara's heart began to pound, and a strange, lightheaded sensation swept over her. She found herself pressing against him until she realized what was happening, then suddenly tore her mouth from his. Her dark eyes probed his face, reading the smouldering passion in his blue eyes.

Sara's breath caught in her throat. Desire and resistance fought within her, drawing her body closer though her hands gently pushed against his chest. . . .

"I know I owe you a lot," Sara said, "but I don't owe you my body!"

CHRISTINE CARSON

LEISURE BOOKS ae NEW YORK CITY

A LEISURE BOOK

Published by

Dorchester Publishing Co., Inc.
6 East 39th Street
New York, NY 10016

Copyright © 1988 by Christine Carson

All rights reserved. No part of this book may be reproduced or transmitted in any form or by any electronic or mechanical means, including photocopying, recording, or by any information storage and retrieval system, without the written permission of the Publisher, except where permitted by law.

Printed in the United States of America

PROLOGUE

Colorado Territory
Winter, 1843

Crying Wind crept through the inky darkness to the red-quarried cliffs above the circle of Conestogas in the grass valley below. The smouldering embers of a campfire gave a feeble glow to the sleeping camp as Crying Wind's dark eyes moved over the wagons, her mind troubled. She thought of the palefaces and the evil spirit they had brought upon Ute land and her dark eyes burned with anger.

Her anger was quickly tempered, however, by the gentle breath of the sleeping babies in her arms. Slowly, her black eyes dropped to the babies, and she lifted first one rabbit skin, then another, peering impassively into the faces of newborn twins—a boy and a girl. The age-old superstition that twins were bad medicine loomed in her mind, and new fear thundered in her heart as Crying Wind stared at the infants. Their faces shone white. Even though the moon was small, it was the color of the palefaces.

She had brought shame and disgrace to her people. These were not cherished Utes, whose births would have been a joyous occasion; therefore, no warrior had brought firewood to her lodge in her final days. Nor had she gone to the birthing lodge where she could kneel on a straw-covered mat for the birth. Instead, she had fled to a secret cave when the ravaging pains began. She had begged the Great Spirit for death but death had not come; instead she had given birth to two healthy infants. Afterwards, she had hobbled to the icy mountain stream to bathe herself and the babies; then she had wrapped them in rabbit skins and crept to the high red rocks. She had intended to offer them to the Great Spirit to purge her sins, but when she reached the jagged rocks, she had spotted the wagons in the valley, and her plans changed.

As she stood gazing at the settlers' wagons, her mind drifted back to happier days, when the Utes had roamed freely from the land of bubbling springs to the open plains. But then the palefaces had come, over Ute trails and across Ute valleys, their greedy eyes seeking the buffalo and the beaver, their careless axes felling the big cottonwoods for reckless fires that blazed high in the night skies.

Tears filled her dark eyes as she recalled the evil man—the strong, fair-skinned man with his hairy face and eyes the color of the forest pine. Her search for pinion nuts had led her into their camp and, too late, she had remembered the warning of her brother Bear Claw, who had cared for her since the death of their parents during the Winter of No Sun.

The man who rode the white magic dog had motioned to her, holding out a shiny wristband of silver. He had dropped down from the magic dog, speaking in a strange tongue, his lips spread in his hairy face. Fear mingled with curiosity; her moccasined feet stilled as he approached. Then his green eyes changed, his lips turned downward. Too late, she sensed danger. The smell of his breath held the fire of the potion the palefaces left as a gift for the braves. They had drunk the firewater when the moon was round, and she had watched with disgust as her people behaved like sick dogs, sprawled in the dust.

A gasp of horror clogged her throat as the evil man reached for her. She wished for enchanted moccasins—like those of the legend—so that she could outrun him. But her moccasins were not enchanted, and her thin body had failed in her battle with the strong paleface.

He had ripped the doeskin skirt from her legs, thrusting the spear of his loins into that special place that all Ute maidens kept sacred. As her skin tore and the stench of firewater stung her face, she had ceased to fight, knowing it was useless, and prayed that the horrible, knife-like pain would also reach to her heart and end its wild beat. He had left her in the shade of the cottonwood, with only the pounding feet of the magic dog to drown out her soft cries of pain.

A deep, wrenching sigh shook her now as she stared at the wagons. She suddenly knew what she must do. She would return them to their people, the nation of palefaces. But life would not be easy for them. They were neither Ute nor paleface. Her eyes lifted to the sky, again seeking guidance from the Great

Spirit. She prayed for their lives, that somehow they might survive in the strange world to which they were going. The little brave would have to be strong and noble, like the wild eagle. The little squaw must have a spirit that would sing even when it suffered, like the little dove.

She opened her eyes and looked at the babies, Wild Eagle and Little Dove. She had named them well, though they would never know their true names; still, *she* would know, she and the Great Spirit.

Crying Wind began to maneuver her way down the rocky path leading to the valley of wagons. Soon the sun would set fire to the mountain of rocks; soon the palefaces would build their morning fires. Her steps quickened.

Farthest from the fire and the man who guarded the camp, two wagons were swathed in darkness. Drumbeats of fear pounded in her chest, and her stomach heaved as if she had drunk firewater. She pushed on, moving like a wispy shadow that melted into the darkness of night as she crouched to place a baby beside the rear wheel of each wagon. Her cold fingers darted inside the blanket, pinching one tiny foot until a small cry rose in protest. Crying Wind turned and fled through the darkness as the cry sharpened to a high, thin wail.

She did not look back until she reached the high red rocks. Below her the camp sprang to life as the small and distant cry of the infant filled the night.

She crossed her arms over her throbbing belly, as blood trickled down her thighs. Biting her lips against the pain, she turned and hobbled up the side of the mountain, then hesitated for one last glance downward where the pale, yellow flame of lanterns wavered in the darkness and loud voices drowned out the baby's cry.

As she watched the babies being lifted from the ground, Crying Wind's body began to tremble beneath her patched, muddy dress. The bad seed that had entered her body had blossomed and sprung to life in the warmth of her womb. She had not wanted the twins who would bring evil to her village, yet her body had nourished them. And her heartbeat had quickened when she felt their movements within her. In a strange way, she had relished the new life, and now she felt as though a piece of her soul had been torn from her and cast into the night, into the arms of the strange palefaces.

For a long time, she stood as still as a spirit, watching the distant camp . . . and the sadness in her soul carved a trail of tears down her frozen cheeks.

1

Dawn at Jackson's Post was bleak and bone-chilling. Fresh snow ccovered the dome of Pikes Peak, blanketed the canyons and valleys, and piled up against fence posts.

The post contained ten square, one-story buildings of slab pine, with a large courtyard in the center of each. Abruptly, the door of the first cabin opened and a large, gray-haired woman stepped out.

Elsie Jackson thrust calloused hands on her plump hips and squinted up at sunny sky. Eighteen years of Colorado weather told her that the week's snow had ended, at least temporarily. She heaved a relieved sigh as her eyes fell to the post, scanning with pride the general store, the blacksmith shop, the guest cabins and the kitchen-dining hall. She and her husband Ernest had built every square inch of the place, starting from nothing. Although Ernest would never admit it, his general store had drawn trappers from the foothills, but it had been Elsie's good cooking that kept them coming back. Now the post was the center of activity between Pueblo and Colorado City.

Elsie turned back inside and lumbered

across the plank floor to a small bedroom. She paused in the doorway, staring with pride at the young woman sleeping peacefully in the narrow iron bed.

Sleek black hair was swept back from an oval face in one long, gleaming braid which, during her sleep, had wound itself around her slender throat. A high forehead, slim small nose, and delicate lips were balanced by pronounced cheekbones over hollow cheeks.

Sunken cheeks, Elsie thought, shaking her gray head. The girl wâs much too thin! As she looked at her, she felt a sudden remorse for being unable to provide a better life for Sara, but she'd done the best she could ever since the baby had been left at their wagon. A baby when her womb was barren!

"Wake up, Sara," she said with a tenderness rarely revealed in Elsie's busy schedule of herding stray chickens, dogs, errant children and drunken traders from her doorstep. "I'm goin' on to the kitchen to build a fire. We gotta fix a bigger breakfast today. More riders come in from Taos last night." She paused to seize a strand of steel-gray hair that dared escape the fierce bun at her nape. "That Missouri family stayin' in the last cabin's been prowling since daybreak. Kids are probably hungry. We've got dough to knead, hoecakes to mix and fatback to fry." Thoughts of hard work sharpened her tone. "Wake up, you hear?"

"Mmmm-hmmm." The dark head tossed on the feather pillow and one long, slender leg twitched beneath the mound of quilts.

"I'm gone," Elsie called, stomping back through the cabin and slamming the front door to underscore her command.

"I don't want to get up!" Sara called after her, as her inky lashes parted and dark eyes roamed the dim room. The thought of leaving her warm nest for another work-filled day brought a heavy sigh to her lips, yet she forced herself to toss back the covers. In her own way, she was as conscious of her duties as her mother.

She was slim and tall, with long, fine-toned legs. Those legs made a swift leap to the small rag rug that offered a patch of warmth to her feet. Shivering into her long flannel gown, she leaned over the chest and plunged her fingers into the cold pan of water there. As she splashed her sleepy face, a blur of hungry faces filled her mind. She could easily envision the crowd at breakfast, elbowing each other around the ten-foot table, grabbing food and talking with their mouths full.

Fifty-niners, they called themselves, though this was '61. But ever since gold had been discovered at Cherry Creek, they'd stampeded the Territory, riding donkeys, mules and horses. Some walked, others rode in sleek prairie schooners. She sighed again, reaching into the chest for her step-ins. Their clothes were mud-crusted and their faces were covered with beards. All had that same dazed look in their eyes when they talked about the diggings—gold fever! She shook her head, mentally scolding herself for complaining. After all, it was miners' money that put food on their table and clothes on their backs.

Her mother's departure had admitted a gust of cold air into the small, drafty cabin and the cold quickened her movements. She yanked on her camisole and wound the long braid into a thick coil at the nape of her neck. From a peg on the wall, she lifted her gray muslin dress and tugged it over her head. The soft folds of the skirt draped over high firm breasts, slid down the tiny waist and gently rounded hips, then fell to the floor, covering her only decent petticoat.

Her cold fingers moved stiffly over the buttons of her dress as she glanced down her shivering body, suddenly recalling those awkward years when she had been all arms and legs, as gangly as the undernourished colts in the overcrowded corral. Unlike her mother, most Colorado women were as thin as a blade of prairie grass as a result of their long, work-filled days. Sara had finally rounded into curves at breast and hip, yet her five-foot, seven-inch body registered only a dozen or so notches over the hundred mark on the scales at the post, and her mother nagged her constantly.

She hurried into the tiny living room, frowning at the disorder that neither she nor Elsie had time to remedy. She pulled on her kid boots, threw her black woolen cape about her shoulders, and took a deep breath. It would be weeks before the winter broke, but to relieve the monotony, her mind seized images of the columbine that would bloom in the meadows, the crystal streams thick with trout, the golden sunshine glinting over the mountain peak. Those images were precious treasures to her during the long, harsh winters, and yet she loved Colorado. She wouldn't want to live anywhere else.

She lifted the door latch and stepped outside, blinking into the morning sunshine. The bright light filled the depths of her dark eyes, and they gleamed like polished onyx in contrast to the pristine snow.

The creak of the gate drew her attention to the guard who was admitting an early visitor. Her eyes widened. She'd always loved horses, though she'd never owned one, but now she was looking at the biggest, most beautiful horse she'd ever seen. It was a black stallion with a white stocking extending to his left knee. Its dark coat gleamed as though oiled in the morning sunlight. After a few seconds, Sara lifted her eyes from the horse to the rider. When she did, she was even more startled.

He sat tall in the saddle, wearing a fringed buckskin shirt and patched trousers. A cap of the same buckskin sat on blonde hair that glinted golden in the sunlight. His face was covered with a dark brown beard, but the eyes were such a vivid blue that even from a distance she could define the color and shape. His attention was centered on the general store, and to her disappointment, he never once looked her way.

"Sara! Sara!" Young Will Brantley had leaped up from his game of marbles and was racing over the snowy courtyard to her doorstep. "Are you gonna think up some kind of game for us today?"

A gentle smile touched Sara's small mouth as she stared at Will, bundled to the chin in his heavy coat, yet already missing his fur hat. Pale brown curls rioted over his thin face, lit by a pair of sharp brown eyes, eagerly awaiting her answer.

"If I have time, Will," she reached out to playfully muss his curls. "I have a busy day and—"

"You better!" The full lips thrust into a threatening pout. "There ain't nothin' else to do at this stinkin' post. Yore pa won't let us have snowball fights or do anything fun."

Sara's smile faded as she darted a glance back toward the general store where the tall, golden-haired man had dismounted and was quietly observing an argument in progress on the steps of the general store.

Ernest Jackson, her adopted father, stood haggling over a team of mules with one of the fifty-niners. Ernest was a skinny, raw-boned man whose oily black hair and large hooked nose made him startlingly ugly.

Will sidled up to her, his brown eyes filled with concern. "He ain't really yore pa, is he?"

The words brought a sharp ache to her heart

as her gaze wavered, then dropped. She had never ceased to wonder who her parents really were. Kidnapped from one wagon train and left at another by Indians, her mother had always told her. Still, she searched the faces of everyone who came to the post, wondering . . . always wondering.

"I'm sorry." The small cold hand touched hers.

She looked back into the boy's sympathetic face and sighed. "He raised me, Will. He's the only father I've ever known. Now"—she forced a bright smile—"you be a good boy, and I'll try to think up something fun for this afternoon."

"Yippee!" Will shouted, racing back across the courtyard to join the others.

A frown gathered between her dark brows as she pulled up her hood against the cold. Ernest Jackson had never wanted her, she had always sensed that. A son would have pleased him, but he regarded a girl as a luxury he couldn't afford. When he considered her worth, he seemed to forget the long hours she worked in the kitchen and the time she spent entertaining the children whose parents were staying at the post until spring break-up. But Elsie always defended her, and it had been Elsie's love that had sustained her for eighteen years, providing the comfort and security she needed when she so often felt lonely, confused and bewildered.

"Them mules is worth more than you're offering, Jackson!" The fifty-niner shouted angrily.

"Take it or leave it!" Jackson countered, raking through his greasy dark hair.

"I'd leave it." A Southern drawl flowed over the sharply spoken words. The handsome stranger, who had been leaning idly against a post, now took a step forward, towering over the other men. "If this man won't pay you a fair price, Abe Williams up at Three Mile will."

Sara's breath caught, and she stared in amazement. Few men challenged her father.

Ernest spat a stream of tobacco juice into the snow. "Fella, what business is it of yores?"

A cynical smile twisted the stranger's lips as his broad shoulders rose and fell in a careless shrug. "Probably none." He turned to untie his horse from the hitching rail, then thrust a leather boot into the stirrup and swung his lean body into the saddle with the grace of one accustomed to living on the back of a horse. "The trappers and fifty-niners are keeping you in business, sir," he called over his shoulder. "It wouldn't hurt you to remember that." He touched a bronze hand to his cap, then turning the big stallion's head, he cantered out of the post without a backward glance.

Sara's eyes followed, widening in curious fascination. He was the most strikingly handsome man she'd ever seen, but what she admired even more was the smooth, soft-spoken way he'd called Ernest a cheat.

"Reckon I'll take that feller's advice," the other man said with a sneer, as his eyes swept Ernest.

Sara grimaced, dreading Ernest's black mood for the rest of the day. She averted her eyes to the snowy path and hurried to the squat, one-room dwelling that served as the post kitchen. She despised the tactics her father used against his traders and was secretly glad he had failed this time. If not for the stranger, Ernest would have bought the man's mules for half their worth, fattened them cheaply, then sold them to the next wagon train.

Where, she wondered as she glanced absently toward the gate, which was closed again, had the stranger come from? Where was he going now? She sighed, trying to dismiss him from her thoughts as her boots crunched over the thick snow. The deep, stinging cold brought to her the familiar smells of the post—hay, leather, woodsmoke. Smells were important to her, giving her a sense of identity. A part of her had never accepted the post as home, or the Jacksons as her family. Of course she knew she was adopted, but something more basic than that bothered her: a sense of belonging. While she had spent her life in the shadow of Pikes Peak, she'd never felt at home. And yet, she'd tried to tell herself, any girl would feel the same, growing up at a rowdy post rather than a civilized town back East or a more comfortable house in Colorado City.

She scraped her boots on the kitchen step, then lifted the wooden latch and dashed into the cozy kitchen.

"It's about time!" Elsie, floured to the elbows, swung her big frame around, her eyes pinning Sara to the door.

"Don't worry, Ma," Sara removed her cape and dropped it on a peg by the door. "We'll get everyone fed." She was never intimidated by her mother's strong voice. It was just her way. Sara could count on her hand the number of times Elsie had spanked her as a child. She could remember many more times when she needed discipline and Elsie had backed down.

"Them blasted roosters!" Elsie's face reddened as the Santa Fe cocks began to crow. "I told Ernest I won't stand for any more cock fights!" Her big hands attacked the ball of dough and the calloused red fingers began to knead.

"Did he agree?" Sara asked, concealing her cynical tone behind an amused grin.

Elsie turned her attention to the flour barrel, avoiding a reply. "Money! That's all he thinks about!" She glanced across at Sara, the flush on her face deepening. "They're gambling and drinking in that last cabin; now if them cock fights continue, there's no tellin' what's liable to break loose. Why, there could even be a killin'!"

"Ma, I'm tired of all these drifters," Sara said as she grabbed an apron and whisked it over her head. "They're rude, they spit tobacco juice on the walk, and they stare and use bad grammar."

"That's why I'm payin' that uppity Eastern

lady to teach you. Lucky for us, her husband got down on his luck and they ended up here instead of Pueblo. She's been a real blessing."

Sara nodded, thinking that Amanda Murray had influenced her life more than anyone she knew. Amanda was soft-spoken, cultured, and once a beauty, though she was quickly aging in the rugged west. Amanda had taught school back in Boston. Deprived of the work she loved, she had viewed Sara as both a challenge and an escape from dull post life. She'd seized the opportunity to pour etiquette, religion, and knowledge into Sara's eager young mind. Sara had thrived beneath Amanda's tutoring in the two years the woman had lived at the post.

"I want a better life for you," Elsie grumbled, more to herself than to Sara, as she kneaded dough.

"Oh, well, maybe I'll meet a rich man," Sara said, her eyes filled with dreams. "He'll fall in love with me and—"

"*Indians!*"

The hoarse shouts of warning reverberated over the peaceful post, bringing Elsie and Sara to the door.

A dozen Indians were galloping into the courtyard, scattering snow, dogs, and children in a wave of panic. They wore fringed buckskin and beaded headbands. One man, obviously the leader, wore a headdress of white feathers.

"They threatened to attack if they can't trade!" the guard at the gate was yelling.

The leader edged his white horse ahead of his braves as his eyes, black as midnight, scanned every building. There was something about him that commanded attention. He held his head high and proud, and his face bore a stony expression. It was an arresting face—lean, taut skin over rigid bones, a prominent nose and piercing black eyes. He drew up before the hitching rail of the general store as his braves fanned out around him.

Ernest Jackson threw open the door and scrambled onto the boardwalk, gaping at the startling sight before him. The cold black eyes that swept Jackson flashed contempt as Bear Claw shifted on his horse and cooly surveyed the gawking crowd. A few brave men took a step closer, curiously inspecting the jagged scar on his right cheek.

Bear Claw was a legend in the Pikes Peak country. The story of the slashing claw mark was spun around many a campfire, and now almost everyone knew about the young brave who had encountered a huge grizzly in the Tarryalls and had been forced to fight it single-handedly. He had escaped with only that deep jagged slash from the bear's claw across his cheek, while the grizzly had fallen to his death beneath the speed and skill of the brave's tomahawk.

The chief was motioning at a young brave behind him, who dropped from his horse and pulled down an armload of buffalo hides. Ernest Jackson's jaw sagged at the sight of the hides, so hard to come by now. Another brave followed with beadwork, water-jug baskets, and wooden flutes.

"You want to trade, Chief?" Ernest yelled, a wicked gleam rising in his narrow-set eyes.

Bear Claw sat rigid on the white horse, whose muscles were twitching beneath the firm hand of restraint. "The young squaw." Bear Claw's deep voice boomed over the courtyard, quiet as death. "We trade for the young squaw."

"*Squaw*?" Ernest croaked. "We got no squaws here!" His greedy eyes returned to the buffalo hides, the handmade pieces that would seduce the miners into parting with their gold dust and coins. But this fool Indian was wantin' some damned squaw!

"Squaw!" Bear Claw insisted with a brisk nod.

Ernest's mouth dropped open as his eyes flew over the crowd. There were no squaws living at the post. Was this savage crazy? But the hides, he had to have the hides!

"What about some white lightnin' from Taos, Chief?" Ernest asked, a sly grin spreading over his yellow teeth.

Bear Claw glared at him. "Trapper Sam tell us papoose left at your wagon. Papoose belong to Crying Wind."

Ernest sucked in his breath as his eyes slid to the kitchen where Elsie and Sara watched from the open door. *Sara*! They wanted Sara! Jackson clawed at the tight collar of his flannel shirt, as he forced a hollow laugh from his tight throat.

"Chief, you got me confused with someone

else! Why, I ain't been in no wagon train. I been at this post for eighteen years!"

The muscles in Bear Claw's face clenched as he ground his jaws together, and a murderous warning leapt into his black eyes.

"Crying Wind leave two papoose eighteen winters past," he countered. "Crying Wind dying. She want squaw."

Shocked whispers flew over the crowd. Heads turned, eyes shot to the kitchen door, suddenly closing.

"You take," Bear Claw said, motioning toward their offering placed on the steps of the general store. "When sun rise again, we come for squaw. No squaw"—he touched the pouch of arrows strapped to his side—"we fight."

He swung the white horse around and motioned to his braves. The hard-packed snow flew into the air, settling again into wet clumps as the horses thundered through the gate. As soon as the gate slammed shut, shouts of panic erupted across the post. Men cursed, women shrieked, and Will Brantley tore out for the kitchen, yelling for Sara.

The sound of wood striking wood captured the attention of the shuffling crowd as the kitchen door was flung wide to bang against the wall. Elsie marched out into the courtyard, her long skirts billowing in the wind, her plump hands still floured, thrust in determined fists on her large hips.

"Nobody's proved Sara belongs to this Crying Wind," she yelled, her pale blue eyes moving over each face in the crowd. "Why, she's lighter-skinned than half of you! They just want her, that's all. They've seen her and they want her."

"Elsie, why start a war over it?" someone yelled. "Couldn't Sara just visit the old squaw? Be nice to her, then return?"

"No!"

"Are you askin' us to fight 'em off, then?" A small, scowling man stepped forward. "'Cause we got a war on our hands come sunrise if we don't figger somethin' out."

"I'll not turn my daughter over to them savages!" Elsie shouted, her voice and her eyes daring anyone to challenge her. "And that's final!" She whirled and lumbered back inside, her large body stiff with pride. But her spine felt the cold breath of terror, a terror that surpassed all the other terrors of her life.

Her steps quickened until she was almost running by the time she reached the kitchen. Her hands trembled on the door, trembled even more as she slammed it and shot the bolt. She turned slowly, dreading to face Sara, who was pacing the floor, wringing her hands.

"Here now"—Elsie laid a protective arm around her shoulder—"don't look so scared, honey. Ain't nobody takin' you away."

"Is it true?" she demanded. "Am I the daughter of Crying Wind?"

"Course not!" Elsie began to pace the floor with her. "They just watched you from the cliffs and wanted you—like all red-blooded males!" She yanked a stray hair back into her bun. "Why, them Cheyennes and Arapahoes are attackin' wagon trains and takin' the women home as squaws. The Utes are gettin' ideas now. But they'll not get you, baby!" She pulled Sara tight against her bosom, heaving with erratic pounding of her heart. "I love you as my own. *They'll not get you!*"

"Ma, I don't want anyone killed because of me," Sara protested, anxiously rubbing her forehead, trying to think. "Maybe I should go."

"No! You ain't no squaw's daughter. And they'll keep you once they get you in their camp. I've heard these miners and trappers a-talkin'. Them Indians want white women." She paused for breath, her head throbbing. "You were kidnapped from another wagon train," she said, her tone more rational. "We all knew that."

A fist pounded on the door. "Open up, Elsie," Ernest yelled. "We gotta do somethin'."

"Them savages may not wait till sunrise," he said as she unbolted the door and he burst into the kitchen. "They may git a hankerin' to come back sooner."

Ernest rarely wore a hat and his thin black hair, always tormented by the elements, now stood on end. He tugged at his large nose, marbled with broken blood vessels. "Her features ain't Indian, and her skin ain't dark, but her hair and eyes. . . ." He was muttering his thoughts aloud, distressing Elsie even more.

Elsie swung on him, her hands clutching and unclutching the folds of her apron. "It's the craziest thing I ever heard, Ernest. Sara, an Indian!"

"Well, she *was* wrapped in a rabbit skin, don't you remember? You always figger't she was stolen, but . . ." his beady gaze attacked Sara's features, then the shape of her long slim body, examining her as though she were a stranger. "How did that devil Bear Claw know a baby was put at our wagon if the ma didn't tell him?" he asked Elsie.

"They just want her and they'll lie to get her!" Elsie snapped, beads of perspiration breaking over her upper lip. "All that matters is, she's *our* daughter now, and so help me, they ain't gettin' her!" She shook a fist at Ernest.

Ernest's eyes narrowed on his wife while his mind pondered the value of those buffalo skins, buffalo so hard to come by now! And the trinkets and beads—hell, he'd sell them in no time!

His steely gaze drifted back to the girl. If she belonged to the Indians by blood, why start a war over it? He scowled and shook his head, and hunching his bony shoulders, he yanked the door open and stormed out, venting his frustration on the door, which trembled on its rusty hinges.

"He'll trade me." Sara's voice was a mere whisper as she stared at the space where Ernest had stood.

"He'll do no such thing!" Elsie shouted, and now the rafters seemed to tremble. "I'm gonna find Trapper Sam, that's what I'm gonna do! I'll get to the bottom of this mess right now."

* * *

Trapper Sam was a slight but hardy man in his sixties. A grizzled gray beard and sideburns covered most of his thin, weather-beaten face. Straggly white hair fell from his coonskin cap to brush the collar of his rabbit-skin jacket. He had survived blizzards, famine on a wagon train, and had even been trapped in a cave to escape a hungry mountain lion, and it all showed in his leathery face.

But nothing equaled the threat in Elsie's face when one rough hand wrung Sam's collar while the other poked a loaded musket into his chest, backing him against the slab wood of the horse corral.

"Tell me what you told them, and for once your lyin' tongue better tell it straight! For if it don't, the next breath is gonna be your last!" She thrust her face in his, her faded blue eyes brimming with hate.

Constant exposure to bitter wind and summer sun had weathered and darkened Sam's skin to the bronze hue of the Cheyenne. All color drained from his face, however, as the tip of the barrel slammed against his breastbone.

"I been tradin' with Bear Claw for years, Elsie," he sputtered. "Ever time I go up Ute Pass, I stop at the bubbling springs where his camp is." He turned his head to spit the wad of tobacco from his jaw. There was a rank taste forming in the back of his mouth, combining with the tobacco juice to make his stomach heave. The woman looked like she'd gone stark crazy, like she'd kill him and never blink an eye! He swallowed again. "Bear

Claw's been pesterin' me about a young squaw that one of his braves seen here at the post," he began, attempting to sound contrite. "I just figger't the brave was hankerin' after her, that's all. I thought . . ." His yellow teeth ground into his bottom lip as he struggled to reason out the words before he spoke them.

"You thought what?" Elsie tightened her grip on his collar.

Sam took a deep breath that made a choked hiss in the tense silence overhanging the post since the shocking news. Everyone seemed to be waiting with bated breath to see what the Jacksons would do.

"I thought if he knew she was forsook by her parents . . . like there was somethin' wrong with her . . . Hell, Elsie, you know how superstitious them savages are. I figger't then he'd stop askin'."

"So did he?" Each word was like a stone hurled in his face.

"No. Hell, no!" A heavy sigh wrenched Sam's thin frame. "Then Bear Claw told me his sister was dying, that she thought all her pain was comin' from the Great Spirit for leavin' them babies." The words fell over his tongue, unchecked. "She never could have babies after them twins, he told me. He said—" he broke off, flinching as the gun barrel poked harder against his pounding heart. If he told her more, she'd probably pull the trigger and blow his innards sky high.

"He said *what*?" Elsie's face was ashen.

Terror, like a hungry mountain lion, was attacking the pit of her belly.

"He said the squaw, Crying Wind, wanted him to bring one of her babes back to the village," he rasped. "She knew about you folks. She must have kept an eye on them wagons, Elsie. She knew one of them twins was here." His words were a mere rasp now as Elsie began to slump, defeat registering in her eyes before she could stop it.

Feeling her grip lighten and seeing the look on her face, as though someone had just dealt her a blow, Sam continued, daring to hope he might now live to hunt that huge elk with the nine-by-nine rack he'd mount and hang at the post.

"Bear Claw said the squaw wants to see that girl before she dies," he continued more calmly. "Maybe that's all there is to it, Elsie."

She sank back against the wall of the corral as a hard pain tore through the center of her chest. Her big hand fell away from Sam's collar as she lowered the musket.

"Elsie, you better get ahold of yourself," Sam said, suddenly concerned. "You look like your heart's about to take out on you."

"Not yet!" she hissed. She had to think what to do—she had to save Sara. But how? She lifted a hand to her heart, pressing against the persistent ache. The damage was done. There was no point in shooting Sam. But he'd pay for his mistake later; she'd see to it.

Sam fidgeted beneath her cold, thoughtful stare. "I'm sorry, Elsie," he muttered softly.

"If only I could have done something to change his mind...."

"You can do something now," she snapped. "You can take her to Colorado City. Tonight."

"Tonight?" Sam choked, his eyes shooting to the mass of dark clouds rolling in on a northern wind.

"You can take the best horses, and I'll pack food and coffee."

"Colorado City?" he repeated limply.

"You'll do it, Sam, and don't tell me you won't," Elsie said, her chest heaving. "You got that poor girl into this mess, and now you're gonna get her out. *You'll do it, Sam*"—she raised the musket again—"or I'll kill you!"

Sam gulped and nodded. "All right. Get her ready. We'll head out right after dark."

Elsie heaved a sigh of relief, then glanced worriedly at the clouds. "There's a Thompson family that lives on this side of the town. They spent a winter here once, and I nursed his wife through a bad stomach ailment. They said if I ever needed anything . . ."

"Elsie, what'll happen if she ain't here when they come back?" Sam didn't want to get killed, but he didn't want to be responsible for an Indian uprising at the post either.

Elsie shook her head. "I don't know, and right now I don't care. I gotta think of Sara."

"Does Ernest know you're planning to sneak her out?" Sam asked.

Elsie glared at him, her fingers closing over the trigger of the musket.

"Oh, hell," he said. "I'll take her anyway."

Sara huddled into the buffalo robe, her teeth chattering, her mind dazed with shock. In the darkness outside the corral, Trapper Sam led out a gentle mare, then turned back to a frisky roan, raising the stirrups to accomodate his short banty legs.

"Now don't waste any time," Elsie whispered through the darkness, tucking a bundle of food in Sam's saddlebag.

"I'll send you a message from town," Sam said, pulling up into the saddle and lowering his cap against the wind.

"You'll be all right, honey," Elsie said, her eyes hungrily searching Sara's face as though memorizing each feature.

"Yes, I know. Don't worry about me," Sara answered, trying to assume the courage for which she'd prayed throughout this day, the most shocking day of her life.

"Sara, you keep a tight rein on that mare," Sam warned from behind her. "We'll just mosey quiet-like out the gate and across them foothills. That's the best way to slip outa this valley."

Elsie's plump hand shot up to grip Sara's arm. "The Thompsons are good people. They'll take care of you, and I'll come as soon as I can."

Sara's teeth were chattering, more from nerves than cold, as she nodded in agreement, glancing one last time at the log buildings huddled in a dark mass against the falling snow.

"Take care of yourself, Ma," she said, her eyes returning to Elsie Jackson, always so strong, yet reduced to heaving sobs now. The sight brought tears to Sara's eyes, but she sank her teeth into her lower lip, refusing to break down. She gripped the reins and kneed her mare into line behind Sam.

The guard opened the gate, a sad smile on his bearded face as he quietly waved them through.

Sara shivered in her buffalo robe, her eyes stinging from the tears she fought to control. Her bottom lip ached from the hard thrust of her teeth as she centered her thoughts on getting to Colorado City. Her eyes were focused determinedly on Trapper Sam, whose cap was drawn low over his gray hair. In the darkness, his earlobes glistened fire-red from the cold.

The mare plodded along, its slow, easy rhythm a soothing distraction to her turbulent thoughts. For the past hours, her mind had been frozen in shock, and she was relieved that Elsie had taken charge, making all the decisions. Now, as she rode along in the darkened night, the cold air had a sobering effect, mobilizing her thoughts again.

What if Bear Claw spoke the truth? she wondered suddenly. How could she know what to believe? Elsie was so certain that the Indians had kidnapped her from another wagon train, but was that what had *really* happened?

They had ridden in silence for almost an hour when Sara sensed a change in the quiet night. She studied Sam, huddled into his coat. He seemed unaware of any change, yet her skin prickled. What was wrong, what was different?

The silence was no longer complete. That was it! She pushed her hood back and strained her ears. Then the change she had tried to identify became apparent even to Sam, who yanked his roan to a halt. The leather of his saddle creaked as he shifted his weight to survey the darkness that enclosed them, a darkness feathered by gently falling snow.

Sara pulled her mare to a halt, following Sam's searching gaze into the black night and seeing nothing. But there was a sound drifting through the darkness, a thudding that grew stronger. Though she had never been pursued before, she knew it was hoofbeats muffled by snow.

"Someone's after us!" Sam called at the moment the realization struck her. "And we ain't hangin' around to find out who! Kick that mare and ride like hell!" he yelled. "We gotta reach them rocks up there so we can hide."

Wordlessly, she obeyed, slamming her booted heels into the mare's side. The horse lunged forward, and the snow spun a white web around her as the mare tore across the frozen earth. Sara's pulse drummed in her ears as she struggled to hang on, while the cold wind stung her face and blurred her vision.

The night was suddenly rent with shouts, words that were foreign to her. Then another sound reached her—a hoarse, guttural moan, wrung from a body in agonizing pain.

Ahead of her, Sam toppled from his horse into a mound of snow, a tomahawk buried in his back.

"Sam!" she screamed, jerking the reins. At her panicked tugging, the mare reared, then plunged again, throwing Sara headlong into the snow.

She was half-buried in a mound of snow that froze her face and matted her lashes. She struggled to get up, impatiently brushing the snow from her face.

Hoofbeats and wild shouts filled her ears as she shook loose the clumps of snow. A rough hand yanked her to her feet, snapping her head back. She was staring into the dark face of an Indian brave.

"Sam!" she screamed uselessly, though she was unable to stop herself.

There was no answer.

More faces crowded in; dark eyes peered at her as though she were a strange creature from another world.

Her eyes flew across the snow seeking Sam. He was sprawled several yards away in a bank of snow that was stained with the crimson pool of his blood.

Sara screamed again, horrified by what she saw.

The dark faces watched her in grim fascination as she struggled to suppress another scream. She tried to hold onto her common sense, to pretend she was not afraid of them. But her body was jerking from head to toe, though she forced herself to meet those dark, peering eyes. As she looked over the strong, cynical faces, her teeth gashed into her bottom lip, and the taste of blood filled her mouth. Then a firm hand gripped her and dragged her back to her horse. There was no point in asking where she was going, for she already knew.

Bear Claw had won, after all.

2

Shane Simmons guided his pinto over a narrow deer trail leading through the foothills of the Tarryalls. The day's hunt had not gone well; the blacktail deer had evaded him again and now there was no meat for supper. He drew rein, leapt down from his horse, and strode quickly to the twin red rocks overhanging his secret cave.

A bitter wind prowled down the mountainside, snatching at his thick dark hair and whistling down the collar of his buckskin jacket. He was eighteen years old and stood five feet, ten inches, with rippling muscles as smooth and hard as a mountain lion's.

There was something about Shane Simmons that commanded a backward glance as he strolled the board sidewalks of mining towns, his spurs jingling rhythmically, his deerskin cap slanted carelessly over his forehead. On second glance, it was the eyes that drew one's attention—dark, flashing eyes that reflected a ready challenge.

The dark hair and eyes hinted of Indian ancestry, but the skin was not the coppery hue of the Utes. It was a deep, golden brown. A low forehead gave way to level dark brows,

followed by a straight nose and full lips. His
rounded chin held just the hint of a dimple,
but that was scarcely noticeable beneath the
shadow of dark stubble. A small scar, shaped
like a half moon, sat in the center of his left
jaw, reminding him to curb his temper, for he
had not always won his fights when very
young. His steps were swift and sure and he
was unquestionably the best hunter in the
area.

He sank down at the mouth of the cave to
wait, drawing from his pocket the button of
peyote that would dull the echo in his mind of
the exaggerated stories of raids on the
ranches in the South Park Valley and the
rumors of rape and scalpings on the plains.
The white man often forgot it was the
Cheyenne, not the Ute, who attacked there.
All Indians were savages, they said. Shane
wanted to forget those stories; he wanted to
forget everything except Star of the Morning,
the beautiful Ute maiden who filled his
dreams.

His eyes grew pensive as he stared at the
valley below, where lanterns glowed in mining
shacks. To the east, in the wooded foothills
along the Peak, the band of Utes led by
Shavano camped, but no lights flickered from
their lodges. His heart ached with the
knowledge that he could no longer come and
go freely among them as he once had. Too
many lies were being circulated about the
Indians, and in retaliation, there was much
bitterness against the white man. Shane was
white.

He chewed on the peyote, waiting for the euphoria that would still his nerves, but tonight the peyote had lost its magic, failing to quiet his fears. If it came to war, as they said it would, he'd have to choose sides. That meant fighting against his best friend Wasatch and his younger sister, Star of the Morning.

Wasatch! The Ute brave he had met at the beaver lakes was the one friend he could understand. Wasatch felt the same eagerness to follow the sun, the wind, the dark and unknown trails that beckoned. Shane had never found this kind of kinship in his white friends, many of whom were sissies, to his way of thinking.

Two winters ago, he and Wasatch had made sleds of buffalo ribs and raced each other down the snowy slopes. Wasatch had found a broken wagon wheel and repaired it. Spinning the wheel down the slope, they each threw lances, trying to pin the wheel to the ground. Wasatch had been very good at "killing the wheel."

Shane sighed. Now he was alone, an outsider at the Indian camps, an alien among the white man who resented his loyalty to the Utes.

Elmer Simmons, his father, had no desire to trade with the Indians or smoke the pipe of peace. Like the other greedy settlers, he had come to the South Park seizing the Utes' prized hunting grounds, trapping their beavers at the streams, aiming their fancy guns at the deer in the valley, the elk and sheep in the foothills. Elmer believed the tales of scalpings, rape and mutilation by the Cheyenne out on the plains, and he suspected the Utes of participating in those horrors.

"Why shouldn't they fight?" Shane had argued back as Elmer spat tobacco juice into the fire. "It was their land first."

"They're just savages," Elmer had roared. "Damned savages—all of 'em!"

It had been their last fight. Shane had packed his clothes and stomped angrily from the cabin, his fists clenched. The knowledge that Elmer was not his real father festered within him, fueling his anger. Who *were* his real people?

Kidnapped from one wagon train and dropped at another, his mother had told him. And so, for the first years of his life, he had eagerly searched the faces of trappers and traders from Colorado to California, hoping somehow to recognize his true father. But he never had found him; he doubted now that he ever would.

He dropped his head, a deep and lonely silence filling up in his heart. Numbly, he tossed the peyote aside, disappointed that it had failed to rekindle the comfort that had died, three years ago, with the death of his mother.

She had been the gentle spirit that held his life together until that freezing winter on the upper Arkansas. In the drafty cabin there, she had taken to her bed with chills and fever until finally her thin, worn-out body had relinquished the fight.

Elmer had grown harder each day, more

desperate for the gold that evaded him in California and now Colorado. He had driven himself, and Shane, beyond all reason, from the first light of day until the depths of darkness.

"Drag the pan again," he would yell. And again and again. Until pitch darkness drove them back to their dismal shack for another tasteless meal of unleavened bread and cold beans.

Shane knew now he'd rather starve in his cave than endure another winter with crazy Elmer. He would never go back to live with him again. Never!

His hard bronze body began to tremble as the cold wind howled louder. The hope that lit his dark eyes began to fade as he scanned the shadows beneath the tall pines. *She was not coming.* His heart was as heavy as the granite rocks surrounding him. He dragged himself up and stared into the still, dark night. The only sound was the jingle of his spurs as he walked back to his horse.

"Shane?" The lilt of her voice was as soft and sweet as a bird's cry. "*Shane?*"

He whirled, his heart pounding, his hopes rising again. Soundlessly, she emerged from the dense pine thicket, a doeskin cape swinging about her small body, raven hair loosened from braids to frame her long face.

With a gasp of hunger, he drew her to his chest, his hands automatically smoothing the silky dark hair from her face, then gently circling her narrow shoulders. He could feel the cold of her body beneath the frayed cape.

lusty and erotic, relieving him of the pain yet never really satisfying the hunger of his soul.

But Star prized her virtue and he would not defy that. She'd spent five years of her life with a missionary woman who had come to the village to pass out Bibles. It was shortly after Star's mother had died of a fever that began to infect Star as well. Star had cried over the kind older woman who had begged Shavano to let her take Star back to the city for medicine and treatment. To everyone's surprise, Shavano had agreed. Star had lived with the white woman until she developed an incurable illness; then she brought Star back to the village at twelve years of age. Although Star had acquired a knowledge of the English language and a firm set of morals from the missionary woman, she still preferred the simple Ute life to the white man's world.

Shane sighed, lifting her hand to his lips. The memory of other girls he had so carelessly taken nagged momentarily as he looked into Star's sweet face. There had been times when he had half-heartedly enjoyed the attention of other women, leading them on, taunting them with his careless charm. What he had discovered in their eager clinging arms had not been love or even tenderness. Only relief.

Since the first time he saw Star of the Morning, at the beaver lakes with Wasatch, he'd felt a strange tugging at his heart, a tenderness that never ceased to amaze and fascinate him. She would not be considered beautiful by anyone else, yet he was captivated by the thin face with the huge dark eyes, the small nose and pointed chin. The eyes held the innocence of a startled doe until he kissed her; then her eyes darkened with desire. Star reached deep in his soul, uncovering a tenderness that surprised him.

He ran his tongue over her thin fingers, treasuring the smell of the pine on her, the taste of wild honey on her lips when he kissed her. What would happen to her, he wondered suddenly? What would happen to the rest of her tribe and to the small encampment here? The Utes, the smallest of tribes when united, were even smaller as they scattered to obtain hunting grounds.

"You are quiet," she spoke at last. Her voice was light and sweet, like rain in the pines.

"Star, let's run away!" he burst out. "We could go to Wyoming."

The slender fingers that rested on his chin now splayed to cover his lips, silencing his words. She shook her head sadly. "There is no place to run. The white man hates us now. He will hate you if you join with us. They never forget the day our people fought back."

Shane nodded, remembering the shocking news of the Ute attack on Fort Pueblo five years before.

"But the military led an attack against your people the next spring," he reminded her. "Then both sides agreed to peace."

"But the peace does not last."

"Star, this land belonged to your people. The settlers have no right to come in and take over."

"Still, my people are wrong to raid your livestock, your ranches. . . ."

"We were wrong to trespass on your land. Please"—he pulled her into his arms—"let's not argue."

Star wrapped herself around him, welcoming the hands that shyly explored her small firm breasts, then molded her waist, her belly, traced the outline of her smooth thighs, muscled from the mountains she climbed and the miles she walked each day in search of herbs and berries.

As he touched her, Star whispered soft words of love, words spoken in her native tongue. Though Shane did not understand every word, he read their meaning in her glowing face.

A northerly wind blasted the half-dozen lodges clustered together, howling like a coyote around the flap of the lodge, but the fire kept them cozy. The blood raced through their veins as Shane dipped his lips to hungrily claim hers.

With tears glistening in his brown eyes, he spoke the words he had never voiced to another human being, not even the gentle woman who had raised him.

"I love you," he said.

Tears flowed from Star's dark eyes to blend with his as she pressed her thin cheek against his whiskered jaw. "And I love you. As the stars love the sky, as the moon loves the heavens . . ."

A horse neighed, then another, confirming the return of the braves to camp. With a heavy sigh, he released her and leapt to his feet. This time he had almost gone too far.

3

Moonlight streamed over the Rampart Mountains, illuminating their snowy peaks as the Indians led Sara's mare into a wide meadow enclosed by dark pines, forests, and jagged boulders. This was the land of the bubbling springs that she'd heard about, where Utes left trinkets for the Great Spirit. She remembered a trapper who had once stolen one of those trinkets and had come to the post with it. Ernest had traded some Taos lightning for it, put it in a jar and told everyone it was a valuable good-luck charm from a medicine man. A Kansas mule skinner turned gold seeker had paid a fortune for it.

Half frozen and numb with shock, Sara stared through bleary eyes to the small, silent village where a campfire threw flickering shadows on the buckskin lodges clustered in a wide circle.

The lead Indian broke from the group and loped into camp, shouting hoarsely as he tumbled from his pinto and raced to a lodge in the center of the village.

Flaps were thrown back, faces peered into darkness, before torches were lit to flare in Sara's pale, terrified face.

Bear Claw appeared, wearing a furry robe and a long, elk-tooth necklace. His black hair hung in thick braids bound by rawhide, which swung about his shoulders as he broke through the gathering crowd and approached her. The cold black eyes held a look of triumph.

"Come!" he commanded.

The deep voice rumbled over her, sending chills down her spine. She dismounted, yanking her robe tightly around her. Every bone in her body ached and throbbed from the long punishing ride and the freezing cold. Still, she held herself erect, sensing she would be watched and judged for her courage. She followed Bear Claw to a tall lodge that held colorful drawings of elk and deer. A large painting in the center featured a grizzly and a young warrior. Remembering the story of Bear Claw's encounter with a grizzly, she assumed this was his lodge.

Nearby, a smaller lodge held only one painting, that of a sad Indian maiden with tears trailing down her cheeks. *Crying Wind*, she thought. Bear Claw threw the flap back and motioned her inside.

Sara hesitated, suddenly apprehensive. Then, feeling the black eyes boring through her, she forced herself to enter. A flickering candle offset the darkness within, and she blinked and glanced around. A young girl sat beside a small, thin body that lay still as death on a bed of animal skins.

"*Crying Wind*," Bear Claw pointed, stepping toward the sick woman.

Sara's heart was in her throat and her feet moved like stones as she crept toward the small woman whose gaunt brown face was as shriveled as a prune. Her hair was gray and hung down her chest. Curiously, Sara took a step closer, carefully studying the blunt nose, pale shriveled lips and sunken cheeks. This person could not possibly be her mother, she thought, sighing with relief.

The woman appeared to be sleeping, but as though sensing their presence, the sunken eyes slowly opened.

The big bronze chief stepped in front of Sara and touched his sister's shoulders. As he spoke to her, the old woman struggled to sit up; dark, pain-filled eyes flew to Sara.

Sara froze as a gnarled hand flailed through the air, and the woman began to babble incoherently. The words died away and she lay with her mouth open, gasping for breath. Sara stared.

"Little Dove. Your name Little Dove," Bear Claw's deep voice broke through Sara's thoughts. "She say your spirit sings even when you suffer. Like the little dove."

Sara's mouth dropped open as her eyes drifted back to the sick woman who was staring at her with a wide, toothless smile.

"But there's been a mistake," she burst out. "I'm not Little Dove, I'm Sara Jackson. And I'm not her daughter!"

Bear Claw's black eyes looked as sharp as knife blades as he glared threateningly at Sara. "Tell her you forgive."

Sara gulped and looked from his stern face

to the suffering woman. The memory of Trapper Sam, lying face-down in the snow suddenly burst into her mind, and she told herself not to behave like a fool.

"I forgive you," she said sweetly, staring into Crying Wind's wrinkled face.

Bear Claw translated her reply and the woman listened carefully as tears filled the dark eyes and rolled unevenly down her creased cheeks as she looked back at Sara.

Watching her, Sara felt a sudden surge of pity for this woman, Crying Wind. Even if she weren't her mother, Sara decided to be kind. She was obviously dying. Her eyes dropped to the brown hand, still dangling in mid-air. She reached out and shyly grasped the cold fingers. New strength seemed to flow through her feeble body and Crying Wind began to babble again.

Sara frowned, carefully studying the sunken eyes, the nut-brown skin. No, this woman couldn't possibly be her mother and yet—how did she know about the babies? *Babies.* Could she be a twin? Did she have a brother someplace?

The trauma of the past twenty-four hours now centered in one blinding pain behind her forehead. She could no longer think straight; how could she know what to believe?

Crying Wind's strange murmurings had ceased, and the grasp on Sara's hand weakened. An expression of peace settled over her features as she closed her eyes and slept again.

Bear Claw nodded approval at Sara, then

turned and swept out of the lodge. Sara's eyes cautiously followed him, and when the flap closed, she gently removed her hand from Crying Wind's. The flap opened again and the girl who had been keeping vigil returned with a clay pot of steaming broth. Sara's eyes dropped to the thin liquid and her mouth began to water as her empty stomach reacted to the flavorful aroma. She was motioned to a corner of the lodge where a smooth rock served as a table. She sank down on a buffalo skin, her weary glance moving from the broth to the dark-skinned girl, who gave her a shy smile before she darted out again.

Sara filled her stomach, trying not to think; but worries, like predators, raced through her mind. Had anyone found Trapper Sam? Had word reached the post? How long would it take Crying Wind to die? A*nd what would happen to her then*?

She glanced around the small lodge, walled with buffalo hides sewn together between long, rigid poles that narrowed into a chimney at the top. The lining of the skins helped insulate the lodge against the harsh weather, but Sara continued to shiver. As her eyes moved curiously about, she could see doeskin dresses, moccasins beaded in flower designs, and baskets shaped like jugs attached to the poles. Along the floor, there were more baskets of various sizes and shapes, and a clay bowl and crude wooden spoon.

Sara sighed and returned to her broth. As she was finishing, the flap parted and the Indian girl returned, carrying a buckskin dress, a pair of moccasins, and several animal skins, which she indicated was Sara's bed.

Bone-weary, Sara sank onto the skins, too numb in mind and body to care what would happen next. The warm broth had filled her hungry stomach, and with only the snores of the sick woman to distract her, she pulled the extra skins over her and quickly fell asleep.

Sara huddled before the morning fire, staring glumly at the interior of Crying Wind's lodge. Absently, she counted the thirteen slim poles that held the dried buffalo hides together. Her eyes roamed to the opening, covered with a flap of skin held by two rigid poles. If only she could walk through that opening and leave this village behind forever! But she was guarded like a prisoner.

She sighed and turned to stare into the fire. She was trapped within this lodge, this village. And to complicate matters, the skinny brave they called White Buffalo had become a stubborn suitor!

How, she wondered, could she continue to avoid him when Bear Claw actually encouraged his repulsive advances toward her. The skin from the rare buffalo had brought him respect among the tribe, but his treasured gift meant nothing to her.

"I hate him," she hissed, whirling to Crying Wind. Only half-conscious, the woman couldn't understand Sara's words, but talking helped to vent her frustration. "I hate everything about him—his hairless chest, his long, pointed face, his secretive eyes. But

Bear Claw has given his approval and White Buffalo thinks I belong to him now."

She turned to stare broodily into the fire. Homesick tears welled in her eyes. Five days had passed, and the tense waiting had drained her energy. The Utes interpreted her silence as submission to this strange life, but they were wrong. She would never accept it! Her mind flew like a wild wind, constantly looking for a way to escape.

The pent-up tears overflowed her dark eyes and streamed down her cheeks when she thought of the post and her adopted parents. Surely by now they had heard of Trapper Sam's death; surely Ma knew they never made it beyond the mountain pass where the warriors waited. She expected nothing from Ernest Jackson, but her Ma . . .

Sara wandered over to lift the flap, trying to push those thoughts from her anguished mind as she studied the inhabitants of Bear Claw's small village. On this cold morning, the men wore animal skin robes over their breechcloths and moccasins. The women wore loose dresses fashioned from skins. Some of the dresses held painted decorations; a few were embroidered with beads.

Near the fire some of the women were skinning a large buck brought in from the morning hunt. Two squaws had cradle boards strapped to their backs. The dark-eyed babies appeared content, apparently accustomed to this kind of activity. The children roamed freely. A few were clustered together in some sort of game with a stick and a rock. Their dark braids bounced against their rabbitskin coats as they raced about.

Strange, Sara thought, how the children here seemed happier than those at the post. None cried or begged at their mother's side. Suddenly, one of the children let out an excited shriek and jabbed a small finger in the direction of the trail leading into camp. The other children joined in the excitement, laughing and yelling as they raced toward the road.

Sara's brow knitted in a curious frown and she ventured outside to investigate. Everyone's attention was centered on the approach of a blond man riding a black stallion into the village.

Recognition flashed in Sara's eyes. It was him! The man who had come to the post. Had Ernest sent him to speak with Bear Claw? For the first time since her capture, her hopes soared.

The children crowded about as he swung down from his horse and reached into his saddlebag. Hands shot out, eagerly awaiting the contents. Obviously, this man was no stranger here; certainly he had been generous in the past. The children shrieked with delight as their small brown hands were filled with peppermint candy and trinkets. A compassionate smile touched his lips as he spoke to them, and Sara stared in awe at this man who had stood up to her father, as few men did, yet who could be generous and caring to the Indian children.

Heavy footsteps sounded behind her, and

she whirled to see Bear Claw sweeping past the lodge. For the first time, there was a pleasant expression on his face as he looked from the man to the children, jumping up and down with glee.

"How!" Bear Claw called, lifting his hand.

The man turned from the children and returned the greeting. The stranger was not intimidated by the Indian Chief, although he spoke with respect, half in English, half in the Ute language, his Southern drawl dominant.

As the sunlight filtered over him, Sara took in every detail of his appearance. His rugged features and buckskin cloths made him the epitome of the western man, yet the startlingly blue eyes held a look of humility and the soft Southern drawl spoke words of kindness. As she stood staring, he turned and glanced in her direction, and she caught a look of surprise on his face. But then Bear Claw spoke, reclaiming his attention.

The brave smile Sara had forced to her lips began to waver. She had expected him to acknowledge her in some way if, indeed, he had been sent to her. A worried frown creased her forehead as she recalled his disagreement with her father. What, she wondered, had Ernest offered him to come on this mission? When he had seen her, his eyes had reflected surprise. Her mind raced, searching for an explanation. Maybe it was part of his plan to appear casual, conceal his real intention.

When he turned to walk with Bear Claw to the center lodge, Sara motioned to Deer Woman.

"Who is he?" she asked, pointing to the tall, handsome man.

"Friend..." The old woman spoke the word slowly, reverently, as she touched a thin silver bracelet on her wrist.

Sara's eyes jumped from the bracelet back to Bear Claw's lodge, into which the men had disappeared, but when a wail of pain pierced the air, Sara turned back into Crying Wind's lodge. The woman's agonizing battle for life appeared to be coming to an end. Her dark eyes rolled back, and the mouth that had issued moans of agony now sagged as Crying Wind sank into death.

Sara stared down at her, dumbfounded at the reality of death, even one so obviously imminent. She heard someone babbling and turned to see Deer Woman's aging eyes widening in stunned comprehension as she stared at Crying Wind's lifeless body. Then she dashed out, shrieking the news.

Gently, Sara pulled the buffalo robe over Crying Wind's still face, and as she did, she was surprised to feel sadness welling up inside of her. She thought of what Bear Claw had said, that Crying Wind was her mother. She shook her head slowly, dismissing that unlikely possibility. There was not the slightest resemblance. It had all been a mistake, as Elsie had insisted.

Bear Claw burst into the lodge, his dark face sorrow-filled at the sight of the covered body. At the edge of the flap, Sara could see the buckskin trousers of the stranger, politely waiting outside. Sara glanced back at Bear Claw, who was momentarily caught up in grief. Seizing the opportunity, she slipped from the lodge and motioned the stranger out of earshot from Bear Claw.

"I'm Sara Jackson," she said, eagerly awaiting his reaction.

"I'm Eric Christensen," he said, removing his cap. Beneath the sun, the blonde hair glinted golden and she was momentarily struck dumb by his strikingly handsome face. A firm jawline, straight nose and sculpted lips were set in a deeply tanned face. A dark beard shadowed his jaws. Her eyes moved down the muscled neck, swept broad shoulders, narrow torso, and long legs, then ended on his dark leather boots. Suddenly aware that she was staring, she prodded her mind back to the question she intended to ask. She glanced over her shoulder to the lodge, thankful Bear Claw was lingering in his grief.

"Did my parents send you?" she whispered, turning back to Eric.

"*Send* me?" he questioned, momentarily taken aback.

Sara swallowed, fighting the sick disappointment that was overtaking her. "I've been kidnapped," she explained desperately. "I'm Ernest Jackson's daughter from Jackson's Post. You were there last week. I *saw you*."

"Kidnapped?" he repeated, as though nothing else she had said registered in his mind. "I can't believe Bear Claw would allow . . ."

"There's been a terrible mistake," Sara interrupted, glancing impatiently toward the lodge. "I haven't time to explain, but you must believe me." Her hand shot out, grasping desperately at his fringed sleeve. "And you must help me! *Please.*"

His eyes widened, taking in every inch of her, from her tangled hair down her buckskin dress to her dusty moccasins, as Bear Claw emerged from the lodge, glancing at Sara. Silently, he motioned to Eric, who continued to stare at her for a moment before he turned without a word to follow Bear Claw back to the center lodge.

Tears of frustration leapt into Sara's eyes as she stomped back inside the lodge and threw herself dejectedly down on a mat. Her frustration soon turned to rage as she realized that Ernest Jackson hadn't sent this man to trade for her. Why, the way Ernest hated Indians, he probably wouldn't even let her come home! She kicked angrily at the earthen floor, wishing it was Ernest Jackson instead.

But Ma! Why hadn't she done something? It was hard to believe that news of her abduction and Sam's murder hadn't reached the post. If Ma knew she was here, she'd do something.

That was it. Ernest had kept it a secret!

She rubbed her nose, sniffed and brushed angrily at her useless tears. She had to help herself now; she couldn't depend on anyone else. Suddenly, she caught sight of her dirt-encrusted hands with the broken, grimy nails. No wonder Eric Christensen doubted what she'd told him. No wonder he was reluctant to help her. She yanked a strand of hair from her shoulder, examining its dull, lifeless color. Why, she looked like a . . . a savage!

Footsteps whispered behind her, and she whirled to see Deer Woman creeping around, gathering up Crying Wind's clay bowl, her beaded moccasins and doeskin dress.

"What are you doing?" Sara demanded, thinking the old woman was stealing Crying Wind's possessions.

Deer Woman motioned to the lifeless body, then held the articles up and indicated, through sign language, that these would be buried in the crevice of the red rocks with Crying Wind.

Feeling embarrassed by her outburst, Sara dropped her head and nodded. Unlike their Cheyenne neighbors, who buried their dead high above ground, the Utes buried their people in rock crevices, and they particularly favored the high red rocks.

A low, mournful wail broke over the camp. Other voices joined in, and the sound of dozens of stamping feet filled her ears. Sara's flesh crawled as the monotonous chant swelled over the village and the dance of mourning began. Then suddenly the flap was thrown back and two braves entered. Sara quickly looked away, unable to watch as they hoisted the lifeless body and carried it from the lodge.

She was alone again, with only her turbulent thoughts. *What will happen to me*? she wondered, knowing if Bear Claw chose to give her to the repulsive White Buffalo, she was doomed.

I've got to do something, she decided. *I've got to*

PASSION'S PEAK   61

persuade Eric Christensen to help me.

Her decision propelled her to her feet, and she flew outside and up the path to Bear Claw's lodge. She burst in, surprising the men as they sat quietly smoking their pipes.

She clenched her fists at her side, summoning all of her courage. "Let me go," she said, her voice shaky yet determined. "Please let me go. Mr. Christensen can take me back to the post. Crying Wind is dead now. There's nothing more I can do here."

Bear Claw's face was a bronze mask. "We trade for you. Now you and White Buffalo . . ."

"Trade?" she echoed, the blood seeping from her face. At the mention of White Buffalo, panic swept her again. "No! I won't stay here. I *won't!*" she cried.

Eric Christensen laid down the pipe and rose to his feet. He stood gazing down at her for a moment, the deep blue eyes filled with questions. Then he cleared his throat and turned back to Bear Claw.

"Perhaps I can settle the problem. I'd like to trade for her, Chief." He reached deep into his jacket pocket. "I worked many suns for this," he said, withdrawing a large gold nugget and offering it to Bear Claw.

Bear Claw's dark eyes held a cunning glow as he turned the nugget over in his palm, studying its soft gleam in the glow of the fire.

For a moment, Sara's dark eyes were frozen in shock as she, too, stared at the nugget; then, slowly, she regained her composure and swung to face Eric.

"You don't have to do that," she said

tightly. "Surely there must be some other way . . ."

As though summoned by the drama involving him, White Buffalo appeared in the parted flap of the lodge. An evil grin slit his mouth as his hand reached out to stroke Sara's arm.

Sara shrank back from him, unconsciously taking a step closer to Eric.

"Don't touch her," Eric said, his voice calm yet threatening. Then he voiced something in the Ute tongue.

White Buffalo's face darkened in fury. His lips snarled, and again he thrust a possessive arm toward Sara.

"Leave me alone," she cried and yanked free of him. "I won't be your squaw! I'd rather be dead!"

She didn't know if he understood her words or merely read the hatred in her face, but this time he could not tolerate her rejection. His hand closed tightly over her wrist, as though preparing to drag her from the lodge.

With lightning speed, Eric's hand shot out and gripped the brave's shoulder, shoving him away from Sara. White Buffalo crashed against a warrior shield in the corner of the lodge. Then he lifted eyes, burning with hatred, to the squaw who had rejected him and to the white man who had pretended friendship. But there was no friendship now—only bitterness that demanded justice.

Eric turned back to Bear Claw, who had watched the scene with a stony countenance, as though contemplating the fate of this squaw who had brought an evil spirit to his village.

"Bear Claw," Eric began again, but his words were cut off by a hoarse battle cry. White Buffalo slammed into Eric's shoulder, knocking him to the ground dangerously near the fire.

Sara's hands flew to her mouth, trying to stifle a scream. The brave threw his body on top of Eric with another ear-splitting yell. He had Eric by the neck, forcing his face closer to the smouldering coals. Sara watched in horror as the two men struggled. She could already smell the burning flesh when suddenly Eric's elbow lashed into the brave's stomach and White Buffalo momentarily loosened his grip. In that moment, Eric broke free and leapt to his feet. White Buffalo rolled deftly out of range and lunged to a squatting position. For a moment, the two men circled each other, their eyes locked as every muscle in their bodies tensed for the next assault.

Like an eagle, Eric sprang through the air and dived into White Buffalo's body. The impact drove them both through the flap into the hard-packed snow. Bare legs entangled with buckskin as the snow covered their faces and clung to their hair.

Terror choked the breath from Sara's body, and her heart pounded louder than the drumbeats accompanying the mourning dancers, who had now ended their dance to stand like totems, gazing at the wrestling men. Sara whirled to face Bear Claw, silently praying he would end the fight, but he sat like a statue, his scarred face impassive except for the cold gaze fixed on her.

"Stop them," she pleaded. "Please stop them!"

He grunted and shifted his eyes back to the bodies rolling over and over in the snow. Eric had pinned the brave with his knees while his unrelenting fist smashed the Indian's face again and again. White Buffalo groaned and sank helplessly into the snow, his face smeared with blood.

"Stop it!" The words that had been gathering in her throat finally burst from her lips. "Don't hit him anymore!"

Eric stood, brushing the snow from his clothes, then smoothing the tumbled hair from his face. His features were clenched determinedly, and Sara shrank back from him as he stepped inside the lodge.

Her pulse was beating like the drums of death as the blood roared through her ears. She knew her fate hung in the balance now.

"Do we trade?" Eric asked.

Bear Claw cast a brief glance in Sara's direction, then resumed his appraisal of the hunk of gold, which gleamed brightly against his dark palm. A slow grin spread over his mouth as he looked at Eric and nodded his head.

"We trade!"

4

Again Sara was on a horse riding through the frozen night. After the exchange of the nugget, Bear Claw suggested they leave. The Utes suspected Sara of possessing an evil spirit, for her presence had caused trouble in their camp.

Sara shivered into her buffalo robe, wondering if the Utes might be right. An Evil Spirit did seem to be haunting her. She hadn't wanted to cause trouble, yet trouble seemed to be waiting at every turn. She glanced at Eric Christensen, riding just ahead of her. He had scarcely spoken to her since they left Bear Claw's camp, and she felt embarrassed and self-conscious.

The memory of the fight sent her glance riveting back to the snow-covered trail. What was he thinking? she wondered. Was he angry with her? He seemed preoccupied, staring up at the sky where a mass of dark clouds had gathered.

She shifted nervously in the saddle. She had to start a conversation; she had to figure out what he was thinking.

"Where do you come from?" she asked.

"Georgia." He drew rein on his horse until her mare was directly beside him. His eyes drifted to hers, but the night's darkness concealed the expression there. "We're in for some bad weather," he said, glancing again at the sky.

His drawl was pleasant, a soothing contrast to the harsh, rapid-fire speech she'd heard at the post. She thought of the post, of Ernest Jackson who'd ignored her, of her ma.

"How far is the post?" she asked suddenly.

"Too far if those clouds break. I have a friend who lives over the next rise. I think we'd better stop."

Sara's head jerked back to him as a new worry took over. She knew nothing about him; how could she possibly stop someplace with him? A friend, he'd said. She looked up at the swirling clouds and realized he was right about the weather. The wind had begun to shriek through the woods, flailing the aspen branches and bending the tops of the tall pines. A blast of wind and snow hit their faces, and she lowered her head against its fierceness.

"We're gonna have to make a run for it," he shouted, whipping his horse. "Stay with me."

Her mare lurched after the big stallion as he broke into a gallop. The harsh wind bit at her face and stung her eyes to tears that quickly froze on her cold cheeks. The ride became an endurance test against the elements, and Sara gritted her teeth, wrapping her fingers around the saddle horn and holding on for her life.

Because she was not an experienced rider, she bounced wildly in the saddle, unable to mold herself to the mare's gallop. As a result, every bone in her body took a pounding.

They tore down a narrow trail that veered from the main road through a deepening woods. Her fears grew with each dark turn. She knew nothing about this man, nothing except that he was Bear Claw's friend and had traded a gold nugget for her! Elsie's warnings flew at her like the debris hurled by the wind. Would she be expected to repay him for the nugget with her body? Ernest and Elsie believed everyone had a motive, that few people acted out of the kindness of their hearts.

Eric was slowing his horse to a trot, and her mare slowed, too. She peered through her tangled curtain of hair and saw that the trail ended in a small clearing. She could see the dim outlines of a cabin, dark and deserted. Her heart sank.

Eric reigned in and bolted from the horse, then reached forward to steady her mare. Sara crawled down, her body almost too stiff to bend. She decided she'd rather take her chances with this stranger than battle the stinging snow and howling wind for another mile.

As her eyes crept over the dark cabin, Eric led the horses around to the back of the cabin, away from the wind, and hobbled them.

"Try the door," he yelled above the howling wind.

Sara lifted her skirts and stumbled blindly up the rocky path. She tripped and barely caught herself against the door frame. Her hands shot out, blindly seeking the latch. She shoved, and, to her relief, the door creaked open. Stale, cold air settled over her like a musty old cape.

"We're in luck," Eric said just over her shoulder, and she jumped before she could stop herself.

She stumbled inside, feeling his breath on her neck. Her stiff knees had begun to wobble as he slammed the door against the wind. She gulped, hugging her arms to her to still her trembling.

"Ben abides by the old wilderness rule of leaving the door unlocked," he drawled, fumbling along a table just inside the door. He came up with a match, which he struck against the wall, while she took a deep breath and tried to calm herself.

She pressed her lips together, planning her defense, if necessary. The heels of her boots were sharp; if she had to fight him off, she could start with her boots!

In the dim light her eyes skittered over the interior. It was obviously a man's place. There was a fireplace, a tiny eating table, nails driven in the wall to hold clothes, a narrow cot. Her eyes returned to the cot, stripped of cover.

One cot.

Sara glanced suspiciously at Eric, who was lighting a lantern. In its amber light, his blond hair gleamed like spun gold, casting shadows in his deep blue eyes.

"Are you cold?" he asked, looking at her.

Cold. Numbly, she considered the question.

"Of course you're cold," he muttered, striding over to the fireplace. She watched him, thinking vaguely how attractive he was. And older than she first thought. At least thirty. She'd heard about Southern gentlemen. She had to believe he was one.

Elsie's stern protectiveness had discouraged most of the single males at the post; she considered none of them good enough for her Sara. There had been only two suitable men, who had stopped overnight with wagon trains. But the trains had moved on, and there was no time for a friendship to develop.

Now she felt painfully vulnerable and inexperienced. She stood like a statue, watching as Eric's tall frame bent over the fireplace.

"Luck's with us again," he said. "There's dry wood in the barrel."

"G . . . good," she chattered. If only she could get warm, she could think straight; but as long as she was frozen, her brain refused to function. She took a deep breath and tried to reason with herself.

Eric Christensen was not a dangerous man, she told herself firmly, watching as he laid thin strips of wood into the blackened fireplace. He was a good man . . . she sensed that in the way he spoke to her, the way he had defended the trader at the post when her father would have cheated him. And he had traded a gold nugget for her! One he had doubtlessly worked hard to obtain.

Her apprehension had begun to fade until she'd remembered the nugget and wondered again about its worth. Well, she'd just repay him and then she wouldn't feel obligated.

Her teeth had ceased to chatter and she decided it was time to clear up this uncomfortable matter. "When we reach the post, my parents will pay you for the nugget . . . and your trouble," she added. She tried to speak with conviction, but her voice sounded uncertain, still containing a slight tremor. She stared at his long back in the buckskin jacket, waiting for him to respond. He merely whittled away at the wood chips, concerned only with starting a fire. He lit a match and the flame caught, crawling over the chips to the layered wood.

He stood again, and Sara's eyes skipped across the broad shoulders that added strength to his tall frame. Her freezing hands clenched at her sides. She was no match for a man so powerful. Yet there were her boots, she reminded herself.

"Are you hungry?" he asked.

"Yes. And I imagine you are, too." Here was a way to begin to repay him. Thank God she could cook. She hurried across to the narrow wooden shelf. "I'll fix supper," she offered, staring doubtfully at the items there. One can of beans and three sprouting potatoes.

She glanced around the room. From the absence of heavy clothing on the wall pegs, it was obvious Ben planned to be gone for a while and had left little behind. She sighed, determined to make do.

She pushed back the soiled lace cuffs of her sleeves and searched for a pot or pan. She located one of each, along with a sharp knife and a wooden cooking spoon.

She peeled and sliced the potatoes while Eric poked at the fire. When she finished, she hurried to the door. As she lifted the latch, the wind seized the door from her grasp and whipped her skirt about her slim legs.

"What are you doing?" he yelled, poking at the fire.

"Getting water for the potatoes," she called, dipping her hand down to a clean mound of snow. Her hand stung briefly before she dashed the snow into the pan and hurried back inside, throwing her weight against the door to close it.

Eric had crossed the room and was frowning down into the pan. For a moment, she forgot what she was doing as she felt herself being drawn to this tall, rugged male who made her anxious and nervous, yet sharply aware of her femininity. It was a strange new experience and her fear of him was giving way to fear of her strong attraction to him, and where it might lead her.

"The snow will melt to water. I'll put the pan on the edge of the fireplace. That's the purpose of that smooth rock there," she inclined her head in that direction.

He stepped aside, glancing back at the fire. "I suppose. But I've lived at this high altitude for two years and I've yet to cook a decent potato. Of course, I'm no cook. It's a bad thing for a man who can't cook to live alone."

His words seemed to follow her as she swept past him and knelt by the fire, placing the pan on the smooth rock. *Alone*, he said. She had been tormented with questions about him, but she told herself it made no difference to her if he were married or a bachelor. All she cared about was getting back to the post. Still . . . it wouldn't hurt to be pleasant, she supposed. He'd given her no reason to question his motives.

"The secret to cooking potatoes is to cut them in tiny pieces," she said in an attempt to begin a conversation. "If you aren't spoiled to well-cooked potatoes, maybe you won't mind if these are half-done."

"I won't mind," he sighed wearily. "I'm going to fetch my saddlebag and bedroll." The door opened and closed, admitting a gust of frigid air. Sara shivered, extending her cold fingers to the fire. A smile of satisfaction curved her lips as the heat of the fire liquified the snow; then she stood up and went back to the can of beans. She frowned at the long Bowie knife, obviously used as a can opener. Summoning her courage, she lifted the knife and tested its sharp blade with a cautious finger.

She set the can on the table and grasped it firmly, stabbing the blade into the top of the can. It penetrated with a light crunch. She was diligently working the metal loose when the door opened and Eric's long shadow fell over the room.

"Wait!" He dropped his bundle and bounded to her side, quickly removing the knife and can from her capable hands.

"I can do it," she protested, proud that she was managing without his help.

"I have no doubt that you can," he said as a slow grin crept over his lips. "But just to be on the safe side, allow me."

The grin unnerved her even more, and the strong hand that brushed hers lightly as he took the knife made matters worse.

"Mr. Christensen, I wish you'd stop treating me like a Southern belle who can't do anything for herself!"

He said nothing until he'd opened the can and wiped the blade of the knife across his sleeve. Then his blue eyes sharpened as he glanced at her.

"What makes you think a Southern belle can't do anything?" he asked. "Have you ever lived in the South?"

Sara stiffened. She knew he was baiting her, just as Ernest baited the traders who came to the post. She had no experience in coquettish banter, as Amanda, her tutor, had called it. She remembered how Amanda had sometimes teased her husband, and Sara shrugged. That wasn't her way. Her eyes drifted from the neatly-opened can to Eric's sculpted lips, lean hard jaw, and wide-set blue eyes.

"I've never been anywhere," she said flatly, "so I don't know how Southern women act." She sighed. "I shouldn't have said that."

"At least you're honest. I appreciate honesty. some *Southern belles*, as you refer to them, are prone to little white lies. At least

Kathleen was," he muttered under his breath as he turned and picked up his blanket and bedroll.

Kathleen . . .

The name seemed to swell in the silence of the cabin as the fire cracked and hissed. *Kathleen*, she thought as she dumped the beans into the pan which she placed near the fire. If there was a woman back in the South, Sara didn't want to know about her. At least, not for a while.

She knelt by the fire, gratefully absorbing its penetrating warmth. She'd never once felt warm in Crying Wind's lodge, despite the animal skins and the low fire always burning on the earthen floor.

"What really happened?" he asked quietly. He was spreading a blanket over the floor, and he motioned her to sit down.

Slowly, she complied, her eyes returning to the fire. "How did I happen to be kidnapped by the Indians? Is that what you mean?"

At his affirmative nod, she wrapped her skirt around her and hugged her knees. "I was hoping you'd been sent to Bear Claw's camp by my father. . . ." Her voice trailed away as she glanced from the fire to his face. "I watched you ride into our post last week," she said. "I admired the way you stood up for the man with the mules. Few men challenge my father like that."

"Ernest Jackson is your father?" he asked again; a disbelieving frown crossing his forehead.

"Yes. I thought, or rather I hoped, my

parents had hired you to come to Bear Claw's camp for me. I assumed they'd heard we never made it to Colorado City, but . . ." She shook her head sadly. "I guess they never found poor Sam."

"Sam?"

"Trapper Sam. Ma persuaded him to take me to Colorado City after Bear Claw and his braves came to the post and wanted to trade for me. He said if I didn't go with them when they returned at daybreak, there'd be a battle." She bit her lip, shutting off her words. She didn't want to reveal to Eric the real reason Bear Claw had wanted her; after all, there had been a mistake. She was certain of that. All of Elsie and Ernest's hostility toward "savages" crowded into her mind.

She thought about how the people at the post had reacted when Bear Claw announced she was the daughter of Crying Wind. Despite Elsie's stern rebuttal, she felt a change in the attitude of those around her. She sensed their doubt and suspicion, even among people whom she considered her friends. For as long as she could remember, people at the post scorned half-breeds. Maybe Eric felt the same way.

She leaned forward to check the simmering potatoes. "Supper's almost ready," she said.

They ate in silence. The hard, freezing ride had taken its toll and now the warmth of the fire and the comfort of food in their stomachs made them listless. Sara began to yawn as her eyes moved longingly toward the single cot. She'd spent a comfortable hour with him, and now her suspicions were fading.

"Here." He reached down to take the tin plate from her relaxed hand. "You take the cot. I'll sleep on my bedroll."

She curled up on the cot and threw her robe over her weary body. In less than five minutes, she was asleep.

Eric, in contrast, sat staring into the fire, watching the flames dance over the wood and seeing in those dancing flames the face of Kathleen, the bride of his youth. And another face, a tiny cherubic face whose golden features matched his own.

Eric's large hand curled into a fist, the knuckles leaping into pearl ridges. His thick brown lashes swept downward like a curtain, blocking the fiery reflections from his tormented eyes. They were gone now and he could only hope to see them again in the Land of the Sun, as the Indians referred to heaven.

He took a deep, long breath, and as he did so the scent of the woman sleeping nearby filled his nostrils. He opened his eyes and looked over at the cot, tracing the outline of her body beneath the robe.

Shame had kept her from admitting she was the daughter of Crying Wind, but he'd already heard the rumor. It had spread like a raging brushfire across the territory. He'd heard a half-drunk trapper repeating the tale on the banks of Fountain Creek a few days before. It was the reason he had believed Sara at Bear Claw's camp, even though at first glance she looked like one of them. After she spoke to him, he knew the truth; still, it had taken some thought on how best to get her away from the camp. The nugget had proven to be the answer.

He heaved a deep sigh and turned back to the fire. He'd take her back to the post; what else could he do? But he dreaded her return, for she was about to discover a truth that was both shocking and heartbreaking. She didn't belong to the Utes, and sadly, she no longer belonged with the whites who knew the story. Her life would be different now, very different.

Eric had slept only a short while when the horses whinnied. He sat up, glancing through the darkness to Sara. The coals of the fire gave a feeble glow to the room, and he could see that she was sleeping soundly. Quietly, he slipped out of his bedroll, wearing only his long johns as he tiptoed barefoot across the earthen floor. He seized the rifle, leaning upright against the doorjamb.

Cautiously, he opened the door and peered into the darkness. The wind was sighing through the tall pines, which were burdened with three more inches of snow. Eric's eyes crept over the clearing, seeing nothing. The horses whinnied again, a nervous sound that signaled trouble. He returned to the fire and shoved his feet into his boots. He glanced again at Sara's still form before he sneaked out the door and crept around the corner of the cabin.

Through the stormy night he could see his stallion rebelliously tossing his head against the rope. Several yards away, the mare was still, but her eyes were fixed on the woods.

Eric listened. A heavy gust of breath sounded in the cold stillness. He squinted. The hulk of a grizzly came into focus as he ambled out of the pines. Eric's heart jumped.

It was not a large grizzly, but Eric knew size was not always a measure of strength and determination. Ever so carefully, he raised his gun and crept around the back of the cabin. His eyes never left the grizzly, whose ribs swelled in a huge breath as he tested the wind with his nose. The bear ambled forward, its dark, glassy eyes trained on the nervous horses. Like a ghost, it crossed the white blanket of snow toward the horses, and Eric took a step forward, hoisting his gun. The bear spotted him and with a mighty roar, plunged straight for him.

He drew a bead on the grizzly and carefully pulled the trigger. He tried not to think of the consequences if he missed. Certain death for himself and Sara, as well. A hungry grizzly denied of food in a blizzard was the most formidable kind of foe.

The boom of the gun splintered the night, followed by a wild bawl of pain as the grizzly reared, staggered forward, then fell, only a few dozen yards from Eric.

Eric lowered the gun and stood shivering as he stared at the dying grizzly. It was a close call; the grizzly had been exceptionally fast.

"Eric? E*ric*!"

Sara's panicked scream cut through the night, and suddenly he was in full control again. He fired another shot, finishing off the suffering animal.

"Eric! Oh no!"

Sara stood at the corner of the cabin, her hands to her mouth, her body trembling as she stared at the grizzly.

"It's all right, Sara," he assured her as he moved to her side. "He's dead."

Sara flew into his arms and began to sob against his chest. He cradled her against him for a moment, a sudden tenderness touching his heart, a tenderness that had evaded him for a long time.

"We'd better get inside before we freeze."

He led her back to the warm cabin and bolted the door. "Don't cry," he said as he tightened his arm around her shoulders.

"I guess my tears are just a way of letting off steam from all that's happened. And the grizzly"—she shook her head, looking up into his eyes—"brought back a terrible memory. Last year a good friend of ours was mauled in the Tarryalls. They only found parts of him."

"Here, sit down," he said. "I'll stoke up the fire."

Sara sank onto the cot, her arms clenched around her trembling body. "I'm behaving like a child," she fussed, suddenly angry with herself. "You're the one who just risked your life. . . ."

"We didn't get gobbled up by the grizzly," he said, grinning at her. "That's all that matters."

"What happened?" she cupped her chin with her hand and stared at him.

"I heard the horses acting up. I thought—" He broke off, unwilling to voice his concern that the Utes might be trailing them. He still remembered the cold hate in White Buffalo's eyes. He stood, staring at the crackling flames as he brushed his hands against his long johns. The feel of the thin cotton under his fingers suddenly reminded him of his scanty dress. Automatically, his eyes flew to Sara.

She, too, had suddenly become aware of his state of undress. Every muscle and bone was clearly outlined in the skin-tight long johns. He whirled, seeking his clothes.

"Well, you saved me again," she said nervously, standing up to divert her attention to the fire while he dressed.

Hell, she was beginning to think of him as some sort of hero, he thought, slightly irritated. He had merely reacted as any man worth his salt would have done. To his astonishment, he realized he *did* care about her. He fastened his pants and tugged on his shirt. Ever since he saw her, bedraggled and wide-eyed with fear, he'd felt an overpowering urge to protect and defend her. Not that he minded defending a pretty woman, but this one was different. She seemed lonely and vulnerable, yet there was a solid strength to her, a spirit not easily broken. His eyes returned to her, his mind puzzled.

She was standing before the fire, her slim fingers extended to absorb the warmth.

"You must be frozen," she said, glancing back over her shoulder.

He shrugged, ambling up to the fire. As the warmth penetrated his chilled body, he slowly relaxed and breathed a low, weary sigh. Tomorrow he'd return her to the post and then his life would be normal again. Or would it?

"You are a good man," she said, her voice a mere whisper above the crackling fire.

He turned to stare down at her. Again that sweet vulnerable expression in her eyes tugged at his heart. Eric swallowed, taking a step closer. The firelight danced over her face, illuminating her delicate features, casting a gleam in the dark eyes. He reacted totally from the instincts of a man who has known many women—and who had too often been without one the past months.

"Maybe not so good," he said huskily, as his arm swept out, pulling her against his chest. The dark eyes that widened in shock did not stop him, nor did the lips that seemed unfamiliar with a man's kiss. As his mouth covered hers, he sensed her awkwardness, then her hesitancy, though she did not pull away from him. If she'd lifted a hand to press against his chest, he might have stopped. But she didn't. Her lips were soft and warm, but unmoving beneath his, as he inclined his head and kissed her gently, tentatively.

Sara's experience with kisses had been severely limited. The texture of his lips was a shock to her; she expected a man as masculine as Eric to have rough lips, like Billy Whitaker who had yanked her behind the blacksmith shop one summer night and pressed his bearded face to hers. She had hated that kiss, and now she knew why. There had been no gentleness—and even more important, no desire—in it.

Her stiff arms uncoiled and suddenly she wanted very much to touch him, to rest her fingertips lightly on the strong muscles of his shoulder and arm, to feel the skin beneath his shirt. She lifted her hands, but her fingers were shy and hesitant. Then the kiss deepened, as the pressure of his mouth parted her lips and she felt the enticingly rough tip of his tongue against her own.

She gasped as his tongue teased hers, then ventured over the velvet curve of her lip. Her fingers crept up his muscled forearm and rested lightly on his broad shoulders. As the kiss deepened, Sara's heart began to pound, and a strange, lightheaded sensation swept over her. She found herself pressing against him until she realized what was happening, then suddenly she tore her mouth from his. Her dark eyes probed his face, reading the smouldering passion in his blue eyes.

Sara's breath caught in her throat. Desire and resistance fought within her, drawing her body closer though her hands gently pushed against his chest.

"Sara, don't be afraid. I would never hurt you." He smiled gently.

She stared at his smile, at the even white teeth, as her mouth still tingled from the warm imprint of his lips.

"I believe you," she answered. "I don't know how or why, but I know I can trust you, no matter what."

There was something deep and strong and

honorable that ruled Eric. Despite her inexperience with men, she sensed this about him. With a regretful sigh, he slowly released her.

"You know just what to say, Sara." He dropped to his bedroll and slowly shook his head. "I would have to be the worst kind of varmit to take advantage of you now."

She went back to the cot and sat down, thoroughly confused. "I never had a beau," she sighed. "Ma hovered over me like a mother hen and Ernest was so mean no one would court me."

Eric's mouth tightened. Jackson was a real jackass. Everyone in the Territory knew that. It would have been easier for Sara to run away with some upstart than to live with that bastard.

"I know I owe you a lot," Sara said, "but . . ."

"But you don't owe me your body." A grim smile touched his mouth as he looked at her. His basic need to protect and defend rushed back to him. It was his Southern upbringing, the strict code of honor his mother had instilled in him and demanded he live by. He'd shed that code of honor many times on occasions when respect was not the issue. But now, all the old-fashioned traits rushed back with the knowledge of Sara's inexperience.

He closed his eyes, trying to gain control of his physical urges. "We'd better get a few hours sleep before dawn breaks," he said. "Then I'll see you safely back to the post."

5

Bitter cold crept through the lodge that Shane shared with Wasatch and Ignacio. Wasatch's friendship was more guarded now, while his father, Shavano, ignored Shane completely. But that would change today, he promised himself, for this would be the day he caught up with the big buck. He had made that pledge to himself upon awakening.

He pulled on his deerskin cap and buckskin jacket, placed his rifle in the leather scabbard he had made, then slipped out into the frozen dawn. The wind bit at his face with the sharpness of pine needles as his boots crunched through the snow to the corral where the pinto's head was lowered in sleep.

Shane had hardened himself to the elements, had learned to endure the cold as the Utes had done for so many years. As he saddled his pinto, he thought of the trappers and fifty-niners, hovered at the trading posts like shivering rats. He snorted when he compared them to Wasatch and Shavano and the other brave Utes.

He stroked the cold neck of his horse, promising food later. "For now, we must find the buck," he whispered, tying his scabbard onto the saddle.

Mounting, he moved quietly from the sleeping camp. Only Shavano watched from the open flap of his lodge, his dark eyes squinting thoughtfully. Shane felt those eyes following him, but he turned his attention toward the eastern sky. He felt the excitement of the hunt again, sharpening his senses and quickening his movements. Hunting was his gift, the one thing he did well.

Though he was impatient with men, he had infinite patience in tracking the animals, in waiting for them to come down from the high craggy rocks to mate and winter. He thought of the bighorn sheep that came to the valley to rear their lambs until the break-up of the ice, when the high ridges would call them back. The other animals did this as well. Shane respected animals far more than most humans, and it grieved him to take their lives, but he'd long ago reconciled himself to the fact that man must have dominion over the animals. It was his means of survival.

Suddenly, a lonely wail rose from a mountain peak, building into a quivering note before falling away into the silence of the valley below. It was a wild and beautiful song, and Shane's eyes swung upward to the craggy hills and moved slowly over each ridge, halting abruptly on the elk standing on the tip of a rocky ledge.

An elk! The king of the Tarryalls and the Utes' favorite meat! His hand crept to the rifle that was his most prized possession. He'd worked an entire summer at Seven Mile Stage

Stop to earn the short, heavy rifle made by the Hawken brothers. Designed for hunting game, it was less likely to break than other rifles.

He kept a firm grip on the reins as he guided his horse up a narrow back trail cushioned by three feet of snow. All the while his eyes were trained on the elk, whose frosty breath sent tiny clouds into the gray morning.

The elk began to move, picking his way north. Shane's eyes raced ahead, noting the wall of rocks that would soon camouflage the elk. If he were to get a shot, it must be in the next few minutes. He reigned his pinto behind a wide spruce and slid from the horse. His movements were cautious and calculated, although the elk was still a hundred yards away. He pulled his rifle from its scabbard and leaned his body against the trunk of the tree. Fitting the rifle to his shoulder, he took aim.

The gun blast shattered the silence and the elk lunged forward. Shane reloaded and fired again. The second bullet found its mark and the big animal toppled. Shane lowered the gun and stood for a moment, staring at the elk. He felt sadness for the animal, but he knew there would be no hunger in Shavano's camp tonight.

He turned back to the pinto, replacing his rifle.

Sitting cross-legged before the fire, Shane's dark eyes held Shavano's piercing stare. Exhaustion claimed his body, yet his mind was too anxious for sleep. He'd returned to camp for pack horses and, with Wasatch's help, brought home the elk. Following the Ute courting ritual, he'd hung the elk carcass on the sturdiest branches of a tall tree near Star of the Morning's lodge. If she wished to accept him, she would skin and dress the animal, then build a fire to prepare the meat in a meal for him.

Shane's heart had ached for Star as she worked tirelessly through the long day, skinning the elk, then roasting some of the meat on a spit above the fire. Her eyes glowed with pride when she glanced over her shoulder at Shane, seated with Wasatch and Shavano, and there was no weariness in her face.

She'd served him the roasted meat an hour before, and now he had to secure the approval of Shavano before their union could be consummated. This was sacred, though there would be no marriage ceremony. If he were joined with Star, he would still be free to leave if he desired, for this was the Ute custom. But he was certain that would never happen.

Shavano sucked deeply of his clay pipe, his stern eyes dropping to the fire. In a corner of the lodge, Wasatch sat, quietly thoughtful. He loved Shane like a brother; the bitterness he felt for the palefaces who seized the Yuuttaa's hunting grounds and streams did not apply to Shane. Nor did the desire for revenge, which burned deep in his soul.

He glanced at Shane, remembering happy days. It had always seemed to him that Shane was more Yuutta than paleface. He'd stared at his blood-brother's dark eyes, observed his gift for tracking the animals and shook his head in disbelief. To his own dishonor, the blood-brother was a better hunter than he. But this time he was grateful. He rubbed his full stomach, remembering the tasty elk.

Shavano spoke, breaking the silence of the past hour. "The Yuuttaa do not wish to mix blood with the palefaces." His strong voice held a deep note of authority, and Shane's heart sank. "But you are brave and strong. You bring food to my people whose spirits are as black as the Misho-tunga. And now you wish to be Yuuttaa?" he asked, his tone less stern.

Shane leaned forward, trying to maintain his composure, yet eager to convey his fierce desire.

"I feel more Yuuttaa than white. My heritage is unknown. I was left beside a wagon train. The paleface who called himself my father believed the blood of the red man ran in my veins." A grim smile settled over his lips. "Before I left his cabin for the last time, he said I was more like a"—he bit off the word *savage*—"a half-breed than a white."

Shavano's dark eyes now held compassion for the young warrior before him, for he knew what it had cost him to speak those words.

"And you wish Star of the Morning to be your squaw?" he asked, studying Shane carefully.

Shane nodded, holding the older man's gaze. "I will take good care of her."

Shavano nodded, rising to his feet. "Then

you shall have Star of the Morning."

Shane pulled himself to his feet, trying to find the best words to express his gratitude, for this was the happiest moment of his life. "For all my days, I will try to live up to the trust you have placed in me," he said huskily.

Shavano clasped his hands on Shane's shoulders. "Star of the Morning waits."

A smile broke across Shane's face as he turned to Wasatch. As their eyes met, Wasatch threw his arms around Shane's shoulders.

"You have been a brother since our knives carved trails of blood that joined us. Now we are Yuuttaa brothers!"

Awkwardly, Shane returned his embrace. His throat was tight, and words failed him as he nodded briskly, then hurried from the lodge.

His eyes flew to Star of the Morning's lodge, and the blood raced in his veins. He hesitated uncertainly at the flap, wondering about Nish-ki, who shared the lodge.

Star had waited eagerly, and the crunch of boots drew her to the flap. The light bounding step so familiar to her sent her heart soaring. She threw open the flap and smiled into Shane's radiant face.

"Nish-ki joins Running Doe in her lodge," she said, gripping his hand.

Shane stared at her. Although it was a Ute superstition not to comb their hair at night, he saw that Star's hair fell smoothly about her shoulders, its gleaming mass framing her radiant face. She wore a white doeskin dress, intricately beaded in a design of stars. On her feet were beaded moccasins, but her brown legs were bare of leggings.

Taking a deep breath, he stepped inside the lodge. A small fire burned in the center of the earthen floor and he saw, despite her weariness, that she had arranged his possessions with hers. His saddle sat by the fire to dry. His gun and scabbard, along with the pinto's leather harness, were tied to the lodge poles. Her moccasins and doeskin dresses hung there as well. In a corner, willow branches were neatly stacked. His Navajo blanket, which he spread beneath his saddle, was stretched across a bed of buffalo skins. He stared at the bed, his heart racing.

Star's slim fingers wound around his arm and he turned back with a smile. Drifting from her was the smell of pine and something more, some special herb that she had dried and saved for this occasion.

"I have bathed," she said. "Nish-ki went to the stream this afternoon, broke the ice there and warmed the water before the fire."

Shane glanced down at the large water-jug basket. Near the basket, he saw a clay dish holding a smooth round stone and something that resembled soap.

"I will bathe you," she said, leading him around the fire. "You are Yuuttaa now. You must learn our ways."

Her fingers slipped to the neck of his shirt, tugging gently. Impatiently, his hand shot out, yanking the shirt over his head and tossing it aside.

She knelt down, cupping her palms in the basket to bring the warm water to his face. Her gentle fingers trailed the water over his dry face, then she dipped her palms again to trickle water over his broad shoulders, down his hair-shadowed chest. Shane watched, spellbound. Her eyes shone with love, and the shyness that had always accompanied their courtship was disappearing.

She reached for the stone and dipped it in the clay pot.

"What's that?" he asked curiously.

She laughed softly. "It will not sound pleasant to you, but it is something you will grow to like. Fat of the deer, dried in the sun and filled with camas bulbs. It is what the palefaces call soap."

As the warm stone made gentle, tantalizing friction down his jaw and neck and across his shoulder, he found the scent pleasant, the bath relaxing. Her fingers darted from his shoulders to the water basket; then she turned to his back, rotating the warm stone in small circles. He breathed a deep, contented sigh.

"You have won my tribe's approval," she said softly, "but we do not speak of that now. We speak only of our love." Her dark eyes returned to his as she finished bathing his back then diverted her attention to his chest, damp and gleaming in the fireglow.

Her hand pressed gently at the firmness of his belly, and Shane felt the blood rush to his groin. Her eyes shot to his and the flames of passion that had begun to smolder in his eyes were reflected in her uptilted face. Her fingers moved lower, dragging at the waist band of his britches.

Their eyes joined in eager anticipation as he tugged the britches off and stood before her, his body proclaiming his need for her. Shane watched with mounting passion as her eyes crept downward and widened. He saw the rapid rise and fall of her chest and her breath quickened. She knelt before him, dipping the stone into the water and soap, then working it gently down his muscular legs, avoiding his manhood.

He stood rigid, unable to move or speak as desire lashed through him like summer thunder rolling over the mountain peaks. He clenched his teeth, wondering if he could hold on until she had finished the bath.

He felt the stone tracing the curve of each toe before returning to the water again. He watched, fascinated. Carefully, she placed the stone in its dish and dipped her slim fingers into the soap. Her touch was featherlight as her hands stroked warm water and soap onto his manhood. The breath rasped through his throat. As she plunged her fingers back into the water and lifted them to rinse him, he could see that the slim little fingers had begun to tremble. It took all of his willpower not to reach down and haul her up to his side, press his mouth against hers, then lift her to the buffalo robe. But Star's pride was a precious thing, and the ritual she was performing had been carefully planned. He would not interrupt until she had finished.

A small, clean animal skin was whisked from a corner and she began to rub his body with more urgency. When he looked into her face, he saw a glow spreading over her cheeks as her dark eyes grew drowsy. Their eyes held in an embrace of longing.

"Star," he groaned, "I can wait no longer."

"Nor can I, my noble warrior." She reached for his hands and placed them on the sides of her dress, with a smile of complete surrender.

He understood the gesture, and gently lifted the dress over her dark head. She took it from his hands and placed it beside his clothes near the fire.

Shane's eyes caressed the body of the woman he had loved and desired for the past year. She was almost exactly as he had imagined. Only he had not, in his wildest dreams, known the effect the dusky brown skin, lit with the glow of the fire, would have on him. His heart leapt in his chest and for a moment it seemed an iron band constricted his breathing. He felt drops of perspiration gathering on his brow and upper lip as she stood with her hands at her side, waiting now for him to become the aggressor.

For a moment he could only stare in wonder at each part of her body. Her shoulders were narrow, her arms long and slender. Her ribs made bold ridges against her smooth skin, but the breasts were perfectly rounded with taut nipples the color of mountain honey. Her stomach was flat, almost sunken, and automatically his hand reached out to press the flatness, wanting to fill it with their child.

The skin was warm beneath his splayed fingers as his eyes fell to the softly rounded muscles of thigh and calf on slender brown legs.

When he had completed his inspection, the breath he hadn't known he was holding erupted from his chest in a mighty groan. His arms wrapped around her, pulling her against him. As their bodies met and his rougher skin pressed into the velvet of hers, her head dipped back and her eyes grew enormous. Her lips parted, begging for his.

He stared at her lips but he did not kiss her. He turned her in his arms and led her to the bed of soft animal skins. Then as they dropped to the bed, his mouth touched hers, his tongue gently parting her lips. Her arms slipped around his chest as his hands gripped her waist, molding her to him.

An exquisite kind of torture weaved through his body as he sought to lead her gently through their joining. This was her first time, and he must remember that. He had waited for so long; it must be perfect.

Beyond the lodge, someone had begun to play a flute, and the mellow notes drifted over the still night. Shane's hands moved over Star, touching, soothing, preparing. But soon her little fingers were tugging at him, and as the flute music grew more tantalizing, so did their lovemaking. The erotic dip and flow of the flute blended with the fierce drum beat of their hearts, the soft cooing sounds from Star of the Morning, the rugged moans that Shane could no longer hold back.

"Star . . . Star . . . I don't want to hurt you," he whispered against her moist lips.

"You could never hurt me." Her voice trembled as her arms reached out to wrap around his glistening back.

Shane moved over her, entering her as gently as possible. His heart pounded. Blood roared through his head like a swift river. He felt the barrier of her maidenhood give way, and he was, at last, inside the warm velvet that tightened while drawing him deeper.

It seemed all the elements of the fiercest storm raged through his brain. The wind tore through his mind, lightning zigzagged his senses, thunder crashed in his ears . . . then, as the note of the flute quickened and ascended into a high wail, their cries of passion flew into the night, drowned by the shrilling crescendo of the flute.

Peace, joy, sweet, sweet release filled every corner of his mind, touched every part of his body. The storm was replaced with golden sunlight, birdsong, a thousand wildflowers dancing on wooded hillsides. Ecstasy filled their hearts and like the eagle they had so often watched from the mountain top, they too circled and soared through space.

Unbound at last. Free.

6

Sara's heart was lodged in her throat when finally her eyes scanned the valley and came to rest on the trading post. Her hand automatically gripped the reins tighter, slowing her mare.

"What's wrong?" Eric asked, noting the change in her expression.

Sara swallowed. "I don't know. I feel . . . uncomfortable."

Eric grinned. "You're the one who insisted on riding sidesaddle."

"Most folks think women should ride this way," she argued. It was now important to abide by what most people thought. She had also retrieved a comb from her scattered possessions and pulled her hair into a sedate bun. Although Sara would not admit it, she was trying *not* to look Indian.

"I feel anxious about returning," she finally admitted. "I don't understand why Ma didn't send someone to Bear Claw's camp. I didn't expect Ernest to do anything, but Ma . . ." her voice trailed away as her eyes focused on the approaching pine buildings, clustered together in the snowy meadow. Smoke curled high in the sunny skies, attesting to the lighter

PASSION'S PEAK 97

air that accompanied warm weather.

As their horses trotted through the gate, Sara's face fell at the meager greeting offered by a small group of stunned faces. Eric's eyes drifted over the men, reading something more than shock in their expressions. Pity? Embarrassment?

Sara drew rein on her mare at the post kitchen and dropped down.

"Ma!" she called, throwing open the kitchen door. She stopped in her tracks as a Mexican woman, years younger than her mother, looked up from the stove.

"Where's Ma?" Sara asked, glancing about.

The kitchen was different in a way she couldn't immediately define. The smells were spicier, pots and pans cluttered the countertops. It was a stark contrast to Elsie's neatness.

She turned questioning eyes to the woman, who stood twisting her plump hands in her apron.

"You are . . . Sara?"

She nodded, puzzled.

The woman dropped her head. "Your mother . . . is not here."

Sara whirled from the kitchen and hurried across the courtyard toward the cabin, her eyes flicking right to left. Where were the children? Where was Will? *Where was her mother?*

"Ma?" she called, bursting into the cabin, ready to hurl herself against the bosom of the woman who had given her so much love. After what she'd been through, she needed Elsie more than ever.

Clothing was scattered carelessly about, and snow clumps had melted to puddles of water on the wooden floor. Lifting her skirts to sidestep the water, Sara peered into a bedroom. She found only an empty, unmade bed. Frustration mounted as she flung open the door to her room.

Her mother was not there; neither were the few possessions that Sara had left behind. A cheap comb and brush and a black-lacquered hand mirror cluttered her tiny dresser.

In shock she walked over to peer into her closet. The heavy perfume of the Spanish woman clung to the unfamiliar dresses hanging there.

A gentle rap sounded at the front door, and she found Eric standing on the slab step, his eyes filled with concern.

"May I come in?" he asked.

She nodded blankly, glancing back at the cluttered room. "I don't know what's going on. Ma's not here...."

The sound of quick steps crunched over the snow beyond the open door, echoing in the tense silence that hung between Sara and Eric. Ernest Jackson poked his dark head through the door.

"Where's Ma?" Sara asked.

Behind the forced smile, her words held the echo of fear, a fear too horrible to name.

Ernest rubbed his hands down the front of his faded flannel shirt and shifted from one foot to another.

"Gone to Colorado City?" she asked as his eyes slid from her face. "She probably went to the Thompsons to see about me," she said, a frown crossing her brow as Ernest's eyes dropped.

Ernest coughed uncomfortably and loosened the tight collar of his shirt.

"Girl, I don't know how to say it, other than give it to you straight out." The silence in the room grated on Sara's nerves as she listened to the steady drip of melting snow on the eaves. Her eyes darted to Eric as he took a step toward her.

"Yore ma's heart give out the night you left," he finally blurted out. "We buried her the next day."

"*Buried her?*" Sara gasped, horrified. Buried her. . . ?

Her hands flew to her mouth to stifle the rising sobs. Through a blur of tears, she saw Eric reach for her hand while Ernest retreated toward the door.

"We never heard nuthin'," Ernest argued. "Figgert you was safe in Colorado City. Thought it was best not to send fer you, all things considered."

"What things?" she choked. "You knew I'd want to be at Ma's funeral!" She couldn't believe that the one person who had loved her was gone. She felt an arm slip around her shoulder, and she leaned against it, fearing her legs would buckle. Her ma *gone. Buried.*

Wiping at the streaming tears, she struggled for words. "Did she . . . suffer?"

Ernest shook his head. "She just come in here"—his eyes slid to the door of the room that had belonged to Sara—"laid down on your bed . . . and died."

Fresh tears stung her eyes. "My bed?" she echoed, scarcely aware she had left Eric's encircling arm and stumbled to the open door of the bedroom. Then her eyes fell on a tattered black lace petticoat and her grief burst into rage. She snatched the petticoat from the floor and hurled it against the wall. Then she spun on Ernest.

"And you moved that—that Mexican slut into *my* room? In Ma's house?" she shrieked.

"Sara," Eric warned under his breath.

"Watch your mouth, girl," Ernest snarled. "I had to have a cook."

"I can cook," she cried. "If only you'd sent for me—"

"I ain't gonna stir up war with them savages! Can't you git that through your head?" His eyes raked her slowly, contemptibly. "Besides, from what Bear Claw said, chances are you *are* the daughter of that squaw."

Blood rushed to Sara's face as she darted a wild glance at Eric. *He knows now*, she thought, waiting for him to react. But his grip merely tightened on her arm.

The room was spinning around her. She felt as though the earth had given way, and she was being sucked down into the recesses of hell. She would not let Ernest Jackson destroy her—she would not!

She forced herself to meet Ernest's hard eyes. This was no longer her home. She knew that now, but she made a valiant effort to stand her ground.

"I have spent the past week at Bear Claw's

camp," she answered more rationally. "That squaw could not possibly have been my mother." She waited for Ernest's reaction, but his expression hardly changed. "Anyway, she died yesterday." Suddenly she remembered Trapper Sam and lowered her eyes, guilt washing over her. First Trapper Sam and now Ma. All because of her!

"You know about Trapper Sam, don't you, Mr. Jackson?" Eric asked, holding Jackson's slithering glance.

"How would I know?" Ernest snapped. "First you come in here running off my customers. Now you're back tryin' to make me out a liar!"

Sara studied Ernest with the wisdom of eighteen years spent cringing under his scowls. Her ma had once told her that when Ernest was caught in a lie, his neck reddened. Her heart sank as she watched the flush form at his throat and spread up his bony neck. He'd known where she was all along and he'd done nothing!

Heartsick, she stumbled to the sofa and sat down, unable to stand on her own another second. "I'd like to have something to remember Ma by," she said dully, staring down at the water-stained planks. "Then I'll be leaving."

If she had looked at Ernest, she would have caught the faint sigh of relief, followed by the twitch of satisfaction on his mouth. Eric, however, missed nothing.

"Her things is in a trunk in the closet," he replied. "You kin have whatever you want."

He paused to clear his throat. "Where're you goin?"

Sara lifted her tear-stained face to him. Where indeed? She tried to think but her mind was locked in disbelief.

"I could take you to that family in Colorado City," Eric offered.

Sara nodded. "That's where we started. Ma and I nursed Mrs. Thompson through a stomach ailment when they first came to Colorado."

She took one long look at Ernest, her last. She had never loved him, but he had begrudgingly provided for her.

"You'll be better off there," Ernest declared, unable to meet her eyes again. "With all this business about Indians, some folks feel kinda diff'rent about . . ."

"Where is everyone?" she asked before he could say more.

Ernest kicked at a loose board. "Half the post left after yore ma died and Carlotta—"

"We'll be leaving as soon as Sara gets whatever she needs," Eric interrupted.

Ernest merely grunted and stalked out.

Sara sat staring at the door. How could any man be so cruel? She gripped her hands, too dazed to open her mouth. She felt the cushions of the sofa sink deeper as Eric settled at her side, but she couldn't face him. She had no idea what to say.

"Sara, I have great respect for the Utes," Eric began.

"But I'm not . . ." Her words died away as her eyes met his and he began to shake his head.

"It doesn't matter to me either way. Your mother's gone. You'll be better off someplace else."

She stared blankly at the cluttered room that seemed so strange to her now. Eric was right. She had to leave the post and it didn't really matter to her where she went. She took a deep breath and looked at Eric.

"What makes *you* so nice?" she asked bitterly. "I've brought you nothing but trouble. Like Trapper Sam, like Ma! You don't have to offer to help. I'll manage."

"Listen to me," he said, gripping her hand. "The trouble in your life comes from circumstances beyond your control. You're worth a hell of a lot more respect than you're getting *here*. It's time to get out of here and find a better life. I'm headed to Colorado City anyway. There's no reason you can't ride along with me."

She looked into his vivid blue eyes and her bitterness faded. She saw a deeply compassionate man strong enough to stand up to Ernest Jackson, grizzlies and snow storms—even the Indians. Yet he was gentle and caring, too. She swallowed, thinking he was the only person in the world she could trust right now.

"All right, but once I'm in Colorado City I can take care of myself," she stated firmly.

"Then get your things and let's go." He stood up.

"There's little to get."

Sara dragged herself to her feet and wandered into her mother's room. She stood for a moment staring at the trunk in the closet.

When she opened the lid, more tears filled her eyes at the sight of the rumpled dresses, the sturdy work shoes, the heavy wool cloak.

Her hands scooped up the dresses and she buried her face in the cold cloth, trying to find a lingering scent to forever etch in her memory. And it was there—the faint yeast-and-onion scent of Elsie Jackson.

Thank you, ma, she thought. *Thanks for loving and caring for me. It couldn't have been easy . . . with him.* She quickly replaced the dresses, poking further into the trunk. Her fingers closed over a small object, loose among the dresses. She stared down at the cameo pin, lifting it gently to her lips. This was the treasure she sought, the one she would keep with pride.

She closed the lid and bundled up the last of her possessions in a clean flour sack from her mother's cupboard.

"I'm ready," she announced to Eric. Her face was pale, haunted, but her chin was set determinedly.

"Then let's go. And incidentally, we'll consider your little mare a parting gift from Jackson. Unless he stops us."

Sara nodded as her eyes roamed over the cabin, silently bidding it good-bye. She hesitated in the door, remembering all the sessions with her tutor and the hopes and dreams of a bright future that she and Elsie had shared. But the hand of fate had smashed those dreams, whisked away everything that had been comfortable and secure. She was alone now, with only her own ingenuity to shape her future, and she knew her future would be difficult.

She was relieved to see that Eric had brought the horses to the door. It would save her the embarrassment of having to walk across the courtyard beneath rude, appraising stares. She tied her knapsack on the saddle, then thrust her boot into the stirrup and mounted like a man.

Eric's lips tilted in amusement as he tossed her the reins and climbed on his black stallion.

Impulsively, Sara jabbed her heels into the mare's side and tore out of the post without a backward glance.

The morning slipped away as they rode in silence. Eric glanced worriedly at Sara, who didn't speak a word after they left the post. Her eyes were distant and haunted but determination sat on her mouth. He knew she was hurting, but he chose to remain silent. Only she could come to terms with her pain, and that would take time.

He turned the leather reins over in his fingers, absently studying them. He was beginning to feel responsible for her, but she'd manage all right in Colorado City. He had to take care of his business, then he'd return to his cabin in the mountains. The nugget he'd left with Bear Claw was impressive, but nothing compared to the one he'd kept. That could be traded for staples and some cash in Colorado City, then he'd be on his way.

"Tell me about yourself."

The shock of her voice after such a long silence brought him upright in the saddle. He glanced at her curiously. "What do you want to know?"

She stared ahead and shrugged "Anything. Tell me about Georgia, your family there..."

"My family? Well"—he leaned back in the saddle—"my ancestors were Swedish."

She glanced at him. "That's why you're so blond."

He grinned. "Yeah. They came to America in search of a better life. They found jobs in New York but quickly moved South after hearing of friends who had settled in Georgia. My grandfather got work picking cotton on a plantation. Over the years, he worked his way up to overseer. Finally, when the owner died, he rewarded Grandpa's years of faithful service by leaving him 100 acres of land to start his own place."

A smile crossed Sara's lips. "That's very touching."

Eric nodded. "He learned how to work the land, to grow quality cotton, and how best to market it. His two sons worked side by side with him, and over the years they expanded their land to about 1,000 acres. My father was the oldest of the two sons and he eventually bought out the other son, who decided he preferred an easier life in Atlanta."

The worried expression that had filled Sara's face all morning was now replaced by a look of interest. "How many are in your family?" she asked.

"There were three boys." He looked out across the mountains and sighed. "We were quite different. We always disagreed, particularly on how to run the plantation. After my father died, I decided to come West and make a new life for myself."

"I see."

His eyes drifted to her, and he felt a sudden urge to explain what he felt. "I never agreed with slavery. The South's in for some hard times because a lot of stubborn people are going to resist the changes." He shook his head and his blue eyes deepened thoughtfully. "I'm not sure how I feel about the threat of war between North and South. I mean, I agree with some of the changes, but I don't see anything civil about a war to settle it."

Sara nodded, thinking of what he had said. Then she remembered his mention of the name Kathleen, and she couldn't resist asking another question. "Did you have a family of your own?"

His eyes lifted to something far away on the horizon, and for a long moment it seemed he wasn't going to answer.

"Not anymore," he finally replied. "I lost a wife and son to the fever a year before I left. It was another reason I needed a change."

Sara's breath caught at this bit of information. "I . . . I'm sorry," she replied. "But now I understand why you are so compassionate. I think that's true of people who have known great sorrow."

They rode in silence, each lost in thought. Sara tried to imagine how Eric's life had been . . . the heartbreaking loss of a wife and child, the difficulty of coming west to start over. . . . Her throat tightened as she thought of this, and a sad silence hung between them. She was relieved to see the distant huddle of log buildings in a flat meadow cupped by foothills and overshadowed by the brooding hulk of Pikes Peak.

Eric's eyes were tracing the outline of Colorado City and he spoke again, in a calm, leisurely tone this time.

"It's a rowdy little settlement that popped up as a supply base for packtrains heading up the Ute trail to the mountains. Ever been here?"

She shook her head. "I've never been anywhere, Eric."

Her eyes wandered curiously over the rows of rough pine buildings, taking in a boarding house, a mercantile, several saloons, a couple of eating establishments, and the stable and blacksmith shop. Side roads led to numerous cabins, all similar in size and shape.

"I wonder how we'll find the Thompsons," she said, looking worriedly at him.

"We'll stop in at Bull Wright's stable. He knows everyone."

Sara fell silent as Eric led the way, drawing rein at the log hitching rail before a large, open-ended building that was a combination of blacksmith shop and stable.

A heavy-set man was laying a hot iron to a horseshoe, but at the sight of Eric, he plunged the iron into a barrel of water and came striding forward.

"Afternoon, Bull," Eric called.

His nickname suited him, Sara thought, as she looked at the man who was well over six feet tall, with large blunt features and shaggy gray hair. He shook hands with Eric, then his eyes moved to Sara, widening with curiosity.

"This is Sara Jackson," Eric said. "I'm trying to help her find a Thompson family." He glanced inquiringly at Sara. "Do you remember the man's first name?"

"Burgess," she answered, grateful for the unusual name which made him easier to track.

"Burgess Thompson?" The big man recognized the name. "Real nice people. But they moved back to Kansas last summer. The missus couldn't take the hard winters here, so they went home."

Sara stared at him, unable to believe her ears. Her hopes began to plummet as she shifted in the saddle and began to appraise the rowdy little town. Well, if she was going to stay here, she'd have to get a job, that's all. She was used to hard work.

"Thanks, Bull," Eric was saying. "Maybe we'll leave our horses to be rubbed down. Darkfire's had a lot of miles lately. In the meantime, we'll grab a bite to eat. Does Mrs. Willis still make those good buckwheat pancakes?"

Bull's slips spread in an approving smile. "They're better than ever, Christensen." He rubbed his sagging belly, then reached up to stroke the black stallion's neck. "Darkfire's a fine horse, yessir."

Absently, Sara stared at the horse, thinking it was the first time she'd heard his name. When she realized Eric was swinging down, she shook her mind back to the present and hopped off her mare.

"No use trying to think on an empty stomach," Eric said as they turned and began to walk across the street. "And I could use a strong cup of coffee. What about you?"

"I suppose," Sara mumbled, too frustrated to say more as they approached the small log dwelling with red-checkered curtains at the window and a hand-painted EATS sign over the front door. Maybe they needed an extra hand in the kitchen, she thought hopefully.

Eric opened the door and they stepped inside. Half a dozen square tables and tall wooden chairs filled the room. At first glance, it appeared all tables were occupied, but Eric located one in the rear. Sara's eyes were boldly exploring the room as Eric pulled out a chair for her.

"Luck isn't running in your favor lately, is it?" A grin curled his lips and Sara realized he was trying to tease her out of her gloom, but it wasn't working.

"No, it isn't," she answered solemnly, "but I'll find work."

A tiny, gray-haired woman with a friendly smile approached their table and nodded in recognition as she looked at Eric.

"Mrs. Willis, do you have any of those good buckwheat pancakes?" Eric leaned back in his chair and delivered a charming smile.

"So happens I do! Two orders?"

"And coffee. Mrs. Willis, I'd like you to meet my friend, Sara Jackson."

"Pleased to meet you, young lady." The woman nodded politely and turned to go.

"Mrs. Willis?" Sara's voice halted the woman in her tracks. "Do you happen to need any help in the kitchen? I'm experienced," she added with a smile.

The woman looked from Sara to Eric then shook her head. "I'm sorry, honey. Half the women in Colorado City are looking for work while their husbands are up in the hills seeking their fortunes! I got a long waiting list if anybody quits." She turned to Eric. "Can you believe how this place is growing? There must be around 300 cabins here now!" Her hazel eyes returned to Sara. "Sorry, dear. Wish I could help you out."

"It's okay." Sara shrugged, trying to hold her smile, but the corners of her mouth felt hard and rigid.

"We'll check the mercantile," Eric offered. "I know the owner."

Sara nodded, her smile now frozen against stiff cheeks. Her pride kept her from crumbling, but the woman's words had dashed her hopes. When the food was delivered, she fell silent, but Eric didn't seem to mind. They were entertained by the lively conversations around them. Sara forced herself to listen in an effort to keep her mind from her problems.

"It's rich diggin's, I'm tellin' ya. But gettin there is the problem," a strong voice behind them was saying. "First, there's that damned rough Ute trail, then there's the deep snow on the back side of the Peak.

Another man interrupted. "Jim, there ain't no point in goin' till break-up, 'cause all the streams are frozen to a solid chunk of ice."

Sara glanced at Eric, measuring his reaction to the conversation. A muscle in his jaw clenched as he listened to the men whose words had obviously set him on edge.

"Kit says by mid-March we should be able to start hacking our way into them gulches. That ain't long."

"Maybe we oughta head down to the Arkansas," another voice entered the conversation. "Speaking of Carson, he was tellin' it at the saloon that another supply town's goin' in at Currant Creek Pass. It'll be an easier route. . . ."

Eric leaned back in the chair and sighed. When he looked at Sara, the tension was gone from his face.

"Were they talking about your creek?" she whispered.

He grinned. "I thought so at first, but now they appear to be heading in another direction."

Sara's eyes lingered on his face, tracing his rugged profile. As her gaze dropped to his lips, she remembered the satiny feel of those lips on hers, and the way his touch had sent her blood tingling through her veins.

She cleared her throat. "What's it like living up in the mountains?" she asked, intent on learning everything about him. He fascinated her and she wasn't sure why.

His eyes drifted over her features. She was a pretty woman but something deeper than beauty tugged at his heart when he looked at her. The loneliness of long months in the mountains hadn't bothered him so much until now, but looking at Sara, he had an idea what he was missing. His eyes dropped to his mug and he sighed.

"What's it like?" he repeated. "I freeze my

rear off half the year panning the streams, and the rest of the time I sit in my cabin watching the snow pile up. When I get a bad case of cabin fever, I come down from the mountains for a while. It's a pretty dull life altogether—or it was until I rode into Bear Claw's village two days ago." He grinned at her.

She tried to smile but her lips wouldn't cooperate. The mention of Bear Claw's village still gave her a chill.

"Well"—he drained his cup—"if you're ready, I have some business to take care of."

While he paid the bill, Sara wandered back to the door and stared out into the crowded streets. Eric would be returning to the mountains soon. *She had to get a job.*

7

The rooms in Mrs. Karraker's boarding house contained only the bare necessities —four iron cots, two washstands, a couple of chairs and a small bearskin rug that covered less than three square feet of the cold plank floor.

Sara tossed and turned on her cot throughout the night, listening to the snores of the three other women who shared the room. It had been a relief when finally, at dawn, two of the woman dressed and left for work. She was left with Mrs. Franks, a matron in her forties who, before breakfast, was drowning her sorrows with a strong gulp of whiskey. Sara could scarcely believe her eyes when the thin, bedraggled woman pulled a flask from her trunk and eagerly tilted it for a long deep swallow.

Mable Franks had a long, heavily lined face, jet black hair and gray eyes that were as lifeless as tombstones.

"We never should of left Independence," Mrs. Franks complained, slumping onto her cot. "But Harold swore he'd strike it rich if we could just sell our little spread and join the wagon train heading to Pikes Peak." Bitter tears glinted in her eyes. "We've run through most of our money and now Harold's living up in those mountains like an animal, waiting for the weather to break so he can strike it rich!" She dropped her head, staring at her hands. "We never should have left Independence . . ."

"Maybe he *will* strike it rich," Sara gently suggested. "I have a friend who got lucky."

The woman's head jerked up. "Then stick with him! Either a fellow's lucky or he's not. My Harold's been unlucky all his life!" The corners of her mouth sagged downward in a perpetual expression of defeat.

Sara thought about Eric and found herself wishing that she *could* stick with him, as the woman put it. Eric had brought warmth and tenderness into her life when she needed it most, and an odd peace had filled her as they rode along in comfortable silence. She felt as though she had known him a long time. There was a strange kind of tension between them, but she had come to recognize that as a strong physical attraction—on her part, at least.

Was Eric affected as strongly? she wondered. She recalled the times she had caught his eyes on her and there had flowed between them an almost palpable surge of desire, before she looked away.

She jerked her mind back to the present. Why was she thinking of Eric? She'd better be worrying about a job.

"I tried to get work but I can't!" Mable continued dejectedly. "It's true what they call us—camp widows!"

At those words the frustration that had nagged Sara since the previous evening returned to haunt her. She and Eric had visited every shop in Colorado City and there were no jobs to be had unless she wanted to work in a saloon.

"No saloon!" Eric had protested. "You'd be expected to do more than serve drinks."

Sara avoided his eyes and changed the subject. She wasn't that desperate; she'd think of something.

"What're you planning to do?" Mrs Franks' question cut through Sara's wandering thoughts.

She got up and went to peer into the smoky mirror above the washstand. "I don't know," she said, adjusting the hairpins in her chignon. She had changed to a long-sleeved, dark print dress that looked to her pitifully homespun compared to the fine woolen dresses some of the ladies in Colorado City were wearing. She turned from the mirror with a dismissive sigh. She had more important things to think about.

"I have to meet a friend," she announced, reaching for her cloak. It was early to meet Eric, but she'd rather wait downstairs than be subjected to more of Mrs. Franks' depressing conversation.

"Good luck, dear." The woman waved a limp hand as Sara hurried out the door.

Sara's kid boots moved quickly over the creaking boards of the narrow hall, and she grimaced at the thought of remaining in the cheap boarding house. She gripped the worn stair rail and for a moment her shoulders rounded beneath the heavy burden. Then she remembered the crazy idea she'd had during her sleepless night. In spite of the hopelessness of her situation, her spirits lifted at the thought of seeing Eric again. It had been a crazy idea, and yet it was an idea that made her happy.

"Good morning!"

The sound of Eric's voice gave her heart an unexpected lurch. She looked up to find him standing alone in the front hall, dressed in a clean flannel shirt and tan trousers, his thick blonde hair neatly combed, and his brown spade-shaped beard carefully trimmed.

"Good morning," she said and smiled. As her foot touched the bottom step and Eric reached out to her, cupping her hand in his, a look of joy lit her dark eyes.

They gazed deep into each other's eyes for a brief moment, then Eric cleared his throat and glanced nervously around. "Hungry?" he asked.

She shook her head. "I'm too indebted to you already."

"Sara, I want to talk to you." He took her arm and led her into an adjoining parlor that was deserted at this early hour.

Sara tried to suppress her curiosity about the subject of his conversation as her eyes darted nervously over the parlor, taking in the threadbare carpet, the marble-topped washstand, even the tintype of a fifty-niner hard at work with a pick and shovel. Had that same crazy idea crossed his mind too?

"Sara, I had another nugget," he confessed.

"This morning I traded it for staples at the mercantile and a little cash. I want to leave you some money."

Her hopes sank. "No." She shook her head and withdrew her hand from his. "I can't accept your money."

At her refusal, a frown clouded the deep blue eyes. "But why not? Think of it as a loan, if you prefer."

Taking a deep breath, she focused her eyes on the fifty-niner in the tintype and decided to be reckless. "Eric, I had a thought . . . well, a crazy idea, perhaps, but I want you to hear it." She bit her lips, scarcely able to believe she was being so bold.

He leaned back against the settee and crossed his arms, waiting. "If you're thinking of the saloon job. . . ," he began, breaking the silence after she continued to hesitate.

"I'm not." Her eyes dropped to her hands, clenched tightly in her lap.

"Then what?"

Her eyes drifted back to his face, lingering on his mouth, and she remembered the way he had kissed her in the cabin two nights ago. She swallowed and summoned every ounce of courage. All he could do was say no. It was worth a try.

"You said you live alone, you admitted that you can't cook. . . ." Her voice trailed away and her cheeks were suddenly hot as he tilted his head, his eyes taking on a twinkle as he listened. "I could cook for you," she forced herself to continue before she lost her nerve, "mend your clothes, clean your cabin. . . ."

"That's a mighty tempting offer," he said, staring at her lips. "In return for what?"

"For . . . marriage." The word was a whisper, but she knew he had heard it for his brows shot up in surprise. "We get along well," she rushed to explain, "and I'd work very hard; I promise I would."

"Sara"—a tender smile touched his lips—"I'm sure you'd be a good wife, but you have no idea what you'd be in for. It's a hard, rough life up there, and very lonely. I'd welcome your company, but it wouldn't be fair."

"Why not? I'd prefer it to here. Not just *here*, this boarding house"—her eyes swept the room—"I don't care for towns. I love walking in the mountains, picking flowers in spring, searching for wild herbs and berries in the fall. I even like fishing the streams! On summer afternoons at the post, I used to take children fishing just to pass the time. . . ." She clamped her teeth together to shut off her impulsive babbling.

His eyes dropped to her lips, making a slow, thorough journey down her slim body. "There's more to marriage than cooking and cleaning," he said, and the sensual huskiness in his voice accelerated the wild beat of her heart.

"I know that." Her voice shook as she added, "and I would be a good wife."

"But do you really care for me?" he asked.

She didn't have to give the question any thought. "Yes, I do," she whispered. "More than any man I've ever known. You're kind and considerate and understanding. But do you. . . ?" She couldn't finish the question.

"Yes, I do." His eyes held hers for a moment. "I have from the beginning." He took a deep breath and stood up. "We'd better give this some thought."

Her eyes followed him as he crossed the room to stare out the window.

"Eric, if you don't want to, I'll understand," she said hastily.

Dear God, she never in her wildest dreams imagined she'd be the one to propose to a man! But then, she'd never imagined she could end up so desperate. But *not desperate enough to beg*, she decided, lifting her head proudly.

"It was just a thought," she finished stiffly.

He had turned from the window to look at her again. Then, without speaking he walked back across the room and reached for her hand, gently pulling her up from the settee. "Maybe this is the best way to decide what we want."

His arm encircled her waist, pressing her tightly against him as his lips covered her mouth. She marveled again at the warm satiny texture of those lips that teased hers in a slow, thorough kiss. Automatically, her hands crept up his chest, her fingers resting on the warm flannel shirt. The tip of his tongue outlined her lips, parted them, and slipped tentatively into her mouth.

She gasped at the strange fever that began to envelop her. Then a strong, firm throat-clearing penetrated her dream-like state.

Releasing her, Eric stepped back; her dark lashes fluttered open, but her eyes, still filled with wonder, failed to focus on Mrs. Karraker in the background.

The matronly woman stood, hands clasped before a full bosom heaving with indignation. "I must ask you two not to behave in such a shocking manner! I run a respectable boarding house."

Eric nodded. "Of course. And I'm sorry, Mrs. Karraker, but you see, we're getting married. Today, if possible."

The woman glanced from one to the other. "I see." She cleared her throat again, with less force this time. "In that case . . ."

"Is there a minister in town?" Eric asked.

"Reverend Black used to be a preacher before he fell to drinking. But of course he lost his wife on the wagon train, still blames himself . . ."

"Where could we find Reverend Black?" Eric interrupted.

"He has a little cabin at the end of the first street here. It's easy to spot because the hitching rail in front is broken in half. One night he . . ."

"Thank you, Mrs. Karraker." Eric turned to Sara. "Get your coat. We've got some shopping to do."

When Sara and Eric stepped into the mercantile, her eyes nearly popped at the endless array of items labeled *Pikes Peak*. There were Pikes Peak guns, shovels and picks; Pikes Peak boots and hats. An outfit displayed with a small sign proclaiming it to be the New American Costume was made of dark calico with a knee-length skirt from which peeped a pair of matching pantalets.

"Is that what you want?" he asked, amused.

"Not yet!" Sara laughed and wandered over to inspect a long woolen dress, the blue of a Colorado sky. Impulsively, her fingers trailed over the soft nubby cloth, even though she had intended to choose something less expensive.

"Try it on," Eric whispered over her shoulder.

Unable to conceal her delight, she grabbed the dress and dashed behind a curtain. The tucked bodice accented the fullness of her breasts, dipped to mold her tiny waist, then swirled in a perfect circle about her feet. When she stepped outside for Eric's inspection, the slow sweep of his gaze down her body brought a rush of color to her face.

"Get that one," he said.

After she changed and stepped out, she discovered him pillaging through an arrangement of lacy underwear. His hand scooped up several pieces, edged in creamy lace, and he shyly laid them on the counter. Biting her lips to restrain her laughter, Sara avoided his eyes as she laid the dress on the counter.

He indicated the underwear. "Don't you need some of this stuff?"

"I suppose." Sara grinned.

"Now what else?"

"Well . . ." Feeling the clerk's eyes raking her curiously, she edged closer to Eric and whispered, "What I'd really like is a pair of long johns, a flannel shirt and thick britches. I know it's not the way most women dress, but I'm cold-natured and if we're going to be living at a higher altitude . . ."

Eric chuckled. "So the lady's practical! Sure, get what you need."

She began to rumage through the men's section, locating the necessary items in a small size. Ignoring the raised brow of the woman behind the counter, she added a pair of thick woolen socks to her other items.

"Now what?" he asked as he paid the bill.

"A bath!"

"And food," he added, rubbing his stomach.

He left her at the boarding house where Sara luxuriated in a soapy bath. While Mable Franks snored on her cot, Sara shyly pulled on her new lacy underclothes. When she caught sight of her half-nude body in the mirror, she paused to stare thoughtfully. She was about to become a bride. Would she be pleasing to Eric? For the first time, a man would see her body, and she felt a stab of panic as her eyes traced the curve of her breasts, round and firm, yet not very large. Her gaze fell to her tiny waist, flat stomach and gently rounded thighs and calves.

She turned from the mirror, too nervous to think. Lifting the blue dress, she pulled it gently over her head. As she smoothed the tucks over her breasts, she ventured another glance in the mirror. This time a pleased smile curved her lips. The dress seemed to transform her into a lady, with the soft blue accenting her dark coloring and complementing the peachy glow of her cheeks. She brushed through her long, dark hair, then quickly wound it around nervous fingers, reshaping her chignon and inserting more hairpins.

Eric whistled his approval when they met downstairs. Her dark lashes blinked rapidly upon sight of him, dressed in a tan frock coat and navy trousers. His blonde hair held a golden sheen beneath the gas lamp, and his blue eyes deepened with desire as he looked at her.

She sighed, unable to believe this wonderful man was going to be her husband.

After they had feasted on roast meat and potatoes, a few persistent inquiries led them to Buck's saloon, where Reverend Black was slumped over a corner table.

Sara's high spirits plummeted at the sight of the inebriated preacher, whose thin brown hair was in total disarray, and his dark suit was rumpled and stained.

"I don't believe it," she whispered to Eric as they stood before the man's table, staring at a flushed face and glassy eyes that were attempting to comprehend the couple's untimely intrusion.

"Hardship can do strange things to people," Eric muttered before ordering coffee for the Reverend.

"Think you're up to performing a ceremony this afternoon?" Eric asked, after the flushed little man had taken a scalding sip of coffee and grimaced at his burned tongue.

"I'm no longer in the ministry," he mumbled, frowning.

"But you can marry us, can't you?"

"I . . . er . . . legally, yes."

Eric tucked Sara's hand in the crook of his arm. "Then we'd be most pleased if you'd marry us—after you finish your coffee, of course."

Reverend Black conquered two mugs of strong black coffee, which eventually softened his glassy stare and repaired his self-esteem. Reeling slightly, he led the way back to his cabin, where he retrieved a dusty Bible from underneath the bed. Unfortunately, the Reverend suddenly developed a spasmodic bout of hiccups, and their vows were punctuated by scarcely muffled *hic's*.

When the Reverend finally pronounced them man and wife, Sara turned to Eric with a radiant smile. Eric pulled her against his chest and pressed his lips to hers in a tender, lingering kiss—until Reverend Black once again hiccuped loudly.

Eric reached into his pocket and thrust several bills toward the startled minister, his eyes never leaving Sara's face. Then, arm in arm, they hurried out into the bright sunny morning, where the dying breath of winter was no longer a threat to their warm bodies.

"And now," he said, pulling her tightly against his side, "it's time for the honeymoon."

8

Since there was no hotel, and neither Sara nor Eric wished to return to the boarding houses, Eric finally located and rented a low, sloping loft lighted by a single window and approached by a rickety outer staircase. Within, the room was warm and cozy. A brass bed, marble-topped stand and rocking chair all gleamed from recent polishing. The pine floor was clean, and there was a small rag rug near the bed.

Once they stepped inside and closed the door, Eric tossed aside their packages and pulled Sara into his arms. For a moment, words failed him as he stood admiring the beauty of his new wife. One strand of dark hair had slipped loose from her chignon and gleamed like sable across her brow. He brushed that strand from her face as he looked into eyes filled with love. There was something so vulnerable about Sara that he suddenly found himself feeling as awkward as a schoolboy.

"Eric, I want to be a good wife to you." Her whispered words filled the silence of the room.

"You will be," he said hoarsely. His hands

cupped her cheeks as his lips dipped to kiss each corner of her mouth before moving to the center. Their mouths clung in warm, sweet agony until the desire that had been building thrashed through Eric with such intensity that he was forced to pull his mouth from hers before he lost control.

She was fragile and sweet, as shy as an animal of the forest, and he must treat her gently.

A soft rain began to fall outside the narrow window, tapping a gentle, soothing rhythm on the tin roof. Eric's eyes drifted to the brass bed, topped with a thick quilt of wedding-ring design. His eyes returned to Sara, catching the slow blush that spread over her face, though her dark eyes were bright and eager. His eyes held hers as he reached down and scooped her into his arms, then bounded across to the bed.

He laid her down easily, pausing to nibble at her neck and earlobe until she giggled. Her laughter broke the shy tension between them, and he stood again, removing his coat and unbuttoning his shirt.

Sara froze on the bed, watching as he bared his square, bronze shoulders, the broadest shoulders she'd ever seen. Her eyes fell to the sparse dark hair shadowing his chest and she bit her lips. She was a virgin and this was all so strange and new, yet she was filled with keen anticipation and aching desire. She had not imagined she could so quickly adjust to this new life with Eric, yet everything seemed right and natural. He was her husband now.

Her eyes remained firmly fixed on his face as she began to unbutton her dress. Mesmerized, Eric watched as she slipped out of the dress, then the lacy undergarments, and lay nude before him.

As Eric's eyes ran over her lovely body, he began to tear the remaining clothes away and stretched out beside her.

"I love you, Eric," she said, as his tongue moved over the curve of her mouth, parted it, then slipped gently into the warm sweetness beyond.

"And I love you, too," he whispered against her lips.

Sara pressed closer to him, wrapping her arms around his neck, as she pulled her mouth from his to speak. "I'm so glad to hear you say it," she smiled into his eyes. "I don't ever want to feel that you married me just because I was . . ." Her words trailed away.

"Helpless and vulnerable," he supplied, his eyes crinkling with humor. "Maybe that had something to do with it, but" — his eyes trailed down her body and the ache of desire filled him again—"but that wasn't why I married you. I love you," he repeated as his lips claimed hers hungrily and she responded with equal fervor.

The rain began to drum harder on the tin roof, and Sara arched against him as his mouth trailed from her lips down her chin, nipping gently at her long, soft neck. Then his mouth slid into the hollow of her throat, where the throb of her pulses touched his lips. His hands explored her round breasts, and the sight and feel of her gave him great pleasure.

Go easy, he told himself, dipping his lips to taste the bud of each nipple. When she gasped, he drew deeply of each as his hand trailed down her slim body.

His touch was tentative, gentle, while his mouth branded hers with such hunger that Sara found herself responding with an intensity that surprised and delighted Eric. Gently, he slid his hands under her hips and lifted her to meet his strong velvet thrust. Both gasped as their bodies joined, and while he watched her face carefully for any sign of pain, he saw only joy gleaming in her eyes as her hands cradled his face.

"Sara!" he moaned. "I don't want to hurt you."

"No," she whispered, "you haven't." Her body relaxed now after that first swift pain. As he began to move slowly within her, an instinct older than time filled her, and she found herself moving too, in time with him. Their bodies and souls seemed to melt together, move and breathe and act as one, as Eric's thrusts became more intense, moving to the very depths of her being.

A moan slipped from her lips as their breathing grew wild and ragged, like the drumming of the rain on the roof. Suddenly both cried out in the sweetest joy imaginable, in a delight that tore all the tension from their bodies and left them molded together as one.

"Oh Eric . . ." Sara shook her head slowly, her dark eyes filled with awe. "I never dreamed . . ."

Eric sighed and nestled her against him. "And it will get better each time. That's the way it is for two people who love each other."

The rain beat harder and soon they were joined again, with a passion that drove them to the heights of ecstasy, then plunged them into total exhaustion. Their bodies curled together as one while their rapid breathing quieted, and soon both were sleeping with contented smiles on their lips as darkness fell over the cozy room, and the rain softened to a heartbeat above them.

9

Everyone in Chief Shavano's camp was excited by the arrival of Kit Carson, or "Rope Thrower," as he was known among the Utes. He had befriended them during his early years of trapping, and despite his marriage to Looking Glass, who was an Arapahoe and therefore a tribal enemy, Rope Thrower was still admitted to their camp.

Shane sat by the fire with Wasatch and the other braves, listening as Rope Thrower related news from the posts. Rope Thrower was not a large man, but he appeared as strong and tough as a rawhide thong. Shane tried to concentrate on the stories that Rope Thrower was telling, but his eyes constantly wandered across the meadow to Star who, with two other women, was skinning a buck from the morning's hunt.

Shane's heart swelled with pride as he looked at his woman. Despite her small stature, she was as strong as some men. His eyes slid down her doeskin dress to her belly, no longer flat, and the corners of his mouth twitched in a smile of pride. In winter, they would have a son; he was certain of it.

His eyes returned to her face. Her dark hair

was parted in the middle and drawn into braids on each side of her face. The face was rounder in cheek, and he felt a surge of pride in the knowledge that he had provided well for her. His hunting, fishing and trapping had brought in more meat than the tribe could eat.

A stillness had settled over the group, the kind of stillness that comes from worry or fear. He looked around him, centering his attention again on Rope Thrower.

"Since Chief Nevava died, some of your people speak of Ouray as a new leader," he was saying.

"No!" Shavano shook his dark head vehemently. "This warrior they call the arrow is young and headstrong. He believes a new treaty with the white man will end our troubles. But we have learned the white man's treaties mean nothing!"

Shane's eyes dropped to the blade of grass he was winding around his finger. He dared not voice an opinion, but perhaps a strong, new leader might be the answer to their trouble, a man who could go to the United States government and speak for the people.

"Now that the snow has melted, will you break camp?" Rope Thrower asked, sucking deeply of the peace pipe.

Shavano nodded. "Tomorrow we go to the soda springs."

"Then perhaps you can unite with Bear Claw's band. There has been much bitterness between the Utes and the Cheyenne and Arapahoe. You must make peace among your tribes; it is more important than ever that you stand together."

"To that I agree! It is the reason we go to the soda springs. Bear Claw is of the same mind on matters concerning our people. We will unite our bands and . . . we will see."

Rope Thrower nodded, then stood. "The sun rides low on the horizon. I must go."

He shook hands with each warrior, then rode off. Shavano stood, arms crossed, his face set in a hard mask as he watched this man who had been the Indian agent leave.

"I have heard this Ouray speaks four languages," Wasatch commented, glancing at Shavano.

Shavano's eyes were dark arrows piercing his son's face. "We do not need one warrior to represent us, we need hundreds! Now we must prepare to leave for the soda springs," he growled, striding angrily toward his lodge.

Later, as Shane and Star sat in their lodge, gloom seemed to dominate the camp.

"What is it, Star?" he asked softly. "You seem worried."

Her small face turned to him and her eyes grew sad as she answered, "I fear for the safety of my people. *Our* people," she corrected herself at Shane's expression of disappointment.

"But it will be good uniting with Bear Claw's tribe, don't you think? Rope Thrower's words are true; we must stand together as one. We must make peace with the other tribes."

Star sighed and turned to stare at the fire burning low on the earthen floor. "It will not be easy, I fear. There is much hate and bitterness already."

"Stop worrying," he said, reaching out to

pull her into his arms. "If you think unpleasant thoughts, our little one will be born with an ugly face!"

Shane pulled her body against his and began to kiss her until they were both desperate to fill their bodies and souls with an intense passion that would wipe away their worries, if only for a while. They made love passionately beside the flickering fire, then slept peacefully until dawn streaked the sky and Wasatch came to their lodge to announce that Shavano was ready to break camp.

While the women removed the buffalo skins from the poles, the men sat around the fire, smoking their pipes. Shane busied himself with tending to his pinto in order to hide his frustration. He agreed with most Ute customs, but not that of having the women do the manual labor. The warriors considered this kind of work beneath their dignity.

With the horses tethered, the women began the tedious work of loading the belongings of the tribe. They tied the thin ends of several lodge poles together, balancing them over the shoulders of the horses. An equal number of poles ran back along either side and the ends dragged the ground. Just behind the horses, they lashed a brace over two bundles of poles, creating an A-shaped frame. This crosspiece served to lock everything in place while forming a platform to hold the rolled-up lodge cover and their personal belongings. They'd been at the task for hours.

Shane glimpsed Star's weary face, and anger welled up inside him when he looked back at the men, lounging lazily around the fire. He clenched his teeth, fighting a strong urge to go over and finish their hard work. But he would lose the respect of the warriors, and he couldn't afford to do that. And Star would be embarrassed. She took such pride in performing her duties.

He heaved a sigh, trying to release his anger as he turned and stomped back over to the fire.

"Soon we will be on our way," Wasatch said, his eyes full of silent understanding for Shane.

They followed the old trail first carved by lodge poles being dragged over the earth during the Utes' treks from one camp to another, running between lunettes of sandstone and granite. There had been a break in the rock wall years before, now affording a narrow pass through the mountain wall, and this led them from the big settlement at the soda spring up to the fine hunting grounds in South Park.

Shane glanced around him, impressed by the beauty of the land. The streams were swollen with snowmelt and the aspen groves along the foothills sprouted tender green leaves. Shane tightened his hold around Star's waist and fought an impulse to bury his mouth in her soft neck. She rode on the pinto with him; in this he was firm. Nish-ki rode with Wasatch, because of her age, but the other two squaws walked beside the ponies bearing the lodge poles and coverings.

"I've never been to the soda springs," he

said to Star. "I went with Ma and Elmer to Pueblo when we first returned from California, but we never came this far north."

"How long were you in California?" Star asked, glancing over her shoulder at him.

"Ten years. Elmer was ready to move on again. Only this time he started backtracking." He chuckled. "We were headed to Kansas to stay with Ma's folks but ran out of money when we reached Colorado. Elmer had heard stories of gold in the streams, and you know the rest."

"Poor Shane." Star lifted a slim hand to stroke his stubby jaw. "Life has not been easy for you."

"Nor for you. But now we will build a good life together."

"Yes," she smiled. "We will."

Shavano's group reached the soda springs late that afternoon. Shane was enchanted with the bubbling waters, cool and crystal clear, as they stopped to graze their ponies in the lush meadows and partake of the healing water.

"Our people believe the Great Spirit dwells in this place," Star explained to Shane.

Immediately he realized what she said was true, because even Wasatch approached the springs with a strange kind of reverence. The stream was surrounded by a wide, lush valley that led to Bear Claw's camp, and Shane could see smoke curls in the distance.

"Come." Star placed her hand in his. "Let us drink from the magic fountain so that we may always have good health."

Shane followed her to the transparent water and saw, on the bed of the stream, bows, arrows, knives, beads and trinkets.

"Our people leave gifts for the Great Spirit," Star whispered as she caught the puzzled look on his face.

Shane looked at Star and noticed she had taken on a special radiance as she walked near the mouth of the stream. Her eyes gleamed like black stones, and her smile was one of joy and contentment. His eyes moved from her to those about them, studying their reaction.

Shavano was standing with his arms raised to the sky, his head thrown back as though awaiting a message carved in the clouds. The squaws were pulling trinkets from their pockets to drop in the crystal water, and Shane wondered if Star would leave something.

Together, they knelt and cupped their hands to the water that was cold, yet deliciously invigorating.

As Shane rose from the stream, he caught a brown flash in the meadow—a startled deer bounding into the forest. He smiled to himself. Truly, this was a special paradise that delighted humans as well as animals.

To the west, the snowy dome of Pikes Peak reached to the clouds, and Shane took a deep breath of the fresh spring air.

"I wish we could stay here forever," he said to Star.

"So do I. But for now I am content to spend the spring and perhaps the summer, if we are welcome. I fear my father will then grow restless for our other camp. We always return in the fall."

He nodded, fighting the urge to remind her that she was his wife, and soon they would have a family of their own. But he was still having to prove himself to Shavano, and he must force his rebellious nature to yield to the older man. He could run no risk of losing Star.

Star was removing the thin silver bracelet he had given her, and her dark eyes silently sought his with the unspoken question. His glance returned to the sacred water, and he nodded.

Eagerly, she dropped the bracelet in the water, then watched until the silver swirled down to the bottom of the stream.

"Now all our wishes will come true," she announced with a radiant smile.

"Star . . ."

"I know"—she pressed her fingers to his lips—"but do not say it."

They climbed back on their horses and made their way across the meadow. Ahead, a dozen buckskin lodges were widely spaced at the end of the meadow. They heard a strange bird cry and looked up. Shane spotted a young brave perched in a tall pine, relaying a warning to the village.

Suddenly the flaps were thrown back, and those not already outside came rushing forth to stare at them. Shane shifted uneasily in the saddle, wondering if this band of Utes would accept him.

A tall, bronzed chief strode out of the center

lodge and in a deep, booming voice issued a welcome to Shavano's tribe. On the side of his cheek was a vivid slash, like claw marks.

Bear Claw, Shane silently acknowledged.

Suddenly the fierce dark eyes of the Indian chief moved to Shane and froze.

Dressed in buckskin, his dark hair hanging to his shoulders, Shane definitely looked part-Indian. But the smaller features, the lighter skin, the other part that declared him white brought a scowl to Bear Claw's face.

Shane's heart sank. There would be trouble for him here; he could already sense it.

10

Eric's rough, slab-pine cabin was situated on a small plateau on the southern slope of Pikes Peak. As they rode into the area, Sara's eyes widened with surprise and awe. She had secretly worried that his cabin in the wilderness, as he so often referred to it, might be a difficult place for her. But the beauty here was absolutely breathtaking.

"This area is level because it was a lake bed millions of years ago. Or so an old trapper once told me. It makes sense." Eric's blue eyes swept the aspen-bordered meadow and lifted to the sprawling range of mountains. "I've never found another area as level as this, so high in the mountains."

The snow was still deep in the woods but in the open meadow the lush new grass was sprouting beneath the penetrating sunshine.

Sara sighed. "I think it's the most beautiful place I've ever seen."

Her eyes traveled from the dense cluster of aspens over the lush meadow, upward to the snowy peaks thrust against an azure sky. A bald eagle soared above a craggy peak, and it seemed to Sara that the eagle symbolized the wild, free beauty of this place.

"I had no idea I'd have any luck on the stream here," Eric was saying as he studied the landscape. "I stopped and made camp simply because I like the view."

Sara nodded, turning to study the handsome features of the man she loved with every ounce of her being. She'd never thought it possible to be as happy as she'd been since marrying Eric, but each day with him was a glorious adventure.

"Beaver Creek is behind that aspen grove," he said. "The creek comes down the west side of Pikes Peak and feeds into this meadow. There's another creek on the north, and I'll try my luck there this fall."

"Eric, I want to pan the streams with you!" Sara announced, her eyes glowing.

Eric chuckled as he drew rein on his horse. "Hell, Sara, that's tedious work, dull and monotonous. It can take days just to rake up a little gold dust. Then again, we might get lucky and find a couple more nuggets!"

He dismounted and extended a hand to Sara as she hopped down. "Well, we're home." They turned, arm in arm, to survey the vast stretch of land before them.

"It's a big, lonely land to some," Eric said, his voice softening with respect, "but to me it's a challenge. This land makes me want to stretch myself, be a bigger man. Make sense to you?" He slanted an amused grin down at her.

She nodded, smiling at him. "It makes a lot of sense to me. And I want to share it all with you." She turned back to take in the wild rugged beauty that held so much promise. "Seems like a good place to put down roots, raise children . . ."

"But when your time comes, I'd want to take you into town," Eric reminded her. "Our closest neighbors are over a mile away."

"Who are our neighbors?" she asked interestedly.

"Rex and Arabella Straum. They've been living up here for several years. Rex was a trapper who got caught up in the gold rush like so many other men. We're good friends, and you'll like Arabella," he added, his eyes moving thoughtfully over her face. "She's Ute."

His words seemed to hang for a moment in the air as Sara's eyes suddenly filled with a distant memory.

"We might as well get something out in the open, Sara. I told you at the post, it doesn't bother me if you have Ute blood. And it shouldn't bother you. They're a very noble breed."

"I really don't know what to believe, or even how I feel," she sighed. "But I'd like to forget about everything that's happened, Eric. I'd like to start over here, in this beautiful place."

"We can," Eric agreed. "But you can't run from a thing, Sara. It's best to face up to it and learn how to deal with what life hands you. We've all had setbacks. We just have to make the most of the circumstances and go on."

"Eric?" Sara looked into his face, probing his deep blue eyes. "Tell me about your family."

Eric found himself wanting to do just what he had asked her not to do, to run from his past, for the memory of his beloved little son always hurt him. As for Kathleen, time had dulled her memory. Time and Sara. He realized now that his love for Kathleen had lacked something from the beginning, but he might never have discovered this if it had not been for Sara.

"I don't know what to tell you," he answered softly. "Her family and mine were neighbors; it was always kind of expected that we would marry. She was the first girl I ever courted, and I never got around to courting anyone else."

Sara swallowed. "Did you love her very much?"

Eric smiled tenderly as he looked into Sara's bleak face. "I loved her, but not the way I love you. We have something very special," he said, his lips claiming hers. She responded with her usual fervor, and when finally they broke free, both laughed to ease the tension between them.

"Ready to see your new home?" he asked, as they turned to face the small cabin. "A trapper built it, a trapper who was also an excellent carpenter. The logs are square-hewn, chinked and plastered with mud. The roof is made of poles spread with brush and topped with dirt shingles. No windows yet"—he looked apologetically at her—"maybe next year. For now it will suit us."

Sara studied the small, squat cabin and saw

that it had been well constructed. "I'm surprised the trapper would part with his cabin."

"I dropped in to visit him one night, caught him lonesome and homesick, and bought the cabin with half my grubstake money. After he left, I got to wondering if I'd made the biggest mistake of my life! After all, I'd come here to strike it rich like the other fifty-niners. I thought, what if the stream he's been bragging about is empty? Then I decided I didn't care; it wouldn't matter. I'd find something else to do. You see"—he looked from the cabin across the quiet aspen grove—"I found something here that I'd been seeking for a thousand miles. I found peace."

"And now I shall find peace here," she said, tears of joy rushing to her eyes.

"Don't do that," he said with a sad smile. "We haven't time for making love. And when I see your face all soft and dewy like that, I want to hold you in my arms and make love to you. But we have to unload and unpack. You're in for some hard work, I'm afraid."

"I don't mind hard work." She hugged him. "I'm used to it."

But when Eric opened the front door and they stepped inside, Sara gasped in shock. It looked as though an angry grizzly had been turned loose inside the small cabin. The eating table was overturned and two three-legged stools were tossed in a corner, along with a couple of chairs. Each drawer in the chest had been yanked out, its contents strewn haphazardly across the earthen floor.

Eric cursed and stomped through the front room, which served as living room, dining room and kitchen. He peered inside the tiny bedroom and swore louder than before.

"Eric, what is it? What's happened?" Sara's question trailed into despair as she surveyed the mattress of the bed, cruelly slashed in several places.

He rushed over to survey the extent of damage. "These look like knife slashes," he said, lifting a handful of feathers. "Apparently someone thought I was dumb enough to hide money or nuggets here."

Sara began to stuff the feathers back in the mattress, her eyes filled with confusion. "But who. . . ?"

"I don't know. News travels fast. Or it could just have been a stranger who caught me gone and decided to rip the place apart."

Sara tried to push aside the mental image of thieves lurking about in the woods, as she glanced at the disorder of the room.

"I'll clean this up," she said. "Why don't you see if anything else is missing?"

"There's nothing of value, unless they needed cooking utensils." He returned to the living room and called out, "Thank God they didn't!" The clatter of tin on wood accompanied his words.

Later, after the mess was cleaned up and they had unpacked, Sara worked like one possessed, unaware of what drove her, until finally she paused to admire the clean little cabin. Then she knew: it was home. Her first *real* home.

There were only two rooms separated by a thin partition of wood. To some people, the cabin might seem pitifully plain, Sara thought, with earth floors, two three-legged stools, a pine chest and eating table, and two straight wooden chairs. The best feature of the cabin was the large featherbed with a wooden frame, but Sara was secretly glad that the cabin was plain. She could add her own special touch to make it homey. She would fill the cabin with wildflowers, and she'd make colorful pillows to soften the wooden chairs and stools. And she'd sweeten the air with the aromas of baking bread, cakes and cookies.

She felt Eric tugging at her arm, and she turned to him, her eyes blank, her mind lost in thought.

"I said, I will build you a plank floor. I do not intend for my wife to walk over cold earth floors."

"It's all right," Sara began, only to be silenced by the brush of his lips.

"No. You'll have a nice plank floor. We'll add other things in time."

Sara found Eric's broad chest a welcome comfort, and she began to sag against him in total exhaustion. He sensed her weariness.

"Want me to open the tinned goods for a late supper? Then we'll get to bed. You look beat."

Sara tried to ignore the ache in her muscles, but it persisted through their quiet meal, and when she stretched her weary body over the featherbed, she was instantly asleep. Although she drifted easily to sleep, soon her body jerked involuntarily, and the first of the dreaded nightmares began.

> She was hovering in the darkness of a tight, musty place. She could hear someone moaning and crying in the back ground, and there were heavy footsteps approaching . . . coming for her. She knew somehow that the steps were coming to claim her. She huddled into a ball, trembling from head to toe, as she waited for a face to appear in the darkness, a face to go with the feet, but the steps went on and on. She began to sweat and cry, but her tears became drops of blood. Finally the steps ended at the door and a face loomed over her—it was Trapper Sam! His face was clenched in pain, his eyes rolling back in his head as he toppled at her feet, a tomahawk buried in his back.

Sara screamed and bolted up in bed, tears streaming down her cheeks, her eyes blank as the nightmare died away in her mind.

"Sara, Sara!" Eric pulled her into his arms, soothing her as she sobbed brokenly against his bare chest. "Honey, what is it?"

She shook her head, dark strands of hair curtaining her troubled face. "It was just a nightmare. I'm all right, aren't I?"

He wrapped his arms tightly around her. "Of course you're all right; I'm right here beside you. Nothing can harm you. What did you dream?"

She took a deep breath, lifting a trembling

hand to wipe the streaming tears from her face. She related the nightmare brokenly, then snuggled into his chest, her body trembling violently.

"It's all right, honey. You've had some bad times, but they're over now. You're safe. I'll take care of you. Always. You have nothing to fear, ever again."

She awoke to the smell of fresh coffee in the air, and she stirred cautiously, aware of the dull ache in her muscles.

"Good morning!"

Her lashes flew open and she gasped. If she had not first looked into the familiar deep blue eyes, her sleepy glance might have given her the impression that a stranger was standing over her bed, for she was looking into a clean-shaven face—and she could only stare in fascination. Eric's thick beard had concealed his lean jaw, even distracted from his sensual mouth.

"Why did you shave off your beard?" She pushed herself up on her elbow as her eyes roamed over his face.

He sat down on the edge of the bed and extended a tin cup of steaming coffee to her.

"I just had a hankering to." He grinned. "Like me better?"

She smiled. "Even better."

He placed the mug in her hand and pressed her fingers against it. Over the rim of the mug, her eyes studied the handsomeness of the man she'd had the good fortune to marry.

"Like my coffee?" His eyes were slowly

taking her in, an amused grin lurking in the corner of his mouth as he reached out to smooth her tousled hair.

"It tastes wonderful," she sighed. "How long have you been up?"

"Long enough to start the fire I banked last night. I'll have to chop more wood today. Pine burns in a hurry."

"I'll fix your breakfast," Sara said, throwing back the heavy quilt.

His hand stopped her. "No need. I'm not hungry. And you look pretty tired." His thumb traced the dark circles under each eye. "Do you feel all right?" She nodded, remembering the nightmare, and a chill swept over her. She swallowed. "It was just a bad dream. I'm okay this morning."

He lifted her hand to his mouth, kissing each finger. "I want you to meet our neighbors, Rex and Arabella. And after the ice breaks up at Beaver Creek, I'll show you where I found the nuggets. You'll be happy here; I'll help you put the past behind you."

Sara nodded, considering his words. The mention of the nuggets sparked a rush of excitement, but the idea of meeting their neighbors left Sara oddly frustrated. She had no desire for a friendship with Arabella.

"Well, there's plenty of time for those things," he said, taking the cup from her hand and placing it on the floor. "For now, let's just enjoy each other in our own little world."

Sara turned loving eyes to him. He was wearing a clean buckskin shirt and trousers, and he smelled of soap, wood and coffee. She breathed a deep contented sigh as she nestled down into his arms. Soon the horror of the nightmare was forgotten as Eric held her close and made love to her. This time Sara reached an even higher peak of ecstasy because it seemed to her for the first time in her life that she'd discovered her destiny. She was Eric's wife; it was all she'd ever want to be.

The next morning, after Eric and Sara had finished breakfast, Sara met her neighbors. The jingle of harness, followed by a soft neighing of horses, alerted them.

A male voice strong enough to penetrate the thick logs of the cabin called to them. "Anybody home?"

"It's Rex!" Eric said, leaping up from the stool and throwing the door wide open.

Sara shrank back, dreading this encounter. Why did they have to come so early? That was rude and inconsiderate. Before she could replace her irritated frown with a smile, a tall, lean man with gray hair beneath his fur cap and a gray-bearded face loomed in the doorway.

"Come in, Rex. Where's Arabella?" Eric asked.

Rex turned and motioned. A plump, middle-aged woman with braided black hair and dark eyes shining in a wrinkled, round face appeared. She was dressed in men's clothing, just as Sara was, and her smile was shy and tentative.

"Rex, Arabella, meet my new wife, Sara."

Eric said, pulling Sara to his side.

"Pleased to meet you!" Rex's dusty boots covered the distance in three giant steps. He thrust out his large hand and Sara hesitated for a second before she shook his hand. It felt rough and calloused.

Her eyes drifted to Arabella. The woman repeated Rex's greeting, her inflections the same as his, and Sara assumed she had learned most of her English from Rex.

"Hello," Sara replied stiffly. Arabella, she thought; that is *not* a Ute name.

"Drag up a chair," Eric said and, turning to Sara, "get them some coffee."

He didn't say *please*, she thought childishly as she searched for clean mugs. She knew she was lapsing into some kind of immature behavior, but she couldn't seem to prevent it.

"Rex, somebody broke in and ransacked the cabin while I was gone!" Eric announced, his face darkening with anger as he recalled how his possessions had been strewn around the cabin, the mattress cut.

"What's that?" Rex growled. "I tried to keep an eye on it, but . . ."

"You're too far away." Eric shook his head. "Guess they were disappointed to go to so much trouble for nothing."

The couple shed their heavy coats while Sara poured coffee, keeping her eyes averted.

"Think they were looking for the nuggets?" Rex asked, concerned.

"Or money." Eric shrugged. "Let's forget it and have coffee. Could just have been a lonely old grizzly." His lips tilted in an effort to make light of the problem.

Sara took her seat beside Eric and darted a glance to Arabella. The Indian woman held herself erect, maintaining a polite expression as she settled into a chair. Her skin was dark, not just from her ancestry, but also from exposure to weather. Deep lines crinkled around her eyes and mouth, yet hers was a happy face. When Arabella caught her staring, Sara's glance fell to her lap.

Rex's eyes made a quick approving sweep of Sara. "Gets lonesome in these parts. Eric's lucky to have found a wife."

"I'm lucky to have found Eric!" Sara answered, too quickly. She'd meant to sound grateful, but her tone was sharp and brittle and her cheeks flushed. She didn't know how to repair the damage, so she concentrated on draining her coffee mug.

Her reply brought an exchange of glances between the visiting couple. Arabella's mouth tightened as she stared into her coffee.

Rex turned to Eric. "What's happening out in the Territory?"

"The biggest news is that South Carolina's fired on Fort Sumter in Charleston Harbor."

Rex'a jaw sagged. "You don't say! Reckon North and South's gonna take arms against each other?"

Eric dropped his eyes, his lips pursed thoughtfully. It was a question he'd asked himself over and over the past weeks. He thought of his brothers and their families, his widowed mother . . .

"I don't know what'll happen, Rex. President Lincoln has appointed William Gilpin as our first Governor."

"Know anything about him?"

"He's supposed to be an expert when it comes to civil government. He's already touring the mining camps, taking a census of the population of the Colorado Territory. There'll be an election to choose delegates to Congress and the legislature."

"Sounds like we're getting too damn civilized!" Rex roared with a disapproving frown. "What's goin' on in Colorado City?"

Eric's glance swept Sara, then Arabella and finally Rex. "More trouble with the Utes and Arapahoes."

Sara released her pent-up breath. She hadn't expected Eric to relate the depressing news of how he met her, and yet it was definitely news.

"The Utes and Arapahoes will never smoke the pipe of peace," Arabella spoke for the first time, startling them all. Her voice was calm and quiet, yet there was suddenly an intense look in her dark eyes. "It has always been so."

Eric nodded. "And I hear the Cheyenne are giving newcomers the devil out on the plains."

"That, too, is as always," Arabella said, nodding solemnly.

Sara kept he eyes on the floor, nervous and anxious. She should be entering into the conversation somehow, adding some sort of comment, but she had no idea what to say. And, if she were to be truthful with herself, she didn't want to talk pleasantly. She didn't *feel* pleasant; she felt uncomfortable.

"Well"—Rex finished his coffee and stood—"I say let them settle it on their own. We're happy tucked away up here in the backwoods." He turned and winked at Arabella.

"Won't you have more coffee?" Eric asked, glancing sharply at Sara.

She rose to get the coffeepot, but Rex shook his head. "Nope. We're on our way down the Ute trail now. Gotta lay in staples before I start pannin' again. How was the road?"

"Rutted bad a quarter-mile down. But you'll have no trouble. Stop in on your way back," Eric invited Rex.

They headed out the door; Sara and Eric followed.

"Need anything?" Rex called over his shoulder. "We can bring back flour, sugar, anything—if you're short, that is."

"We stocked up, thanks. Have a good trip," Eric called.

"Good-bye," Sara called after they'd mounted their horses and jog-trotted toward the main road.

Eric thrust his hands onto his hips and turned to Sara. "Weren't you a bit unfriendly?"

She swallowed, averting her eyes again. "No, I don't think so."

"Well, I do," he said, unable to hide his anger. "Look, Sara, they're my best friends. I want you to like them."

"I can't!" she snapped. "They make me feel uncomfortable."

His mouth dropped open, and he stared in disbelief. "How? They're very easy to be with."

"Maybe for you, but not for me!"

His brows lowered over his eyes, narrowing on Sara. "It's because Arabella is Ute, isn't it? You resent her. How the hell can you be so prejudiced?"

"I'm not prejudiced!" she cried. "I'm just"—she paused, taking a shaky breath—"I just haven't recovered from my experience at Bear Claw's camp."

Eric pressed his lips together as his eyes flicked over her, and he tried to understand her feelings. "Well for God's sake, don't take it out on Arabella," he said, shaking his head in dismay, as he turned and stomped off to the meadow where the horses were grazing.

Sara fled back inside and burst into tears. She went into the bedroom and threw herself on the bed, angry with Eric but even angrier with herself.

She heard Eric's footsteps bounding back inside the cabin. Suddenly, his blond head was thrust around the door. There was no longer any anger in his face, only a sheepish grin.

"Guess we've had our first argument," he said. "I've saddled the horses. Want to go for a ride?"

That night Sara slept fitfully and again the nightmare returned.

> She hovered in the darkness of a tight, musty place. From somewhere behind her a woman moaned and cried. This time she knew it was Crying Wind, and Sara tried to call out for help, but her lips froze. The woman was dying, but she did nothing. Then she heard footsteps approaching, drawing closer and closer, coming for her like before. Sara tensed, crying tears of blood. This time two faces appeared in the darkness. Trapper Sam and her mother's. Both frowned and shook their fists at her.

Sara screamed out, again and again, and it was several minutes before Eric could wake her. When he did, she collapsed against him, her body heaving with broken sobs.

"Another nightmare?" he asked gently, pushing her hair back from her face.

She nodded. "The same nightmare, only this time . . . Ma was with Trapper Sam and they . . . they . . ." She was sobbing wildly. "They were shaking their fists at me!"

Eric turned her to face him, tilting her chin back until she was forced to look into his eyes. "You've got to stop blaming yourself. That's what you're doing. Somehow, deep in your mind, you've convinced yourself you're responsible for their deaths. *You're not*, do you hear me?"

She pressed her lips together and jerked her head in an affirmative nod.

"You had no control over what happened.

You had nothing to do with any of it. Don't you understand that, honey?"

"I suppose," she answered weakly, feeling drained of all emotion. She slumped back onto the pillow, curling against Eric's shoulder. She closed her eyes, pretending to sleep, but for a long time the image of her mother and Trapper Sam still haunted her. Both were shaking their fists at her, their faces filled with hate.

The next morning, Eric saddled the horses and they rode all day long. He had hoped to get Sara's mind off the nightmare, for ever since she'd awakened, she had moved about in a fog, a look of depression filling her eyes.

"How far is the Straums' cabin from here?" she asked, breaking her silence for the past hour.

Eric jerked his head around in surprise. "It's just over that next rise. Why?"

She looked at him and smiled tentatively. "I'd like to go visit."

His lips spread into a pleased smile. "All right, we'll do it."

The cabin was nestled in a grove of pines and surrounded by a large corral of split logs. Both horses were grazing, and in the distance Sara saw a small, crude stable with tin roof and open ends.

"We need to build one like that," she said absently, staring at the make-shift stable.

"I'd had the same thought. Just hadn't gotten around to it."

"Then I'll help you," she said, pleased with the idea. There had been no more sign of thieves, but Sara often feared they might come by night and sneak the horses from the pasture.

The Straums greeted them with a look of surprise but quickly invited them inside.

The cabin was large and rambling, and Sara could see that Arabella was a good housekeeper. They were seated at the table, and soon thick slabs of homemade bread were placed before them. Sara recalled her reserve and felt even guiltier now. She tried to smile and be talkative both to Arabella and Rex, but her words sounded stiff to her ears, and at last she settled for just listening to their conversation with an occasional smile when it was warranted.

Arabella and Rex were polite, but they, too, seemed uncomfortable now, and the friendship became strained.

Eric was silent on their return. He did not scold her this time, for he knew she had made an effort. Sara, however, felt restless and displeased with herself. What was wrong with her? Why was it so difficult to strike up a friendship? She'd never had trouble before.

"Eric, I want to invite them over for dinner sometime," she said optimistically.

A puzzled look arched his brows, but then he shrugged and smiled. "Sure. Any time you want to."

"Okay," she nodded, smiling. But as time went by, Sara found she could never get herself in the right mood. Her good intentions were finally forgotten.

Spring flowed into summer, taking the last

snowmelt from beneath the thick stand of pines and turning the meadow grass to shimmering silk. Sara wandered through the meadows, happy and content, while Eric hammered away at the plank floor. He worked long and hard, refusing her persistent pleas to let her help.

"You'll splinter your hands," he'd reply firmly. "I can do this job better on my own."

At first Sara had been slightly offended, but finally she realized it was his own special gift to her, and he wanted to do it without any help.

Many afternoons she sat in the open door, watching with love and pride. She was glad, now, that she had not protested this new floor, for she needed something better than an earthen floor in coming months. She needed wood over which she could lay rag rugs for a baby to play on.

She smiled with happiness, choosing just the right moment to tell Eric the good news.

11

"Sara, how can you be sure?" Eric gasped when she told him the news.

"A woman has her ways of knowing," she replied. "And I'm sure."

The look of complete awe and bewilderment on his face brought laughter to her lips. He watched her with wide, fascinated eyes, as though she had suddenly taken on a special kind of power.

"I'm sorry, I don't mean to laugh at you." She lifted a hand to tenderly stroke his jaw. "It's just that you looked so . . . well, so much like a little boy being told he could have the whole jar of peppermints! Oh Eric, I love you so much," she said, wrapping her arms around his neck.

He looked down into her adoring face, his eyes holding an expression of deep tenderness. "Sara, I can't tell you how happy this makes me," he said with a catch in his throat. "More than anything in the world, I've wanted a child with you."

That night they dined by candlelight on trout and fresh-baked bread. Eric easily provided them with fish and game and he'd wisely stored up enough staples to keep them fed for a long time. Sara had begun to wonder if they'd ever diminish his supply of dried beans.

Eric reached across the table and touched her hand. "Now that we've honeymooned for two months..."

"And worked some too," she reminded him, laughing.

"Yes." He turned to study the clean plank floor, pleased with the joining of the planks and the fit of the corners. He leaned back in his chair as his eyes moved over the cabin that had been so lonely before Sara came. She had stitched pillows from one of his torn red-flannel shirts, she'd cleaned the walls and floors until not one speck of dirt remained, and most of all, she put some order into a cabin where pots, pans, boots and hunting gear were usually tangled together.

"Well"—he raised her palm to his lips—"it's time for me to start panning Beaver Creek."

"I can't wait till we start," she responded eagerly.

Eric's face held a blank expression for a moment before understanding suddenly dawned in his eyes. "We?" He gripped her hand tighter. "Sara, you have to be careful now that we have a little one on the way. I hate to remind you how far we are from a doctor, but you have to be practical. Those stream beds can be mighty treacherous, honey."

Her hand stiffened in his before she removed it. "Eric, don't punish me for being pregnant!" she snapped. Then, seeing the stunned look on his face, her voice softened. "I have sturdy boots and work clothes. Please Eric, I've looked forward to this."

"All right," he relented with a grin, "if you promise to be careful. And now"—he stood and pulled her to her feet—"let's forget work. Let's forget everything except loving each other."

That night he made love to her with such exquisite tenderness that Sara cried out with joy. Afterwards, as they huddled together, waiting for the wild beat of their hearts to calm, Eric tilted her face back and looked down into her eyes.

"I never told you about my little boy, but he was the dearest person in the world to me. It felt like my heart broke when he died in my arms. . . ."

"Oh, Eric!" Sara sobbed, tears filling her eyes and pouring down her cheeks. "To think you endured such a terrible thing." She reached up to press a kiss onto his lips. "But we'll have lots of children. And I pray this first one will be a boy. Not that he would replace your first son," she added quickly, "but to fill that void in your heart."

As Sara pressed her cheek to his, she could feel the dampness of his tears mingling with her own.

"We're going to put the old life behind us," she whispered, "and build a brand new one. A much better one."

A beautiful summer morning dawned, inspiring Eric and Sara to head for Beaver

Creek. Dressed comfortably in trousers, shirt and boots, Sara trudged through the thick meadow grass, feeling as excited as any fifty-niner in Colorado.

"I'm eager to learn to pan," she told Eric.

He placed an arm around her shoulder and shifted his gear to the other hand. "It can be fun, until you wake up with a damn cold and your hands swollen from hours in cold streams. Then you wonder if you haven't gone crazy! I just wish my cradle wasn't broken."

She merely smiled now, although she had laughed the first few times he referred to his *cradle*. She had since learned that the apparatus the miners used was called a cradle because of the rockers on the bottom and the way it was used to "rock out" gold.

"It'll be fun to pan," she replied.

"But it's much tougher than using the cradle."

"Well, you started out panning, so that's the way I want to learn. Come on"—she poked him in the ribs—"we may be about to really strike it rich!"

Eric chuckled, turning loving blue eyes to her. He had made an excellent choice in a wife, he decided. Every day they learned new things about each other. He knew, from living with Kathleen, that marriage was a risky business. As well as he thought he knew Kathleen, he'd discovered that one person didn't truly know another until they had lived together. But to his surprise and delight, Sara was turning into the perfect companion.

They had reached the edge of the stream;

Eric dropped his assortment of tin pans and turned to Sara.

"All right, ready for your lessons?"

"Ready!" Her dark eyes reflected her intense anticipation, and she listened carefully as he handed her a pan.

"Gold is usually concentrated around bedrock. I found my first nugget at the bottom of the stream right where it makes a bend. The second nugget was in a dry creek bed where the stream had shifted its course. Here's how you do it."

He leaned down and dipped the pan in the swirling crystal water, going deep enough to scoop up some soil.

"You want the pan to be about three quarters full of dirt from the creek bed. Then hold the pan level just under the water so the dirt clots can be broken loose. Shake the pan counterclockwise to loosen the gravel." He demonstrated several times. "Then rotate it so the water and gravel can move about. This washes the lightest pebbles and sand over the edge."

Sara nodded, watching eagerly as he pulled the pan above water.

"Rotate it real quick so the heavier gold and sand settles again. Now submerge the pan with the edge raised just a bit to let more loose sand go over the edge. Keep rotating back and forth until the dirt collects in the crease of the pan. It'll look like this. . . ." He extended the pan to show her. The dirt had formed a crescent shape in the crease of the pan.

"Hold the pan level, add a little water, then tap the pan with the palm of your hand to resettle the dirt. The lighter soil will rise to the top. Let the water swirl clockwise. The heavier soil should collect on the right side of the pan while the lighter soil will be on the left, like this. And after all that trouble, you pray to God there's gold in that dark soil!"

Both studied the dark mass, their hopes sinking, as there was nothing visible but slick dark mud.

Sara tried, feeling awkward at first, but slowly catching on until she felt confident enough to ask Eric how she was doing.

"You've taken to it like a true fifty-niner!" he laughed.

The morning passed quickly but Sara began to tire around noon, and neither had found one particle of gold dust.

"Who taught you to do this?" she asked, hoping a little conversation would keep up her enthusiasm.

"The trapper who owned the cabin. The poor guy had been wading icy water for months with no luck, living on sourdough and salt pork. He had developed scurvy when I met him, which was another reason he was ready to quit and return to an easier life."

Sara nodded. "And how long before you got lucky?"

"A few weeks after I came here. I'd overheard a fifty-niner bragging at a saloon in Denver. He'd found a big nugget at a bend in the stream. I looked this creek over, and decided to follow it a mile or so. Two miles down, it makes a bend, and sure enough, that's where the nugget was."

Sara's mouth opened as her glance darted downstream.

"No point in going back there. I spent weeks in that spot; there was nothing else. And you look tired," he observed, his tone softened. "Want to call it a day?"

"Well, I *am* getting hungry. How about a picnic?"

"A better idea than panning here. There's nothing. Tomorrow I'll take my cradle and ride over to Rex's place. I'm sure he can show me how to repair the hopper on it."

They gathered up their pans and headed back across the meadow. Sara tilted her face back to absorb the penetrating rays of sunshine and she sighed contentedly.

"Eric, I've never been so happy," she said.

"Nor have I." He leaned down to kiss her cheek.

Arm in arm, they hurried on.

Sara felt queasy and nervous upon waking the next morning. Her hand flailed across the bed, reaching for Eric but she found only emptiness. Then she remembered. He'd slipped out of bed early to ride over to Rex Straum's cabin to see about repairing his cradle.

She sighed, curling into a ball, as an odd depression crept over her. She felt weak, desolate, and jumpy.

"But I'm not alone," she reminded herself. She touched her stomach and thought of the baby. How happy she would be to place their baby in Eric's arms; she hoped and prayed it would wipe away the pain of his first loss.

Her efforts to go back to sleep were all in vain, and she finally forced herself from the bed. Was this strange shaky feeling due to Eric's being away? Was she afraid to stay by herself? she wondered.

She dressed quickly in her trousers and shirt, feeling the need for sunshine and fresh air to offset her unaccountable gloom.

As she pulled on the mud-caked boots she'd been too weary to clean the night before, she remembered her lesson in panning yesterday and an idea sprang into mind.

She'd go down and pan by herself! Wouldn't Eric be surprised and pleased when he came home and she presented him with some gold dust! Maybe even a nugget!

Her spirits lifted as she gathered up a couple of pans and set off at a brisk pace through the aspen grove leading to Beaver Creek. While her dreary mood vanished, her body continued to feel sluggish and unnatural. A dull ache began in the pit of her stomach and then moved to her back.

She reached the stream and began to dip, hoping to forget her aches and pains. But again the gold evaded her, and in her frustration she turned too quickly and her right foot caught on a boulder that sent her tumbling headlong into the cold water.

She came up thrashing and moaning and fought her way back to the bank. The ache in her stomach had become a fierce throbbing pain, and her teeth began to chatter as she gathered up her gear and angrily headed back to the cabin.

"Obviously, I should have stayed in bed," she muttered, stomping along.

Then suddenly she was aware of a warm stickiness between her legs and she froze in her tracks.

"Oh dear God, no! *Please!* N*o!*" she cried, trying to pace her steps cautiously. But there was no longer any question of what was happening when the blood seeped through her trousers, plainly visible.

She tried to run but her legs felt as though all the strength had been drained from them. With her eyes clinging desperately to the dim outline of the cabin, she felt something break loose inside her, and she fell to the ground in pain.

"Help!" she screamed. But there was no one to help her. She tried to think, but her mind was frozen in horror. Eric was miles away; she could bleed to death if she didn't get back to the cabin and somehow stop the bleeding.

Her head swam; nausea bolted through her. She managed to push herself upward to a crawling position and inch her way across the meadow. The back of the cabin was only yards away when she heard the jingle of harness.

"Eric!" she screamed. "*Eric!*"

It was not Eric, but rather Arabella who found her writhing in pain.

Arabella leapt down from her horse at the sight of the crumpled woman. She raced to her side, and immediately realized what was happening. Arabella knelt down and pulled Sara up, hooking the limp woman's arm around her own strong shoulder as she grasped her dangling hand.

"Just lean against me, little one," she said soothingly. "We will make it. Do not worry."

Sara's body was dead weight, but Arabella hung onto her until they reached the cabin. There, Arabella stripped the wet clothes from Sara's body and washed away the blood. Even after the mass had been dispelled from Sara's womb, she continued to hemorrhage.

Arabella plundered the kitchen, locating flour and grease to make a plaster to seal off the bleeding. Pleased when her remedy worked, she checked Sara's forehead, distressed by the burning skin against her calloused palm.

Arabella frowned as she pulled a clean gown over Sara's head and laid her back against the pillows, her mind seeking a solution. Then she remembered the herbs in her saddlebag and raced out to get them. She brewed a strong dark tea for Sara, poured it in a tin cup and pleaded with her to sit up. Half delirious, Sara refused the tea at first, but Arabella's steady patient voice ultimately won her over. Sara drank one cup, then another, before collapsing on her pillow in a deep sleep.

While Sara slept, Arabella remained at her side, wiping Sara's face with a cool rag, offering more tea. When at last she heard hoofbeats on the trail leading to the cabin, she breathed a deep sigh of relief. The crisis was past, and Eric would be spared some of the pain of seeing his wife suffer.

Wearily, Arabella pulled herself from the chair and met him at the door. She put her fingers to her lips to silence the question forming on his lips, as she motioned him outside.

Eric stood rooted in shock, wanting to press a hand to the Indian woman's lips, halt the words she was speaking in kindness and love. But he knew he had to face the truth—and it was a hot spear tearing through the center of his heart.

He leaned against the cabin, his eyes resting on a distant pine while his voice was lost behind the huge lump in his throat.

"The fever has broken now," Arabella was saying, "she will be all right."

Eric nodded slowly, wondering how long it would be before he could speak again. Finally he forced his voice around the lump in his throat, and though his words were weak and raspy, they were sincere. "I don't know how to thank you," he began.

"It is not necessary to thank me. I thank the Great Spirit for sending me. I had this"—she shook her head, trying to find the words—"this craziness to ride over and visit her while you men worked on the cradle. I am glad I did." She glanced inside the door, then turned back to Eric. "Just do not let her work the streams for a while. She might fall again."

"Again?" he said, staring at her.

Arabella nodded. "First she fell in the

stream. Then she fell again"—she pointed —"out there in the meadow. She had been panning," she explained hastily. "Her foot must have slipped on the rocks."

At those words, Eric's eyes deepened to a hard glare while his mouth tightened in a grim white line. Again he had lost his voice, but this time in silent rage.

When Sara awoke, she sensed it was night even though there were no windows to reveal the darkness. And it had turned colder, she remembered, stirring sleepily. She felt a hand pressing on her shoulder, and her matted lashes dragged open.

Eric stood over her, a strange expression on his face.

"Lie still," he said. "Arabella said you should stay in bed for a day or two."

For a moment, Sara's mind was completely blank. Then, ever so slowly, a painful memory returned as her confusion cleared, like fog blowing off the mountain top. She bit her lip, remembering the horrible ordeal, Arabella's help, and finally the bleak knowledge that she had lost the baby.

"I . . . I'm so sorry," her voice made a strange rasping in the silent room.

She expected Eric to pull her into his arms, comfort her, say something to ease her pain. But his eyes moved over her head, as though staring at some distant object.

"Try to sleep," he said, straightening again. Then he turned and walked over to stoke up the fire.

Her eyes followed his tall, broad frame while her mind reeled with another shock. How could he be so unfeeling? Didn't he understand the pain she had suffered? Didn't he know she had been desperately ill?

She swallowed, her eyes filling with tears as she watched him probing at the fire, then reaching for the woodbox. Without a word, he trudged out of the room.

She stared at the ceiling while tears rolled down her cheeks. She had never seen Eric this way. What was wrong with him?

She turned and buried her face in the pillow, muffling her broken sobs.

Eric heaved the ax into the wood with a ferocity that sent splinters flying in all directions. His brawny arms lifted the ax and heaved downward, again and again. He was scarcely aware of the anger he was venting until the handle of the ax broke in half, and a splinter of wood gashed his palm.

His shoulders rounded, and he stood, chest heaving, staring through a fog of tears at the stack of crudely chopped wood. He lifted a hand to cover his face as the cold darkness swirled over him. *It just isn't meant to be*, he thought, tormented by this knowledge. *I'm not meant to have a child.*

He dropped the broken ax and gathered up the wood. If only she'd stayed in the cabin; if only she hadn't gone off on her own, trying to act like a damn fifty-niner. What the hell was she trying to prove, anyway? And she had fallen . . .

The door crashed open beneath his booted

kick. He lumbered across the room and stretched out his arms, dumping the wood into the woodbox. The heavy thudding sounds finally penetrated his own distraction and he flinched. He turned and glanced worriedly at the bed. Sara was lying still, as in sleep. He drew a deep, ragged breath and silently cursed his loud entry.

Dropping to his knee, he began to stack the wood. He would not chastize her, or even argue with her, until she was well. Then this matter would have to be settled.

Why had she gone down to pan the stream? Why had she been so careless? Didn't their baby mean more to her than that? The confusing questions swirled around and about, like aspen leaves in a snowstorm.

He glanced over his shoulder to the still, slim body. He loved her as he had never loved another human being. Not even his first son. But he was angry with her now. He hated himself for it, but there was nothing he could do to stop it. Nothing, until he confronted Sara with a few questions.

After another day of lying in bed, Sara could no longer stand the inactivity. Eric had dutifully brought meals to her and had courteously inquired if there was more he could do. But his smile was stiff, his words too polite. He spoke as though she were a mere acquaintance, not his wife. And he didn't mention the loss of the baby. She lay back against the pillows, pale and stunned. As he maintained his remote behavior, she too slipped into a shell of surface responses, polite and formal, while the pain and anger began to fester within her.

Her dark eyes narrowed on his form as he sat beside the fire, smoking a pipe. He rarely smoked, and the smell of strong tobacco wafted over the cabin, washing her with a wave of nausea.

She threw back the covers and swung her slim legs onto the plank floor. The plank floor the baby would have crawled over.

Her eyes settled on the clean wood as a dark feeling engulfed her, a sadness that went straight through to her heart, leaving her weary and desolate.

"What are you doing?" He was standing over her, his blue eyes still distant and cold.

She looked into his face, trying to read his thoughts. Suddenly, she realized she didn't care what he was thinking; she wanted to flee from the bed, the room, the cabin.

Shakily, she got to her feet. His arms were around her shoulders, steadying her. She stiffened beneath his grip as her eyes darted about, searching for shoes.

"I suppose it would be all right for you to sit by the fire for a while," he said, his tone more sympathetic now.

"I don't want to sit by the fire," she snapped. "I want to go outside and breathe some fresh air. Your tobacco smoke is making me ill!"

She had never spoken to him with a sharp tongue, nor had she ever been angry with him. Until now.

Her words were a slap against his pale,

drawn face, but he took the blow with quiet dignity.

"All right, but let me get your shoes." He knelt by the bed, seeking her boots.

Sara's eyes were dark fire as she watched him methodically lift each foot and place her boots on. Rigidly, she waited.

"You won't need a coat," he said. "It's a warm day. I just kept a fire in here because I thought you might get chilled."

She crossed her arms and plodded toward the door, avoiding the curious look on his face. When she stepped outside, a brilliant morning sun greeted her. She tilted her head back, absorbing the sun's healing rays. The air was fresh and sweet, and from a tall pine, birdsong drifted down to her.

She was more surprised than Eric when sudden tears filled her eyes and trickled down her cheeks. She closed her eyes and squeezed them tightly, hoping to ward off the tears that would not stop, but soon her shoulders were heaving, and she felt as if her heart would break.

Strong arms encircled her, pulling her gently against his chest. The smell of wood and tobacco filled her nostrils, but she didn't mind. She needed the solid strength of his body, the comfort he offered to soothe the pain in her heart.

"Why, Sara?" His voice was a tentative plea. "Why did you go down to the stream that day? You knew it was dangerous; I warned you." His voice grew hoarse, ragged. "And damn it, you knew how much I wanted this baby!"

"*You*?" Her head flew back, her eyes shot to his. Through a blur of tears, she saw the awful pain in his face, but her temper had snapped, and she was blind to all pain but her own.

"You? Is that all you can think of, what *you* wanted?" She was sobbing wildly, but she could not stop the flow of angry words. "How do you think I felt? Or do you even care, damn it!" She flung his arms from her shoulders and stepped back from him, one hand dashing up to wipe the tears from her face.

"My past is a blank," she continued. "I don't know who I came from; I don't have any heritage, only one huge question mark that's always there in my mind. Don't you see what this baby represented to me? It was much more than a symbol of love; it was the first time I had a blood tie to *anyone*!"

At those words, Eric's face changed; the frustration and anger were swept away, replaced by a look of agony.

"Oh God, Sara. I've been so selfish." He lifted a hand to rub his aching forehead. "I just wanted the baby so bad, and I thought you'd been careless. . . ."

Her outburst had freed some of her anger and torment, and now she was left with the awful hurt that continued to bring tears to her eyes. But she had begun to listen to him, really listen, as she noted the change of his expression and heard the pain in his voice.

She frowned, trying to concentrate on what he'd been saying to her.

"I wasn't careless," she finally responded. "I

woke up feelng nauseated and aching. I went down to Beaver Creek hoping to forget how bad I felt." She paused, taking a long, deep breath as her eyes wandered slowly toward the aspen grove where she had fallen, where her blood had seeped into the cold earth. "I was already in pain . . . I would have lost the baby anyway." She turned her tormented gaze back to Eric as a shudder rippled over her body. "I . . . I'm sorry," she whispered, drained of all anger and frustration. She felt exhausted, totally exhausted.

He took a step forward, sweeping her into his arms again. "You're all right; that's the most important thing. I love you with all my heart, more than I've ever loved anyone! I don't know what I'd do if I lost you. . . ." His voice broke as he pulled her tightly against him.

Suddenly she understood, and her love for him flowed through her anew, wiping away the anger and hurt. They had each other; it was all that really mattered. And she loved him so much, she could forgive him anything.

"It's all right," she said, wrapping her arms tightly around his waist. "I know what you must have thought." She took a deep breath and tilted her face back to him. "Maybe we can start over."

He nodded, lowering his mouth to hers. Their lips seared together in a passionate kiss, one that deepened and sent a wave of desire to the center of their being. But then Eric forced himself to pull his ravishing mouth from hers and press her head gently against his chest.

His eyes wandered over her dark head to the peak of the mountain, where only a light powdering of snow remained.

"You're not well yet. We must not let our passion lead us into carelessness."

His fingers wound through the dark silk of her hair, smoothing it back from her face.

"Now come back inside. I want you to eat. I want you well and strong again. We have work to do."

That night the nightmare returned to haunt her.

> She was huddled into a dark, musty place. She could hear cries, but this time it was the faint, weak cry of a baby. She heard steps approaching and she began to cry—not blood, this time, but real tears. As she waited for the face to appear, she began to tremble from head to toe. To her horror, Eric's face loomed through the darkness, angry and accusing. He was shouting at her, cursing her, and she froze in shock.

This time she did not cry out; she merely awakened with a start and whirled to see if Eric was awake. He was sleeping peacefully and she heaved a deep sigh of relief. She thought of their argument, remembered Eric's disappointment and wondered if he was secretly still angry with her. She sank onto the pillow and stared at the ceiling. When was she going to stop being so hard on herself?

As soon as Sara felt strong enough, she

cooked a venison roast and rode over to visit Arabella. She had to thank her for what she had done, and now she wanted and desperately needed her friendship. As much as she loved being with Eric, she'd missed other people, particularly a woman to talk with. She was sorry she'd let her personal feelings interfere before, and she was determined now to make amends.

"I wanted to show my appreciation in some way," she said, as Arabella invited her inside. "After all, you saved my life."

There was deep sadness in Arabella's eyes as she looked at Sara. "I grieve for you. I, too, have lost little ones. Then there were no more."

The thought brought a tinge of panic to Sara, but she pushed it from her mind as she set the food on Arabella's table.

"But you will have other babies, healthy babies," Arabella spoke reassuringly.

Sara's eyes returned to Arabella with a look of anguish. "What makes you say that?" she asked.

"Because you are young and healthy. I was not healthy."

An awkward silence stretched between them as Sara pondered whether to question Arabella further. But then Arabella would have the right to return the questions, and Sara was not ready to discuss her past. Instead, she changed the subject.

"I understand there are people who are trying to grow lettuce up here in the mountains. Have you had any luck?"

"None." Arabella slung her long braid over her shoulder and crossed the kitchen to lift the coffee pot. Sara settled down at the table, grateful for a cup of strong coffee. "I have no luck at growing things," Arabella sighed. "My grandmother taught me well, but I forget. It has been . . . many years."

For a moment, Arabella's dark eyes lingered on Sara's face, and Sara had the uncomfortable feeling that Arabella knew more about Sara than she had acknowledged.

"How long have you lived up here?" Sara asked, her eyes lowered to her coffee cup.

"Five winters now. I marry Rex when he came to my village, and that would be"—she paused to count—"twenty winters ago. We find this place, and it is home. Our best home."

Sara nodded and smiled across at Arabella. She was torn between asking more questions and remaining ignorant of Arabella's past. Finally, she chose to ignore Arabella's heritage, just as she had chosen to ignore her own. She felt it was the only way to bridge the barrier that had existed between them.

"Arabella, I haven't been a good neighbor," she said, staring into her coffee. "I want to do better."

There was a moment of silence as Arabella's dark eyes studied her thoughtfully. "You will be a good neighbor," she said. "The mountains take getting used to, that's all."

Sara nodded and smiled. "Well, I mustn't tarry. Eric will worry." She drained her coffee and stood. "He's working Beaver Creek again today."

"How is the panning?" Arabella asked, rising from the table to remove the empty cups.

"No luck. But perhaps that will change."

"And for us too, I hope. Rex is having no luck at West Creek. I wonder if the miners have not taken all that was here."

Sara hesitated in the door and shrugged. "Well, come to visit," she called, waving as she hurried out.

As she rode back to the cabin, Sara thought of Crying Wind for the first time in weeks. She remembered the wrinkled brown skin, the sagging mouth, the quiet pleading eyes and a feeling of pity swept over her.

"But she wasn't my mother," she said aloud, her eyes rising slowly to the dome of the Peak. "I felt sorry for her, but *she was not my mother!*"

Then who was? came the hauntingly familiar question.

The next week, Eric gave in to Sara's badgering and allowed her to return to pan with him again. Luck seemed to have run out at Beaver Creek, and he suggested they pack gear for camping and venture north to the other creek he'd been anxious to explore. Sara eagerly agreed, feeling a change would improve their mood. She found herself occasionally sinking into a depression that confused and puzzled her. Their love was as strong as ever, and certainly Eric was all she could ever want in a husband and more. At times, she felt a deep sadness settle over her, but she refused to give in to a whim to sit down and stare into space. Eric observed these moods and assured her she was having a delayed reaction to all the heartache she'd experienced in the past year.

She decided he was probably right, but still there was an emptiness within her, a feeling that she had lost something very precious. Then she would remember the feeling of joy that had filled her when the small new life began to form within her. Eric had been very cautious with her on the few occasions they had made love since she lost the baby, but now she felt physically strong again, and she was determined to have another child. As soon as possible.

The woods surrounding Oil Creek were dense and thicky populated with animals. Eric had stopped to study deer and elk tracks along the way, and now Sara stared with amusement at a black squirrel playing on the branch of a tall pine.

They had reached the area late in the day and set up camp. Now there was only a blanket of stars overhead, the sound of a beaver hard at work in the distance, and the occasional snort of the horses, hobbled nearby.

Eric doused the fire with a few handfuls of dirt than came to stretch out beside her on the bedroll.

"Happy?" he asked, lifting a strand of hair from her brow and winding it around his long fingers.

"Very happy," she whispered, turning to stare up into his face.

The moonlight filtered over his face, outlining his profile. Her hand reached up and touched the broad cheek gently, as she studied the long nose and sculpted lips. The blue eyes were violet in the moon's glow, and suddenly her heart was beating rapidly as she watched his eyes creep down to her breasts and linger there.

He lifted his hand to the buttons and began to work them loose, slowly and lazily. When her breasts were bare in the moonlight, he sat for a while admiring their rounded silken curves. Then he lowered his lips to each nipple, and his tongue traced slow, maddening circles.

Sara's hands wound through the thick blonde hair that gleamed like molten gold in the moonlight. Her body responded with a heated throb that began at the center of her being and radiated outward. His mouth moved lower, nipping at her shoulders as her clothing was cast aside.

The cool night air was a welcome caress on her heated body as Eric continued to explore with hands and mouth until Sara was writhing in a kind of agonized ecstasy that demanded relief.

"Eric, make love to me," she whispered.

Quickly he shed his clothes and settled down beside her, but to her surprise, he did not do as she asked.

"Wh . . . what are you waiting for?"

His eyes were making a slow, thorough journey down her body as a sensual grin tilted his mouth. "I like to look at you before my mind goes into somersaults." She wrapped her arms around him, silently expressing her need for him.

With a moan of pleasure and pain mixed as one hoarse sound, he did as she had asked and Sara responded wildly. Her fingers massaged the tense muscles of his neck, soothed his chest where the rapid beat of his heart drummed against her fingers.

He held back his own pleasure in the intense desire to give her all the joy possible. His movements were slow, deliberate, searing the depths of her being until she cried out his name into the velvet darkness broken only by the silver gleam of the moon. The look in Eric's face was one of pure ecstasy as he watched Sara's eyes fill with tears of joy. Then slowly he closed his eyes, drawn into the spiraling ache that weaved throughout his body as he gripped her against him and a strong hard quiver shook his entire body. Neither could move; neither could speak. The pleasure was exquisite, a kind of sweet torture that demanded more. And more.

"I can never get enough of you," he sighed into her soft neck. "Never."

A bright morning sun fell over their faces; Eric stirred and came awake slowly. Sara's body was molded into his side, and he was sleeping on his back, one arm around her, one arm stretched out to the side. He looked down at her and smiled.

Her dark hair was tumbled about her face,

which appeared soft and vulnerable in deep sleep. Gently, he brought his free arm over to smooth back the hair from her oval face. In the bright light, her skin was a deep olive, and he stared at her with pride.

Love made a man stronger, he decided, while gentling him as well. He could never do enough for Sara, and this made him aware of how unselfish true love could be. He felt desire sweeping through him again, but he forced himself to slip out to build a fire; he wanted to have hot coffee waiting for her when she awoke.

As they sat before the breakfast fire sipping coffee, Eric stretched his long legs and looked at her. "I seem to have forgotten why we came here. All I want to do is make love to you."

Sara laughed, uncoiling her slim body in the rays of sun that beamed over them. "Perhaps we needed a special place like this to make our time together more . . . exciting."

Eric chuckled. "My heart can't take much more excitement. And so"—he pulled himself up from the ground—"I think I'll get out the cradle and see if I can locate a good spot at the creek. Why don't you sit and relax for a while?"

Sara nodded, watching contentedly as Eric lifted the heavy pack propped against the trunk of a large spruce. He lifted out a wooden apparatus, similar to the few Ernest sold at the post. This one, she soon realized, was constructed of better wood than Eric's old one. The cradle was actually a strainer build on a rocker with holes in its hopper bottom to allow dirt, but not heavier matter like rocks and gold, to pass through to a canvas apron.

"I'll come along too," she said, leaping to her feet. "I want to see how the cradle works."

She followed Eric down to the stream and they tracted its winding course for quarter of a mile until they came upon a sudden bend.

"I'd never get lucky a second time at a bend in the stream," Eric laughed, wading out into the water.

"You never know. Maybe this will be our lucky day!" Sara called, anxiously watching as he lowered a tin pan into the water, scooping up soil from the bed of the stream. He waded back to the bank and slowly poured the contents of the pan through the upper channel of the cradle. Sara knelt and began to work the cradle while Eric waded back out to the deeper part of the stream.

Sara began to work the wooden handle back and forth to rock the cradle. As she watched the loose sand disintegrate and fall through the strainer, she thought of a different kind of cradle that she wanted to rock, but then she sighed and pushed all sadness from her mind as she concentrated on her task.

At first she felt awkward turning the handle, unable to get the right rhythm to loosen the debris from the clear, cold water. It splashed in her face when she rocked too hard, but when she rocked too slowly there was not enough force to separate the rocks and debris from the water.

She gripped the handle tighter, straightened her shoulders and tried to work at a moderate pace. This time she got it right, and she studied the loose gravel falling into the cradle's apron. When the last of the debris had fallen and nothing caught her eye, she glanced at Eric with a shake of the head and a light shrug.

"We're just getting started," he called to her, an encouraging smile on his tan face. "Watch carefully. Sometimes nuggets are covered in so much dirt they're hard to spot until they're washed clean."

"Whatever you say," she said, her brows lifted teasingly. She felt good this morning, better than she'd felt in a very long time.

Eric waded up the bank, boots sloshing with water, and poured another pan of water and sand into the cradle. Water sprayed over her, but she merely laughed, not caring if he drenched her. The penetrating sun would soon dry her clothes.

She began to rock the cradle again, her eyes moving over the matter in the hopper. Then her gaze began to widen, and she stopped rocking, and merely stared. Her mouth dropped open as she plunged her hands into the apron of the cradle, scooping up a handful of nuggets. If Eric hadn't warned her to watch for a pale gleam in the mud, she might have missed the first one, but the others were so large it would have taken a blind person not to recognize the quality of the rocks in her hand.

She gasped as the sunlight caught their golden glitter and reflected it back to her.

"Eric!" she screamed. "*Eric!*"

Her eyes filled with wonder as she sought the hopeful face of her husband, plunging out of the creek and leaping the bank.

"What is it? What have you found?"

"Nuggets, if I'm not badly mistaken. And don't you dare tell me this is fool's gold!" she threatened breathlessly.

Eric stood over her, water dripping onto her clothes, but neither cared. His wet fingers scooped up one huge rock, nearly as large as a gold dollar, and turned it against the sunlight.

"Pure gold, Sara. *Pure gold!*"

She was reaching for a clean pan to place the nuggets in when Eric's hand cupped her radiant face and his cool, moist lips covered hers with a triumphant kiss.

"I always knew I needed a partner," he said, beaming down into her shining eyes.

"Well, now you have one. And now that I've touched gold, I may never be the same again! So why are you standing there dripping on me, husband? Get back to that water and start panning!"

He chuckled as he turned and bounded back into the creek while Sara examined the remaining debris one more time, trying to be certain she hadn't overlooked a smaller piece. There was nothing else, however, even though she rocked the cradle again and again, straining her eyes.

After several hours of dipping water and rocking the cradle, Sara and Eric had to give up hope for further nuggets. They had struck a bonanza on the second try. Eric estimated several hundred dollars worth of nuggets were rattling around in the pan.

"Not a bad day's work," he said, smiling at her. "I'd say we've earned ourselves a trip to Denver—and a celebration!"

12

Shane sat under a cottonwood tree, staring morosely across the lush meadow leading to the soda springs. From the village came the sound of chants, flutes and stamping feet, but he had turned angry eyes from the celebration taking place. He gritted his teeth against the sounds and his lean jaw clenched, accenting the moon scar on his cheek.

He had not been accepted in Bear Claw's camp. There was a stiff politeness among the tribe when he came around, but he was smart enough to sense and respect their reserve. They followed the example set by their Chief, Bear Claw, who had ignored Shane after the first scowling glance, when he saw that Shane possessed white blood. Shane had been at camp for two weeks now, and though he'd tried to make friends, he was still an outsider.

"Shane." Star of the Morning's soft voice sounded behind him, and he jumped nervously and spun to face her.

Star's eyes were filled with pain as she looked at him. "Why do we not join the dancers? This is the Mamaqui Mowats, the Bear Dance. It is a time to be happy, to sing, to call forth the spring. The squaws invite the braves to dance." Her eyes twinkled as she extended her hand. "It is an insult to be refused."

Shane did not share her humor, though he tried. His patience had been stretched to the limit. Even Wasatch, who was now his brother, seemed to have changed toward him, and to Shane this was the worst kind of rejection. Resentment festered and fueled his now hair-triggered temper, leaving it ready to snap like the cottonwood twigs he'd idly broken with restless, impatient hands.

"I'm not wanted here," he growled.

Star sank down beside him, absently lifting a broken twig. "Give them time. I told you it would not be easy. There is so much bitterness. . . ."

"What have I done to make your people bitter? I fed them when they were starving—even now, I would hunt night and day to feed Bear Claw's tribe, but I sense that my game would not be welcome."

Star sighed and tilted her head back to close her eyes. Again, she chose not to reply, knowing it would be useless. She, too, sensed the cold feeling among Bear Claw's tribe where Shane was concerned, but she knew no way to change those feelings. She felt split in half, her loyalty still with her people, yet her love for Shane threatening to overshadow all else.

Shane turned and leveled his angry stare toward the celebration taking place within a circular enclosure of pine branches. Through an opening, he could see the medicine man cracking a willow whip over the dancers who were lined in parallel rows, the women facing the men. As he watched them move three steps forward, three steps backward, he began to share the trancelike state that enveloped the dancers. In the background, a slowly beating drum ground out a monotonous rhythm. Shane shifted his position on the hard ground, suddenly experiencing a strange desire to join the festive dancers. Perhaps they would accept him if he showed skill in the Bear Dance. His feet were quick and sure on high mountain trails; he was certain he could dance as well as any of the braves.

"All right." He glanced at Star, whose closed eyes indicated she must be begging the Great Spirit for his compliance. "We'll dance," he announced, forcing a smile as he stood and extended his hand to her.

Joy lit her face as she took his hand and jumped to her feet, not so lightly as before, for now a dizzyness often accompanied sudden movements. Automatically her hand touched her stomach and pressed gently against the little bulge. That gesture always filled her with pride and strength, for she had never been happier, knowing she was carrying Shane's child.

"Life will be better," she promised, entwining her fingers in his.

They hurried across the meadow to join the dancers, quietly slipping through the opening of the branches; but as soon as they positioned themselves in line, the drum beat stopped. Shane glanced toward the medicine man, who had dropped the whip and was leveling an icy stare at the couple.

Shane's eyes narrowed and swung down the long line of dancers, meeting in every eye the same chilling stare. He turned and strode away from those silently condemning eyes, his booted feet stomping out his anger as he hurried to the north end of the meadow where the horses were corraled.

"Shane!" Star caught up with him as he was leading his pinto out of the corral and tugged desperately at his sleeve. "Where are you going?"

"I don't know." He saddled his horse and tossed the reins around his neck. "Maybe I'll go to a white man's village. Maybe that's where I belong." He was beyond all logic. His muscled body was rigid with a fury that would explode on the first man who crossed him. He had to get away for a while.

Yanking the reins of his horse, he wheeled the pinto around and jabbed his heels into its side. The horse tore across the meadow as Star stood watching, her eyes filled with tears.

Shane had treated his horse unmercifully, he realized with a guilty heart when he finally trotted into Colorado City. The pinto was heavily lathered and thirsty, and his eyes were wild with fear from the slashing reins and the cruel jabbing of his rider's spurs.

A wooden trough near the blacksmith shop offered fresh water. Shane directed his horse to the trough and slid off, regretfully rubbing down the sweat-covered neck.

"Sorry," he muttered. It was unforgivable to

treat his horse in such a manner; he must not vent his anger this way again.

He lifted his buckskin shirt sleeve to swab across his perspiring face, then turned to survey the strange town. He'd merely followed the rutted trail, having no idea where it led. His eyes roamed the false-front stores, ending up on the bat-wing doors of a saloon. Turning back to his horse, he waited patiently until the pinto had drunk his fill. Then he led him across to the hitching rail before the saloon.

Dusk was settling over the town, and with the end of day came the invitation to enter the saloon for gambling or wetting the whistle, as the sign over the door proclaimed.

Shane tied his horse, then paused on the sidewalk, smoothing back his long dark hair and straightening his clothes. He was vaguely conscious of a few bold stares from passersby, but he ignored them. He was in no mood to argue; he wanted a strong drink, one that would burn his throat and leap into his blood, soothing all that had gone wrong.

He pushed back the swinging doors and stepped into a huge, crowded room. A narrow bar ran the length of one side with the remaining space cluttered with chairs and tables. Oil lamps hung from posts, casting a pale yellow glow. The smell of tobacco smoke, whiskey and cheap perfume drifted through the air, and he saw the room was filled with men dressed in rough work clothes. In the center of the room, three women, dressed in colorful satin dresses with feathers in their hair, strolled from table to table. Their faces were heavily rouged, and their eyes held a glazed look, as though something stronger than drink had dulled their minds. Greedy hands snatched at their breasts, then their swaying hips, as they lingered at tables.

Shane turned toward the crowded bar, angling his way between the shoulders of two men dressed in flannel shirts and trousers patched with buckskin. He looked neither right nor left, but sought out the small, balding man who was busily filling glasses.

The man's eyes lingered on Shane and a wary expression crossed his face. Shane nudged in to the bar, feeling the heated glare of other eyes as the bartender paused before him.

"Whiskey," Shane spoke up, reaching into his trousers for his sparse change, acquired from the rabbitskins and furs he had sold at a trading post along the way.

The bartender nodded, as though relieved that his tone held the relaxed enunciation of the white man.

Shane plunked down the coins indicated on the mirror behind the bar where all drinks were priced. Then he lifted the glass and tossed down the amber liquid, enjoying its bracing effect.

He motioned the bartender and dropped another coin. His glass was refilled, again and again, until his shoulders rounded as he hunched over the bar, feeling the sting of the alcohol in his blood. His nerves were lulled and soothed, and he leaned down on his elbows, his dark eyes fixed dully on the empty glass. He now felt numb to the anger and frustration that had driven him for miles.

"What tribe you with?" The question was half slurred, yet strong, and underlined with contempt.

Slowly, Shane rounded on the man standing next to him. With growing hostility, he looked at the man with the dirty white skin.

"Ute," he replied. "I am Yuttaa."

"Yuu . . ." the man broke off and sneered, baring dark, broken teeth behind his leering grin.

"Hey, fellas"—he looked over Shane's head to the other men—"we got us a real live Ute here. A savage who got dressed up and come to drink with us. We oughta—"

Shane's fist slammed into the grimy teeth, and the man's head jerked backward as though he were a puppet yanked by a string. His arm flailed across the bar, knocking glasses to the floor with a splintering crash.

Shane's anger was a fever that took possession of his senses, pumping fire and ice into muscles that coiled and readied for the attack. He dived into the white man's stomach, driving him backward to the floor. Before the wild-eyed victim could retaliate, Shane straddled him and began to pummel the sneering white face. Blood spurted from the nose, and a tooth broke on Shane's swift, hard knuckle. Shane's blood roared in his ears so that he was not immediately conscious of the bodies closing in around him until a heavy hand seized his collar and dragged him backwards. A blow struck the side of his face, stunning him momentarily. He blinked against the dizzying blow, and in that split second of hesitation, a boot caught him low in his back, grinding his kidney.

Shane crumpled in pain. Then the tobacco-sweat of the man he had fought filled his nostrils as other hands seized him and dragged him out the back door.

"Hold him, Luke!"

The man who had suffered a quick and fair beating from Shane now crouched like a predator on the attack, his hair hanging in his blood-smeared face. "I'm gonna teach this bastard to stay where he belongs."

Star knelt beside the crystal stream, dropping a trinket into the clear water as her mind groped with the black feeling that had seized her upon Shane's departure. Fear mingled with a terrible kind of apprehension that made her heart race while her body shook. A bad spirit was upon them; she felt it.

She lifted her tear-stained face to the sky and began to speak Yuuttaa words to the Great Spirit, but soon she was forced to turn and flee back to the village. The feeling she sought to dispel at the soda springs had grown stronger as she communicated with the Great Spirit. *Shane was in trouble; she felt it; she knew it.*

Wasatch! Her brother was Shane's best friend. He must go in search of him, because death's devil danced around her, the same devil spirit that had seized her as a young girl when she went racing to her mother's lodge and found her lifeless on her bed, her face on fire with the fever that soon closed her eyes forever.

Since then, Star had listened to the warnings that came to her, often mysteriously. She would beg Wasatch to ride after Shane. He must catch up with him before the dark spirit of death claimed her beloved.

Hours later, after Wasatch had followed Shane's trail into Colorado City, he found him in a darkened alley, bleeding, half conscious, and struggling for breath. Shane was vaguely aware that his brother knelt over him, but their midnight ride back to the village was obscured by the pain that drove him in and out of consciousness. Pain was the only reality he knew, the pain that beat against every bone and muscle of his body. Wasatch begged him to hang on, but each step of the pony shot the pain deeper into his body until Wasatch's words faded into the darkness. Finally, he passed into merciful unconsciousness.

Star continued to bind Shane's broken ribs with strips of softened doeskin, though he lay in a stupor, scarcely aware of what she was doing. He had suffered a severe injury to his head which confused his thinking. His slim, straight nose would be forever crooked, and three teeth were missing from the right side of his mouth.

Bruises covered his body, his eyes were

swollen shut, his breathing was heavy and labored. But Star knew he would live because *she refused to let him die.*

Beyond their lodge, a mournful wail rose from the dancers, and from the medicine man who had come to press herbs into Star's hand. Together they lifted Shane's head and poured the special potion down his throat. A lesser man would have died; a lesser man could not have survived that first terrible night. But Star of the Moring's love was as bright and eternal as her name, and she worked tirelessly with him, never once relinquishing hope that he would live.

By the fifth day, he was able to sit up, feed himself and speak again, though his heart was too heavy for words. His spirit was beaten and broken, for now he lived in a dark and lonely place, separate from everyone he knew. He did not belong with the Utes, nor could he ever again live with the whites. A deeper wound festered and bled inside him which, unlike his body, worsened with each passing day as he thought over his life and wondered what demon spirit had cast him on the earth to live like a tortured animal.

Star watched the change with grave concern, noting the spark that had been ignited in the brooding eyes and that burned low and steady, giving him an expression she had never seen.

"Our people suffer for you," Star whispered, as her slim capable fingers rubbed salve into his wounds. "The night my brother brought you home, the medicine man led them in a dance of healing for you. They danced until the moon gave way to the sun, and you grew stronger afterwards. You are better each day now; soon you will hunt the elk again." She smiled, though her dark eyes held sadness still.

"Better?" Shane snarled. "I think I'm worse, Star! There are wounds that your loving hands cannot reach."

"But my love can," she said, wrapping her arms around his shoulders and pressing her soft cheek against his bearded jaw. "My heart aches for you, and my body has known pain each time I look at your wounds. Can't you see that you *are* my life, that if you die inside, I die as well?" She paused, pressing her body against his. "Here, I will give you half of my strength to heal those broken places—but only half! I cannot spare more, because our son awaits his birth when the trees lose their leaves and when the north wind starts to howl. We both need you. You cannot fail us!"

Some faint emotion began to stir deep in Shane's cold heart, and with her soft weight against him, Shane closed his eyes, absorbing her words like the rays of the sun. With his last ounce of strength, he would protect Star and their baby. But what sort of life would his son have? he wondered miserably. Would he be beaten and dragged off to die because he was a *savage*, because the white man held a strange contempt for those born to another heritage? Did they not understand that the Indian had no more control over his birth than the white man?

"What are you thinking?" she asked, pressing a kiss to his lips.

Her fingers, as light as a summer breeze, soothed his clenched jaw as the question, and her touch, wrenched a heavy sigh from Shane's sore body.

"The white man thought I was Indian. I was *proud* to tell them I was Yuuttaa," he replied, slowly opening his eyes to focus on Star's slim face. There were dark circles beneath her eyes, and her mouth was drawn in a tense pale line. "One of them called me a savage and I hit him. I would have won the fight had it been fair, but that is not the white man's way. They dragged me outside . . . three men, and held me while . . ."

Star's fingers splayed across his lips, silencing his bitterness. "It is over. It will only please the Misho-tunga—the bad spirit—for you to remain in the dark world of anger."

Shane stared at her, annoyed that she wanted to forget the lesson he had learned —even worse, that she expected him to.

"Please, Shane, let us put this terrible thing behind us. The spring sun rides high in the sky, and soon the warm summer will be upon us. A better time is coming for us. Let us try to be happy."

Tears were shining in her dark eyes, and as always, Star's tears began to work their magic on him, softening his heart with love.

His lips formed a kiss against her fingers, and he tried to nod his head in an attempt to be agreeable, but that slight movement sent sparks of pain deep into his brain. For a moment, hatred and bitterness shot to his mouth in a strong taste of bile. But deep in his heart, he knew that Star was right. He could not forever lie on his bed, nursing bitterness and anger. It would only give more power to what the white men had done to him. He must be useful again, for Star and for their baby.

"Shane, I have something to tell you," she was saying, a look of concern on her face. "Bear Claw wishes to speak with you when you are strong enough to walk to his lodge. He, too, is angry that you were hurt by the white man."

"Why?" Shane scowled. "He resents me. He doesn't want me here in this village."

"That has changed." She lifted his hand to her lips. "Nish-ki told one of the squaws how you were left beside a wagon. That squaw had a very strange story to tell."

"What kind of story?"

Star hesitated, her dark eyes caressing each feature of his bruised face. "I have sworn not to speak of it. Not until Bear Claw smokes the pipe with you."

"Does this have anything to do with us?" Shane stared at her, his curiosity mounting.

"Perhaps with you, my strong warrior." A wide, proud smile stretched her small lips. "Perhaps you are more Yuuttaa than you know. It is a strange story, but one you must hear only from Bear Claw. He is the one to tell you. Then you can decide for yourself."

Star seemed to be talking in riddles, saying words that made no sense to him. He studied the gleam in her eyes, the radiant smile on her face, as he sank back on his bed wondering what he would have to decide.

"Is this good news I will hear?" he finally asked.

"Yes, my beloved, it is."

For the first time in many days, his full lips quirked in the hint of a grin, one that deepened the dimple in his cheek, and crinkled the moon scar on his jaw.

And for the first time in days, Star breathed a deep sigh of relief.

13

Shane's curiosity now helped to speed his healing, and by the next afternoon, he was hobbling across the village to Bear Claw's lodge.

He walked with his head up, his body stiffly erect. His pride would not allow him to acknowledge the pain that still accompanied his movements.

The squaws looked up from the baskets they were weaving, their gazes sharp and curious. The braves milled about the fire and offered a friendly greeting as he passed. Shane noticed the change in their expressions, but he was still wary of Bear Claw as he approached the chief's lodge. He hesitated at the flap, but it was soon thrown back as Bear Claw stepped out to greet him. Shane squared his shoulders and forced his vision to the piercing black eyes of the man who was taller and heavier than he.

"You are better?" Bear Claw inquired in his deep booming voice.

"I am well," Shane replied. Not having seen himself, he was unaware of how much the blue skin of his face denied his proud reply.

Bear Claw nodded and motioned him inside.

With the warm spring weather, a fire was no longer needed, but scarlet embers burned low in the center of the lodge. Two pipes were filled with tobacco, ready to be smoked. Shane now understood the reason for the fire, and was pleasantly surprised that Bear Claw had gone to this trouble for him. The Utes preferred to smoke their pipes around a fire.

Bear Claw sat down and lifted his pipe, motioning Shane to do so as well. Shane obeyed, glancing apprehensively at the chief. The vivid scar of the grizzly's claw covered half of Bear Claw's jaw, and though Shane tried not to stare, he longed to hear the story of the fight. In all of his hunting, he had never killed a grizzly.

Bear Claw's strong voice broke the silence. "The white man speaks with a forked tongue. You learn this?" he asked, lighting his pipe and sucking deeply of the tobacco as he surveyed Shane through a cloud of smoke.

"I have learned what I always suspected," he replied.

Bear Claw nodded and the silence lengthened. Shane sensed he was being tested, and he decided to speak only in reply to Bear Claw's questions. He wanted to earn the chief's respect, and his instincts told him that Bear Claw, like himself, did not care for useless words.

"You are a good hunter?" Bear Claw inquired.

Shane felt more comfortable to speak of animals than of men, yet he did not want to boast. "Hunting has been my gift," he answered as he sucked lightly on the pipe.

Bear Claw nodded slowly. "Like the wild eagle."

Shane frowned, then nodded. He supposed it was true.

"It is a gift from the Great Spirit," Bear Claw continued. "Shavano says you fed his people."

The chief removed his pipe and studied Shane for a long silent moment. "What do you know of your birth?" he asked suddenly.

Shane was taken aback by the question, and he frowned as his eyes drifted to the embers of the dwindling fire. "The white woman who raised me told me that two babies were left at their wagon train. Two couples traveling west did not have children. Those two took the babies. It happened that I was placed at the wheel of the Simmons wagon and they took me."

"And the other papoose?"

Shane shrugged. "I don't know. The train broke up when they reached the Arkansas River. The people who kept me wintered there, but some of the others moved in different directions. I don't know where the other papoose went."

"Where the white woman say you come from?"

Shane had never given the matter much thought, but now he tried to remember everything he had been told. "My mother said she thought the Indians had kidnapped the babies, then decided not to keep them and gave them back to the wrong wagon train."

Bear Claw leaned back and crossed his arms over his bronze chest. "What winter was this?" he asked.

"1843. My birthday is the day I was left at the wagon. November 5, 1843."

"Crying Wind was Yuuttaa," Bear Claw began, staring into the dying embers as though the memory was hidden there. "In her twentieth winter, a paleface spoke to her with forked tongue."

The chief's voice deepened and an angry fire began to blaze in his eyes. "Two papoose born. The paleface call them twins."

"Twins?" Shane frowned, trying to piece together the news he was hearing.

"Before the sun come up, Crying Wind go to red rocks and see wagons in our valley. She leave papooses with this train you speak of. The Winter of Dark Moons."

Shane's heart was hammering wildly in his chest, as he sat there stunned, wondering if it were possible.

"Rope Thrower tell us the palefaces called Winter of Dark Moons a year, 1843."

Shane groped for words as he stared with disbelief at the bronzed, weathered face of the chief. "Did he say the month was November?" he finally asked.

Bear Claw shook his head. "Not know. There had been red and gold in the trees, and now the color was dying. We built our winter fires."

"That's the fall of the year. *November!*" Shane said, a wild, wonderful joy sweeping through him. All of his life, he'd moved in a confused and lonely world that held no answers to his many questions. Now the secrets were being revealed to him, forever freeing him of the dark uncertainty of his life.

"What happened to Crying Wind?" Shane asked anxiously.

A deep frown rutted the heavy lines in Bear Claw's brow. "She cry many tears. She never have more papoose. She say the Great Spirit curse her for leaving papooses at wagons." He shook his head. "No happy days, much suffering." He was looking over Shane's head to some distant place, where his thoughts lay. "She beg for the squaw, Little Dove."

"Little Dove?" Shane echoed.

"She name the papoose before she leave them. Wild Eagle and Little Dove. Their spirits would match their names, she say. We bring Little Dove here, but she no claim her people. She is bad medicine for my village."

He scowled. "When Crying Wind die, a paleface trade for Little Dove. Trade gold nugget. They leave . . . no come back ever."

Bear Claw's eyes wandered to the open flap and he thought of White Buffalo, sullen and angry most of the time.

Shane stared at him as his thoughts tumbled like snowflakes in a northerly wind.

"This Little Dove is my sister?" he repeated.

"But she is bad medicine."

Shane laid down his pipe on the glowing coals and leaned forward. "Crying Wind died?" he repeated.

Bear Claw jerked his head in a stiff nod.

Shane sighed. Again fate had cheated him. Bear Claw stood and Shane assumed this signaled the end of their talk. He pulled himself to his feet, his mind a fog of confusion.

"Crying Wind lived here?" he finally asked.

Bear Claw nodded again. "And now we speak of Wild Eagle. And *me*"—he pounded his chest with his fist—"Crying Wind . . . my sister!" A slow grin broke over the leathered face, and he stretched out his hands to clamp Shane's shoulder. "We are blood."

Shane stared at the chief he had feared and respected, who was now—his *uncle*! As he absorbed the good news and felt the weight of Bear Claw's strong hands on his shoulders, his chest swelled with pride. "I will try to be worthy," he said. "And my name is now Wild Eagle. I must be worthy of that, as well."

14

Star lay in Wild Eagle's arms, sleeping peacefully on their bed of animal skins while Shane stared at the small opening overhead where the lodge poles were joined. The first gleam of morning light drifted down through the smoke hole, and he studied the dim gray rays as he lay thinking. Again, he marveled that the courageous Bear Claw was his uncle!

A pleased smile lifted the corners of his mouth as he thought of this tribe to which he belonged. He now understood his restless nature, his compelling urge to follow the wind, explore every forest trail, seek out Wasatch and Star of the Morning. Everything made sense for the first time in his life. He understood why he'd always preferred the company of the Utes to that of the whites at the trading posts and villages.

A strange sound penetrated his happy thoughts, and a wrinkle puckered his low brow as he listened. Another unnatural bird call echoed across the stillness of early morning. From the confinement of the corral, a horse neighed, then another.

Gently, he freed his arm from Star's shoulder and crept to the flap of the lodge.

When the strange call sounded again, he identified it as the mimicking call of one Indian giving a signal to others. And it was not the Ute call, which closely resembled that of a mourning dove.

Unmindful of his nude body, Shane bolted outside and glanced cautiously around the wide circle of lodges; no one was stirring. He flattened himself against his lodge and scanned the meadow and the low, pine-studded ridges. His keen eyes caught a movement in the pines and he squinted. He could dimly make out a horse and rider slowly advancing through the pine thicket. His eyes swept the ridge and he made out another, then another.

Arapahoes!

He inched his way back along the side of the lodge, moving slowly, cautiously, until he reached the front. Then he dashed inside and threw on trousers and boots, then grabbed his gun. Crouched, he made his way to the nearest lodge where Wasatch and Shavano lay sleeping. He shook them awake and related the distressing news.

Their eyes snapped open and widened with alarm as their minds registered his warning.

The men bolted to their feet, scrambling for weapons. But already hooves were cutting up the soft earth of the meadow as two dozen Arapahoes charged into camp, flailing tomahawks and aiming arrows.

The excitement of battle shot through Wild Eagle's body, yet the disciplined calm of his hunting nature took over. With careful precision he raised his rifle and took aim.

The crack of fire jerked one of the Arapahoes from his pony, but now other riders circled the village, lying on the outside of their horses and shooting underneath.

The Utes erupted from their lodges whooping war cries and waving tomahawks. Wild Eagle raced after one of the Arapahoes, yanking at the buffalo-hide rope on the horse until it reared. The rider toppled and Wild Eagle struck him.

Clouds of dust rose up, stinging his eyes as the Arapahoes raced around the circle, firing guns and shooting arrows. The Utes fought back, never once yielding to the surrounding enemy, though two braves and a squaw were pierced with arrows and staggered into the swirling dust.

The battle lasted only a few minutes, but to Wild Eagle it seemed to go on forever. He'd never imagined that one tribe would fight another with such vengeance. The Arapahoes retreated, but Wild Eagle saw, with sickening horror, three scalps dangling from their belts.

He lifted his rifle and picked off another disappearing rider. Then he whirled, seeking Star. She was standing just outside their lodge, her face deathly pale. Wild Eagle pushed through the hysterical group of women around her and reached out to Star, pulling her into his arms as he spoke words of comfort.

"But it is not over, Wild Eagle." She began to cry softly as she pressed her cheek against his heart. "My people will not rest until three

Arapahoe scalps are taken. You see our dead?"

Eagle nodded sadly. She was right; there would be no rest until the three deaths were avenged.

For three days and nights, the village mourned. On the fourth day, the braves painted their faces and bodies yellow and black to prepare for battle. They dressed in buckskin leggings and capes, and gathered their war spears, shields and tomahawks.

Beneath the light of a pale quarter moon, the warriors rode out of camp, intending to surprise the Arapahoes at daybreak. Wild Eagle had already scouted the trail and marked the route of the Arapahoes. They would find the enemy encampment beyond the red rocks on a flat, distant plain.

From the high rocks, they spotted only a few animal-skin lodges, with half a dozen more made of brush and sticks tied together and half covered with robes or blankets. In the graying dawn, Bear Claw's white horse led the way, with Wild Eagle and the other warriors fanned out around him. When they approached the steep ravine leading down to the plains, the riders formed a single line as they picked their way down the rocky trail, then forded the narrow stream at the foot.

Wild Eagle fixed his eyes on the huddle of lodges as the icy water splashed over him. He was oblivious to anything but the coming battle.

The Arapaho horses had eaten most of the meadow grass and now the earth, moist from snowmelt, sucked up the plodding hoofbeats of the Ute mounts.

No one spoke. Only the occasional snort from one of the horses broke the silence of early morning as they advanced toward the sleeping camp.

Then Bear Claw silently lifted his arm and the line halted. He pointed toward two Arapahoes, slumped beside a small nest of coals with only a tiny orange flame still glowing in the embers.

Beyond the lodges, ponies were hobbled and Bear Claw pointed in that direction. Three Ute horses were hobbled there. At the signal from Bear Claw, two braves turned and loped toward the corral to reclaim the horses.

Shavano and Wasatch began to pull their arrows out and fit them to the bows. Eagle loaded his rifle, knowing he was far more adept with his own weapon, though he was slowly becoming skilled with bow and arrow.

Because the sound of their approach could no longer be silenced, Bear Claw gave the signal to charge.

The horses tore across the plains, their hoofbeats throbbing in Eagle's ears, mixing with the roar of his blood. The braves had reached the corral and were attempting to free the Ute horses. An arrow whizzed through the air from the cluster of lodges, finding its mark in one of the braves at the corral.

The Utes charged the Arapahoe camp, surrounding the half-awake Arapahoes who were rushing from their lodges. Arrows and

PASSION'S PEAK

spears sailed through the air. Eagle rode low on his horse, firing as an Arapaho lifted his tomahawk. His bullet was true, knocking the enemy to the ground in a pool of blood. He reloaded and fired again. Vaguely, Eagle was aware of his brothers bounding from their horses to claim Arapaho scalps; but, as planned, his job was to fire, reload and fire again his trusty Hawkin rifle.

The war whoops of each tribe filled the air, along with the hysterical cries of squaws yanking frightened, wide-eyed children inside the lodges.

A strange calm settled over Eagle in the face of battle. The age-old instinct of a true warrior burned in his blood as the Yuuttaa battle cry automatically erupted from his dry throat.

Without their horses, the Arapahoes were at a disadvantage, as the Utes had been when the Arapahoes burst into their camp, killing three of their braves and stealing horses. A few of the Arapahoe braves now fled in fear, but most stood their ground.

Then suddenly Bear Claw's deep voice boomed over the other shrieks as he commanded his warriors to retreat, having avenged the three deaths.

Eagle looked back to see the Arapaho horses bounding freely across the plains, while only a few warriors continued to fight. He turned his pinto's head in the direction of his retreating tribe, glancing left to right to survey the number and strength of their men. Then his heart sank. Shavano slumped over his horse, an arrow embedded in his back.

Eagle seized the trailing reins of Shavano's horse as the older man's hand fell limply. Eagle yelled to Wasatch and they drew rein abruptly. Eagle leapt from his horse, unable to catch Shavano before he toppled face down in the dirt.

Eagle and Wasatch reached him at almost the same moment, but it was Eagle who, as gently as possible, removed the deeply-embedded spear of the bloody arrow. As he did so, he felt the tearing of flesh and bone.

Wasatch turned his father over, staring with horror into his dying face. Bubbles of blood filled his mouth with each labored breath as Wasatch stood rigid, valiantly withholding his tears.

The Utes were less likely to take scalps than the other tribes, Eagle knew, but he glimpsed three scalps dangling from bloody hands. His eyes roamed over the assortment, his jaw clenched in bitter satisfaction at the sight of them. Yet Shavano's killer still ran free!

Star had been right, he thought grimly. This was only the beginning.

15

At last Sara and Eric spotted the sprawling settlement of Denver, built out in the flats with the jagged, frost-glistening peaks of the Front range as a backdrop. They had boarded their horses in Colorado City and taken yesterday's coach to Denver. Sara had never traveled and she'd sat staring out the window as wide-eyed as a child for most of the trip.

Mountains gave way to hills with table-flat summits and sandstone ridges as the country opened up, stretching out before them. Occasionally, an antelope or deer bounded across the meadow or darted daringly in front of the stage.

The stage stop where they had spent the night was a rambling log dwelling that served fried venison, creamed potatoes and thick gravy in large bowls on one long table. Everyone huddled on narrow wooden benches that ran the length of the table and drank mug after mug of strong black coffee. The tales of travel were as plentiful as the coffee and Sara listened in utter fascination.

Overhead, a sleeping loft divided by curtains separated the cramped area into three tiny enclosures with scarcely enough space for a narrow cot and straight-backed wooden chair. Neither Eric nor Sara could move without bumping the other while the gusty snores of exhausted travelers filled their ears and ricocheted off the pine rafters. Still, the friendly, fun-loving couple who owned the stage stop compensated for the crowded quarters and there was a spirit of adventure among the travelers that was infectious. Eric struck up quick friendships while Sara sat in awe of the rip-roaring stories that were told.

Her mind drifted back to the post and the years she had spent there. It seemed like another lifetime, and not a happy one, compared to the life she now had with Eric.

The stage was rattling into Denver, and Sara blinked. Her eyes felt gritty from trail dust, and she longed desperately for a bath, but those discomforts were forgotten as she stared around her.

"That's Cherry Creek," Eric said, pointing to a narrow stream threading its way between two rows of cabins built of cottonwood logs and roofed with earth and grass. "When I first came to the Territory, that creek was the dividing line between two settlements, Auraria and Denver. Folks cussed and fussed and occasionally fought each other for the miners and settlers' trade. Finally they realized that the only way either could succeed was to bury the hatchet and join forces as one town, Denver City.

"What was it like when you first came?" she asked interestedly.

"It was like one giant ant heap!" he

chuckled. "People were crowded into tents and crude shacks, even sleeping under wagons. Half of them were ready to turn around and head home. At a boarding house in Auraria, I met a man who owned two hundred and four lots in Denver and Auraria. He was so homesick he offered to swap all his lots for a good horse with a saddle and bridle! Too bad I didn't take him up on that offer."

The quiet older couple sitting opposite them had been napping, but their arrival in Denver City stirred them. They peered sleepily through the stage window, listening to Eric.

"Yessir, young man, you should have traded with him!" The older man confirmed. "Prices have shot sky high!"

"I've had to pay as much as $15 for a sack of flour," the woman added, clearly outraged.

Sara smiled politely but quickly returned to the view beyond the window. Log buildings with false fronts held brightly lettered signs advertising the wares within. A funny little sign hung in one window and when Sara read it, she couldn't suppress a laugh.

Any man who won't eat prunes is a son of a bitch!

"There's a shortage on fruit," Eric whispered, chuckling.

The stage bounced on, giving them a blurred view of a gun shop, a carpenter shop, a hardware store that boasted stoves made of sheet iron, a meat market, bakery, saloon and gambling hall, and barber shop. Graham's Drug Store offered watches and jewelry made to order from native gold.

"Now I can buy you a wedding band," Eric

whispered, touching the bulge in his coat pocket. Tucked away in a buckskin bag were the gold nuggets. He'd left the two smallest ones at the cabin, safely hidden. The medium-sized one he'd traded in Colorado City for new clothes and traveling money.

He was taking the three large nuggets, weighing several ounces each, to an assayer in Denver.

As the stage rocked to a halt before the hotel, Eric turned to Sara. She was smoothing down her dress, a printed blue-and-white cotton with full sleeves and lace collar and cuffs. The bodice hugged her breasts and emphasized her tiny waist, while the full skirt, over a stiff new crinoline, flared about her slim ankles. New black patent slippers encased her feet. Eric's eyes swept back to her face. Since marriage, she'd gained a few pounds that were becoming to her. Her cheeks were no longer thin, and her glossy black hair was swept into the popular chignon with soft ringlets falling about her cheeks. She was a beautiful woman.

"Wait," Eric said as the older couple climbed down. "It's been too long since you've kissed me."

Her eyes widened in surprise but she ignored the crowd gathering about and leaned forward to press her mouth to his in a deep, lingering kiss.

Eric stared into her dark eyes, delighted as always by the smell and taste of her. She was a stronger tonic than any liquor or tobacco he'd ever sampled—that and his crude comparison raised a grin as he released her and stepped down from the coach.

Their trunk was retrieved and placed at their feet as they waited with their hands shading their eyes against the penetrating glare of the July sun. Denver was hot compared to their cool haven on the back side of Pikes Peak.

"It's good to stand on solid ground again," Eric said as he stretched his muscles and glanced up and down the crowded street.

He was a striking figure, dressed in a dark broadcloth suit with a starched white shirt and gleaming black leather boots. For a moment, Sara allowed herself the pleasure of gazing at him through eyes of love. The fashionable new round hat was dark, like his suit, and sat on gleaming blonde hair, neatly trimmed about his ears while brushing his shirt collar. His face was deeply tanned from many hours in the sun, accenting the vivid blue of his eyes. He had grown a beard again, spade-shaped and well trimmed.

Sara ventured a curious glance at the people crowding the sidewalks. The men were dressed in red shirts and buckskins, others in dark business suits. All wore mustaches or luxuriant beards. She turned back to Eric.

"You're the handsomest man around," she whispered.

He didn't seem to hear. He was staring down the street. Sara followed his line of vision and her breath caught in her throat.

Two young Indian boys, filthy and wearing only loin cloths, stood on a corner, their hands outstretched.

Eric sauntered down to them, reached into his pocket and dropped a coin in each eager hand. Sara followed, surveying the children. When they turned haggard eyes to her, there was a look of stark desperation in their young faces. She gave them a sad smile, but already they were glancing hopefully at other people passing by. When ignored, their faces fell and their fingers closed tightly over the coin Eric had given them.

"They're Ute, aren't they?" Sara whispered.

Eric looked quizzically from Sara to the children. "I'm not sure. Maybe."

"They are," Sara nodded, staring at them. "In fact, they resemble two of the Indian children I saw at Bear Claw's village." She glanced at Eric. "After you're around them for a while, they no longer look the same. You see the difference in their features and expressions."

Eric shoved his hands in his pockets as his eyes wandered back to the children. He judged them to be seven or eight years of age.

"What do you suppose they're doing here by themselves?" Sara asked.

An older woman, dressed in a calico dress and a bonnet, stopped on the sidewalk upon hearing her question. "They were captured by the Arapahoes, poor little things." She shook her head.

"How many others are there?" Eric asked.

The woman shrugged, her gray eyes sad in a heavily lined face. "Don't know. Two nights ago, some Arapahoes pitched tents out on the edge of town. My husband says these children are Utes, that the Arapahoes captured them after a battle. You know how those Indians are always at war with each other!" The woman turned and ambled on down the board sidewalk.

"You were right." Eric looked from Sara to the children, who were still begging. "They *are* Ute."

Her eyes were held by those gaunt, hungry faces, and a wave of compassion swept over her. She had always loved children and still grieved over the baby she had lost and her inability to become pregnant again.

"I feel so sorry for them," she sighed.

"They can buy food with the money I gave them." Eric linked his arm through hers as they walked on. "Come on, we'd better hurry and get a room before the hotel fills up."

Sara glanced back over her shoulder; the bleak little faces made a permanent imprint in her mind as they walked away.

While Denver was still a young town, the large frame hotel promised the best in comfort and luxury. Brass spittoons and hand rails, velvet settees and chairs, and a few fancy rugs offered reminders of what civilization had been like for those uprooted from North, South and East for the adventure of living out in the Territory.

In the lobby an argument was in progress, drawing the attention of those checking into the hotel. An older, distinguished-looking gentleman was stoutly defending the issues that had led the Southern states to secede from the Union. At his words, Eric's expression turned grave, and Sara remembered how distressed he'd been on hearing the news of Fort Sumter. She bit her lip, wondering how this war would affect Eric. The possibility that he might return and fight alarmed her, and she tried to dismiss the man's words from her mind.

"The people here dress well, don't they?" She pressed Eric's arm, attempting to divert his thoughts from war news.

"Yes," he agreed absently, still observing the quarreling men.

Sara sighed and glanced around at the women, abandoning her effort to distract him. The women wore fine silks and dainty bonnets. Patent leather gaters peeped from beneath hoops and crinolines. Their fair skin had been shielded from the sun, and their cheeks were delicately rouged. Diamonds and rubies glittered at their throats and on their fingertips. In comparison, Sara felt extremely plain.

But then her eyes wandered back to Eric, lingering on his strong profile. She was content with her life. She didn't need to own fine clothes and jewels to be happy. What she did need was love, and she'd found the true meaning of love as Eric's wife.

"I'll get a room," he muttered, an angry frown knitting his brow as he stalked toward the desk clerk.

Sara bit her lip, glancing back at the men who had adjourned to the bar to continue their discussion. She hoped the war news wasn't going to prey on Eric's mind; she didn't

PASSION'S PEAK

want anything to spoil the good time they had planned in Denver.

Eric obtained the last available room in the hotel and they hurried toward the stairs, but their attention was quickly drawn to the adjoining gambling hall. Through the open door, they could see the roulette tables filled with eager gamblers. Sara glanced at Eric. "I hope you aren't a gambler," she teased.

"Staking my life on nuggets is the extent of my gambling," he answered with a grin.

Their room was the last one at the far end of the second level. When Eric unlocked the door and they stepped inside, Sara was pleasantly surprised. There was only a brass bed, dresser and night table, but the furniture was cherrywood, obviously shipped from the States, and a fresh, clean smell drifted through the air. The blue satin spread matched the draperies covering a single long window. Sara peered out.

In the street below a train of wagons was unloading dry goods, groceries and crockery at the store on the corner.

"Want to rest, or shall we get something to eat?" Eric asked.

The mention of food brought a sudden rumble to Sara stomach. The jolting ride to Denver City had robbed her of her appetite, but now she pressed her hand to her stomach and smiled. "I'm starved!" she admitted. Another growl reached Eric's ears and they both laughed.

He pulled her into his arms and pressed his lips to hers in a gentle kiss. "All right, food it is. And the rest. I'll be glad to stretch out in a comfortable bed, won't you?"

Remembering the narrow lump mattress at the stage stop, she quickly agreed. But then a warm light flared in Eric's eyes as his lips sought hers again, and she knew he was thinking of more than a comfortable bed.

"Food . . ." she murmured against his mouth, her hands pressing gently against his broad chest.

Reluctantly he released her and nodded solemnly. "Food."

They dined at the Tremont House at a table elegantly decorated with bouquets of Pikes Peak flowers, but the dinner Sara had so eagerly awaited was clouded by the memory of the hungry Indian children. As she lifted her fork to spear the golden-baked trout, the sad dark eyes and hungry faces flashed into her mind, and her fork halted in mid-air. She stared at the generous serving of food on her plate, and her heart sank. It seemed so unfair for innocent children to be victims in the battles of adults.

Catching Eric's quizzical expression, she hurriedly dipped the fork in her mouth and murmured approval. But pity welled within her and she chewed slowly. To her disappointment, her appetite vanished, and the food lay like rocks in her stomach. She felt guilty in ways she couldn't begin to understand.

Walking back to the hotel in the soft golden twilight, Sara found herself searching the street corners for the Ute children, but they were nowhere in sight.

"They already have two churches here, even a school," Eric was saying.

Sara nodded, glancing from one building to another. At the end of the street, she spotted the assay office. "Look Eric," she tugged his sleeve and pointed.

"I know. But I'll wait until tomorrow to conduct business. Tonight is for you."

And Sara discovered that she was as eager as he to climb into the comfortable bed and make love. For a moment, it seemed strange to lie in Eric's arms and hear voices out in the hall, or the drumming of hoofbeats on the dirt street below. But soon her tense body relaxed as she gave herself over to the sweet pleasure of giving and receiving love.

"Sara, I love you so," he whispered as their bodies melded together and the beat of their hearts and the rhythm of their bodies soon drowned out all else.

Sara curled against his side, her arm around his waist as they drifted off to sleep. And for a while the Ute children were forgotten.

Eric was the first customer to arrive at the assay office the next morning. His spirits had been high as he strolled down the sidewalk, his head tilted back to study the busy little town. The air was filled with the smells of early morning—bacon frying and coffee brewing from the restaurant on the corner; dust mixed with tobacco smoke in front of the saloon where a few loyal customers still lingered; and finally the smell of printers ink and a type of mineral he couldn't identify as he passed the tiny newspaper office and turned into the assay office.

In addition to the three nuggets, he had several pinches of gold dust which would only go for twenty-five cents each, but his interest was in discovering the quality of the gold dust at Beaver Creek. But gaining knowledge on his gold appeared to be more difficult than he'd imagined as he faced a thin, sallow man with a sharp, pointed face and watery blue eyes surrounded by bags and shadows.

Eric soon dispensed with chit-chat, since the man hardly responded. He withdrew the buckskin bag from his pocket and placed the nuggets on the counter. Then he emptied the gold dust into his hand. The assayer maintained an air of cool indifference, as he carelessly picked up the nuggets and weighed them on his scales. The nuggets came to a total of fourteen ounces, which Eric was careful to watch and count for himself.

"I'll pay $8 an ounce," the assayer informed him in a toneless voice. "And the dust"—his bony shoulders lifted in a disinterested shrug—"just standard pay. You'd be better off to trade it for something at one of the stores."

Eric's temper blazed while his large hands curled into fists at his sides. "The hell you'll pay me $8 an ounce! That was the going rate *last* year for adulterated gold! My gold is *not* from Cherry Creek, or anywhere in this area. This is Pikes Peak gold." He ground each word through snarled lips as an angry fire leaped in his blue eyes.

The man took a step backward, awkwardly

cleared his throat, and lifted the nuggets again, studying them more carefully this time. He turned them over in his hand, weighed them again then sidled a glance at Eric.

"I see that you're right. The nuggets are more valuable than I thought." Again, the indifferent shrug. "I'm afraid I've become a bit jaded from dealing with so many miners who've tried to pass off tiny pieces filled with black sand and quartz. It pays to be careful. . . ."

Eric glared at him, not bothering to reply. He suspected the miners had been deceived far more than the assayer, and that suspicion was like gravel in his gut. He thought of his hard-working friends wading in icy streams to their waists, freezing their fingers off in the winter for one gold nugget, then sweltering beneath a blistering summer sun. It was no wonder so many dragged back to wherever they had come from, broke and disillusioned, their dreams forever lost.

His muscled hands clenched and unclenched, as a strong, almost overpowering urge to smash the ugly face in front of him took hold. He forced himself to turn from the man and stare dismally at the cracked wall, attempting to regain his composure.

"Fifteen dollars an ounce," the man finally rasped in a voice tight with greed.

Eric stared at him, suspecting his offer was like pulling off a layer of his skin, but Eric knew his gold was pure. He shoved his hands in his pockets and turned to stare out the narrow window, his eyes fixed on the morning traffic in the street.

If he were single, he'd take his gold and leave; he couldn't trust this man. His reason for bringing the nuggets all the way to Denver, rather than Colorado City, had been for an honest evaluation of the gold. But the man would not give him that, and he was left with the choice of taking his offer or heading back to Colorado City, where he might get a fairer price. His fingers closed over the loose coins in his pockets and he thought of Sara. He had wanted to buy her some pretty clothes, spoil her a bit. The look of little-girl joy on her face had reached deep into his heart, touching him almost to tears. She'd spent her life at that damn post, cheated out of the things she deserved by a man more greedy than the assayer who was now clearing his throat and repeating his offer.

Eric heaved a resigned sigh and turned back to the man. "All right, I'll take it."

The days that followed were a very special time for Sara as she and Eric sampled the wares Denver had to offer. First, Eric had taken her to the best store in town and bought her a blue silk Parisian gown and matching slippers. He tried to persuade her to get another, but she had adamantly refused, asking again for trousers and flannel shirt, to which he agreed. She'd also bought two pretty calico dresses, which were lightweight and suitable for summer weather, but then she'd drawn the line once more, insisting Eric buy clothes for himself. He'd argued that he had all he needed, and instead, they had compromised on a sluice box for his mining.

The highlight of the week was the play they saw at the Apollo Hall, performed by a troupe recently arrived in Denver. Eric had paid their admission in gold dust, weighed on the scale at the box office, and they had joined a large audience to see *Richard* III acted out on a stage illuminated by candles, which added to the romance and intrigue of the story.

Afterwards they had returned to the hotel where Sara had dabbed herself generously with the perfume Eric bought for her. She felt as though she were wallowing in luxury, having tubs of warm water sent up for nightly baths, dressing in fine clothes and wearing perfume. Every night they had eaten at a special place and yet, in spite of the wonderful time, she missed their special little cabin in the mountains and had even begun to look forward to their return.

"Having a good time?" he had asked as she dropped her crinoline and began to peel off her stockings.

"A wonderful time," she had sighed, as his hands gently brushed hers aside and he took up the task of removing her stockings. As he did so, he leaned down to brush his lips across her calves, her knees, her thighs. Sara's breath lodged in her throat as her heart began to race madly. Wherever Eric touched her, he lit a fire beneath her skin, and by the time he had removed her corset and camisole, she was practically writhing beneath his teasing hands and mouth.

Finally, when he lifted her nude body and

placed her on the bed, she was more than ready for his love. She lay on her side, curled like a sleek little kitten as he slowly dropped his clothes, his blue eyes searing over her.

The candle on the nightstand cast a wavering gold glow on her skin. Eric stood in the shadows, staring at her. Her breasts were fuller, her waist as tiny as ever.

He stretched out beside her, his eyes lingering on the creamy skin of her belly. He reached out and with one broad palm cupped her belly as his thumb traced circles around her navel.

"You know what would make me happier than anything in the world?" he asked huskily.

"Wh . . . what?" her question was a throaty rasp, for already the blood seared through her veins as her body throbbed and ached for his love.

"For my baby to be there . . . again." He removed his hand and lowered his mouth to the creamy flesh of her stomach as his lips roamed over her, defining the area that was sacred to him.

Finally, when Sara could no longer stand his gentle caresses, her arms shot out to his back and her nails traced the blade of each strong shoulder, then pulled his arms around her.

"Not so fast," he teased, as his body joined hers in a slow and patient rhythm. Then as she tightened against him, he changed his gentle caresses to deep, velvet thrusts of searing passion. He held back his own pleasure in the intense desire to give her all the joy possible. Her arms wound around his neck, pulling his

mouth to hers as her tongue thrust into his
mouth, matching the thrust of his body until
she cried out his name against his parted lips.
The look in Eric's eyes was one of pure
ecstasy as Sara's eyes filled with tears of joy
while her lips silently formed his name again,
with her pronouncement of love for him, over
and over. When finally her words drifted away
and she relaxed against the pillow, Eric closed
his eyes, drawn into the soft velvet world of
Sara, the smell and taste of her beneath him.

The familiar spiraling ache weaved through
his body, filling him, drawing his very soul into
the act of love until pleasure exploded
throughout his body, sending ripples of
ecstasy through every muscle, every pore.

"Oh, Sara. *Sara!*"

He plunged his mouth to hers, drawing the
sweet honey of her kiss over his tongue as his
tense body relaxed against her. Her hands
cradled his perspiring face as their passionate
kiss gentled to one of sweetness. Then,
wearily, they curled together, slipping into a
totally relaxed euphoria that quickly
deepened into a sound, dreamless sleep.

On the day before their departure, Sara and
Eric were taking a late afternoon stroll around
Denver, needing exercise after dining lavishly
at the Apollo Hotel.

As they reached the end of Larimer Street,
they spotted a crowd gathering around two
men dressed in buckskin and leather, with
long hair and beards and dusty felt hats
perched low on their heads.

"That's Kit Carson over there," Eric said, staring curiously at the man. "Let's saunter over to the edge of the crowd and see what's going on."

Sara tried to stretch her legs to keep up with Eric's long stride. As they drew closer, they saw the object of attention—the ragged Ute Children. At the sight of them, Sara's heart ached with pity.

"The Ute's and Arapahoes are at war," the man Eric had identified as Kit Carson said, drawing Sara's attention.

He was rather short, with bold features and keen eyes. "Last year, when me and Jim Beckwourth tried to persuade the tribes not to fight, we had no luck. Now, I'm askin' some of you to help these young-uns. They're at the mercy of the Arapahoes, and last night I saw a sight that made my blood run cold." He paused, adding to the dramatic hush that had fallen over the crowd. "Around their campfire out yonder on the edge of town, the Arapahoes forced a Ute squaw to dance around the scalp of her husband! And they've mistreated Ute children. These two deserve better. Can anyone give them a home until we find their tribe?

The hush had dissolved into a flurry of whispers, but no one stepped forward. Sara's eyes shot to Eric as she bit her lip. If only . . .

Then the matronly woman she had seen on the street they day they arrived in Denver slipped to the front of the crowd. "Me and Horace'll take care of them. Temporarily, that is."

Eric turned to get Sara's reaction and saw a look of anguish on her face. Slipping his arm around her waist, he gently pulled her away from the crowd. "Let's go," he said. "There's nothing we can do now."

Sara was frozen with horror at the words Carson had spoken. Her mind raced back to Bear Claw's camp. What if one of the squaws so mistreated was someone she had known there, someone who had shown her kindness?

She felt sick at heart as they walked back to the hotel. She recalled her resolve not to believe she was half Ute. But what if she was? If so, these were *her* people who were being treated like animals!

Tears glazed her eyes as she looked at the store they were passing. She tried thinking of something else—of her new clothes, of the elegant meal they'd eaten—but a feeling of despair haunted her.

She couldn't forget the Indian children, or what Kit Carson had said about the poor squaw. Compassion tugged at her heart, and she found herself wishing she could help. In the past, she'd been as prejudiced as Ernest Jackson about Indians. She realized now how unreasonable she'd been.

"God, forgive me," she silently prayed. She'd never really understood their plight, how cruelly they had been mistreated, not just by the white man, but by other tribes as well.

"What is it?" Eric asked quietly. "What are you thinking?"

She inhaled a deep breath of the stale dry air. It was extremely hot in Denver and she longed for the fresh cool breezes of their mountain home.

"I don't know," she looked up at him. He was her husband; why couldn't she be honest? Her eyes wandered back to the crowded sidewalk as she lapsed into silence.

Instinctively, Eric respected her silence as they returned to the hotel. The lobby was crowded with people exchanging the latest news and rumors.

"Let's not go up to the room yet," he said, his eyes darting over the crowd. "I want to hear what they're saying."

Sara wanted to object, but she had no right to interfere with his interest in the news from the South. It frightened her to think of war there and how Eric's family was being affected. The chances of her ever meeting his family were unlikely, but she knew he loved them despite their differences in the past. *Would he want to go home?*

She thrust that thought from her mind, unable to imagine its consequences. Mutely, she followed him, straining her ears to hear what was being said.

As they approached, it was apparent that a heated argument was developing.

"This should be interesting," Eric muttered under his breath. "A Southerner and a Yankee expressing their views on the issues between North and South."

"I tell you, sir, that I was in New Mexico Territory several weeks ago and there is a lot of sentiment for the South. They're even talking of organizing a group to align with the

Confederate States. Not everyone, as you prophesy, will jump in with the Federal Government."

"I didn't say everyone!" the other man fired back. "I said even though Colorado Territory is split, most everyone will go with the regiment of volunteers that Governor Gilpin is organizing!"

The argument accelerated, but Eric had heard enough. He shook his head as he grasped Sara's elbow and hurried across the lobby and up the stairs.

Sara frowned, troubled by his irritation, and he was venting that irritation on her arm.

"Eric!" she finally tugged her arm free and glared at him. "You're hurting me."

He turned blank eyes to her, as though he were incapable of understanding what she had said. Then, slowly, his eyes dropped to his hand, hanging limply in the air after she had removed her elbow from his steely grip.

"I . . . I'm sorry," he muttered huskily as they trudged down the hall to their room.

A gloomy silence hung between them as he opened the door for her. The cozy bedroom where they had shared such passion now seemed dark and sad. Sara lighted the candle as Eric stretched out on the bed, locking his fingers behind his head as he stared at the ceiling.

She studied his thoughtful face and tried to think what to say. She wished they'd never left this room!

"Eric," she began tentatively, "are you worried about your family in Georgia?"

He turned to look at her, and she could see the pain in his eyes. "They're reporting casualties, and I can't help worrying about John and Bill. I know they'll join the Rebels; I just hope they haven't left Mother alone at Pine Hill."

Sara felt a rush of apprehension. "They wouldn't go off and leave her alone, would they? Surely there's someone . . ."

"There are the wives and children still there, but I was thinking of a man to protect them. I'm going to send a wire before we leave. I have to hear something from them. Funny thing," he rubbed his furrowed brow. "I've never missed home until now."

Home . . .

The word pierced her heart, and she suddenly felt as though she were no longer a part of his life. She sank onto the bed, her eyes dropping to her hands. *But we have a home,* she wanted to cry out, *and someday we'll have a family!* Someday . . . a useless word right now. She was too hurt to speak her thoughts, too numb to cry. All the old fears came rushing back, and she wondered if he truly loved her, loved her deeply enough to forget his past. Yes, even his family. For how could they build a future together when he was still tied to memories and people she was no part of?

Darkness fell outside the window. Now only the feeble glow of the candle lit the room. Neither had spoken for several minutes.

"Maybe I should make a trip back to see. . . ." Eric began tentatively.

"No!" The word burst from her lips before

she could stop it. She bit her tongue, trying to find a way to make him understand the cold terror that iced her heart at the thought of his leaving. But when she shifted on the bed and faced him, she saw a look of stunned disbelief.

"Eric, I don't mean to be selfish, but you're all I have. I can't let you go. Please don't ask me to!"

He reached across and covered her trembling hand with his. "I won't ever leave you, Sara. Not for long, anyway. Maybe you could go with me." His brows rose hopefully, then fell just as quickly. "No, that wouldn't be wise. I can't haul you across country to face a senseless war." A wrenching sigh shook his long frame. "I won't go. Maybe the war will end soon; at least we can hope for that. But . . ."

"But what?" Sara probed, needing to understand what he was thinking.

"It's just that when I hear folks talking about fighting the Rebels, something within me rises up in defense. I guess I'm still a Southerner at heart."

Sara stared at him, unable to respond. For the first time, she felt an invisible barrier dropping between them, one she couldn't penetrate. She'd never thought much about their different backgrounds, even though it had bothered her in the beginning that Eric might be prejudiced against Indians. But his tolerance had warmed her heart, had given her the courage to believe they could make a happy life together. And they had until now.

"I suppose we both have to come to terms with who we are, don't we, Sara?"

His quiet, honest question left no room for anything but truth, and she turned troubled eyes to him and slowly nodded her head.

"But I can't help wondering how this will affect our marriage," she whispered.

He leaned up on his elbow and lifted his hand to touch her cheek. "You're the most important person in the world to me. Far more important than the family I left behind, or any damn war going on. Nothing will affect our marriage or our love for each other!"

"Oh Eric," she pressed her cheek against his hand, "I want so much to believe that! I *have* to believe it. I can't imagine life without you! You've been so good to me . . ."

Again the tears filled her eyes, but he pulled her into his arms and gently wiped them away as he kissed her forehead.

"Don't cry. You have to believe that our love will abide longer than the problems." He lifted her chin and looked deeply into her eyes. Tears still shimmered on her inky lashes. "And you must trust my love enough to discover for yourself who you *really* are and *be* that person. Don't try to be what you think I expect you to be; no one has a right to make a person change from their true nature—especially when their nature is as sweet as yours."

Sara's eyes dropped to the pillow. "Are you saying that . . . if I am Ute, I must accept that and . . ."

". . . And be proud of your heritage.

Ignorance and prejudice have made you believe otherwise, but that was wrong, Sara. Very wrong. I saw the look on your face today." He tilted her head back further so that his lips could kiss away each trailing tear. "Whether you want to acknowledge it or not, you care about the Indians. You care very much, don't you?"

She laid her head against his shoulder and thought for a moment. "Yes, I do care, Eric. I think . . . I almost . . . love them. And I'm not sure why, unless I am one of them. Perhaps the blood in my veins and the instincts of my ancestors, rooted deep in my being, are finally speaking to me." She took a deep, long breath and when she spoke it was little more than a whisper. "Maybe I *am* Ute."

16

The return trip was uneventful and Sara and Eric were exhausted by the time they turned their horses onto the trail leading to the cabin.

Their joy at returning home was short lived, however, for when they stepped inside the cabin they were greeted by two masked men—and a rifle pointed straight at their hearts.

"Come in, Mr. and Mrs. Christensen. We've been waitin'," the taller man ordered. He was dressed in dusty trousers and a patched flannel shirt. His hair was straggly brown and his eyes above the mask were narrow-set and gray. The man standing slightly behind him was short and stocky, but it was his eyes that Sara noted with mounting fear. They were green and bloodshot . . . and mean. She reached for Eric.

Eric appeared cool, unthreatened, as he squeezed Sara's hand reassuringly and faced the marauders with unwavering eyes. "What do you want?" he asked bluntly.

"Heard you got lucky again. Luckier than before. Maybe this time you wouldn't mind helpin' out a coupla guys who're down on their luck."

"Help you *how*?" Eric challenged, his jaws drawn tightly against clenched teeth. He thought he remembered them now; the two tramps who hung around the saloon in Colorado City. They'd probably heard about his strike the first time he'd gone to town and then ransacked his cabin looking for gold. This time, they'd waited in Colorado City for the stage to return from Denver, then lit out ahead of Eric and Sara. If that were true, they might believe he had sold *all* the nuggets.

"Just close the door and come on inside," the tall man snapped, motioning Eric and Sara toward the kitchen table.

Reluctantly, Eric kicked the door closed. If not for Sara, he'd take a chance. Throw them off somehow, then make a dive for the rifle. But he couldn't risk her safety. Gripping her hand tightly, he led her to the table. She sank into the chair, her face deathly pale, while Eric stood behind her, one hand resting lightly on her shoulder.

"If you're looking for nuggets, they're all gone. I traded them in Colorado City and Denver. And I didn't come out with much cash after paying expenses and buying supplies we needed."

"Damn it, Christensen, I ain't no fool!" the leader threatened angrily.

Sara's indrawn breath made a hiss in the tense silence that followed. The tall man glanced at her sharply.

"Sit down, Christensen," he said, waving his rifle.

Eric frowned, unsure what was going to

happen, but he hesitated only a second before taking a chair opposite Sara.

"Now listen to me, Christensen, you got money and you still got two nuggets. I won't be greedy. I'll just take the nuggets, and maybe a little travelin' money, and I'll leave you with your wife and your nice little place here." His dark eyes raked Sara, lingering insolently on each part of her body. "You got more than most men," he remarked.

Eric leapt angrily from the chair, but the rifle swung around, its long stock catching him full in the face. Blood spurted from his nose as he staggered backward.

Sara screamed, only to be silenced as the tip of the rifle pressed against her heaving breasts.

"Sit still and behave yourself, missy. I ain't gonna hurt him unless he makes another stupid move."

One of the men tossed Eric a dish towel to mop his bloody nose and Eric glared into each man's face, studying them carefully. He would know them without their masks if he ever saw them again. He sat rigid, continuing to study the shape of their foreheads, the color and set of their eyes.

"Maybe the missus here knows where the nuggets are," the leader taunted, trailing the tip of the rifle over Sara's breasts, outlining each rounded curve. She remained stock still, her dark eyes boring into the man's leering face.

"Come on and tell us," he said, jabbing the rifle tip into her breasts. She tried but could not suppress a grimace of pain.

"She doesn't know anything!" Eric shouted. "I have the money. It's inside my coat pocket. Take it and go!"

The short man cackled loudly, plunging a dirty hand into Eric's pocket. He waved a handful of bills. "Lookee, T.C. . . ."

"Shut up!" The other one snapped. "Give it here." He reached across and snatched the bills from the hands of his careless accomplice.

"Keep your mouth shut," he growled. "Now listen here, Christensen, I'm gettin' tired of foolin' around. We've got the money, so after you give up them nuggets, we'll be on our way. We ain't wantin' to hurt nobody unless you get dumb and don't co-operate."

Eric stared at him, determined somehow to outsmart them. He decided to take another risk. "I took two of the nuggets to Colorado City and the rest to Denver," he said. "They were small. Why are you so interested?"

"I got my reasons! I need them nuggets more'n I need your money. But I'll take money, too," he said with a hoarse, ugly laugh.

Eric sat, watching him through hate-filled eyes. The man read that hate but merely shrugged and turned back to Sara. "Come here, missy." He grabbed her wrist and yanked her to her feet, twisting one arm behind her.

Eric's heart hammered. Two damn nuggets, no bigger than gravel, weren't worth having the man's filthy hands on Sara!

"Turn her loose," he said quietly. "I'll get the nuggets."

The man's eyes crawled down Sara's body as though he thought he might have his fun with her first.

"I said, turn her loose," Eric ground through clenched teeth, "or I just might change my mind."

The man shoved Sara back into the chair and turned to glare at Eric. "So where are they?"

"They're hidden down near the creek. I'll have to show you."

"Liar! He wouldn't do anything that dumb," the short man accused him in an annoyed whine.

"It was my way of marking a lucky spot," Eric answered cooly. "And burying them was the best way to hide them."

The two exchanged glances. "That's why we didn't find nothin' before, T. . . ."

"*Shut up!*"

Sara looked across at Eric, her eyes round with fear. She tried to swallow, but her throat was as dry as trail dust. What was Eric going to do? The nuggets weren't hidden there, of course; he was trying to get loose and lead them away from the cabin. Because of her!

"Eric, no!" she burst out. All eyes shot to her. "Don't go down there with them," she added, trying now to control her voice. "Please . . ."

"Oh, we ain't gonna hurt him," the tall man taunted. "All we want is them nuggets!"

"Why are they so important to you?" Eric

asked. "You've taken more money from me already than the nuggets will bring."

"I got my own scheme," the man replied. "And I need nuggets to convince." He broke off, snarling. "It ain't none of your damn business what I want with 'em. Now git out of that chair and let's go walkin'. You stay here with her," he added as an afterthought.

His partner heaved an objecting sigh, obviously disappointed that he wouldn't get to see the lucky spot Eric had described.

Eric hesitated, studying the short, slow-witted man. "I don't want him here with her. She's not going anywhere. You won't, will you, Sara?"

Her eyes were frozen on Eric's face, her mind tormented by the knowledge that Eric was taking a foolish chance. She wanted him to give up the nuggets without a fight, but she didn't know how to tell him. If only she could speak with him in private, convince him that his anger was making him unreasonable.

She shook her head, finally. "No, I . . . won't go anywhere. Eric," she pleaded, clenching her hands tightly, "don't do this." He would understand her meaning, while the others would merely assume she was being selfish.

His blue eyes darkened as he looked at her in quiet warning. "It's best, Sara. It's the *only* way."

"But . . ." her voice trailed off as the man thrust the barrel of the rifle in Eric's back. "Let's go, Christensen."

Still Eric hesitated, his eyes swinging toward the other man. "If you touch her, I'll kill you."

he said, and it was the deadly calm of his tone, as much as the words he spoke, that made the repulsive little man squirm. But as soon as the door was closed, the puffy green eyes shot back to Sara.

Sara fidgeted in the chair, growing more uncomfortable beneath his crude stare.

"You and me oughta git to know each other while they're gone," he said. He sauntered over to stand beside her, and the smell of unwashed flesh filled her nostrils. She felt nauseated; if he touched her, she'd scream before she could stop herself.

But she had no sooner thought that than she felt the fat grimy hand on her neck.

"Ye got soft white flesh," he rasped as his breathing grew loud in the tense silence.

Sara stiffened, trying to handle this situation the best way. She tilted her head back and looked up at him, and for a moment she froze as she stared at the repulsive face. The mask had slipped but he seemed not to care in his greed to touch her. His face was half bearded with a nasty stubble, his thick jaws sagged, his lips curled thickly.

She swallowed. He was the most repulsive looking man she'd ever seen. And now his hand was plundering her breast, and she cried out.

"Have you forgotten what my husband said?" She shrank back from him, wishing she were strong enough to fight him off, but wisely sensing she was not, not when he already had her cornered. If only she could get out of the chair, she'd at least have a better advantage.

"I ain't worried 'bout what he said," he sneered.

A sudden idea hit her. "Do you like whiskey? If you'll let me up, I'll get you a drink of whiskey."

His brows shot up as his short fingers ceased to jab at her breasts. "Whiskey? Well, you're a mite smarter'n I thought. Yeah, I'll have me a snort."

"Then let me up," she said, dropping her eyes.

He stepped back from her and she darted out of the chair. As she reached the kitchen cabinet, her eyes shot back over her shoulder. If she could catch him off guard for just a moment. . . .

"What're you waitin' for?" He grinned, his eyes raking her trembling body.

"Nothing," she murmured, turning to the cabinet.

She began to open and close the doors, taking her time about finding the bottle. "He's got it here somewhere, just give me a minute," she said.

But his heavy steps were already jarring the plank floor as he lumbered to her side. "Ye wouldn't try to trick me, would you? 'Cause I'll tell ye a little secret. Yore man ain't comin' back. T.C.'ll kill him soon as he gets the gold. That's how T.C. is."

Eric walked slowly, his movements denying the speed of his thoughts as he formed a plan. He led the man east, so that the slanting rays of the sun would be in their faces, and he chose the steepest, rockiest path to the stream. He knew every square inch of the mile that ran along the stream bank, and that knowledge gave him the advantage.

They picked their way down the hill, the man cursing when he nearly stumbled, but Eric deliberately let this chance go by, hoping to put him off guard. At the end of the path, a pine sapling had been uprooted during a storm, and he was counting on the obstruction to provide the right opportunity.

It happened as he had planned. Eric pointed toward the creek, saying he was at this spot when he found the nuggets. Intrigued, the thief's greedy eyes swept the creek, failing to note the uprooted sapling. His foot caught on a branch, throwing him off balance. Eric swung around and threw his boot out to trip the man and he toppled headlong down the bank. The rifle flew out of his hand, and Eric pounced on it, slamming its stock across the back of the man's head. He rolled forward, then lay still as death.

Eric did not tarry to see if his blow had been fatal, but turned and raced back up the hill, the rifle tucked securely in the crook of his arm.

When he burst through the door of the cabin, the sight that met him jerked his heart to his throat. The thief had Sara down on the floor, and he was kneeling over her, one hand fondling her breasts while the other pinned her arms over her head.

Her dress was ripped from the collar to the waist and she was kicking at him helplessly while tears of rage poured down her cheeks.

"I'll kill you," Eric said, raising the rifle to the shocked man's face.

"I ain't done her no harm," he whined, lumbering to his feet.

Eric's eyes crawled down his thick body, noting that he was still fully dressed. Then he looked at Sara who was struggling up from the floor, rubbing her wrists.

"Eric, don't shoot him," she sobbed. "He isn't worth it."

Eric fought an almost overwhelming desire to pull the trigger. For a moment he was certain he would do it.

"Trash like him doesn't deserve to live, Sara," he said, his eyes narrowed and boring hatred through the man.

The man was panting loudly, already excited by the feel of her soft breasts in his palm. He was almost beyond logic and reason, certainly beyond caution.

"He won't kill me," he whined. "I ain't armed."

"Then I'll make it fair," Eric snarled. "I'll lay down the rifle and beat the hell out of you! Get outside!"

"Eric!" Sara screamed.

For once, Eric ignored her, knowing he would have no peace until his knuckles slammed into the protruding belly, smashing the sneering face.

The man's face held a look of fear as he stomped around the table to the door, then impulsively dived for the rifle. He was no match for Eric's strength, but in the shuffle that followed, the rifle exploded and the thief staggered back and slumped to the floor as a wide stain circled his chest.

Sara's hands flew to her mouth as Eric knelt beside the man, seeking a pulse. After a long moment, he looked up at Sara and shook his head. "I didn't mean to kill him."

"But you did! And now the other one will kill *us*"

"No, he won't. I left him unconscious. But I want you to ride to Rex's cabin for help. Tell him to get over here as fast as he can, and you stay with Arabella."

Sara changed her clothes hastily, then stumbled from the cabin, numb with shock. It had been the worst hour of her life! She hobbled to the shed for her mare as Eric looked around for the men's horses. They were gone. Then he decided they must be hidden somewhere in the woods.

He watched Sara mount her mare and turn its head west. "Sara, be careful," he called after her.

She nodded and wildly jabbed her heels into the mare's side. For a moment his eyes followed as the mare tore across the meadow. Was he crazy, sending her the distance alone? One man lay dead in the cabin, while the other could be anywhere by now.

He glanced back toward the woods, then the cabin. He couldn't leave; he had to let her go alone.

He gribbed the rifle and raced back through the meadow to the stream, his eyes scanning every shadow in the distant woods. When he reached the bank of the stream, the man was gone. He scouted for tracks, but he found nothing. He had been right in assuming they had tied their horses up the road and walked in. Finding the man could take hours. He only hoped he hadn't gone in the direction Sara had taken. Now he cursed his stupidity in sending her off alone. But the thief was more likely to head down the Ute trail to Colorado City than to linger in the mountains. He obviously cared nothing for his partner, taking off without him.

By the time he dragged the dead man into the woods and buried him, Rex had arrived with Arabella and Sara, who had not heeded his advice to stay with Arabella at the cabin. Arabella insisted on brewing tea to calm everyone's nerves. The men gulped theirs down and went to search the woods again. Sara drank her tea through chattering teeth as she cleaned the bloodstains from the plank floor. All the while she scrubbed, the memory of the man's dirty hands on her breasts tormented her. If Eric hadn't returned, she'd have been no match against the man's brute strength. She shivered, just thinking of the repulsive man and the look of animal lust in his eyes when he mauled her.

"Have more tea," Arabella coaxed gently, noticing Sara's pale face.

Sara raised bleak eyes to her. "Arabella, have you ever been robbed?"

Arabella nodded thoughtfully. "Once. Many winters ago some trappers were camping in the woods near the meadow where we built our cabin. Nothing since. We are hidden in the woods like the deer and elk," she said with a laugh, "and I think that thieves cannot find us."

Sara bit her lip, seeing in her mind the nearness of their cabin to the road. They were easily accessible to outlaws and murderers. She shivered again.

"Maybe Rex and Eric will find the other man and the trouble will end," Arabella suggested, pouring more tea.

"I hope so," Sara sighed. "If they don't find him, it won't be easy to lie down and sleep peacefully." She thought of the nightmares that haunted her, imagining that now she would see the repulsive man's face looming over her, the man Eric had killed.

The men returned after dark with no news of the disappearing thief. Everyone ate in weary silence. After Rex and Arabella left, Eric stood in the open door of the cabin, staring across the moonlit meadow. His eyes traced every outline beneath the dense pines, but there was no movement. Only the gentle sigh of the summer wind occasionally stirred the trees.

Sara walked to the door and put her arm around his waist. "We have each other. That's all that matters."

He shook his head. "Sara, we'll have a hard time making it through the winter now. Of course I'll take the other two nuggets in and trade them for staples later on, but without the money . . ."

"But you have a knack for finding gold. And we have the new sluice box."

He hugged her against his side. "You're

right. We'll find more gold soon."

For the next few weeks, Sara carefully concealed her own doubts in order to cheer Eric. A trip to the Colorado City Sheriff's office had been fruitless. Two men fitting the descriptions of the thieves had been seen loitering around town, but no one had seen the tall, straggly man lately. It was plain he had taken the money and left the area.

The assumption that he was no longer around gave Sara a sense of peace at last. Eric's mood did not improve, however. She sensed there were many things on his mind, though he did not speak of them. Each time they went to town, he bought a newspaper and pored over the latest war news. Sara knew he still longed to return to Georgia, though he said nothing to her. And that silence was becoming a barrier she was unable to break. She was still a bride, still learning many things about her husband. The long, entertaining conversations they had shared on so many evenings were replaced by brooding silences. And to her disappointment, she had not become pregnant again.

Autumn came early that year, drifting lazily into the high country to trail gold and crimson across the woods and meadows. The aspens turned a luminous gold and deepened in breathtaking splendor.

"We're taking the afternoon off," Eric announced after a futile morning with the cradle and sluice box. "I'm in the mood for a picnic."

Sara quickly agreed and they changed into dry clothes after wading the cold streams for hours. Sara wore trousers and flannel shirts every day but Eric never seemed to mind. She packed beef jerky and coffee, and added several slices of pound cake to their knapsack. They chose a sunny spot near their cabin with a panoramic view of the valley and mountains. Sara stretched out on a blanket and gazed at the shimmering gold aspens in reverent awe.

"Eric, such beauty!" she sighed. "I wouldn't have missed living up here for anything in the world."

"I hope you really mean that," he said, looking at her gravely.

"Of course I mean it! Why wouldn't I?"

He took a deep breath and looked out across the valley. "You've worked as hard as I have. I wanted you to have an easier life than the one you left behind."

Sara's mouth dropped open as she thought about what he had said. Then she lifted her hand to touch his bearded jaw. "Eric, my work here has been a labor of love, don't you understand that? We're building a future together and nothing is more important than that. I *love* our little cabin; most of all, I love being with you."

To emphasize her words, her hands slipped to the neck of his shirt and began to knead his broad shoulders while her mouth declared her love to his parted lips.

His arms cradled her as the leaves rustled gently overhead, and the smell of autumn wildflowers and sun-kissed pine drifted over them.

Eric lay back on the blanket and kissed her with renewed intensity. Away from work and worry and sheltered by the friendly woods, his passion was stirred to new heights.

Sara felt this too, and any thought that they might be seen making love on a mountaintop was cast aside. Slowly, they undressed each other, pausing to nibble at bare skin until they could wait no longer.

This time Sara was the aggressor, even though Eric wanted her as badly as she wanted him. But her keen desire to drive all worry from his mind made her bolder than ever, and she stretched out on top of him and began to kiss him with an even deeper passion.

His arms wrapped around her slim, nude body, pressing her breasts against the roughness of his chest, molding her torso to his, as she tucked her bare feet underneath his legs.

When his manhood pressed against her, she took him in, and both gasped in pleasure as the autumn breeze sifted over their heated bodies, and they experienced the new thrill of making love in a world of molten gold.

All worries were forgotten, and they knew only joy and keen ecstasy as they passed the afternoon in each other's arms.

Too quickly, the leaves were whisked from the trees by strong winds and an early snow. As Sara stood in the door of her cabin, watching the aspen leaves drift down from the bare trees, she thought of the afternoon they had made love in a world of shimmering gold.

She was grateful for the memory. Like the animals of the forest who stored up for winter, she gathered pretty memories to offset the bleakness of long gray days when she'd be forced to stay inside. That glorious Sunday afternoon became one of her treasures as the winter wind howled down the canyons and ripped across the brown meadow grass.

Eric worried about the low supply of staples and rose each morning in the first light of dawn, dressed warmly, and hunted for deer as they came out to feed. He made snares and placed them in the woods to catch rabbits. He'd chopped a hole in the icy stream to set fishing lines, which he anchored to a low-hanging pine branch.

They still had an abundance of flour, and Sara experimented with different kinds of breads and cakes. After adjusting her recipes to a higher altitude, she had become an excellent cook.

For Sara's birthday, in November, Eric made a special sled for her. It was constructed of aspen logs tied together with strips of rawhide. He had trimmed thin slats of wood and fastened them beneath the logs to serve as runners. Sara was delighted. They spent their afternoons sledding down the mountainside, and on winter nights, if there was no wind, they went for moonlight rides. Sara had never in her life had so much fun.

The thief had not been seen in Colorado City, or anywhere else, and Eric and Sara soon forgot him. Nevertheless, Eric had been made aware that news of the nuggets could present a threat to their safety. He gave Sara his pistol to protect herself, then proceeded to teach her how to hold and use it. He had blazed a twelve-inch circle on a stump in the yard, and when she could consistently hit the circle from twelve paces, he breathed a sigh of relief. Sara was proud of her skill with the pistol and took target practice regularly.

Eric rarely left her alone, however, except for quick hunting trips or forays to check snares and fishing line. Until she mastered the gun, he was tense and anxious, always relieved when she returned and found her safe.

As another diversion, on an exceptionally clear December day, he took Sara with him to set traps for the animals whose fur could be sold or traded in Colorado City. Sara had her own special trap but while Eric regularly caught beaver, coyote and weasels, Sara's trap remained empty. Then, to her surprise and delight, one morning her trap held a fat mink. When Eric asked what she planned to trade the pelt for, she merely shook her head and gave him a mysterious little smile. But her secret slipped out the next afternoon when she made a casual inquiry about a trip to town for Christmas shopping.

On the week before Christmas, a northerly wind swept down upon them, bringing with it three feet of fresh snow. The wind held, while the temperature continued to drop. No one was safe outside. The snowshoe rabbits burrowed deeper into their holes; elk and deer ambled down from the mountains in search of food. From their front door Sara and Eric often watched the big animals that stood like silent sentinels beneath the pines, while snow salted their thick brown coats.

The blizzard raged for two days, and when finally it had spent itself, the deep snow half buried their cabin in its pristine blanket.

"Sara, we can't make it into town for Christmas," Eric said to her as they sat before the fire drinking coffee. "I'm sorry."

Her eyes revealed her disappointment, though she forced a smile. "It's okay."

But Eric knew it wasn't. He knew how special it would be to her to see the colorful handmade decorations the shopkeepers strung up and to smell the blocks of peppermint candy and the fresh fruit, if the merchants were lucky enough to get a shipment on the stagecoach.

He sighed and shook his head. "This is one of the disadvantages of living up here. We never know what the weather will do. It just isn't safe to start out, honey."

"Eric, I said it's *okay*," she answered crossly, but her mood quickly changed as an idea struck her. "I'm going to make our own decorations. I did that to entertain children at the post who were bored to death and homesick for some place back East."

"Then I'll get us a tree. It may be small, but we'll have a tree!"

Eric kept his word the next afternoon when, bundled from head to toe and fighting the stinging cold, he took his ax and waded through knee-deep snow to the woods. It had taken an hour of searching, chopping and dragging, but he had returned with a stout little fir, beautifully shaped and a perfect fit for the east corner of the living room.

"Eric, it's beautiful!" Sara exclaimed and began making decorations with the pine cones she had gathered in the fall. She made dough, flattened and shaped it into stars and circles, even an angel, then baked her creations. On their last trip to town, she'd purchased a yellow vegetable dye for pillow fabric, but she found a better use for it in dying her tree ornaments. And then, remembering how the gold dust had stuck to the lining of their pockets, she went through all their trousers and shirts and came up with enough gold dust to stick to the end of her thumb. She made a paste of flour and water, glued the sparkling dust to the angel and placed it on the top branch.

Eric stood before the tree, his hands on his hips, staring in amazement at her handiwork.

"It's the prettiest tree I've ever seen," he announced with a wide smile.

"Well, not the fanciest," Sara said, laughing, "but it's pretty enough."

On Christmas Eve, she baked a pound cake and laid a tiny wreath of holly and red berries across the top of it. Even though there were no guests, for not even Rex and Arabella dared brave the elements, Sara and Eric were not lonely this Christmas. They found joy and contentment in being snowbound in their little cabin with only the two of them to stretch out before the fire and talk, or make love, or simply admire the tree.

"Merry Christmas," Eric said at midnight on Christmas Eve. "I'm sorry I have no present for you."

"Oh but you do," she smiled into his blue eyes. "Your love is the best present I've ever had. I would feel guilty asking for anything more. Eric, I've never been so happy."

"Nor have I," he said with a catch in his voice as his eyes wandered back to the tree and they stood with their arms wrapped around each other while the snowflakes continued to fall, enveloping them in a magical winter wonderland.

17

Wild Eagle sat beside his beloved Star, feeling deep anguish each time her small body heaved and contracted in its painful struggle to give birth. Eagle had followed the Ute custom of leaving the birthing lodge when Star's labor began, running through the hills until he was exhausted. The Utes believed that when a father did this, the baby would be strong and a good runner as well. Unlike the other warriors who stayed in the main lodge until the mother came to present him with the baby, Eagle, hearing Star's muffled cries of pain, had raced over the snow-covered ground to the birthing lodge.

Nish-ki sat faithfully by her side, speaking softly to Star as she placed cool cloths on her sweat-drenched forehead. When Eagle burst into the lodge, she read the agony in his face and silently handed him the water basket, then slipped to a corner to wait until she was needed again.

Star's labor had gone on for twelve hours, and Eagle could see that she was weakening. She lay on her bed of animal skins, her heaving body covered with his Navajo blanket.

Dark circles underlined her eyes and her lips had begun to bleed as she bit back her cries of pain.

Eagle took her perspiring hand and tried to smile bravely. "Do not be afraid to cry out, Star. Perhaps the little one will hear you and hurry up!"

Her lips quivered in an attempt to smile, but then another pain gripped her, and her stomach contracted into a huge round ball. He watched her struggle with the grinding pain as her eyes rolled back and her teeth wrenched her bleeding lips. Her nails dug half circles in her palm, and Eagle clutched her fingers. He felt a strength there that surprised him when he considered the length of her labor.

Then the pain subsided, rolling off her parted lips in a scarcely audible moan. Eagle frowned, glancing across at Nish-ki, whose gray head rested on her chest while she dozed in exhaustion, having nursed Star through the long, pain-filled night.

Impulsively, Eagle flipped the blanket back and parted Star's legs to see for himself if the birth would be soon. To his shock, he saw that the birth passage was wide open, yet the baby was not coming through. Then he saw something that made him squint, then stare in horror as he recognized the edge of a tiny shoulder.

He gasped and stared. He knew little about birthing, but he did know the baby was in the wrong position. He jumped up and shook Nish-ki's shoulder, motioning her to come.

PASSION'S PEAK

The sight brought a ghastly look to her face and a stream of incoherent babbling.

Eagle yanked the blanket from Star's body and pushed her legs up so that her knees were bent. Blood began to ooze from her body as another hard pain ripped through her mercilessly.

"We need Shamus. . . ." Nish-ki was moaning and wringing her hands before her. "And he goes . . . until the next moon. He no think Star . . ." Her voice trailed away as she clamped her aged eyes together and pleaded with the Great Spirit.

"Listen to me!" Eagle gripped the old woman's shoulders. "We can't wait for the Medicine Man! We've got to help her. There's no one else. I thought you knew what to do."

She jerked her gray head in a succession of sterm affirmative nods. "When it is right, I know."

Eagle stared into her wrinkled, leathery face, trying to make sense of her babbling. "But you don't know what to do if the baby is turned the wrong way?"

She shook her head, tears welling in her eyes.

The jagged cry Star fought to smother erupted from her bleeding mouth, and Shane knew he could stand no more. He had to do something, even if he had to do it alone.

"Once I see . . ." Nish-ki began, frowning down at Star.

"*What* did you see?" Eagle demanded anxiously. "*Tell me!*"

Nish-ki studied the birth passage, her brow

wrinkled in thought. "The birthing squaw..." She lifted her hands to gesture, and Eagle realized immediately what she meant.

"Turned the baby around?" he interpreted.

She bobbed her head again, her eyes flying back in horror to the little shoulder, clearly visible now.

Eagle dropped to his knees beside Star and gently brushed the damp strands of hair from her gaunt face.

"Star, the baby is not in the right position. I must turn him so he can be born. I will try to be gentle, but you must be brave. Do you understand?"

Eyes glazed with pain searched his face as she slowly absorbed his words. "Do what you must," she answered weakly.

He stood again and lowered his voice to Nish-ki. "Stand beside her, hold her shoulders if you must, but keep her still. I'm going to turn the baby."

The old woman's eyes widened but she did as she was told. As Eagle leaned over Star, a film of sweat broke over his face when he considered the complications if he did the wrong thing. But as he had told Nish-ki, there was no one else.

He took a deep breath and forced his hand into the birth passage, trying as gently as possible to turn the baby. This time Star could no longer hold back a scream, nor did she try. Her pain was a spear in his heart, but if he didn't do something she might die. She and the baby. He gritted his teeth and tried again, and the baby moved slightly. Encouraged by that, he tried to shut out Star's screams as ever so gently he gripped the tiny shoulder and turned again.

This time he could feel the soft fuzz of the baby's hair. Star's passage opened wider and now he was touching the little head, and he paused, waiting, while to the blessing of baby and mother, Star's body heaved in a mighty contraction and the small head came through.

Tears filled Eagle's eyes as he cradled the baby's head while more contractions followed, slowly thrusting the baby from Star's bleeding body.

Suddenly Eagle was holding the baby boy in his arms. He motioned to Nish-ki, who rushed to his side, grabbing the infant and turning it upside down to swat its backside. A healthy wail followed. Nish-ki gestured that she could complete the task and pointed to Star. Eagle wiped his hands on a clean cloth and hesitated only a moment to be sure Nish-ki had the sharpened knife and the clean bandages she needed to finish the birth. She was cleaning the baby now, and Eagle knelt by Star's side.

"We have a son, Star!" His voice shook with pride as tears filled his eyes again.

Her dark lashes parted and haggard eyes sought his face. "A . . . son?" she repeated in a thin whisper.

"And he sounds healthy." Eagle chuckled as the gusty little wails continued. Nish-ki had cleaned the baby, wrapped him in a blanket and now laid him across his mother's breast.

For a moment Star could only gaze in

reverent awe. Then her weak arms reached out to cradle him, while Eagle stuck his thumb into the little palm that curled possessively.

"I'd like to name him after your father," Eagle said, staring into the wrinkled little face. While the baby's skin was a shade lighter than Star's, he had black hair and eyes and somehow reminded Eagle of the noble Shavano.

Star's eyes widened at this announcement, for they had not spoken of names. It was one of her superstitions and Eagle had affectionately humored her in this.

At the mention of her father, sadness, crept like a shadow over Star's face, then quickly passed, replaced by a proud smile. "He would be honored. His name will be Shane Shavano."

Eagle grimaced, recalling his old name, and shook his head disapprovingly. "I don't think . . ."

"Y*es*!" Her features tightened in determination.

He shrugged. "Shane rather than Eagle?" he asked curiously.

She nodded slowly. "Just as I am proud of my Yuuttaa heritage, you must claim the white man's blood as well. Now it runs through the veins of our little one. He must know that he is both and we will raise him to have honor, not shame, in his heritage.

Eagle looked down at Star with love and pride. "I thought it would not be possible to love you more than I did. But now my heart nearly bursts with love for you." He lifted his hand to gently brush her hair from her face, then his fingers trailed down her jaw and cupped her chin. "You are the one with honor, my sweet Star," he said, lowering his lips to hers as gently as possible, for they were torn from her suffering.

His lips moved over her cheek and touched each eyelid before dropping to the baby at her breast. He kissed the small dark head and again he was overcome with emotion.

When he raised his eyes to her again, he smiled. "We will call him Shavano," he insisted.

"Shane Shavano," she repeated stubbornly, a weak grin forming on her lips as she caressed the strong baby boy. "For I think he will be very much like his father!"

The following night Eagle stood outside the lodge, staring with wonder into the starry heavens. He thought of this fresh new life and what it meant. His son! Then slowly his mind drifted back to Shavano, and the other brave warriors who had lost their lives in the past year. Had their souls gone to that distant Happy Hunting Ground they believed in? As he thought of life and death, he wondered what would happen to him when he died. He knew nothing of the spirit world. Maybe he should talk to Star about this.

A lone coyote howled in the breaking dawn. It was an eerie sound that had once made him lonely, but his heart was too full now for loneliness.

His eyes drifted over the other lodges, all quiet now, after a day of feasting and dancing in celebration of his son. He sighed. It was good to be back in the mountains. Although Eagle secretly longed to remain at Bear Claw's village down the Ute trail in the grass valley, he and Wasatch were now in command of Shavano's small tribe, and he had followed their ritual of migrating to their mountain home in the fall.

He crossed his arms against his buffalo robe and tilted his head back to study a pale and distant star. Bear Claw had treated him with respect, and his pride in his nephew was no secret. This had healed a deep hurt in Eagle's heart, and he was happier than he had ever been in his life, despite the seemingly endless battles between the Utes and Arapahoes.

To complicate matters, the Cheyennes sided with the Arapahoes more often than with the Utes. The Yuuttaa hunting grounds and soda springs were a source of deep envy in the other tribes, but had always belonged to the Yuuttaa, and Eagle intended for the land to remain in their possession. This was a constant worry, for now he was one of their leaders, and he knew he would give his life, if he must, to preserve the land of his people. Just as Shavano had so bravely done. He had a squaw and papoose to think of now, and while this made him more cautious, he was still a noble warrior, unafraid to charge into battle when it was necessary.

Footsteps whispered behind him and he swiveled, his keen eyes relaxing at the sight of Wasatch.

"My brother, you startled me," Eagle laughed.

"I awoke early. When I looked out I saw you standing alone. Come to the lodge, I have peyote."

Eagle hesitated. Star would not approve, but she was fast asleep, her son tucked beside her in his rabbitskin bed. And Eagle's nerves were too taut for sleep. He grinned at Wasatch.

"We will not let the peyote lead us into trouble?" he asked, his expression reluctant though his feet were already moving toward Wasatch's lodge.

"We will be strong," Wasatch said in mock seriousness, slamming his fist against his chest as he often did before riding into battle.

Eagle's spirits were already soaring in space; he didn't need the peyote, but he suspected that Wasatch did. Strange, Eagle thought, that his and Star's happiness sometimes left Wasatch moody and frustrated. He knew Wasatch was happy for them, yet he suspected this pointed up his own deep loneliness.

As they walked along, Eagle glanced thoughtfully at Wasatch, whose profile was cut against the thin gray light of dawn. He knew each feature almost as well as his own. Brown skin was drawn tightly over rigid cheekbones and a broad nose, and the wide mouth was shaped in a cynical twist. His eyes were darker than Star's and held a piercing light that seemed to come from the deep and often hostile thoughts that haunted him. Wasatch was a few inches shorter than Eagle, and his muscles were strong and hardy, but Eagle was several pounds heavier, and his muscles were tighter. He attributed his advantage in strength to hauling deer and elk out of the mountains. But he did not allow his mind to dwell on any advantages over his blood brother as their boots crunched over the cold ground to Wasatch's lodge.

Within, a fire burned low on the earthen floor, yet Eagle felt the chill of the night in his bones. Wasatch retreated to a darkened corner to prowl through his possessions. He returned with a large peyote button. He took his knife, cut the button in half, and shared with Eagle. They dropped down before the fire and sat in silence for a while, sucking deeply on the button that would calm their nerves and lift them to a special dream-like state where there were no battles or bloodshed or hunger. Only peace.

Eagle thought of Star and his baby son and looked across at Wasatch with a twinge of sadness.

"You should find a squaw," Eagle finally spoke. "One that would be good to you, one you could love as I love Star."

Wasatch shook his head vehemently. "That is not the life for me. Long ago, I chose the trail I will take until I go to the Happy Hunting Ground. There is no squaw and no papoose on my trail."

Eagle leaned back on the earth floor and crossed his legs. He felt warm and content, eager to listen and understand his friend and brother.

"What is this trail?" he asked.

Wasatch's dark eyes held a mystic glow as

he stared into the dwindling fire and breathed deeply of its pungent pine aroma. "When it was time for my test, I climbed to the top of the mountain and spent three suns with the Great Spirit." He paused, deep in thought.

Eagle waited, eager to hear the story Wasatch had never told him. Eagle knew the custom of Ute braves going to a remote spot to meditate and seek a vision from the Great Spirit before they became warriors. He had wondered what happened to Wasatch during that time, but he had never asked such a personal question. He was pleased that Wasatch now wished to confide this experience.

"I did not eat or drink, and the sun was a fireball upon my face. Finally the Great Spirit spoke to me, taking me back in time to a hole in the earth, showing me how the first Yuuttaa came up from this hole and looked upon the green forests and knew this was his land! This land that we now fight for." The cynical twist of Wasatch's mouth curled his lips upward in bitterness.

"Then I saw myself in battle fighting, always fighting." He released his breath in a deep sigh. "In my vision, there were no squaws, no papoose. I was a warrior, and I will be a warrior to the end. And when I journey into the land of the sun, I will go alone."

Eagle stared at him with deep sadness in his heart. It seemed so unfair that Wasatch should miss the joy of a squaw's love, the happiness of holding a papoose in his arms, a happiness unlike anything imaginable.

"The first of my years were happy," he said, as though reading Eagle's thoughts. "There were many happy hunts with Shavano."

Eagle nodded, thinking of his dismal life with Elmer Simmons.

"Eagle, did you ever wonder about your real father?"

The question startled him at first. He looked across the fire at Wasatch, and he realized that since Wasatch had revealed to him the most personal experience of his life, he felt he could ask this kind of question now.

Eagle took a deep breath as his eyes drifted from Wasatch to the dwindling fire. "Until I was about ten or twelve years old, I looked for him always, in every stranger's face. Then I gave up ever knowing who he is. After I learned that he raped Crying Wind, I am glad I will never know him. But somehow—" He hesitated, wondering about the wisdom of his words. Yet Wasatch was his friend; he could say anything to him tonight.

"Somehow I know in my heart that he no longer lives. I think he may have been killed years ago." A sad grin touched his mouth. "Do not ask how I know that, I just do."

Wasatch nodded, needing no further explanation. He watched a worried frown form on his blood brother's face and he leaned forward. The peyote made him feel happy and free, and he did not want to see this frown.

"What do you think that makes you look like the angry grizzly?"

Eagle looked back at him, unable to grin at

his joke. "I did not follow the custom of going to the mountains for three days to get my vision from the Great Spirit. Maybe I have not found my work. Is it too late?"

Wasatch leaned back on his elbows and grinned. "You have done what your vision would have told you. You are serving your people well; no warrior could do more."

His words eased Eagle's guilt and now he relaxed completely. For the first time in twenty-four hours, his eyes felt heavy. But he was not yet ready to leave his brother.

"I will fight beside you," Eagle vowed, "until the end."

Again, Wasatch's lips curled bitterly. "The red man or the white man? We do not yet know who will cast the deadly weapon to the backs of our heads."

Eagle pursed his lips, considering Wasatch's words.

"Perhaps the white man will have to fight his own wars," Eagle replied. "The battle in the South is already taking some of the whites from the territory. More will go, it is said."

Wasatch sat up, lifting his shoulders in an indifferent shrug. "We will still fight them; we must. It is our land. As my father said, their treaties mean nothing. Their words are like the morning dew that vanishes when the sun turns hot."

Eagle frowned. Wasatch grew more bitter each day. He thought of Shavano and the battles they had fought with other tribes.

"The Arapahoe are our enemy too," he countered. "At least the white men do not kidnap squaws and papooses!"

"But they rape our women!"

The words were spoken from a deep bitterness that had been a part of Wasatch since the first white settlers came to take over the meadows, the hunting grounds, the streams.

Eagle sighed, understanding his bitterness and taking no offense at the words that described his own birth.

"We fight again," Wasatch muttered, glaring into the darkness as though he could envision the battles taking place. "When our people are strong in number, we fight again."

The magic of the peyote had worn off, and Wasatch's bitterness, like a blanket of gloom, settled over the lodge. The gloom was an unwelcome visitor on the night of his son's birth, and Eagle nudged Wasatch and smiled.

"What do you think of my little papoose?"

Wasatch's eyes seemed to make a long journey from a fire that was mere smoke now to the radiant face of his brother. A begrudging grin broke over his mouth.

"He will be a mighty warrior, like his father—like his *uncle*!"

They both laughed together, breaking the dreary mood, and Eagle slowly pulled himself to his feet. "I'm going to my lodge now. Rest well, my brother." He clamped a hand on Wasatch's shoulder and left. Outside, his eyes shot eagerly to his lodge, where he knew he could find peace and contentment. He wanted to forget the hate and anger between the red man and the white man, for now his heart was filled with love as he hurried to his family.

As the winter days passed, the small tribe that was now the responsibility of Wasatch and Eagle was strangely content. The snows were deep and heavy, but Wasatch and Eagle kept their people in meat. It was a good year for hunting, and Eagle had located a lush valley near a stream which drew game down from the mountains. Wasatch was always at his side, observing Eagle as he studied the direction of the wind, identified the tracks of each animal of the forest and stalked them all with infinite skill. Wasatch, too, became a very good hunter.

After their hunts, Eagle would stretch out before the fire in his lodge, watching his baby son in wide-eyed fascination, or talking with Star as she wove her baskets or cured the hides of animals for lodge covers and saddles. Bones were converted to skinning blades and cooking and eating utensils.

Both waited impatiently for Star's weak body to heal, and the need for denial made their desire even stronger.

"I know you grow restless, Eagle," Star said, laying down her work to touch his arm. "But Nish-ki says we must wait until the moon is full on the western horizon. It will not be long."

Eagle groaned, extending his hand to touch Star's breast, enlarged by the nourishment his son so eagerly suckled. Eagle had been filled with tenderness as he watched the baby's greedy little mouth clamp over her brown nipples. When Eagle looked at Star, her slim face glowed with a beauty that was almost etheral as she nursed their son.

"Sometimes I feel jealous," he teased. "My son gets to lie at your breast while I am forced to wait and watch for the damned moon to grow full! Perhaps I could get our people to do a dance for me." He grinned at her to emphasize his joke, yet what Star had said was true. He was restless all the time now, starved for the feel of her body beneath his, for her silken nipple against his tongue.

Finally, when his frustration drove him from the lodge, he would seize his rifle and stalk about in the night, eventually ending up in Wasatch's lodge.

"Tomorrow I go to the mountains to track the grizzly," he announced when he saw the moon rounding out and knew he must keep himself occupied.

Wasatch sat before the fire, content after his peyote. His eyes held the eurphoric gaze that filled them often now—too often, Eagle silently concluded. Wasatch needed to be more active during the long winter days, and Eagle decided to keep them both busy.

An anger lurked in the depths of Wasatch's eyes, an anger that sought relief in the action of battle, but the fighting had ceased until spring. Now they must replenish their meat and keep their tribe warm and healthy.

"Do you want to go with me to track the grizzly?" Eagle repeated the question to Wasatch, who seemed not to have heard.

"The grizzly will eat you one of these days,

my brother!" Wasatch sneered. "It is your pride that drives you to do battle with the grizzly; you want to prove that you are as brave as Bear Claw!"

Wasatch's words, embarrassingly true, touched a spark of anger in Eagle. "Are you going with me or not?" he growled. "I track the grizzly for myself, not for Bear Claw!"

Wasatch threw back his head and laughed, amused that his brother was stung to wrath over the simple truth. "I track with you."

"Then we leave at the first light," Eagle snapped and bounded back to his lodge.

As the darkness of night melted to a soft gray, Eagle and Wasatch guided their horses up the steep trail leading ito the rugged Tarrayalls. Eagle had overheard a miner, full of Taos lightning, speak of a grizzly that ranged low in these mountains. Eagle intended to find him this day.

They rode in silence, each lost in their own sleepy thoughts until Eagle's eyes moved searchingly over a pine thicket and halted abruptly. He squinted, trying to identify the brown woolly animal that should have appeared smaller with distance, yet was huge. He was grazing and only a part of the body could be seen through the trees. Then Eagle spotted the tell-tale brown mound that gave the animal a hunch-back shape.

"Wasatch!" he whispered, hoarse with excitement. "Look. A buffalo!" He pointed to the pine knoll up the mountainside.

Wasatch's indrawn breath made a sharp hiss in the cold morning. There had been no buffalo for two winters after the influx off trappers, miners and settlers, all of whom had chased, tracked and slaughtered the herds until they were forced to seek refuge higher into the Rockies.

Wasatch's mind tumbled back to happier days when the buffalo had been abundant, when the huge animals had provided food, shoes, lodges and rich robes for his people. They had never gone hungry with the buffalo! A wide smile curved his mouth. His arrowheads were tipped with sharp bone and would penetrate the thick woolly fur easier than a bullet, would even produce more blood to slow down the retreating animal. And the fifty arrows in his pouch would find a broad, easy target! This time he had the advantage over Eagle, who had never hunted Buffalo.

They reined their horses to a slow walk as they studied the big animal whose head was still lowered, nuzzling through the snow in search of cured grass.

"Maybe we should stalk him . . . *her*," Eagle corrected himself when closer range indicated a cow.

"But if we miss, if the buffalo charges, we may arrive too soon in the Happy Hunting Ground," Wasatch whispered.

"The *real* hunting ground?" Eagle queried with a grin, his eyes never leaving the animal. "She's going to hear us if we stay on the horses."

The soft carpet of snow cushioned the horses' hooves, but there was still the danger of the animals' spooking or neighing, or the cow might hear them too soon. Eagle considered the alternatives and decided the surest method of slaying the cow was on foot.

"Let's stalk," Eagle repeated, slipping down from the horse and removing his rifle.

Wasatch was solemn, remembering other hunts when he had seen warriors die beneath the charging buffalo, gored or trampled under their pounding hooves. But he could be no less brave than Eagle; he would rather die than have a coward heart!

Wasatch dropped down, reaching quickly for his short bow and his pouch of arrows. Wasatch and Eagle positioned their weapons, creeping silently across the frozen white earth. Suddenly, the buffalo lifted her head and turned glassy eyes in their direction.

Wasatch began to launch his arrows. Eagle hesitated, giving Wasatch the first opportunity, though his rifle was aimed at the buffalo's heart. But the arrows whizzed through the air and sank cleanly between the buffalo's ribs and the wounded animal began to froth blood from its mouth and nostrils.

"Aren't you going to shoot?" Wasatch shouted as they raced up the steep hill.

"No need, brother. You have him!"

The cow had been felled and now wallowed to its death in a pool of crimson that stained the pristine snow. As its eyes rolled back in death, Wasatch dropped his head and repeated the Ute prayer spoken upon taking the life of an animal.

Eagle stood silently by, respecting this

custom. Animals were sacred to the Yuuttaa. Unlike many hunters, the Yuuttaa killed only for survival.

Wasatch knelt by the cow, stroking its rough fur.

"It weighs near a thousand pounds," Eagle said, clamping his hand on Wasatch's shoulder. He grinned. "I am no longer the hunter of our village. Killer of Buffalo is more important than Wild Eagle!"

As Eagle spoke these words, he knew this was a way of easing some of Wasatch's bitterness. He needed to feel that he had accomplished something special for his people. Eagle had Star and little Shane; Wasatch had no one. He needed this deed to build his pride.

Wasatch threw his arms around Eagle's shoulders and tried to hide the sudden rush of tears to his eyes. "The buffalo has been missed by my people. It brings good health and long life to us. Eagle, my heart bursts with happiness!"

Eagle gripped his brother tightly against him, sharing in his joy. It was the first time in months that Wasatch had looked happy, and Eagle sensed that he was thinking of his father now, wishing he could have killed this buffalo during Shavano's lifetime, but it would do no good to feel sad about that now.

"We will need help," Wasatch said, turning to stare again at the buffalo.

"I will ride back to camp," Eagle offered. "You stay with your buffalo. We will return with ponies and travois. It will take a long time to cut up the buffalo and transport it."

"Her death will have purpose," Wasatch said gravely. "We'll use the hair for rope; we'll tan the hide for new lodge covers. The bones will make more knife handles, and from the rib bones we can make a snow sled for little Shane. The meat will nourish our tribe."

There was a great celebration in camp over the next days. The warriors made several trips to transport the meat, and everyone rejoiced in the task.

The tongue and heart were boiled and eaten by all in a sacred feast. Afterwards, the men joined the women in butchering, for the task was mammoth. While Eagle and Star rejoiced with their people, the moon lay full on the western horizon, and another celebration was about to take place.

The village slept as the moonlight sifted through the smoke hole of Eagle's lodge, dusting its pale irridescence over the nude bodies of Eagle and Star.

Eagle's eyes darkened with passion as Star came to him, her body bathed by moonlight and fireglow to a burnished amber, her black hair falling in silken strands to her narrow waist. Eagle took a long moment to admire the full breasts that nourished his baby, the nipples ripe and peaking; the narrow waist above the small mound of her belly, which had been the nesting place for his baby; the dark, glossy V that had taken the seed of his loins into her womb; the strong slim legs, the tiny feet.

Slowly, his eyes made a tortuous return to her face, where an expression of longing suffused her small features. Her eyes grew drowsy as they crept over his body, examining the hard muscles, the sparse dark hair on his brawny chest, the slim torso that held his desire, and the long firm legs, as strong as the trunks of the forest spruce.

Star's moist lips parted as she stretched out on their bed and reached for his hand, lifting each finger to her lips. His other hand traced the rounded curve of her hips, the hollow of her waist, the thin wall of ribs. Then his fingers scaled the rise of her thrusting breasts. He touched a nipple lightly, and it warmed against his hand. The nipples were already stimulated from nourishing the baby, and Eagle's lightest touch sent slivers of lightning radiating into their fullness.

When Star kissed his lips a look of mingled pleasure and pain tensed his features. She lifted her finger to trace the curve of the half-moon scar on his cheek before her hand roamed over the roughness and velvet of this man who had been forced from her bed during her long healing period.

He moaned against her lips and her eyes caressed his face, seeing how clearly the waiting was hurting him.

"Now," she whispered, not caring that they had taken no time for gentle caresses.

He shook his head, his fingers paving the way for his manhood as he clenched his teeth in an effort to control the torrent of desire that lashed through him.

PASSION'S PEAK

Star saw the anguish in his face and pressed her lips to his muscled shoulder. "Eagle, I want you *now*."

"Wait," he said, gently unclasping her arms from his neck so that he could reach back and grasp the soft fur of the huge white snowshoe rabbit.

He slipped the downy fur under her bare hips and pressed her gently into its warm, velvety depths. The fur pillow lifted her body and now he eased into her, carefully, gently, mindful of her healing body. But as soon as their skin touched and melded in warm heat, he was spiraling into the heavens, unable to wait for her. It brought soul-wrenching thunder in instant, intense release. There had been many slow, star-filled journeys of their souls before their ecstasy was reached, but this time his need was so urgent and overpowering that the release in his body was violent.

When finally he caught his breath again, he kissed her tenderly. Then his tongue dove into the velvet of her mouth, joining with hers in bold thrusts of passion. Star moaned and wrapped her arms around his back, pressing every inch of her body to him in pleading desire.

He lifted her against him, filled her again, and brought her to the peak of passion with gentle erotic thrusts that had her crying his name until he smothered those cries with his own. Tears streamed down her face as the fires of love danced, blazed, then gently smouldered in the darkness of her eyes.

"Star of the Morning," he whispered against her lips. "I love you, love you, love you. . . ."

"And I love you, Wild Eagle. With all of my body, my heart, my soul. . . ."

Their love words filled the lodge as the gentle breathing of their baby sleeping contentedly nearby added to their happiness. It was the most perfect night of their lives.

18

The long winter was at last giving way to spring when Eric received the second letter from his mother. The first one had come soon after he sent the wire from Denver. She had assured him she was all right and expressed hope that the conflict would soon end. John and Bill had both joined the Confederate Army, and their letters were cheerful and optimistic.

This letter was different. It was delivered by Rex on his return from Colorado City.

"Joe at the mercantile said this came for you two weeks ago, but since you hadn't been to town . . ."

Eric reached for the letter, a feeling of alarm slivering down his spine at the sight of his mother's shaky scrawl, a drastic change from her usual meticulous handwriting.

"Joe also said to tell you he knows a miner lookin' for a cabin up here if you have any inklin' to sell."

Eric looked back at Rex, who was leaning over the pommel of his saddle, his felt hat riding low on his wrinkled forehead.

"Rex, that offer is pretty tempting right now. That damn stream has dried up."

Rex nodded, looking out across the quiet meadow. "Me and Arabella are thinking of moving over to South Park. They're finding some mighty pure gold in them gulches around the Tarryals. That is"—he hesitated, lowering his eyes to his hands and toying with the leather reins—"if I don't join the Colorado Militia."

Eric looked up quickly from the envelope and stared curiously at his neighbor and friend. They would be on opposite sides if they went to battle, and the thought saddened him. He felt the light pressure of the letter in his palm and sighed.

"Thanks for bringing the letter, Rex. I haven't heard from her since she congratulated us on our marriage—and insisted we pack up and move to Pine Hill!"

"Rex, won't you come in for coffee?" Sara called from the door.

"No, thanks. Gotta get home. Arabella will be worryin' if I'm not back before dark." He grinned at Eric. "Women are funny like that."

Eric smiled and waved as Rex kneed his horse and cantered off. He began to open the envelope as he went back into the cabin and sat down at the kitchen table. The paper held the faint lilac scent that his mother dusted on everything, and he found himself suddenly homesick for her and for Pine Hill.

"It's dated January," he said, frowning, "over two months ago. Still, I guess I'm lucky to have received it at all with the war going on."

He scanned the letter, his heart in his throat,

fearing it might relate the death of one of his brothers. To his relief, there was no news of tragedy. It was, instead, a compelling request for him to come home.

As he read, Sara held her breath, her eyes searching his face as a perplexed frown wrinkled his forehead, then gave way to a look of sadness as he laid down the letter and looked across at her.

"John and Bill are in Virginia fighting. Their wives and children have moved into the big house with Mother, but there are no men there. The overseer John hired before he left finally took up his gun and joined the war."

He raked through his hair and stood, his hands shoved deep in his pockets as he nervously paced the floor. Sara watched him with bleak eyes, knowing he would not refuse to help his mother if she needed him.

"Maybe the war will soon end," she said.

He shook his head. "That's what everyone thought in the beginning, but the battle continues. Sara, there is no man at Pine Hill to protect the women from deserters and thieves who always prey on innocent people in time of war."

"But . . . do you have to go? I mean, could you. . . ?" Her words trailed away uselessly. Of course there was nothing else he could so.

He looked at her with his jaw set, his eyes filled with worry. "I couldn't live with myself if something happened."

"But will you stay at Pine Hill?" she cried. "Or will you join your brothers in battle? Eric, I know you too well. You're not going to sit around the house with the women while all the other men are out fighting a war!"

He walked across the kitchen and flung the door wide, staring out at the mountains for a long moment. "I have to go back, Sara. If I find a competent, dependable man to hire as overseer . . ."

"Don't you think those *competent, dependable* men are already gone, Eric? For God's sake, don't try to trick me."

"*Trick you?*" he repeated, his eyes glittering with anger. "Sara, don't talk crazy. Why would I trick you? I'm trying to be honest with you, but I do have a family to think about. I can't pretend they don't exist when the Union troops are charging into the South killing our men."

Sara sank into the chair and dropped her head to her hands. Tears of frustration filled her eyes. Deep in her heart, she knew he was right, but she couldn't let him go. She just couldn't. If only this stupid war hadn't started. If only . . . their marriage seemed to contain too many *if onlys*. She thought of the baby they had lost, the money that had been stolen, the man Eric had killed and the dark mood that had followed.

She felt his hand on his shoulder. "Come on, let's take a walk and clear our heads," he said.

She lifted her head and looked into his face. His eyes held the pain that tore at her heart and she pressed her cheek against his hand. "All right," she said, as he lifted her from the chair and they walked outside.

With her arm linked in his, she knew she

couldn't stay mad at him for things he had no control over. Did she want a less honorable man, one who wouldn't respond when he was needed, one who was afraid to fight for his land?

Sara looked up at the aspen tree in the yard. A light wind was blowing the new green leaves, spinning them like tiny wheels on their branches. She had watched those leaves blaze to splendor, die, then be replenished again. She longed to be strong in her soul, like the aspen tree, so delicate and fragile, yet able to endure the winter winds that ripped at its slender trunk.

She took a deep breath and turned to Eric. "I understand how you feel. You were right, I'm being foolish. And selfish."

He pulled her into his arms and pressed her head against his broad chest. His own unique scent filled her nostrils, and the thought of giving him up, if only for a short while, was a pain too deep to hide. Then, as though her mind refused to deal with such pain, the answer to their problem came to her.

She tilted her head back and looked up into his face. "I know what to do. I'll go with you. Please don't say no," she said, lifting her fingers to his lips, which were already forming a protest. "Other people are returning to their homes; we heard about that when we were in Denver. Please, Eric. I'd rather take my chances *with* you than to suffer being without you."

A smile began to form in the corners of his mouth as his eyes worshiped her upturned face. "All right, I won't say no." He bent down to kiss her briefly, then his glance drifted over her head to the cabin.

"What do you think about selling the cabin?" he asked. "It wouldn't be wise just to lock up and go off and leave it for an uncertain time. Besides," he added, "I think we've exhausted the supply of gold in these streams. You know we've had no luck since . . ." He heaved a sigh. "After the war's over, I'd like to come back to Colorado, maybe buy some land over in South Park. There's some good grazing land over there, and who knows? There may still be some gold in the Tarryalls."

"If you want to," Sara said. It didn't really matter where she was as long as she and Eric were together.

As soon as the decision was made, they began to pack. Sara found her heart growing heavy again, however, as she stood in the kitchen, trying to decide what to take and what to leave. "Maybe I should just give our cooking utensils to Arabella," she said.

Eric shook his head. "They're leaving, too. And if Rex joins the army, they'll have the same problem we have of trying to sort through their things."

Sara crossed her arms and looked at Eric. "Doesn't it bother you, Eric? That you will be fighting on opposite sides?"

His eyes dropped to the floor. "I've thought about that, but we won't be in the same part of the country. And as you said before"—he looked at her hopefully—"maybe it will end soon."

She nodded and turned to survey the little cabin that had been home for the past year. She'd accomplished what she'd dreamed of doing when she first arrived and surveyed the plain rooms. Wildflowers overflowed baskets, colorful pillows and throw rugs revealed her flair for sewing and knitting, and there was warmth and a homey feeling everywhere. Absently, she wandered to the bedroom and looked at the featherbed, where they'd once had to keep stuffing feathers back inside the mattress. But then she remembered all the nights she'd slept in Eric's arms and awakened to his kisses and his touch and the special lovemaking that started their day off right.

"What are you thinking?" he asked, standing beside her.

She turned twinkling dark eyes to him. "I'm thinking that before we leave this cabin and all its furnishings to the person Rex mentioned, I want you to make love to me in that bed—right now, with the sunshine spilling over the plank floors you worked so hard to build, with the smell of mountain air and fresh pine filling our senses . . . and with the bittersweet ache in our hearts of knowing we're leaving for good."

He scooped her into his arms and carried her to the bed. His lips sought hers tenderly, gently, as her hands wound through his hair, relishing its thick texture. He lowered her to the bed, his mouth never leaving hers. For a long time they lay in each other's arms, reveling in the way their lips could convey their love so well. Eric leaned on his elbow and traced the curve of her cheek with his thumb, as his eyes moved over her face . . . the high forehead, the dark brows with their delicate arch, the wide, deep eyes that were sometimes black, sometimes dark brown, but always a mirror of her soul. Her inky lashes blinked and he lifted his thumb to touch their velvet fringe.

"Do you know," he said, "when we're not together I can close my eyes and see you as clearly as if you were standing before me? I know the set of your mouth when you're angry, or happy, or passionate. I know the way those thick lashes can cast dark shadows on your cheek. I know how your skin turns from olive to pale yellow when you're tired, or worried, or when I've made love to you too often. . . ."

"Eric!" she laughed, grabbing his thumb and lowering it to her teeth. "You are a tease." Her teeth sank gently into his thumb.

"Never," he said, unbuttoning her blouse and smoothing it back from her camisole. "Never a tease." As his lips nibbled at her neck, then followed the rise of her breasts, she tugged at his shirt. He paused, his tongue trailing into the valley between her breasts, before he reached back and yanked his clothes off. Sara did the same.

"Stand up," he said when she had finished undressing.

A curious look filled her eyes but she complied. With a grin, he yanked the thick quilt from the bed and tossed it over his shoulder. "We have enough memories of this bed," he said, reaching for her hand.

"But what—where—?" She giggled as he led her through the parlour and out the front door.

"Eric!" She began to laugh, pulling back as he tugged at her. "I'm not going out in the yard nude."

"All right," he released her, and swept the quilt down from his shoulder and swung it around her. "Feel better?"

She began to giggle, suddenly delighted with his game. It was just what they needed to break the tension and worry that had dominated their minds.

"I, my lady, am less shy." He stood before her, broad-shouldered, tan and muscled, dark hair on his chest gleaming in the sun. Her eyes dropped lower to the dark nest of his manhood, then the long dark legs that were towers of strength. When her eyes dropped to his feet, she giggled again. "Have I ever told you how ugly your big toe is?"

Her question left him indignant, since she'd obviously overlooked his other attributes. "Woman, you'll have to pay for that remark!" He faked a dark scowl, then reached forward and, in one mighty swing, lifted her off the ground and onto his shoulder.

"Eric," she cried, laughing and tugging his hair playfully, "you've lost your mind!"

"It's your fault," he called to her, as his long legs stretched into swift strides. "You've driven me beyond all reason with that enticing body of yours, and those dark eyes that tease and taunt and . . . beg," he finished huskily, lowering her from his shoulder.

Wiping the tears of laughter from her eyes, she glanced nervously around and saw that there was an emerald carpet of moss beneath her feet. They had reached the edge of the woods, where the stream seeped underground to provide the moisture for dense growth. Tall spruce and lush-leafed aspens surrounded them, and in the distance she could hear the rush of water over stones. Somewhere a bird was singing its heart out.

Eric spread the quilt and pulled her to him. She forgot her modesty as their bodies entwined in the forest, and the sweet rapture of passion took over. In the distance the grand hulk of Pikes Peak looked down on them, the last traces of snow melting down its sides.

Sara wrapped her arms around Eric's warm back and looked at the beams of sunlight slanting down through the age-old spruce. As she kissed his shoulder and neck and hugged his face, her eyes drifted toward the distant mountain range.

As their bodies claimed and possessed, and their hearts raced like the surge of the stream, Sara moaned against his lips.

"I think," she said breathlessly, "that the Peak is watching us."

19

The trip to Colorado City seemed unusually long and tiring to Sara, and by the time she arrived she was so nauseated that she had to skip dinner. The sale of their cabin the next morning was overshadowed by another sick stomach, and then other symptoms began to cause concern. The doctor confirmed her suspicions the next day.

She was pregnant.

She and Eric were silent as they strolled back to the boarding house, both filled with conflicting emotions.

"We've wanted a baby so badly," he said, squeezing her hand as they crossed the busy dirt street, rutted with potholes from a bad winter.

"Yes, more than anything," she quickly answered. "Only . . ."

"Only now you don't know about making the trip," Eric finished for her, nodding gravely.

"When the doctor heard about me losing the other one, he said a long, hard trip would be risky." As they reached the boarding house, she turned large, tear-filled eyes to him.

"Oh Eric, I can't take the chance. I can't go!"

"Then I won't go either!"

They were silent through the evening, picking over their meal at Mrs. Willis's cozy little restaurant.

"Remember the first time we ate here?" Eric teased her as they toyed with the thick buckwheat pancakes drowned in maple syrup.

Sara leaned back in her chair and looked across at him, nodding with a smile. "I was about as desperate as a lady could be! No I wasn't," she quickly amended. "I was about as *lucky* as a lady could be . . . because I had met you. Oh Eric," she sighed, "you were so good to me."

He took a sip of his coffee and grinned. "Well, first of all, I felt sorry for you. And second, no woman had ever affected me the way you did!"

Sara's smile faded as her eyes traced his strong profile, the wide-set blue eyes so blue that everything else dimmed in comparison, the chiseled lips in the clean shaven face. Again, he had decided to dispense with his beard.

"Eric, what will we do now?" she asked quietly.

He shrugged, staring at his cup as his thumb traced a circle around the rim. "We've got money from the sale of the cabin. Maybe we'll just take it easy for a while, maybe stay here in town until the baby's born."

"Will you be happy doing that?" she pressed.

He pursed his lips. "I can be happy for a

while, then I'll get restless. After the baby's born, maybe we can go on to South Park."

Sara listened, appreciating his attempt to convince himself and her that everything would be all right. But she knew him too well.

She thought of his mother, alone and desperately needing Eric's help. She thought of the intense way he had spoken about his obligation to return. And she thought of the days dragging on for him here, with nothing to do. She knew what she had to say, but she could not bring herself to say it until the next morning, after they'd spent a sleepless night, too despondent even to make love.

"Eric, I have a suggestion," Sara began, as they were dressing for breakfast. "Maybe you should make the trip back, see to your mother, then come back."

He turned to look at her as his fingers moved over his shirt buttons, then halted. "I don't know if I could do that, Sara. I'm afraid once I got there, I might catch this war fever and join up with the Rebels." He sighed. "I'd better not take that chance."

Sara opened her mouth then closed it again. He was right. And she'd done the noble thing, so now perhaps her conscience would give her some peace.

After breakfast, they went in search of a decent place to stay, one that would see them through until the baby was born. After looking at several dreary rooms, they located a small apartment in the home of a respectable family. The house was a rambling frame structure within walking distance of town, and the small living room, kitchen, bedroom and bath were nicely furnished in simple pine. They settled in, but as the days passed, Sara began to sense Eric's restlessness, though he never complained.

On her next trip to the doctor, she was pronounced healthy and quite likely to carry the baby full term. When she returned, she found Eric standing out under a pine tree, looking blankly at the horizon. It broke her heart to see that despondent look on his face. She knew what she had to do.

She walked over to link her arm through his. "Hello, darling."

He whirled in surprise, then his eyes skipped down her flowing pink dress and returned to her face. He smiled.

"You're even more beautiful since motherhood has put a bloom in your cheeks," he said.

"Eric"—she hesitated, then forced herself to complete the sentence—"the doctor says I'm in perfect health and there shouldn't be any complications this time. And so," she continued over his exclamation of approval, "I want you to pack and take the next stage out to the states!"

His face went blank for a moment, but this time he did not offer a protest. "Are you sure?" he asked finally.

She nodded. "I love you too much to stand by and watch you tear yourself apart inside. You feel guilty over not going back, yet your loyalty to me is too strong to permit it. So now I insist. I'll be fine here," she assured him, as he lifted her palm to his lips. "There's the Freeman family on the other side of the house, and they'll help me if I need it. I like my doctor, so that eases any worry over my health. And I feel marvelous." She fought the ache in her throat as his lips trailed from her palm to each finger. "I'm afraid, Eric, that in time you'd start to resent me, perhaps even the baby, if we keep you from doing what you feel you must."

He looked into her eyes with love and an expression of gratitude. "Sara, I appreciate this. I know how it must cost you to be so generous. . . ."

But Sara had only a vague sense of the cost she would pay until until the next afternoon, when she stood in the dusty street waving goodbye, fighting back her tears until the stage rolled out of town. Then she gave way to deep, wracking sobs, wondering suddenly if she would ever see him again.

She walked back to her apartment feeling a heavy sadness like none she'd known before. Eric had waited until today to leave, and they had made passionate love throughout the night, but now the forced smile and strained cheerfulness fell away.

She lifted her face to the sky, absorbing its hot, merciless glare. Summer was approaching, and she felt sluggish and heavy already, though she was only three months into her pregnancy. But as her feet plodded on, she knew it was the weight of her soul, rather than the baby, that made her so weary.

As she turned into the yard, Mrs. Freeman

stood on the porch, her hands thrust into the pockets of her apron. She was in her early forties, with dark blond hair and sympathy in her blue eyes as she looked at Sara.

"Bless your heart, my dear. It must have been terrible saying goodbye to him, not knowing when—"

"He'll only be gone a few months," Sara said, her lips forming a tight smile. Absently, she brushed at her eyes, hoping the tears had dried by now.

Mrs. Freeman nodded. "Exactly what are his plans?"

Sara reached the porch and sank into a wooden rocker. "He'll travel by stage to St. Louis—there'll be some stopovers of course, and he'll change stages too. But when he reaches St. Louis, he plans to buy a horse and work his way South." As she spoke those words, the impact of the danger Eric would face hit her solidly for the first time. Surely Eric had already thought of this and concealed his concern from her. If he wore no uniform, he could be ambushed by either side as he traveled into the war zone. He might even be mistaken for a spy, for why else would he not be serving either the Union or Confederate army, as young and healthy as he appeared?

She lifted a hand to rub her throbbing forehead.

"This war makes no sense a'tall," Mrs. Freeman grumbled. "What are they thinking of, for heaven's sakes? Slavery, taxes, all the reasons they give—is it worth them murdering each other?" She bit her lip and touched Sara's shoulder. "Come inside for some tea, dear."

Sara rose on wobby knees. "Eric says Abraham Lincoln is trying to end the war quickly. . . ." Her voice was as weak as her knees, and she ceased trying to carry on a conversation. She let Mrs. Freeman serve her tea and chat about a benefit cake sale the Ladies Missionary Society was planning, but Sara scarcely heard a word. She soon pleaded weariness and turned down the hall to the back of the house where her apartment was situated.

The rooms felt cool and dim after the hot hour she'd spent on the streets, waiting for the stage to depart. She undressed and sank onto her featherbed.

She lay there for two days, getting up only for light nourishment and to relieve herself. It was as though something inside her had ceased to function, and she couldn't pull herself out of this dreary mood.

On the third day, a persistent knock on her back door dragged her to her feet. Arabella stood in the open door, a wide smile on her wrinkled face. She was even wearing a dress, a dark, simple calico, and her long braid was coiled into a tight bun on her nape.

"Arabella!" she cried, hugging her. "What are you doing in town?" It was so good to see a familiar face, to have someone call on her.

"Rex buys a new horse." Arabella's round black eyes saddened as she looked at Sara. "The man at the stable tell us you did not leave with Eric to go South. He tell me where you live, and I come to see about you."

Sara nodded. "Our plans changed abruptly when I discovered I was pregnant." She smiled sadly. "You know how badly I wanted a baby. I just wish this little one"—she tapped her rounding belly—"could have waited a while longer."

Arabella's smile sent deep wrinkles into her round jaw as she reached forward to grip Sara's hand. "It will all work out. I am happy for you. My news is that Rex is joining the Colorado Militia. The crazy fool!" She shook her head, her eyes holding a smile, though her words were spoken sternly.

Sara stepped out of the door. "Come, I'll make us some tea."

Arabella located the cups while Sara put the teapot on the stove. "I just wish this crazy war hadn't started," Sara complained, glancing over her shoulder at Arabella, taking her seat at the tiny table.

Arabella shook her dark head. "Men are all warriors at heart. They have to have the gun or the tomahawk in their hands, drive their horses into battle, sit at the fire boasting of their victories or complaining of their losses. It is the way of all men."

Sara looked at her curiously, realizing the white man was not so different from the Indian after all. "When is Rex leaving?" she asked, pouring the tea.

"Today," Arabella sighed.

"I'm sorry," Sara said, taking her seat at the table. "What are you going to do?"

She shrugged. "Find a room in town. We've closed up the cabin, but we do not sell yet. My noble warrior may discover he does not like being with this Colorado Militia."

Automatically, Sara glanced around her living room, thinking. There was an extra bed and plenty of room. She turned back with a bright smile. "I have an idea—why don't you stay here with me? There's plenty of room."

Arabella looked surprised at first, but then she began to shake her head. "No, I will find a room."

"But *why*? You'd be doing me a favor to stay, Arabella," Sara implored. "I need someone with me to keep me from feeling so sad and lonely. First, Eric decided he wouldn't go South when we learned I was pregnant. But he was miserable here, doing nothing. I couldn't be that selfish, Arabella. I know he has a responsibility toward his family, and even his homeland, but I've been crying ever since he left. I know that isn't healthy."

"No, it isn't." Arabella answered, staring intently into Sara's face and seeing the heartache in her pained expression. She turned and surveyed the apartment for a quiet moment, then looked back at Sara. "All right, I will stay if you let me do the cleaning and some of the cooking."

"Of course!' Sara laughed softly. "Right now I haven't the heart to do either one. Oh Arabella, I'm so glad you came," she said, smiling again as a look of peace softened her face. "Eric would have felt so much better about leaving me if he had known you would come."

"And Rex will be glad," Arabella said. "When the baby comes, I will help you care for it," she added tenderly. "I always wanted a little papoose. Maybe I can claim just a little bit of yours."

"The baby will be born in January. I hope Eric will return by then, but somehow I feel that's doubtful."

Sara leaned back in the chair and sipped her tea, feeling more content now that Arabella would be staying with her.

"It will work out for both of us," Arabella said, taking the teacups to the sink to wash them, already feeling at home.

Sara was beginning to feel anxious about Eric, not having heard from him, when an elderly man arrived on her back doorstep early one morning. In his hands was a letter, and when Sara recognized Eric's familiar scrawl, she practically yanked it from his hands before he could speak.

"I'm too old to fight in the war," he explained hoarsely, as if Sara expected him to take up arms. "I've come West to invest in land, but I help the soldiers when I can. I met your husband at a stage stop in St. Louis, and when he heard I was coming here, he dashed off this letter."

"Thank you so much!" Sara beamed. "The telegraph lines to Missouri have been cut, and I was frantic to hear."

The man nodded knowingly and turned to go. "Good day."

Sara sat down by the light of the window to read. Arabella had gone to town and Sara cherished this private time to read Eric's words and share his thoughts. It was as though she and Eric were united again, shutting out the rest of the world.

"My dearest Sara," he wrote, "I can never express how much I miss you. The trip was long and hard, but uneventful, thank God. There were no raids on the stage by the Cheyenne or by army deserters, who seem to be everywhere. Two other men rode with me, both returning to their home state because of the war. One was a Southerner from Mississippi, the other a Northerner from Pennsylvania. Strangely, we did not argue over the issues that started this war. There was a common bond among all of us to reach St. Louis safely.

"There are Union soldiers everywhere. Nathaniel Lyon overcame the Rebels here and took prisoners, parading them through the streets of St. Louis. A small group of Confederate sympathizers rallied back in anger at the humiliation of our troops. As a result, a riot broke out and some were killed and wounded.

"I am purchasing a horse and intend to start South today. Don't worry about me. I will remain safe, for I have no intentions of letting anything stop my return to you and our baby."

As Sara read, she could almost hear Eric's voice in her ears, feel his hands on her body, taste his lips, and it brought a sharp ache to her heart. She shook her head and sighed. "Oh Eric, I do miss you so much!" She read the letter again and again, drawing strength and courage from his words. She had to be brave, just as Eric was, but at times it was very hard.

She pressed her lips to the letter and kept it by her bed, reading it every morning when she awoke, every night before she went to sleep. And most nights she dreamed of holding Eric in her arms.

Life for Sara became predictably routine despite the drama of war. She and Arabella lived quietly, avoiding the shops and streets of Colorado City where the war talk was at fever pitch. Sara tried not to worry about the war in the South, but all sorts of fears lurked in her mind. Did Eric reach Georgia? Did he join the Confederate Army? If only she could hear from him again, but there was little hope of receiving another letter soon.

She told herself she would make herself sick from worry, but she could not control it. Finally, when her appetite waned and she feared for the baby's health, she turned to Arabella for help. Arabella taught her to weave baskets, and they spent many pleasant hours together. During that time Arabella talked about her childhood, when she had been called Running Doe. She and her tribe lived on the western edge of the Territory, far from Colorado City, near a mountain shaped like a saddle horn.

"It was wild horse country," Arabella said. "The braves spent most of their time catching and taming the horses. Our lodges were on a high slope that faced the morning sun, but we always fight with the Cheyenne and Arapahoe. There was never peace."

"How did you meet Rex?" Sara asked interestedly.

Arabella's weathered brown face softened momentarily as her eyes drifted toward the ceiling and her mind returned to the memory.

"He came to our camp. Wanted to trade beaver hides and tobacco for some buffalo meat. He was very hungry, and he had the long beard. He was like a wild man," she remembered and laughed. Arabella's laughter always amused Sara. It was deep and throaty, and she laughed only when she thought something was very funny. "Next time he come, he trade for me!"

"How did you feel about being traded?" Sara asked curiously.

"I felt happy! I was only sixteen winters. When he rode into our camp, my heart was like my name—Running Doe. It run away before I could stop it!" She picked up her basket and began to work again. "We have been happy," she said.

Sara lay down her work and looked at Arabella. "Did you ever know the warrior Bear Claw?" she asked. "His village is at the soda springs in the high red rocks. About a half day from here."

Arabella's eyes darkened as she looked solemnly at Sara. "I know of that tribe, but I do not know Bear Claw."

Their eyes met and held, and Sara sensed

that Arabella already knew about her, had known all along. A look of compassion crossed Arabella's face as she waited for Sara to continue.

Sara leaned back in her chair and began the story, but she had not gone far when Arabella began to nod. "I know of this. Eric told Rex two winters ago. He wanted me to understand you. What do you think now, Sara?" she asked gently. "Do you believe you are Ute?"

Sara looked into her teacup, considering the question. "I could believe that more easily than I could believe I was Crying Wind's daughter. I know that sounds strange, but there was no resemblance between us. I was so certain . . ." Her voice trailed away. "And now it's too late."

Arabella leaned forward, her dark eyes intent. "It is never too late. Everyone, red or white, wants to know this thing. Who they are. If you are Ute, make peace with yourself, then worry no more."

Sara nodded thoughtfully. "Knowing you has changed my thoughts in many ways. Thank you, Arabella."

They laughed then and talked of other things. Sara was fascinated by Arabella's superstitions and her use of nature for remedies to illness. While Sara had conquered morning sickness, she was often bothered by an upset stomach. Arabella browned flour in a frying pan, added water and gave it to her. Afterwards, she felt better. If Sara worried about Eric and awoke with a headache, Arabella would slice potatoes and soak them in vinegar and press them to Sara's forehead. The headache went away. And Arabella's persistent toothaches were alleviated with a thumbful of tobacco packed around the decaying tooth. Once, when Arabella had a sore throat, she used a remedy on herself called *sat ma que*. She swabbed her throat with baking powder, which bubbled and loosened the infection.

These remedies fascinated Sara, and she began to see that the Utes were ingenious about dealing with illness. When Sara thought of the birth of her baby, she was relieved to have Arabella with her. If the baby became ill, she was certain Arabella would have the right remedy. Her body ripened with motherhood; her breasts grew full above the mound of her growing belly. And when the baby began to kick and roll about in her stomach, tears of joy filled her eyes, for it was a living symbol of the deep love she and Eric had shared.

One hot August afternoon, Sara grew restless with the apartment; even the small yard outside her door, where she often sat on a quilt, staring up at the lofty mountains, bored her. On this afternoon, Arabella had been nursing one of her toothaches, and Sara had walked to the market alone. As she glanced at the sun, already casting red fingers across the western horizon, she began to wish she had not waited so long to leave. An uneasiness crept over her, even though she knew she had not enough time before dark to stop in at the mercantile, then go on to the market for supplies.

Day was giving way to evening, and ragged men, some glassy-eyed, lounged in doorways or on street corners. The number of saloons had doubled since the influx of miners, and now the saloon business was the liveliest and healthiest in town. Her steps quickened as she passed a bat-wing door leading into a saloon, from which the tinkling of a piano and hoarse laughter drifted to the streets. In her pocket was the pistol Eric had given her. By habit, she kept it with her, though she had never had an occasion to use it.

She averted her eyes to the dirt street, carefully negotiating her way over a buckled plank in the sidewalk. She decided to skip the mercantile and merely get the necessities from the market and hurry home. But halfway back, as she passed the last saloon, she felt a pair of eyes following her and she cast a quick glance to see who was staring.

Her eyes widened and locked on a tall, straggly man with narrow-set gray eyes. She remembered the eyes and placed the man immediately. Her breath caught in her throat and she considered making a dash back to see the Sheriff, but it was already too late. He came swaggering toward her, and the scent of whiskey and tobacco reached her nostrils. She lifted her skirts and turned her eyes straight ahead, pretending not to see him as she hurried on.

Heavy booted steps pounded in he ears as he fell into step behind her. She glanced around and saw that she had left behind the shops and people; now there was only the dusty road leading to the house where she lived. Her eyes darted toward two strange men lounging at the horse trough. Would they help her, or were they likely to side with him? *What could she do?* Did she dare go on, and thus lead him right to her apartment? No. She stopped walking and turned to face him, summoning all of her courage.

He drew up a few feet behind her, watching her with a repulsive snarl to his lips.

"What do you want?" she asked bluntly.

His eyes crept down her body, lingering insolently on her protruding stomach. "Maybe just that money you was going to spend in town," he said.

"Have you already spent the money you stole from us?" she asked coldly. "You were luckier than your friend, you know. *You* got away!"

Sara's anger made her careless, but she was not afraid of him. He would not rob or rape her here on the street with two men watching. Her eyes flew back to the men at the horse trough, but she saw they were mounting their horses, ignoring the conversation.

He closed the distance between them, seizing her wrist and twisting hard. "What're you talkin' about?"

"Let go of me or I'll start screaming!" she threatened, glancing around her. "Maybe I'll yell for the Sheriff and tell him the man who robbed us is still here in Colorado City!"

"Just walk," he muttered under his breath, and she felt something sharp piercing her ribs.

Her eyes flew to his hands and she caught the glint of metal in the fading sunlight. His left hand still gripped her wrist, but his right held a knife.

She glared at him. "Do you think I'll do what you say when all I have to do is scream for help?"

The gray eyes bored into her face. "I think you're smarter'n that! By the time that first scream comes outa your throat, this here knife will be deep in your ribs. I've killed before, I can kill again, if it means savin' my own neck. Don't be a fool!"

Her heart began to jerk. The truth of his words lay in the cold, hard eyes and contemptible snarl of his lips. He was right; if she screamed he would probably kill her. But then, he might kill her anyway. She took a deep breath, trying to conceal her growing fear.

"All right, what do you want?" she snapped.

"Jest walk, I said."

"If it's money you want, I'll give it to you. Just let go of my arm."

"*Walk.*"

She cursed her foolishness now. Of all the places he might have accosted her, this was the one area that would be to his advantage. Here the road was rough and steep; no one had built a cabin or shop in this rocky stretch.

"Where do you live?" he demanded, pressing the kife blade near her ribs. She kept hoping they would meet someone who would see the knife he had concealed under his arm, but there was no one in sight.

"I'm staying with a respectable family here," she snapped, hating his unclean smell and the leering expression on his face. His clothes were torn and ragged, his flannel shirt was faded and colorless, his trousers patched. "You can't bully your way into their house."

"You mean you ain't livin' with your husband no more?"

Her breath caught in her throat, and again she cursed her stupidity as she struggled for an answer. "Of course I am. And he won't be as easy on you this time," she said, glaring at him.

He stopped walking and stood swaggering over her. The dust of the street filled her nostrils and she sneezed. For once, she was grateful for the dust, and she lifted her hand to her face, faking another sneeze. "My handkerchief," she said, jerking her arm loose.

She knew she would have to react with lightning speed, but she was prepared to do so. He had stepped back to watch her curiously, the knife still concealed.

As soon as she reached into her pocket, her hand closed over the gun, her finger curling around the trigger. Her eyes never left his watchful face as she slowly withdrew her hand and aimed the gun. He lunged at her and she fired, scoring a wide red circle in his chest.

His face contorted in shock, then pain, and finally death as he fell backward.

She stood frozen in her tracks as a crowd began to gather. With amazing speed, the Sheriff arrived, took one look at the dead man sprawled in the dust with his knife nearby, then placed a gentle hand on her arm.

"You all right, ma'am?"

She nodded slowly, then turned to look at the Sheriff. He was a middle-aged man whose deep-set blue eyes had investigated more shoot-outs than he cared to remember. This one would be quickly resolved, however.

"I . . . I'm Sara Christensen," she said, her voice weak, yet controlled. "Eric Christensen is my husband."

"Yes'm. I know Eric. Gone South to check on his family, hasn't he?"

She nodded, glancing back at the man on the ground. "This was the man he told you about, the one who came to our cabin and robbed us. Just now he saw me walking home . . . and tried . . ."

"Save your breath, Mrs. Christensen. It's plain to see you were only defending yourself."

The Sheriff took her home, and Arabella threw her arms around her when she heard what had happened. Sara thought she had managed the crisis remarkably well until she sat down on her bed and began to tremble. Then, in spite of Arabella's comforting words and soothing teas, she trembled and cried throughout the night. Finally, as dawn sifted its feeble light through the bedroom window, she lapsed into the deep sleep of exhaustion.

20

Again, Eric tried to push Sara from his tormented mind as he rode doggedly through the stormy spring night. He'd never known it was possible to miss one human being so much that it added another physical ache to his exhausted body. And yet it had been thoughts of Sara that kept him from obeying the compelling urge to join with the Confederate troops in Missouri. One look at the gaunt faces and disease-ridden bodies of those men had shot guilt so deep in his gut that he could only lower his head in shame.

He blinked his sleepy eyes and squinted into the dark night. There was only a pale quarter moon for light, and now that moon was obscured by wind-driven clouds. He blinked again, and something scratched against his eyeball, a particle of dust from the Kentucky backroads, which were a dense tangle of briars and vines. His right cheek bore the slash of a sharp branch, and his clothes were clotted with debris and broken vines. Still, he preferred this to the gunfire of Yankee troops, or even of his own army. Every day men out of uniform were being shot from their saddles as deserters. Neither army could bear the sight of a deserter, or even a strong, able-bodied man not fighting, not impassioned with this war fever that bordered on insanity. He sighed. Once he made it to Pine Hill, satisfied himself of his mother's welfare and the safety of the plantation, he'd take up arms. He could never live with himself otherwise.

He shifted in the saddle, and his worn pants and shirt, washed in creek water, scratched stiffly against his sore body. He now looked like a deserter, too. His beard, like other men's, was thick and unkempt; his blond hair grew low on his neck beneath his battered felt hat. Twice he'd been forced to fight for his life, once with a Yank in St. Louis and more recently in the woods with a stray Rebel soldier. He'd merely knocked the boy out, then shoved his own strip of jerky in the soldier's thin hand before he rode off. Now his stomach twisted with hunger pains, yet he craved water even more.

A rustle in the dense woods behind him turned him in the saddle. He saw the crack of fire a second before the pain tore sharply through his side. He reacted purely from instinct since there was no time for logic. Toppling from his saddle, he lay face down on the hard, rough ground. Still and silent, his hand under his chest, he allowed his fingers to inch toward the Le Mat revolver tucked in his waistband.

In total darkness, the assailant watching him had the advantage. There was no point in firing blind, Eric told himself; he'd merely be wasting his few precious bullets.

He kept his breath sucked in so there would be no movement along his rib cage. The mould of decayed leaves and rain-soaked earth reeked in his nostrils, along with the sweat of his horse, nervously stamping the ground just behind him. At last he heard the cautious approach of footsteps. His hand tightened over the Le Mat as he waited, his chest nearly bursting from his indrawn breath.

The steps ceased. He heard the creak of a saddle. Flinging himself over, he fired, but in his care not to hit his horse, he'd fired over the thief's head. And now the horse was being whipped into speed, and the rider was disappearing into darkness. Grimacing at the pain that shot through his side, Eric leapt to his feet, took careful aim, and fired in the direction of the disappearing rider. But the dense woods had swallowed up the thief *and* Eric's horse, his second mount since reaching St. Louis.

Cursing his luck, he kicked angrily at the ground as the hopelessness of his predicament struck him. He was wounded, on foot, with no help and no real sense of direction. He staggered onto the road, hoping the clouds would slip away from the moon so he could see how badly he was wounded. Gently, he probed his side as warm blood rushed over his hand. The bullet had penetrated just below the rib cage, which he supposed was better than an inch higher or lower.

He yanked the ragged shirt from his back and ripped it up as best he could, then bound himself tightly, hoping to check the flow of blood. Without the knife in his saddlebag, or any object with which to remove the bullet, he had few alternatives. If he could slow the bleeding, maybe he could get to a farmhouse. As he turned to plod slowly down the muddy road, he now welcomed the memory of Sara, for it gave him the strength and courage to keep on moving.

Sara! Oh God, what would happen to her? And to their child? For the first time since he left, he doubted the wisdom of his long journey. He had underestimated the difficulty of escaping not only the soldiers, but worse, the deserters and thieves who prowled the night for money, guns, and horses.

The night grew darker—or was he about to faint? He squinted through the deep woods on both sides of the road, his ears strained for the beat of horse's hooves. Suddenly, an acrid smell floated through the trees, wafting beneath his nostrils, already filled with thick breath from his tightly squeezed chest.

He cocked his head and sniffed again. Smoke! Had the Yanks burned a farmhouse, or was he getting the drift of a campfire? He stopped walking and turned his head from right to left, trying to identify the direction of the smoke. His senses drew him to the right, to the depths of the woods bordering the road. He had no idea how far he'd have to stumble to locate the source of the smoke or who might be at the campfire. It could even be the man who'd shot him and stolen his horse! But he had no choice. He'd bleed to death if he didn't get help. At least he'd die making an effort, rather than slumping down in the darkness and relinquishing himself to a coward's death. The thought of Sara drove him.

He stumbled through the woods, his body moving by sheer determination as his mind drifted in and out of consciousness. More than once he fell, and when he did, the temptation to lie there was almost overpowering. But then Sara's sweet face would fill his mind again, and somehow he'd find the strength to push on.

The sticky blood filled his shirt bandage, and the whirling dizziness in his brain was worse than the darkness and the vine-tangled path. He caught sight of a tiny patch of orange through the darkness and plunged on, finally coming upon a small circle of men seated around a fire. He would be either Yank or Rebel, whichever role was required. To his relief, the men wore gray uniforms. He made no effort to silence his thudding steps as two soldiers bolted to their feet, their rifles drawn.

"Don't shoot!" he gasped. "I'm a Rebel."

He had taken only a few more steps when the curious faces faded from his vision, along with the glowing fire that promised warmth and perhaps food. The muddy ground sucked him up as he crashed forward, the blood gushing from the crude bandage.

A sharp pain seared his side, a rotating pain that cut off his breath. His matted eyes dragged open, and he was looking into a lantern, then a bearded face above it.

"Lie still," the man commanded in a Southern drawl. "Jim's diggin' the bullet outa your side. It may hurt a mite, but if he doesn't get it out, you're gonna die."

"Thanks," Eric rasped, unable to say more. He gritted his teeth as the sharp gouging continued. He hadn't the strength to tell them about himself, to convince them he wasn't a deserter or a spy, but someone worth saving. All he could show them was courage, and he ground his teeth into his lower lip, determined to do that. As the man said, he might die anyway; he might as well die with dignity.

He opened his eyes again and concentrated on the face above him. Bold blue eyes above a dark beard showed keen intelligence. Eric sensed the man was not a private soldier, though he couldn't see the chevrons on his uniform. Dark brows slanted over his eyes and the black hair beneath his Rebel cap was thick and curly.

Eric sighed and closed his eyes. He had no choice but to trust them.

A pleasant smell penetrated his deep sleep and he lay motionless. It occurred to him there was no pain now, and for a moment he lay reveling in the freedom from that pain. A breeze rustling the oaks picked up the drifting aroma and automatically his mouth watered.

Slowly, he opened his eyes to a thin gray light. Dawn. In the distance, he could hear low voices, whispers. Again his stomach twisted with the pain of hunger, and he now understood why starving men ate whatever they could lay hands on.

He pushed himself up on his left elbow, but the right side resisted, and he felt the stabbing pain again. His eyes dropped to his bare chest beneath the frayed blanket and he saw a neat row of bandages covering his body.

He lifted his head and squinted at eight men seated around a morning fire. With surprise he noted the men were no longer wearing gray uniforms. Had he merely imagined that last night with his vision blurred and his mind desperate? They were dressed in old clothes, similar to the ones he wore. Suspicion and doubt warred within him, until he remembered they had saved his life. Whoever they were, they were his only friends right now.

"Mornin'," he called weakly.

The men whirled at the sound of his voice, and the blue-eyed man got to his feet. He was not a tall man, nor was he muscled, but he moved with the agility of a forest animal, bounding quickly to Eric's side.

"We were wonderin' last night if you'd ever see daylight again. Who are you, and what happened?"

"Eric Christensen," he replied. "I've been in Colorado Territory for the past five years. I'd started back to Georgia to Pine Hill, our plantation." His voice was so weak he doubted that he sounded convincing. "I intended to join the Confederate Army as soon as I checked on my family."

A muscle twitched beneath the man's thick

beard and his blue eyes were now as cold as frozen seas. "You waited a long time to come home, mister."

Eric nodded. "I was one of the fifty-niners. Bought a place out in the Territory. Married. Never thought of coming South again, but after hearing stories of the war, I had to come back. . . ."

"Well, I tell you what. . . ." The man stroked his head thoughtfully. "If you live, and I think you will, you can forget goin' South for a while. I doubt you'd get far alone. And as for joinin' the Confederates, you've just been drafted. I'm Captain Thomas Hines of the Ninth Kentucky. If you want to serve your country, you can start right now. We need you *here* to push the damned Feds back."

When Eric considered his circumstances, he knew he had no choice. Not just his pride and dignity were at stake—his life might hang in balance as well.

He'd already heard too many stories about deserters being shot by their own men, and while Captain Hines' tone was deceptively soft, Eric had seen the cold look in his eyes when Eric admitted he was not yet a member of the Confederate Army. Eric knew he couldn't just get on his horse and ride off. And then he remembered—he had no horse!

"All right. I'll join up with your men. I'm a good shot, I just got ambushed in the dark."

"We'll see how good you are, *Private* Christensen," Hines added, with a wry twist of his lips.

Eric would learn, in time, the reason the

men changed clothes as regularly as a company of traveling actors. They were a select group of General Morgan's men, or Rebel Raiders, as they were known throughout Kentucky. Morgan had been a skilled cavalryman, but he excelled in more than cavalry tactics. He was a master at conspiracy, a trait that seemed to distinguish the magnetic Hines, as well.

As Eric healed, he tended the horses, kept a good campfire and cooked for the foraging men. While he'd joked with Sara that he couldn't boil water, he quickly learned to prepare the thin, watered-down broth composed of whatever could be killed or foraged along the way. As soon as he could ride, he joined the Raiders in destroying Federal stock, burning bridges, and destroying railroad tracks to slow down the advancing Union troops.

Eric admired the courage and dedication of Morgan's troops, but he didn't agree with some of their tactics. When he complained, Hines snapped that this war had to be ended at any cost.

Morgan increased his raids, scattering Union troops and lifting Confederate morale. Hines followed suit. Throughout the freezing winter, Hines drove his men on, taunting them when they slid, exhausted, from their saddles into the snow, begging for a brief rest.

The pounds fell from Eric's already lean frame, until he was a gaunt shadow in the gray winter light. He wrote faithfully to Sara, though his doubts that the letters would ever reach her were well-founded. He had forgotten the luxury of a full stomach, or a peaceful night's sleep, or the beauty of a landscape unmarred by battle trenches and unstained with blood.

"Glad we saved you," Hines drawled one morning when Eric was the first to bolt from his bedroll into the frozen dawn and saddle his horse. "You've become one of my best troopers."

Eric forced a grim thanks but responded no further. He rarely talked now, conserving his energy for the battles they faced daily. He was determined to survive and return to Sara and the baby.

The miserable winter finally gave way to spring and the raids became even more ruthless as a lost war closed in upon Hines and Morgan. Eric grew resentful, bitterly wishing he were fighting with the Home Guard in Georgia, or battling with Lee in Virginia. He disliked the looting and burning that often seemed unnecessary to him.

Hines' troops pressed into Ohio and fought bravely until the hot July day at Buffington Island when they were finally captured. Eric, ill with fatigue and exhaustion, felt only a numb relief when his part in the raids ended.

The relief was short lived, however, when the Confederate prisoners were loaded onto boats for a three-day journey to the prison at Cincinnati. As Eric huddled among the jostling bodies, the dull fog of exhaustion cleared from his mind, and the truth of his circumstances hit him with sickening clarity.

His chances of reaching Pine Hill had been slim before; now they appeared impossible.

His group was met by jeering mobs in Cincinnati who hurled rocks, spat at them and shouted taunts of "Hant them . . . hang them . . ." A guard shoved him into an overcrowded cell, and in the privacy of the midnight darkness, Eric wept bitter tears. He had come back to fight for Georgia, to save Pine Hill, to care for his mother. He had done none of that, and despite the hard months he had served in Hines' regiment, he believed he had failed in his mission.

Eric's spirit was too strong for defeat, however; in a few days he was prowling his narrow cell, seeking a means of escape. He paced and thought, his eyes focused blankly on the iron bed and straw bedtick. The prisoners were confined to their cells, except for meals. Twice a day they were marched to the horse trough to wash, then they were taken to the jammed dining hall where "Morgan's horse thieves" were separated from the rest of the group. Although they were not permitted to talk with each other, some of the men used their utensils to communicate, carving words in the food. The message Eric read in Hines' mashed potatoes brought hope rushing back to his heart. Hines had devised a means of escape—a tunnel to be dug under the dirt floor of the cell next to Eric.

Eric knew it would take patience, determination, and a reckless disregard of the consequences to attempt this escape. But those were the very qualities that had taken him from Georgia to Colorado, held him in freezing water to his waist, and kept him loving Sara with all of his heart, when the chance of ever seeing her again appeared hopeless.

He moved his head in a cautious nod and Hines grinned. Eric knew he would do whatever it took to escape. He would still go to Pine Hill, he would fight again in the war . . . and someday he would be with Sara and their baby. Nothing would stop him.

21

While war raged in the South, the Colorado Territory was torn with conflict between Indians, settlers and outlaws. Several thousand men had left to enlist in the army, while Civil War deserters and refugees flooded into the territory. It was a poor exchange, for the mines and gold mills fell to skeleton crews, while stealing and shoot-outs became commonplace in the streets of Pueblo, Colorado City and Denver.

Out on the plains, the situation grew worse. The Cheyenne and Arapahoe attacked stages, freight trains, mail coaches and outlying ranches. Cattle and horses were seized, and innocent people killed. This incensed the settlers against all Indians and endangered the Utes even more. Now they had to be on guard against an ambush from white men as well as Cheyennes and Arapahoes.

Wild Eagle and Wasatch had taken their small band of Utes to Bear Claw's village in the spring and the journey, this time, had been treacherous. Their party had been fired upon by men, who, fortunately were poor marksmen. Wild Eagle and Wasatch had drawn their weapons and taken aim, but the men quickly fled behind the high red rocks, disappearing into the mountains. The incident reminded them of the constant danger their tribe faced. They decided to remain at Bear Claw's village until some of the unrest between whites and Indians was settled. There was strength in numbers and their tribe had grown smaller each year. Now only a dozen or so remained, and they knew they were safer with Bear Claw and his warriors.

Wild Eagle sat in the lodge, smoking his pipe and staring into the warm fire. He was as skilled as ever with his rifle, and even, after much practice, with the tomahawk; but he found that his heart had softened. He turned and glanced at his young son, whose features so closely bore the stamp of his own, and his heart filled with pride. His eyes moved lovingly to Star as she tucked the blanket around their sleeping baby. He knew happiness and peace, despite the war cloud hanging over their lodge, threatening to burst and rain trouble upon them.

He sighed. Bear Claw had said there would be no more fighting. Consequently, Wasatch sulked most of the time. The thirst for battle ran deep in Wasatch's blood. Wild Eagle believed it was because Wasatch knew only hate and vengeance, and that the love of a good squaw would change his saddened heart.

He laid down his pipe and looked at Star, reflecting on how she and the baby had changed him.

"When will we have another son?" he

asked, his eyes roaming over her slim body, clad in soft doeskin.

"*Another?*" she whirled in surprise. "Little Shane is not yet one winter."

"But he needs a brother," Wild Eagle teased, pulling her down to the blanket and wrapping his arms around her.

"Eagle," Star sighed, snuggling against him, "there is so much war now. Life is uncertain . . ."

"But in our lodge there is only love."

His mouth seized hers, his tongue probing deeper and deeper, until she moaned beneath him, quickly catching the fire of passion that burned through his loins. His strong hands pushed her dress back and grasped her muscled thighs, slim yet firm. She wore no undergarments and his eyes dropped to her nudeness while her legs entwined around his waist. He had intended to be gentle with her, to tell her how much he loved her, how much her love had meant to him, and the many ways she had made him tame when he might have been as wild as the grizzly.

But now he was on fire for her, unable to slow himself down or take time and patience. He flicked his loin cloth aside and lifted her to him.

He was insatiable at first, kneading her flesh, thrusting himself deeper and deeper into her soft womb as his breath grew as ragged as wind in a snow storm. The heat that had ignited in his loins spread through his entire being, consuming his body, his mind, his soul.

The heat burst into flames that sent sparks into the very core of his being as he moaned her name and gripped her to him.

Her legs tightened around his waist, her arms wrapped around his shoulders as she pulled herself upright against him. Again, he moaned as their bodies clenched, drawing the last burning seed from his body.

His eyes drifted open and he stared with wonder into the small loving face below him. His mouth was too dry to speak, and even if he could, the words would not come.

Gently, he unwound her legs and lifted her small body onto the blanket. He dipped his lips to hers, nipping gently at her cheeks, her ear lobes, her neck. Her hands swept up to heave her dress over her head and toss it into a darkened corner.

His eyes devoured her smooth tan skin as his lips trailed down the small globes of her breast. Her nipple swelled in his mouth as he took in more of her breast. Her breast was small yet firm after the birth of his son, and he could contain most of it in his mouth. He sucked gently, as gently as a baby, until the nipple hardened even more and she began to moan.

His hand cupped her belly, kneading the skin and torturing her sensitive places until she began to whimper. Her legs stiffened beneath his, and he knew she wanted him now.

He slipped into her, moving gently at first as he watched her face. Her eyes grew drowsy as her arms circled his neck, pulling his mouth to hers.

Their mouths joined and the rhythm of their bodies increased until she was crying out with joy as he continued to please her. Then again he was swept up in a fever of passion that shook ever fiber of his being.

Slowly, their passion subsided and he sank against her, weak yet thoroughly satisfied.

"Eagle," she sighed, "that papoose you wish for is now in my womb. There can be no doubt. . . ."

Later, as Star was dozing in his arms, Wild Eagle lay wide awake, staring at the smoke curling through the smoke hole overhead. His heart was filled with peace and joy as he thought of his future with Star and little Shane and—he grinned to himself—another papoose, maybe. He wanted to give them a good life, a better life than the one he'd had. He'd heard people were farming the land in the San Luis valley. He thought of the vast plains of South Park, dappled with cloud shadow. Why couldn't this flat land be put to use farming? He had to find a dependable means of acquiring the necessities for his family. The Indian way of life was changing; he could no longer depend on hunting, trapping and trading. The white man was raping the land of game. He was a good hunter, better than most, but he needed something more to do.

Buckskin Joe's lay west of their camp, in the mountains. Life was more peaceful there. The rugged Ute trail into the mountains had served as a barrier. There were occasional battles when the Cheyenne and Arapahoe ranged wide in their search for food, but generally the valley was peaceful.

His dark eyes lit with new hope. It would be good to grow things in the soil, to work with his hands, to plant and harvest vegetables, then fish and hunt for meat.

The stamp of horse's hooves interrupted Eagle's thoughts and he gently removed Star's arm from across his chest. He threw on his loincloth and moccasins and tiptoed to the flap to peer outside.

The braves stood around the campfire outside Bear Claw's lodge, staring at approaching riders. Wild Eagle hurried outside.

Rope Thrower and two strange white men were dismounting. Bear Claw lifted his hand in greeting, but Rope Thrower's face held a dark, worried frown. Eagle sensed trouble.

"Bear Claw, I bring bad news for your people," Rope Thrower began, dismissing the offer of a smoke from the pipe. "A family has been murdered and scalped on their ranch, a day's ride from here. The news has spread alarm to Denver and Colorado City, and now"—he shook his head sadly—"it is a bad time for all Indians."

The faces of the braves were impassive as they heard the news. "It is Arapahoe and Cheyenne," Bear Claw said. "My people not murder and scalp now."

Rope Thrower nodded. "We think it is Mad Dog, the Cheyenne who is the Devil himself. The First Cavalry is scouring the country for him, but I came to warn you of two things. First, do not let your people go to town now.

The white people are scared and have taken up arms."

"Against the Yuuttaa, too?" Bear Claw did not raise his voice, but the long jagged star stood rigid against his clenched jaw.

Rope Thrower hesitated, glancing over the sullen group. "The other thing I want to warn you about is Mad Dog and his warriors. They'll murder just for a meal! And now they need food and fresh horses, bein' on the run."

"We will watch." Bear Claw nodded solemnly as Rope Thrower turned and bounded back to his horse.

Wild Eagle turned to Bear Claw. "Do you know this Mad Dog?"

Bear Claw jerked his head in an angry nod. "His heart is as black as the Misho-tunga. And now our people are cursed because of Mad Dog!" his brown lips twisted bitterly as he spat the name.

"What can we do?"

"We can fight!" Wasatch shouted, striding forward. "We can kill Mad Dog and his warriors who bring shame to our tribe."

Bear Claw's black eyes swung to Wasatch, as his wrinkled brow furrowed in contemplation. "It is not for us to settle what is between Mad Dog and the white man. But if he comes near us"—Bear Claw's brawny hand curled into a fist that slammed against his chest—"we fight to the death!"

To the death . . .

The words echoed into the darkness, adding a chill to the winter night.

"I'll stand guard," Wild Eagle offered. "The

rest can sleep."

"I will stand guard with you," Wasatch said, stepping to Eagle's side.

Bear Claw nodded, his arm swinging through the darkness to dismiss the other braves.

After the village had settled into sleep, and only the crackle of the low fire and the drifting snores of some of the braves filled the silence, Wasatch reached over and gripped Eagle's shoulder.

"We fight to the end," he repeated.

Eagle frowned. "Only if we must. And *then* we fight to the end."

They sat staring into the fire, their thoughts drifting back to the battle a year before when Shavano was killed. There had been two other skirmishes since then with marauding bands of Cheyenne and Arapahoe, but the knowledge that Shavano's killer ran free still haunted Wasatch.

The hours slipped by and they took turns dozing, their heads resting on their chests. It was a cold, windy night, though not cold enough to turn the falling moisture to snow. The rain began to drizzle over them, spattering into the campfire.

Eagle slipped back inside the lodge for a blanket to shield them from the falling rain. They hovered under its warmth until the rain began to soak through, and Wasatch was contemplating returning for a heavy robe.

Suddenly a horse whinnied from the corral, then another. They tossed back the blanket, grabbed their weapons and crept toward the end lodge for a clear view of the corral.

The pole corral had been built a hundred yards from the lodges, but even through the darkness and distance, Eagle sensed the tension of the animals.

"Something has spooked them," he whispered.

White Feather lived in the end lodge, and upon hearing them, he slipped outside.

"There may be someone at the corral," Eagle explained to him. White Feather was a strong brave of thirty winters, one of Bear Claw's best warriors. He rushed back for his weapons.

Wasatch and Eagle stared through the gray curtain of rain. As their eyes adjusted to the darkness, Eagle watched his pinto. The horse was sensitive to anything out of the ordinary, and now he tossed his head and whinnied again.

White Feather had joined them again, and now the three braves flattened themselves against the cold ground and began to crawl through the meadow.

The wind had picked up, howling like a wild animal through the trees. Eagle didn't like the feel of this, pursuing an enemy through the darkness and rain.

A sliver of lightning gashed the black sky, and in its brief flash of light, Eagle caught the silhouette of three forms only a few feet from the corral.

"Did you see them?" Wasatch whispered.

"Yes," Eagle answered. "We'll have to split up. You and White Feather take the east side of the corral, I'll take the west. Maybe we can surprise them before they open the gate."

For a moment, Eagle considered summoning the other braves from their lodges, but there was no time. As soon as the men, whoever they were, caught any movement in the village, they would flee into the darkness, and there would be no hope of catching up with them. If it were possible that these three were a part of Mad Dog's tribe, or if Mad Dog himself was with them, they must be captured!

As he drew closer, Eagle could see the forms more clearly. They were Indians. The one in the center was whispering orders to the other two, who sneaked toward the gate.

Eagle stopped crawling and lifted his rifle. It was difficult to sight them through the darkness, but he counted on his skill to judge the target. His finger curled on the trigger, but before he squeezed, he turned his head to be sure of the direction Wasatch and White Feather had taken.

In the next instant Wasatch's arrow sped through the night and embedded itself in the throat of one of the Indians. He made a hoarse wheezing sound before he fell backward, clutching at the arrow.

The other two turned and fled through the woods. Eagle leapt to his feet, aimed and fired, but to his disappointment, neither fell.

Wasatch and White Feather were hovering over the dying man.

"Cheyenne," Wasatch spat. "I've never seen him before."

Eagle leaped the fence and grabbed for his pinto. Wasatch and White Feather followed.

"We can't let them get away," Eagle called as White Feather opened the gate. "I think they're with Mad Dog—look at the way that one's painted."

As they led their horses through the gate, their glances fell on the dead man, painted in hideous stripes with a shriveled scalp dangling from his belt.

They kicked their horses into a full run and tore across the meadow. The two they were pursuing had already reached the dark mass of pines, and Eagle held up his hand to slow down Wasatch and White Feather.

Their eyes scanned the impenetrable black of the woods as the rain continued to fall, matting their hair to their faces.

White Feather glanced over his shoulder. "They've heard the shot at the village. Maybe our people will come to help."

Just then a horse neighed from the depths of the woods, and again they dug their heels into the ribs of their mounts, aware again the men were getting away. As they reached the woods, they came upon an Indian just beyond them, struggling to mount his wet horse.

Wasatch's arrow sailed cleanly into the Indian's back and he dropped.

The sound of hooves beating the earth alerted them to the escaping Indian.

Wasatch spotted him first and pushed his horse to a full run, but then a war hatchet hurtled through the darkness. Eagle heard a deep, wrenching moan and saw Wasatch's back stiffen. They had left the woods and were in open ground now, as the first graying of dawn was slipping over the land.

Eagle caught up with Wasatch and saw, to his horror, that the war hatchet was buried in Wasatch's chest. Before Eagle could catch him, Wasatch toppled to the ground.

Eagle jumped from his horse and fell beside Wasatch. He leaned over him and tried to gently wedge the steel blade from his chest. Even in dawn's feeble light, Eagle could see the massive hole from which Wasatch's lifeblood drained away. Eagle gripped his hand, fighting back the tears.

"I go to the happy hunting ground," Wasatch gasped.

"You go as a warrior," Eagle said, his voice trembling. "You killed two of our enemy tonight."

"It is . . . as planned. . . ." The words ebbed weakly into the night as the hand went limp in Eagle's grasp.

White Feather had caught up and was now kneeling beside Eagle. Both stared in numb shock as Wasatch took his last breath and his lips widened into a faint smile.

The rain washed over them, blending with the tears on Eagle's cheeks. For a moment, the world seemed to spin around Eagle, as the wind and rain beat upon him, and he gave up his best friend, his blood brother.

Then rage burst through him as he whirled and seized the war hatchet, still dripping with Wasatch's blood. Eagle wiped the steel blade on the grass and lifted it high in the air.

"I swear vengeance," he said through clenched teeth. "Mad Dog will die by his own weapon. I *swear it*."

Their horses had returned to their side and stood cropping grass. Eagle stood, glancing toward the distant mountain as he thrust the handle of the war hatchet in his belt and turned to White Feather.

"I know the trail he has taken," he said. "It leads into the high rocks above the soda springs. I'm going after him." His eyes fell sorrowfully to the still form at his feet. "You take Wasatch back to the village."

"We will follow," White Feather called after him as Eagle swung onto his pinto and kneed him into a gallop. As he rode through the tangle of trees, where dawn was sifting through the dimness, Eagle cocked his ear, straining for the faintest sound. The wind had died away, which was good, for now he could hear the breath of the warriors in the stillness. But there were no sounds around him.

His rifle hung in the crook of his arm, and the steel blade of the war hatchet pressed against his side, the weapon that had taken Wasatch's life and would now kill the enemy just ahead.

Eagle glanced at the gray sky, thankful that dawn was breaking. Ahead, the red rocks crouched against the sky, but there were deep crevices and hidden paths where the enemy could hide.

Eagle tried to remind himself that Wasatch had died with a smile on his face, died as a brave warrior as he'd dreamed. But the thought offered little consolation. Eagle's body was on fire with the fever of revenge, and he knew that fever would drive him on and on, until he tracked and killed Wasatch's murderer.

He reached forward to stroke his pinto's neck. "It's a steep hard trail, but we will make it," he whispered. "No horse is better than you at climbing mountain trails."

He straightened and squinted into the foothills, listening intently for loose rocks, moccasined feet on rocky ground, anything to alert him to a man hiding in wait for him. He switched the reins to his left hand, while his right hand hoisted the rifle, ready to get off a quick shot when needed. The cool dampness of daybreak washed over him, and the morning was so still now that his own breathing seemed to be magnified.

His eyes flicked over the red boulders lining the narrow trail as his pinto clawed his way upward. The trail made a sharp turn, and suddenly the pinto stumbled. The next instant a body slammed against Eagle, knocking him from the horse. The rifle clattered down the red rocks, out of reach.

Once his head hit the hard ground, he was again covered with a body; bare brown skin that was hard as gun metal, but moved with the fleetness of a deer. They rolled over and over, and the man's odor filled his nostrils, as Eagle fought to hold onto the body that evaded him, while a fist pummeled his head.

Eagle heaved his strength into his right arm, breaking the iron grip of the man's wrist.

Eagle's fist shot forward, slamming into the face above him. The body toppled backward and Eagle sprang to his feet, drawing the war hatchet from his belt. For a moment, he felt only surprise as he stared at Mad Dog. He was the same height as Eagle, but several pounds thinner. He had dark hair and eyes, but his skin was lighter than usual for a Cheyenne. Like Eagle, he was a half breed—and in the tense moment Eagle looked into his face, he understood the bitterness and hate that had driven this man.

His hesitation brought a cruel grin to Mad Dog's lips, baring teeth that were sharp as fangs, revealing the origin of his name.

Mad Dog's eyes flashed to the war hatchet in Eagle's hand, and he sneered, as though only he had the power to bring death with his hatchet. He crouched low, wrinkling the stripes of war paint on his leathery body that was covered only by a breechcloth. From the scabbard at his side, he withdrew a long knife, its sharp blade glinting against the sun as he tossed it backward in his hand so that he was grasping only the tip.

Eagle froze, scarcely breathing, as he watched Mad Dog's eyes, his face, for the slightest change. He was gambling that there would be at least a flicker in those eyes before he released the knife. Eagle had hoisted the war hatchet, and although Mad Dog was twelve feet away, he was confident his aim would be true. His fear was not of Mad Dog now, but rather of the speed of the knife over the speed of the hatchet. A cold sweat broke over Eagle's forehead, but he did not blink an eye, and his hard gaze never wavered.

As soon as Mad Dog's black eyes widened and his lips parted, Eagle let go of the hatchet. Both weapons sailed through the air, but because Eagle's reaction was quicker, Mad Dog's knife merely sliced Eagle's shoulder, while the hatchet buried deeply in Mad Dog's chest. Eagle gripped his bleeding shoulder as Mad Dog stumbled backward, shock frozen on his face before he toppled from the ledge. There was no cry of terror to rent the still air; even in his death, Mad Dog's pride kept him silent.

Eagle took a cautious step toward the edge of the cliff, as his eyes sought and found the still body of Mad Dog, broken against the jagged rocks far below.

Eagle closed his eyes, sickened by the waste of so many lives. But he had avenged Wasatch's death, and now he breathed a relieved sigh. He opened his eyes and looked down at the knife blade lodged in his shoulder. He gritted his teeth and tried to remove the blade as gently as possible, but the blade tore more flesh and sinew as Eagle drew it out.

Eagle leaned down to wipe his scarlet blood from the blade, then inserted it in his scabbard. As he did so, his eyes fell on something at his feet and he hesitated. The head of an eagle had been carved into a round piece of silver, and the sight of the eagle brought a strange feeling to him.

He reached down and lifted the medallion

strung on a thin strip of lariat. He turned it over in his hand and found it still warm from Mad Dog's skin. He remembered that it had gleamed at Mad Dog's wrist when he flashed his knife. An eagle, like his name. He chose to think of this as a good omen, for it had fallen from Mad Dog's wrist and landed at Eagle's feet in the scuffle. He placed it on his wrist, and for a moment he seemed to feel new power surging through his body. But the wound began to throb deeply now, so he climbed the rocks and searched wearily for his pinto.

Wasatch's death had been avenged, but a heavy gloom hung over the village as Star dressed Eagle's wound and he rested in his lodge. There had been so much suffering and death, and the sadness was like a curse on Bear Claw's tribe.

On the third day, Bear Claw came to Eagle's lodge. "I had a vision from the Great Spirit," he said. "You must go to the palefaces in their town. You must tell them the devil warrior has met his death at your hands."

Eagle frowned, dreading to return to Colorado City.

Bear Claw's flowing robe brushed the dirt of the lodge as he stepped forward and rested a gnarled brown hand on Eagle's shoulder.

"Our people must be free of his shadow so that no more blood is shed."

Eagle looked from Bear Claw to Star, whose dark eyes seemed to reflect Eagle's doubts. He felt an ill omen at the thought of returning to the town of palefaces, yet Bear Claw's words were true. As long as the palefaces feared Mad Dog, their weapons would be raised against all tribes.

"All right," Eagle agreed. "I will go with the morning sun."

As Eagle prepared to leave the next day, Star flew into his arms, burying her sobs against his chest.

Eagle held her close, touching the dark, gleaming head. "The curse upon us has ended. Do not cry," he whispered to her.

He could feel the soft mound of her belly through the doeskin dress, pressing gently against him, and his thoughts were tender for the papoose growing inside of her. Star had grieved deeply for Wasatch, and now Eagle knew she was in constant fear for his life as well.

"The palefaces will not harm me." His hand cupped her chin, tilting her tear-streaked face back as he lowered his mouth to claim her lips. "Do not worry," he repeated softly. "The Great Spirit gave me power over Mad Dog. I now wear his lucky charm." He lifted his wrist, and the silver eagle gleamed. "Surely the Great Spirit rides with me now."

Star nodded, yet she continued to cling to him as though she could not bear to let go. Then, slowly, she unwound her arms from his waist and stepped back.

"Please be careful, my Wild Eagle," she said, smiling through her tears.

"I will be careful"—he grinned—"and I will expect a good rabbit stew upon my return."

He opened the flap and stepped out into the crisp morning. A young brave handed him the reins to his pinto, already saddled and waiting, and he swung astride.

All the eyes of the village followed him, a look of pride and admiration on their faces, as Eagle rode out of the village.

22

"Take care of her while I'm shopping, Arabella."

Sara leaned down to kiss her daughter's rosy cheek. Her new baby was her entire world now, and she loved her so dearly that it almost brought a pain to her heart.

She had named her Elsie Marie, after her adopted mother, but she chose to call her Marie. For a moment, Sara lingered over the cradle, gazing affectionately at the baby's oval face, a tiny replica of her own. Sara's expression turned wistful as she looked at little Marie. She had hoped and prayed the baby would resemble her father; instead, the hair and eyes were as dark as Sara's, and the skin was only a shade lighter.

Sara lifted a finger to gently trace the delicate little nose and rosebud mouth. It had been months since she'd heard from Eric, and though she fought to keep her spirits up, doubt gnawed at her constantly. She was beginning to wonder if Marie was all she'd ever have of Eric. The thought brought tears to her eyes.

Footsteps shuffled behind her, and Sara straightened from the cradle, wiping the tears from her eyes. She sniffed, hiding her face from Arabella, who had been so brave during Rex's absence. The two women tried to support each other with smiles, cheerful countenances, and conversations filled with hope rather than despair. At times it was difficult.

"You not want to go alone?" Arabella asked, as Sara continued to dawdle.

"Oh no, that isn't it," Sara said, trailing her fingers over the baby's silky hair and giving Arabella a confident smile. "I'm not afraid to go alone."

The two rarely spoke of the day when Sara had been forced to shoot down the man who had stolen from them and would have killed her. She had trembled for days afterward, but as the baby grew within her, her thoughts shifted to preparing for its arrival. She and Arabella had weaved a basket cradle, knitted blankets and designed baby clothes. The birth had come two weeks early and had been surprisingly easy for Sara and for Arabella, who had proven a skilled midwife.

"I could go with you," Arabella offered.

"No. We've already imposed on Mrs. Freeman to sit with Marie twice now. I'll be fine."

She pulled her woolen cape tightly around her and hurried out the door before Arabella could see the apprehension creeping over her face. As the cold wind struck her, she shivered into her cape and stepped quickly along the cleared walk. A week of heavy snow had been followed by a week of sunshine, which had melted most of the snow.

The crisp air was a pleasant caress on her face, and Sara felt a sense of pride that she'd been able to put behind her some of the unpleasantness and go on. She missed Eric desperately, but she'd found a strength within herself that had infinitely surprised her. Throughout her pregnancy Arabella had hovered over her like a mother hen, and Sara had allowed it, feeling it was probably good for both of them. It made her think of the days when Elsie was rearing her, when she'd smothered her with protection.

As she thought of Elsie, her eyes deepened with sadness. How proud her mother would have been to hold Marie, to boss everyone about her care. . . . But there was no point in thinking of that now.

How strange life is, Sara thought. How very strange. Her life had been filled with twists and turns the past three years. It seemed that her dreams kept being snatched from her, just as her loved ones had been.

She lifted her eyes to the distant, snow-ringed mountains. She thought of their cabin up in the mountains and wondered if the people who had bought it were happy there. She felt a twinge of nostalgia for the cabin and those mountains where she and Eric had spent to many happy days.

Oh God, take care of him, she silently begged. He'd been gone for almost a year. It had been months since she'd heard from him. She'd sent two telegrams to the small town near Pine Hill in the beginning, but there had never been a response. She'd written a dozen letters that were never answered. The mail was not getting through due to the war; she knew that, but still she wrote and hoped.

Will he come back? she wondered desperately. She forced herself not to ponder the answer to that question as she glanced ahead to the street corner where several men had gathered. With her hood drawn low on her forehead, her beauty was half-concealed, yet several hungry eyes followed her.

She turned into the door of the mercantile, relishing the warm gust of air that greeted her as she opened the door. As usual, the mercantile was crowded, although there was not as much buying now that freight and food-supply lines were being raided out on the plains, sending prices sky-high.

She gathered up a few items, quickly paid for them and hurried out of the market. She glanced down the street to the stable where Eric's horse was boarded. They'd sold her mare because she was getting old, but Eric could not bring himself to sell Darkfire, and she had insisted on boarding him here where she could occasionally see him.

As she headed toward the stable, she could see through the cracked doors that several men loitered about inside. She hesitated.

"Mrs. Christensen!" Bull spotted her and hurried to the door. "Come on in," he insisted, then lowered his voice. "These men are all respectable. No need to be nervous."

At those words, she averted her eyes, embarrassingly aware that everyone in town knew of her encounter with the thief. She swept past the men to the back stall where Darkfire was kept. His head was lowered as he chomped idly on some grain.

An affectionate smile touched her lips as she looked at the horse that was so dear to Eric. She clucked to him and extended her hand. He had obviously been cared for because his coat gleamed like black satin, and the blaze on his foot was a clean, pure white.

She began to stroke his neck. "If only I had a place to keep you," she whispered. It seemed so unfair to confine him to a stall when he had spent such a free life. As he turned his head and fixed pleading, brown velvet eyes upon her, her heart ached for him. She decided she simply must find a good owner for him if Eric hadn't returned by warm weather. Bull had promised to exercise him, but Sara could see that he was too busy to do that often.

She sighed and dropped her hand, her eyes still fixed worriedly on Darkfire. Eric wouldn't want him to remain caged like this. Troubled, she turned and walked out of the stable, her head lowered.

The clomp of horse's hooves brought a half-hearted glance from her. Then her eyes widened as though seeing someone she recognized. She was sure she'd never seen the Indian riding into town, yet as he glanced her way, there was something about his face that seemed familiar.

He rode a sturdy pinto, and the man's hair was long and black, secured at his neck with a strip of rawhide. He was not a tall man, but he was heavily muscled. He wore a fringed buckskin shirt and trousers and black boots. A Navajo blanket was tossed carelessly over his shoulders. Her eyes followed as he turned into the hitching rail before the Sheriff's office. He sat on the pinto for another minute, as though he was reluctant to dismount. But then, with the grace of one who has spent his life on a horse, he swung down. The spurs on his boots jingled softly as he stepped up onto the boardwalk and entered the Sheriff's office.

She'd never seen him before. Why did she think she had?

Eagle sat on his horse for a moment, casting a suspicious glance around him. A year before he'd been unwelcome in this town, had been beaten half to death behind the saloon. Now he'd killed another Indian, and he wondered if this would change their attitude toward him. He thought of Wasatch, who had given his life in the battle against Mad Dog and his warriors, and Eagle's jaw clenched. He rarely allowed himself to shed tears, but each time Wasatch's memory came to him, a rock-sized lump filled his throat, and he could almost feel the weight of tears on his cheek, though he was careful to hold them back.

Wasatch had died in battle as he'd always predicted he would, and Eagle had tried to find consolation in remembering Wasatch's dedication to his people, his willingness to die for a worthy cause. But fighting and dying made no sense to him now. He wanted to end it here.

He swung down from the pinto and tied the leather reins to the wooden rail. As people edged cautiously past him, he could feel their eyes, narrowed and suspicious, upon him. He stepped onto the boardwalk and glanced around. A cowboy leaned against a door frame just down the street, and as his eyes met Eagle's, his hand flew to the gun at his belt.

Eagle merely turned in disgust and faced the dark boards of the door leading into the Sheriff's office. He took a deep breath and pressed the wooden latch.

As the door swung back, two faces jerked up in surprise. The Sheriff, a robust man in his fifties with gray hair and a heavily lined face, sat behind a cluttered desk. A younger man, who had been leaning against a corner of the desk, jumped to his feet and stared wide-eyed at Eagle.

Calmly, Eagle closed the door, suddenly conscious of the small, tight room where a burning wood stove, a brass spittoon, several chairs and a coat rack were jumbled together. Posters filled the walls, images of men wanted by the law, and his eyes made a quick sweep of the strange faces, ending on a poster with no face, merely some words printed there.

Eagle's dark eyes returned to the man with the Sheriff's badge, who was now standing, eying him curiously.

"What's your business, stranger?" The Sheriff asked, his hand lingering near the holster where a large, pearl-handled Colt rested.

Eagle cleared his throat. "I came to tell you I've killed Mad Dog."

A hiss of indrawn breath accompanied his announcement, but the two men's faces still held suspicion and distrust.

"That so?" The Sheriff reached down and lifted a long dark cigar from a box on his desk. He thrust the cigar between his teeth, then struck a match against the side of his desk.

"It is so." Eagle nodded, his gaze moving to the younger man, who also wore a badge—that of a deputy. He was thin and lanky, with quick green eyes that were now fixed on the bracelet Eagle wore. At that instant, the deputy's hand shot to his holster and in a flash, his Colt was aimed at Eagle's heart.

"Too bad for you, we already met up once, Mad Dog!" he sneered, licking his lips nervously as his eyes darted back to the Sheriff. "It's him, Will. He's Mad Dog come to claim reward money for his own life!"

"I am *not* Mad Dog!" Eagle protested through clenched teeth. "I told you, I *killed him*. He and his warriors attacked my people."

"Funny thing you're wearing his bracelet. And funny thing you ain't got his body!" The deputy laughed nervously, gripping his gun tighter as he took a step closer.

The Sheriff blew a thick haze of cigar smoke across the room, and his boots made hollow sounds on the wooden floor as he stepped over to yank a poster from the wall.

"You seen this?" he asked, studying Eagle suspiciously as he handed him the poster.

There was no face there, only words. Eagle's reading was limited but he squinted at the poster, trying to make out the words. Finally he looked back at the Sheriff, shaking his head.

"I can't read," he said.

The Sheriff nodded thoughtfully. "Maybe that explains why you didn't know anybody who claims the reward money for Mad Dog has got to have proof they've killed him. Either his body, or a witness."

"It's him, I tell you, Sheriff!" The deputy was only two feet away from Eagle, and the sweat of his body filled Eagle's sharp senses as his dark eyes swung over the deputy.

"I would not be so foolish as to walk into such a trap," he snarled. "I am Wild Eagle, the nephew of Bear Claw. Our camp is up at the soda springs. My people know I have avenged the loss of our braves."

The Sheriff chewed on his cigar, his eyes wandering up and down Eagle, returning to his eyes, trying to read the expression there.

"I know how we can find out for sure," the deputy raved on. "If you won't take my word—and I'm tellin' you, Will, this here's the guy we had hemmed up in the Rampart Mountains six months ago. But if you don't believe me, there's another fella can identify him."

The Sheriff removed his cigar and stared at his deputy. "Who?"

"Slim Lewis! He was on that stage Mad Dog and his warriors attacked! Was lucky he got out alive."

The Sheriff frowned and turned back to Eagle. "Until you can prove you're who you say you are, we're gonna have to lock you up."

Eagle tensed, darting a glance back at the Colt aimed at his heart. There was no point in going for his gun or his knife.

"Lean up against the wall," the Sheriff ordered.

Eagle, rigid with anger, obeyed, allowing the Sheriff and the deputy to search him and take his gun and knife. He was only a few yards from the door, and a wild urge to run seized him, but he forced himself to remain rational. He knew he'd be a dead man if he made the wrong move.

I'd rather be dead than locked up, he thought, but then the image of Morning Star's sweet face filled his mind. And he thought of little Shavano, and he stood still until they had run their hands up and down his legs and back, then turned him to search his waist and chest one more time.

"All right, in you go." The Sheriff inclined his head toward the open door leading to the cells.

Eagle's dark eyes bored through each man, silently conveying his hatred, but he said nothing. The deputy's eyes had taken on the kind of hungry sheen Eagle had seen in a wolf's eyes. The deputy wanted to be the one to kill Mad Dog, but Eagle knew he would outsmart them somehow, and that would give him great satisfaction.

They entered the room of cells and Eagle's

breath caught in his throat, though he kept his face impassive. As the first cell was opened, he hesitated, then he felt the nudge of the gun in the center of his back.

The heavy clang of the iron door raised the hair on his neck, but he kept his expression coolly aloof. He was not afraid of them, and he'd not give them the satisfaction of humbling or humiliating him.

"Go find Lewis," the Sheriff barked at his anxious deputy. "Not that I'm doubting your word, but it'd put my mind at peace knowin' another man can identify him."

Eagle stood in the center of the cell, glaring at the deputy as he bounded off. Then his eyes moved to the Sheriff, who was lingering by the cell, studying him thoughtfully.

"Sheriff, I am not Mad Dog," Eagle said quietly.

The Sheriff's gray brows jerked downard in contemplation. "If Lewis says you're not, then I'll question my deputy's words. But if you are . . ." the words trailed into the air as the Sheriff's boots echoed over the concrete of the cell room. He returned to his office and slammed the door.

Eagle turned and studied his steel trap, feeling the frustration of a caged animal. His breath began to shorten as he looked back at the parallel bars, which seemed to grow larger and wider as he stared at them. He turned and sank down on the cot, dropping his head to his hands as he closed his eyes to shut out his painful surroundings.

A series of short, heavy rasps filled the

room, and suddenly he realized it was his own breath jerking through his body. He began to feel as though he were smothering, and he leapt from the cot and forced his eyes upward to the small, high window, where a thin ray of light filtered through. He stared longingly at the sunlight, his ears strained for life beyond that window. He could hear the distant clomp of hooves on the road, and as he concentrated on the window, he heard the voice of a child calling to someone.

He gritted his teeth and tried to steady his erratic breathing as he looked at the sunlight and listened to the child's cry. Again he thought of Morning Star and Shane Shavano, and his racing heartbeat began to calm. Everything would be all right. The Sheriff would soon discover his deputy had made a mistake.

Loud voices and the approach of the deputy with a stranger, who began to nod his head upon sight of Eagle, soon shattered his hopes. The man was of medium build and heavyset, with a shaggy brown beard and a funny-looking eye. He was dressed in a patched shirt and trousers with a stained felt hat that swallowed half his forehead.

Cautiously, he inched his way toward the cell and squinted at Eagle. Eagle glared at him, and the man took a step backward, as though he expected Eagle to plunge through the steel bars and grab him. The man's funny eye was a lighter shade of blue, compared to his other one, and it seemed to roll slightly in its socket as he stood, head cocked to one side, staring at Eagle.

He nodded again, with more assurance this time. "It's him," he said to the Sheriff, who stood in the background curiously watching. "It's the one who held up the stage and shot those people."

"You lyin' bastard!" Eagle sprang from the cot, unable to hold his temper for another second.

"He's Mad Dog," the man repeated, backing away from the cell, his eyes averted as though he could not face Eagle's hot black stare.

Eagle gripped the steel bars, unable to believe what was happening. His hands tightened on the bars, and for an instant he was so filled with rage that he almost believed he could rip the steel from the concrete.

The men hurried out, slamming the door. Again, the sense of being trapped brought on the sick dizziness that shortened his breath. Eagle tried to think what to do, but his head was throbbing as though someone was pounding on his temples with the stock of a rifle.

If only he could get word to Bear Claw. . . .

But the palefaces would not believe his people either; they would only cause trouble for them. He leaned his throbbing head against the cool steel and tried again to calm his breathing, but nothing seemed to help. Clutching his head with both hands, he stumbled back and fell across the cot. From the Sheriff's office, the excited voice of the deputy penetrated the closed door.

"Some of them men at the saloon are getting pretty excited, Sheriff. They say we oughta hang him before his tribe comes chargin' into town!"

Eagle's head throbbed harder. He did not hear the Sheriff's cool reply.

"I don't hold with hangings, Williams. He'll get a fair trial like any other man."

Daylight faded to darkness, and the long hours of night dragged for Eagle. He lay on his cot, his hands behind his head, his eyes focused on the tiny window above him. He could see a few stars twinkling high in the sky, and he forced himself to think of the many nights he'd lain out beneath the stars, breathing freely of the cool air.

Free.

Would he ever be free again? Would they hang him at dawn? The hours dragged on and he could not ward off the fear of a noose around his neck. Was there no justice in the world? he wondered. He was to be hanged by palefaces, even though white blood ran in his veins, and this knowledge sickened him even more. For now he felt such rage for the white people that his hands curled in fists, begging to strike them. It had been a white man who raped his mother, whose cruel and careless act had created him, a half-breed forced to live out his life in one endless battle. A white man had tried to raise him, but now, comparing the love he felt for his son and the treatment he had received from his adopted father, he knew he had been a slave to him, no more.

He closed his eyes, trying to form some sort of prayer in his mind, but he was too desolate to pray. He wasn't even sure the Great Spirit heard him anymore.

Loud voices approaching the cell startled Eagle. He sat up on the cot, rubbing his eyes, surprised that he had managed to sleep after all. Morning light flowed through the high window.

The Sheriff stood before his cell with a small man in a dark suit and hat, who peered curiously at Eagle from behind thick spectacles.

"This is Wilbur Collins, owner of the newspaper," the Sheriff announcced. "He wants to talk to you."

Eagle merely stared at the man, saying nothing.

"I want to write your story, Mad Dog. The people are curious about you," he said, extending his hand for a handshake. Eagle's eyes dropped to the bony hand as his mouth curled in contempt.

"I am not Mad Dog," he replied finally. "My name is Wild Eagle, and I am a member of Bear Claw's tribe. They have made a mistake, but no one will listen to me." His eyes held the man, who inclined his head and adjusted his spectacles for a closer look.

"That so? Then I *must* write your story. Maybe it would arouse some local sympathy."

Eagle knew better than to trust or believe

him, yet there was a slight chance that his story might reach someone who knew him—Rope Thrower, for example.

He stood and lifted a hand to smooth back his long, tousled hair. As he approached the bars where the man waited, an idea suddenly came to him.

"Do you know Rope Thrower?" he asked. "The white people call him Kit Carson."

The man's eyes widened behind his thick spectacles. "Of course I know Carson. If I'm not mistaken, he's supposed to be here in a week or two for a meeting with the rangers."

A week or two. Would he still be alive then? Maybe a story in the newspaper would help, but he wasn't about to give out any information without extracting something in return.

"I will give you a story, a damn good story, if you will contact Kit Carson for me. He can identify me as Wild Eagle; he knows I am not Mad Dog."

The man had whipped out a short pencil and a thin pad from his coat pocket. "I'll contact Carson. Maybe I can get two stories out of this! Go ahead, Wild Eagle, or Mad Dog, or whoever you are. Tell me all about yourself."

"I will tell you," Eagle sighed. "But no paleface will believe me."

Sara sat rocking Marie and humming softly while Arabella prepared a beef stew. It had been a long week and Sara had grown restless. Another snow had fallen over Colorado City, and she resented having to stay inside when her taut nerves could have been soothed by fresh air and a long walk.

Arabella had grown anxious as well, often dropping pots and pans and staring morosely out the window.

A hard knock hit the door and both women cast nervous glances at each other, then at the door. Darkness had fallen, and no one ever came to visit after dark. Before Sara could stand, Arabella had rushed to the window to peer out. She let out a yelp that sent Marie into a startled wail.

"Who is it?" Sara asked, trying to soothe the baby as Arabella recklessly threw open the door and a heavily bearded Rex bounded inside.

They fell into each others arms, and Sara quickly looked away, touched by their emotion.

"Hello, Sara!" Rex slammed the door and looked across the room. His eyes fell on Marie and he hurried over to peer into her tiny face, rumpled in a scarlet protest.

"What a pretty little thing," he chuckled. Rex's beard was so thick it resembled a small gray bush, and his hair sprang in all directions from under his cap. Sara tried to conceal her amusement as Marie's wails grew louder upon sight of him.

"It's good to see you, Rex," Sara said, extending her hand to shake his.

"Have you heard from Eric?" he asked, glancing from Sara to the baby with concern.

She shook her head. "Not a word."

Rex pursed his lips in a thoughtful silence.

"The South's losing the war, Sara. I hear it'll be over soon. He might even be on his way back now."

Arabella put her arm around his waist. "What are you doing here?"

"The Cavalry's moving from Pueblo to Denver. I got a pass for the night." His eyes warmed as he looked into Arabella's face. "I've missed you, woman."

"Come have stew and coffee," Arabella motioned him to the kitchen. Sara's eyes followed them wistfully as they hugged each other and fell into conversation.

She thought of Rex's prediction that the war would soon end as she lifted Marie to her shoulder and began to pat her tiny back. If only he were right! Seeing Rex struck a pain deep in her heart, reminding her of Eric and how much she missed him. She shut her mind against the possibility that he might not return. She glanced at Rex and Arabella, whose faces were wreathed in glowing smiles. Sara knew a part of her would die if she lost Eric.

The couple went to the hotel for the night, and Sara and Marie were left alone. Sara thought of Eric and cried desperately. She ached to wrap her arms around his neck, press her mouth to his. He had to be alive, he had to be!

That night she put Marie in bed with her and snuggled against the tiny body for warmth and comfort. She hadn't slept long when the old nightmare returned, with a different twist this time. It was Eric who was huddled in a dark musty place with tears glistening on his cheeks. He seemed to be listening, waiting, as the footsteps drew closer and closer. A man in a blue uniform appeared, a rifle pointed at Eric's head.

Sara screamed out, waking herself. She bolted upright in bed and glanced nervously around the still room. Marie stirred beside her, and Sara clamped her hands to her mouth to silence herself. It had taken too long to get the baby to sleep, and she was in no condition to hold and rock her.

Quietly, she slipped out of bed and padded barefoot across the floor, her heart racing. She sat down in the rocker and began to rock, trying desperately to calm herself.

The piercing eyes of the Union officer loomed in her mind again, and she lifted her hand to her mouth, biting her knuckles. What did it mean? Why was she having this nightmare? Oh Eric, she whispered into the darkness, be careful. *Please be careful*.

Finally, she tiptoed back to the bed and tried to sleep, but she tossed and turned most of the night and was relieved when a thin ray of dawn slipped through her window. She got up, built a fire and made coffee. As she sat at the tiny table, sipping the hot coffee that seemed to thaw her frozen body, she thought of her finances and began to worry. She was getting low on the money Eric had left her. She needed to think about obtaining work. She hated leaving little Marie, but Arabella would gladly look after her. Sara could even pay her if she had a job.

She sighed, placing the coffee mug on the table. A job would be good for her, to occupy her mind and calm her nerves while she waited for Eric to come home.

The next afternoon she returned to the mercantile and spoke with the owner, who'd become her friend over the past months. They'd even laughed together over the day Sara and Eric came to shop for her trouseau. She'd chosen a flannel shirt and warm trousers, while Eric selected dainty lace underwear for her.

"I'm so sorry, Sara," Alma Wilkerson sighed. "I just can't afford to hire any help, though God knows I need it desperately. But with the war going on and the miners leaving, and goods hard to come by . . ."

"I understand," Sara said. "Just thought I'd ask."

"Wait!" Alma glanced through the narrow glass window of the store. "I just remembered there's a new photographer in town. He's set up shop in that little building next to the newspaper office. He has no help. Why don't you talk to him?"

Sara located the photographer's shop, or "gallery" as the sign read, and quickly decided to work for whatever he could pay her. She needed money and she also needed something to occupy her mind.

She stood for a moment before the false-front shop, taking a deep breath. She'd never had a job, and for a moment she felt rather foolish; but then a funny little man opened the door. He was small, with brown eyes and hair and a long nose above a handlebar moustache.

"Come in," he said, beaming and eager for business.

Smiling, Sara strolled inside, glancing interestedly at the cozy front room. An exhibit of photographs covered the wall. The photographs were good, Sara thought, looking at views of mountains, miners at work, and for contrast, a busy Eastern city.

"You do nice work," she said, glancing at him.

"Thank you." He bowed. "Allow me to introduce myself. I'm Andrew Hall from New York."

Sara's eyes took in his slim, small frame —he was no more than an inch taller than she, which seemed short in comparison to Eric. He was dressed in a dark suit, obviously tailor-made, because it fit him to perfection.

"I'm Sara Christensen," she began.

"You'll make a lovely photograph! I'd be most eager—"

"I'm afraid you don't understand," she interrupted, looking embarrassed. "I stopped in to see if you need someone to work for you." At his shocked expression, she glanced around the room, trying to think how to win him over. "'Where do you make the pictures?" she asked.

"In here," he said, opening a door. "There's a tiny dressing room back there, the room just off the parlour, and this is my laboratory."

Through the open door, Sara could see a dark room covered with orange cloth.

"Orange light does not harm my glass plates," he explained.

"I see. You have some expensive equipment here, it seems to me. Don't you need someone to watch your gallery if you have to be away?"

"Well . . . yes, I do. I've been wanting to go to the mining camps to get pictures of the miners. They love to send photographs back home to prove, I suppose, that they're making a go of it."

"Then I could watch the store for you! I could also keep the place clean, make tea for your customers . . ."

He withdrew a gold watch from his vest pocket and stared at it. "Miss Christensen . . ."

"*Mrs.* Christensen," she gently interrupted. "My husband is fighting in the war."

"Mrs. Christensen," he repeated, shaking his head regretfully. "Well, Mrs. Christensen, I do need a helper, but the wages would be small in the beginning."

"It doesn't matter," she smiled. "I need to work. I have a baby to support and I don't know when my husband will return."

"Very well." He glanced back at his watch, then returned it to his vest pocket. "I'm due at the bank for a meeting. You can start to work right now. If anyone comes for a photograph, don't let them leave until I return!"

Sara's mouth fell open as he grabbed his hat and sailed out the door. Then, quickly recovering, she removed her cloak and gloves and sat down to wait for the first customer.

* * *

The beat of horse's hooves echoed in Eric's ear as he jabbed his mount again and thundered along the back roads of Georgia. He'd already heard that Atlanta was burning, and now he could smell the acrid smoke riding on the night wind. His heart wrenched within him as he thought of Pine Hill and wondered if it would be a bed of ashes when finally he arrived.

He leaned low over the saddle, slashing the reins left to right, as the wind whipped over his torn Union uniform. The pants were too tight and ended six inches above his ankle. The coat was ripped across the back where his broad shoulders had strained and torn the woolen fabric. He didn't care. He was disguised in clothing that would improve his chances of getting to Pine Hill, and that was all that mattered.

Heavy clouds swelled about the moon, making the night even darker. He blinked, and the sickening dizziness swept over him again. His body was slashed with briar cuts and an infection was starting in his right elbow where he had gashed it on a sharp object as he dragged himself on his belly through the long tunnel. Sheer desperation for survival had given Eric a strength he feared forever lost after so many sleepless nights of digging. He and the three other men, as weary as he, had even managed to overpower some dozing Union soldiers in the woods near the prison. Their presence had been a godsend, giving the escapees clothing and mounts, and they'd quickly said good-bye to each other and torn out for their respective destinations.

Sherman's march to the sea would, Eric hoped, veer just far enough south to miss Pine Hill. The night ride seemed endless, but when finally dawn broke, Eric guided his weary mount up the pine-bordered road leading home. No smoke tainted the air here, and his hopes began to rise. The land around him had been grossly neglected, but the soil had not been torn up by the cavalry.

Slowly, his horse gained the top of the rise, and Eric's breath caught in his throat. The two-story Colonial house still crowned the grassy knoll. The sight of it, through the gray light of dawn, brought tears to his eyes. He slid off his tired horse and walked wearily up the narrow dirt road past barren cotton fields, farmed for so many years by his family. Just the sight of them brought many memories flooding back.

Eric walked slowly up the long oak-lined drive, his heart in his throat. At the end of the drive, he tied his horse to a fence post and tried to summon strength back to his bones. His eyes were bloodshot and burning as they moved over the tangled shrubbery, the foresaken flower beds. Apparently, his mother had given up on everything.

The frame house was sadly in need of paint, and the closed green shutters had loose boards and appeared near to falling down. The board steps creaked beneath his boots; through the holes in them, he could feel the cool wood on the blistered soles of his feet.

The veranda was stripped of all its furniture, and it almost seemed as if no one lived here any more.

Cautiously, he approached the wide front door and lifted his hand to knock. Then suddenly he remembered he was wearing the Union uniform. He reached up and yanked the cap from his head to better reveal his hair and face, and he began to call to his mother.

There was no response; he knocked again, wondering if William and Susie, the faithful black couple who'd taken care of the house for so many years had gone away.

Finally, he heard the distant patter of steps in the hall.

A key rattled in the lock and the door opened just wide enough to admit the barrel of a rifle through the crack.

"What do you want, soldier?"

The female voice did not belong to his mother, or to anyone else he had known here. He strained to see who held the gun.

"I'm Eric Christensen," he said, lifting his hands high in the air. "The reason I'm dressed in a Union uniform is merely for protection until I could reach Pine Hill. Who's there?"

The door opened wider and he could see a tall, dark-haired woman whom he judged to be in her mid-forties. She was dressed in a nearly new blue dress that was a contrast to the ragged clothing most Southern women were now wearing.

"I'm Julia Anderson," she replied finally, the gun still pointed at him. "My husband bought this plantation a few weeks ago, after Mrs. Christensen passed away."

Eric heard the words and suddenly the world seemed to spin. He reached out to grip the door frame for support, and the woman cocked the rifle.

"Sorry about your mother, but I'm afraid we're not too trusting of anyone these days, even though you say you're a Christensen. I think you'd better be riding on."

Eric raised a hand to his brow, trying to think. "What about my brothers?" he asked weakly. "My sister-in-law?"

There was a brief pause, and this time her voice held more sympathy. "I'm sorry to tell you that your brothers were killed in battle. There was only one sister-in-law living here after your mother died. She needed money, and we'd just come down from Washington."

For a long time, Eric merely stared, scarcely able to comprehend the terrible things she was saying in a voice he now recognized as not completely Southern. She had once been a Southerner before moving to Washington, he concluded.

His brothers! Dead! Tears glazed his eyes before he turned and stumbled down the steps. Before him, the land blurred through his haze of tears.

"I'm sorry," she called to him. "Perhaps you would feel better to know that your mother didn't suffer. She just died quietly in her sleep."

Of a broken heart, Eric thought bitterly.

He remembered her last letter, begging him to return home, yet he had waited several weeks before leaving. And he'd never made it to Pine Hill! He had sent a letter to her, but he wondered now if she even received it.

One last thought occurred to him, and he paused on the bottom step, staring bleakly at the terraced lawns where he had spent so many happy, carefree hours. "How did you happen to choose Pine Hill?" he asked, turning his head slightly, but not looking at her again.

"My husband is a land speculator," she replied, her tone more businesslike. "He bought up this plantation, and a few others by paying off the taxes. We intend to fix the place up, make it a showplace like it once was."

Back taxes . . .

Eric gathered his remaining strength, though it was scarce, and walked back to his horse. There was nothing he could do now. It was too late.

Too late. The words seemed to mock him as he swung into the saddle and cantered down the drive. He would have come home sooner, if not for Sara and the baby. And his brothers had died unaware that he had finally joined the Confederate Army at the end of the war.

Bitterness rose up within him, filling his mouth with a bitter taste and knotting his insides until he began to heave. For one insane moment, his hand crept to his gun as a sudden urge to withdraw his weapon, bury it against his heart and pull the trigger, seized him. But then rational thought returned and he pulled his horse to the edge of the road and slipped down. He was trembling from head to toe, and he could no longer force himself to go on. He crawled into the knee-deep grass that bordered the road beyond the driveway and stretched his weary body. He could not take his own life, but if he gave over to the terrible ache that filled him, the task might be taken care of anyway.

As his face, wet with tears, touched the soft meadow grass, and he breathed into his nostrils the familiar smell of Georgia clay, he felt his heart turn over and break. Nothing mattered anymore. Nothing!

23

Sara sat gripping the newspaper, her mind reeling with shock. She'd read the story over and over, and still she couldn't believe it. The notorious Mad Dog had been arrested two days before, but was now claiming to be Wild Eagle, the nephew of Bear Claw—the son of Crying Wind.

Sara continued to stare at the newsprint before her as she thought about the story. Was it possible? Was he telling the truth? *Was he her brother? Was she Little Dove?*

She remembered the Indian on the pinto and the odd feeling that she had seen him before. Maybe he really was her brother.

Sara leaned her head back against the settee and closed her eyes, trying to think clearly. She could never resolve the matter in her heart or mind. She had felt a strong pull toward the Indian children, but she loved all children. She felt a sisterly rapport with Arabella, who was Ute, but she would have grown to love Arabella regardless of her race.

She tossed the newspaper down and began to pace the room. If she could see this man again, this Mad Dog or Wild Eagle or whoever he was, maybe she would know. She trusted her instincts. If she could see him again, talk with him, she *would* know. In her heart she would know!

But how could she get in to see him? What would she say?

She could always go there on the pretense of representing her employer. She stopped pacing and glanced around the shop, her eyes lighting on the variety of photographs displayed on the wall.

Her mind raced, devising a plan. She could pretend that Mr. Hall was interested in photographing the famous Mad Dog. Since Hall was out of town for the day, he couldn't deny wanting such a photograph. Come to think of it, he'd probably commend her for the idea.

She began to pace again, thinking that she'd feel foolish standing before the man's jail cell, staring at him, asking if he would agree to have his picture taken.

She sank onto the settee and tried to force herself to forget the whole thing. But she couldn't. Finally, she knew she would have no peace until she saw this man, no matter what she had to do.

She took a deep breath and reached for her cape. As she locked the shop and hurried to the jail, her heart began to hammer. She'd never done anything quite so daring. Still, she forced her feet to keep moving over the boardwalk. She had to find out, she had to see for herself.

She paused before the Sheriff's office, glancing toward the hitching rail, remembering for a minute how he had sat on his pinto as though debating the wisdom of going inside. She couldn't believe, if he were Mad Dog, that he'd be bold enough to ride into town to try to claim his own reward. It didn't make sense, and the idea that an innocent man, whether he was her brother or not, might be falsely convicted, gave her the courage to press the latch and enter.

The Sheriff's office was quiet for once. There were no townspeople loitering about; even the deputy was out.

She breathed a sigh of relief as the Sheriff rose from his chair and nodded to her.

"Mornin', Mrs. Christensen."

"Good Morning, Sheriff."

Sara smiled warmly, glancing toward the closed door leading to the cell. She glanced back at the Sheriff, aware that he was waiting for her to state the reason for her visit. "Sheriff, Mr. Hall was wondering if he could get a photograph of your famous prisoner."

A disapproving frown was already forming on the Sheriff's face.

"Do you mind if I ask him?" she pressed, with a gentle smile.

"I wouldn't do that if I were you," he advised her, shaking his gray head. "He's not very accommodating."

The Sheriff was suddenly staring at her, and she wondered if he was recalling the day she had shot the man in the middle of the street. She knew she'd have to proceed tactfully. He was a man who was not easily fooled.

"The problem is, Sheriff, Mr. Hall had to

leave this morning, and he insisted that I come down here and just speak to the man. All he can do is say no," she finished with a light shrug of her shoulders.

The Sheriff pursed his lips and reached for the ring of keys. "I reckon it won't hurt to ask, but I'll walk back there with you."

Sara could feel a cold sweat breaking over her lip and forehead. Her heart leapt in her chest as they stepped into the dismal cell room. Then suddenly she saw him, standing against the wall, his gaze fixed on a high window. She stopped walking and just stared. The Sheriff glanced back at her, his brows jerked upward in a quizzical frown.

She tried to give him a reassuring smile, but a very strange feeling had swept over her, one she couldn't identify.

At their approach, Eagle whirled in surprise and stared straight into her eyes. She felt a shock of familiarity as her eyes ran over his face, analyzing each feature and seeing a masculine likeness to herself.

It was strange that there could be a likeness, for his face was round where hers was oval, and his skin was darker. Perhaps it was the set of his eyes, the shape of his nose and mouth, or merely something in his face. She couldn't say.

"This is Mrs. Christensen from Andrew Hall's photo gallery," the Sheriff explained. "Hall wants to take a picture of you."

Eagle had been staring rather curiously at her until the Sheriff spoke, but now the lips curled cynically and he looked away. "No," he replied, his eyes fixed on the upper window.

Sara glanced anxiously at the Sheriff. She had to find an excuse to linger, to draw this man into conversation.

"Guess you got your answer," The Sheriff told her.

"I'd like to talk to him for a minute," she said calmly, trying to ignore the Sheriff's startled look. He hesitated, his gray brows lowered contemplatively as he shot a glance at Eagle, who had turned to stare at the window again.

"It's all right, Sheriff. If he won't talk to me, I'll leave. You can go back to your desk." She touched his arm and smiled. "Don't worry."

Eagle stood staring up at the window, as though he were alone in the cell room. Sara took a step closer to the steel bars, wondering what she would say to him.

"Wild Eagle?" she called his name softly.

His facial muscles tightened but he continued to stare at the window, still ignoring her.

"I want to talk to you," she said, gripping the bars with nervous hands, "but not about making your picture. I want to talk to you about Bear Claw and Crying Wind."

Slowly, his eyes moved over the room and halted on her, measuring her from head to toe.

When he refused to answer, she spoke more harshly. "How do you *know* you are Crying Wind's son?"

His eyes narrowed, and when she was

certain he was not going to respond in any way, he spoke in a low pained voice. "I believe Bear Claw," he said.

She stared at him, then swallowed. "Did he say you were the only baby left at the wagons?"

A dark light sparked in his eyes as he looked at her more closely. "I don't remember," he finally answered.

"Yes, you do," she challenged him, her eyes pulling at his. "You most certainly would remember something that important."

He shrugged and turned again to stare at the window. "Maybe."

"Don't you know why I'm asking?" she pressed, her voice tense and anxious. "Can't you *see*?"

"I see that I have been tricked by palefaces. I *will not be tricked again*." He turned his back to her and stared at the window again.

Sara knew he would say no more, but she had to try. "Please talk with me. I have to know!"

The door opened and the Sheriff poked his head through. "Are you all right, Mrs. Christensen?"

She heaved a sigh and dragged her hurt gaze from Eagle's still form. "I'm all right," she said. "I was just leaving."

Her eyes lingered on Eagle, hoping for one final response, but there was none. She walked back into the Sheriff's office, her head down.

"He wouldn't co-operate, would he?"

"What?" She glanced at the Sheriff, her

expression blank. "Oh. No, he wouldn't co-operate. Thanks anyway, Sheriff."

She let herself out the door and started up the sidewalk as a cold gust of wind struck her. The shiver that went down her spine was not from the wind alone, but also from a chilling sensation that would not leave her. If she were to follow her instincts, believe her first reaction, the man in the cell was her brother. She hugged her arms around her waist as the wind snatched at her cape. If he was her brother, she must try and help him. She'd already heard rumors that some of the men in town wanted to storm the jail and hang him before his tribe found out where he was and rode in on the warpath. What if that happened?

She swallowed, nodding absently at those she passed on the street. If he were hanged, she'd always have to live with the knowledge that she might have saved his life. She found it difficult to believe that he was Mad Dog, passing himself off as Wild Eagle. There was a directness to his gaze, an even tone to his voice, that made her believe he was telling the truth. And there was that shock of recognition she had felt even though she did not know him. For a moment, he had looked at her with the same curiosity, but he had quickly shuttered his eyes and turned impassive again.

She unlocked the shop and stepped inside, lost in thought. What if she went to the Sheriff and told him what she knew of Crying Wind and the birth of her twins? What if she admitted she was the other baby left at the wagon, and that only Wild Eagle could tell such a story? What if she asked the Sheriff to take a long hard look at her, and then at Eagle, and see if he couldn't notice a resemblance?

The weight of her burden sent her to the settee, and she dropped her head in her hands. If she admitted to her heritage, she'd be snubbed, or perhaps banned from Colorado City. The townspeople hated all Indians after hearing of the brutal scalpings and murders of so many white people. But these people tended to forget that for every white person murdered, twice as many Indians had lost their lives, and in many cases merely in an attempt to protect their land and their families.

If she backed up his story, would they believe him? Would they believe *her*?

She bit her lip, suddenly thinking of Bear Claw. She was certain he did not know what had happened to Eagle. If he did, he'd have ridden into town to try to reason with the Sheriff. But what could anyone do when, according to the newspaper article, the deputy and Slim Lewis had both identified him as Mad Dog.

Her thoughts were suddenly interrupted as the door flew open and James Young, the shopkeeper next door, burst in, his face jubilant.

"Mrs. Christensen, have you heard the news? The South has surrendered. The war is over!"

"Over?" she gasped, staring wide-eyed at the smiling man.

"Yes'm. Just came in over the wires at the telegraph office!"

She rose to her feet, her thoughts flying in all directions. Eric! Would Eric be free to return now? Was he alive? How could she find out?

"Does that mean I can send a wire, Mr. Young?"

"Sending a wire won't be the problem. Getting one back may be, but I hear they're already restoring the service, even in the South."

The news sent her present problem to the back of her mind as she reached out and touched the older man's hand. "Thank you so much for bringing me this news. It's the best I've heard in a long time."

She flew out the door and raced across the street to the newspaper.

"*Mrs. Christensen!*"

An angry voice stopped her. She whirled, sidestepping a thundering team of horses and an angry driver who was swerving to dodge her.

Andrew Hall was dismounting from his horses, looking dusty and trail-weary. "May I ask who's tending the gallery?"

Her eyes flew back to the door, standing wide open, and she bit her lip. "Mr. Hall, I just learned the war has ended. I'm going to the telegraph office to try to get a wire through to my husband's family. Please understand." She turned and hurried on to join the crowd gathering before the telegraph office.

The office overflowed with people standing in line to send wires back home. While she waited, she mentally wrote the message. *Desperate for news of Eric. Please wire immediately.*

When finally it was her turn at the clerk's window, she related the message.

"No point in waiting around," he said, busily scribbling. "Just leave a place where you can be reached, and I'll send a messenger to you if we get a reply."

"*When* you get a reply," she amended stubbornly. She rushed back to the gallery, her hopes soaring. But then, as her eyes swept the town and ended on the Sheriff's office, she thought of Wild Eagle and a small cloud of gloom hung over her moment of happiness. She took a deep breath, thinking she'd talk the matter over with Arabella. She was wise; she'd help her figure what to do.

Crowds were clustered together on the sidewalk now, with the news of surrender filling the air like a charge of electricity after a lightning storm. She could hear snatches of conversation as she passed, and she smiled to herself. The group of men knotted together near the saloon, however, wore sullen expressions on their faces.

"I say, git him now," one grumbled. "The Sheriff's gonna git us all killed by them savages. There ain't no point in waitin'. I say hang him *now!*" he repeated, his voice rising in anger.

Her steps slowed and she looked at the men, her dark eyes filled with worry and disbelief.

"Typical half-breed," another one snorted. "Speaks soft and low and kinda polite, while the eyes say something else."

"It's him, I tell ya," Slim Lews vowed, a whiskey bottle tilted to his lips. "And if he breaks outa that jail, he'll be comin' for me first thing. I ain't forgittin' the way he looked at me. He'd scalp me in a minute!"

A boldness Sara never knew she had suddenly rose to the surface.

"Mr. Lewis?" she called to him.

He broke from the crowd and sauntered over to Sara, and she could see by his loose, careless gait that he was more than a little drunk.

"Mr. Lewis, how can you be so sure he's Mad Dog?" she asked, her eyes pinning his wandering glance.

" 'Cause I wuz on that stage! If you coulda seen the way he killed them people—"

"Why did he let you go?"

Lewis reached up to push his stained hat back from his forehead with the tip of the whiskey bottle. "Don't rightly know. But the way I know it's him is that bracelet he's wearing."

"What?" she gasped. "You identified him solely because of the bracelet?"

His glass eye rolled in its socket as he took a step backward, finally aware that this pretty woman was not impressed with his story, was even challenging it, in fact.

"Naw, he looks like 'im too. He's a half-breed."

"Mr. Lewis,"—Sara was incredulous—"many half-breeds have a similar look, because their skin is a shade lighter than a full-blooded Indian's skin, and their feature are sometimes smaller. But surely you wouldn't say for sure he's Mad Dog unless you're certain? He claims he's someone else, you know."

He tilted the bottle and took a generous swig. Sara watched in repulsion as his Adam's apple bobbed up and down.

"Deputy says so, too," he answered thickly, wiping his mouth on his sleeve. "And Deputy's gonna be Sheriff one of these days . . ."

Sara stiffened, gathering her skirts. "And I can see how he intends to pump up his importance around here with this incident."

She swung around and left the man gaping after her, wondering why she was so angry. There couldn't be another bracelet just like that one; the deputy had already told him about it. He turned and staggered back to the crowd before the saloon. By midnight there just might be a hanging.

By the time Sara left work to head home, she was in a mild state of panic. As she hurried up the sidewalk, her head down, she bumped into Wilbur Collins.

"Mr. Collins," she said, grasping his coat sleeve, "you wrote the article on Wild Eagle, didn't you?"

Collins fixed startled, then impatient eyes on Sara. "That's right. Only he's Mad Dog. Whoever heard of such a cock-and-bull story?

Nobody believed it."

"I do," she replied. "I happen to know his story is true."

"That so?" The little man adjusted his spectacles for a sweeping glance at Sara. "How do you know?"

She swallowed. "I once talked to the chief, Bear Claw. He told me the same story."

"Hmph." Collins dismissed it with a wave of the hand. "Probably some cock-eyed story they all tell when they get juiced up. Don't fret about it, young lady." He turned and stalked on down the sidewalk and for a moment, her eyes followed him.

"Mr. Collins?" she called, a thought puzzling her.

He turned, not bothering to hide his impatience this time.

"How did you get him to tell you such a story? I went to inquire about making his photograph, and he wouldn't speak to me."

"I agreed to contact Kit Carson. He said Kit Carson would identify him."

Sara breathed a sigh of relief. "Did you contact Mr. Carson?"

"Sent a messenger. But it'll be a week or two before he's in town." His eyes strayed to the unruly crowd before the saloon and Sara knew what he was thinking.

"Mr. Collins, he may not be alive next week," she said, pointing to the crowd.

His brows jerked together in a frown, then he shrugged. "And by next week, we may be attacked by savages."

Tears filled Sara's eyes as she stood on the

sidewalk, glancing from his departing back to the crowd. Slim Lewis was staggering drunk, and now the deputy had joined them. But instead of quieting the mob, he was chuckling at their antics, almost encouraging them.

She turned and began to walk toward the Sheriff's office, not really sure what she was going to do, but knowing she had to do something. She was certain he was Wild Eagle now, and if he was, he was her brother—Little Dove's brother, she amended, frowning.

The wind slapped at her face, and she shivered into her cape. How long must she go on battling the truth, when she knew, deep in her heart, what that truth was? Perhaps she had always known, but she was too proud, or too stubborn, to admit it.

She sighed, pressing the latch of the Sheriff's door and slowly entering. The Sheriff was seated at his desk, staring at some papers. When she entered, his look of surprise quickly turned to one of curiosity. He glanced at his pocket watch.

"Shouldn't you be getting home, Mrs. Christensen? Soon be getting dark. It's not safe out on the street after dark. You should know that," he added, his voice lowered.

Silently she walked across to his desk and stood looking down at him, wondering if she could possibly convince him.

"What is it?" He tilted his head and looked at her curiously. She was pale enough to have one of those fainting spells, like some women were prone to do.

"Sheriff, I have to tell you something." She

hesitated, swallowing. She had to speak quickly before anything happened to change her mind. "The man in that cell, whom you call Mad Dog, is really Wild Eagle, as he claims to be. He's told you the truth. Do you realize that your deputy and Mr. Lewis are relying only on that bracelet to identify him? Couldn't he have found it, or perhaps taken it from Mad Dog?"

The Sheriff nodded. "Claims that's what he did. Took it from Mad Dog after he killed him. You know how superstitious Indians are; he probably thinks the bracelet is some kind of charm." He crossed his arms and frowned. "But my deputy is smarter than to identify him just on a bracelet."

"Is he? He wants to be Sheriff pretty bad, you know."

A flush of anger crept up his neck as he glared at Sara. "You got anything else to say, Mrs. Christensen?"

She nodded. "First, I must speak to him in private." She went to open the door to the cell room, then closed it behind her as she walked to Eagle's cell. He stood with his back to her, as before, his eyes fixed determinedly on the window above him.

"Wild Eagle?" she called softly.

His back stiffened, but he did not acknowledge her in any way.

"I was here before and should have told you what I have now come to confess." She hesitated, hoping he would turn to face her. When he remained impassive, she took a deep breath and continued. "I am your sister,

Little Dove."

She stood waiting, hoping, expecting some sort of reaction from him. She held her breath as her heart beat fiercely.

He did not move, he did not speak.

"I just wanted to tell you that, and now I intend to tell the Sheriff. Perhaps it will help to convince him that your story is not so farfetched, after all. It may not change anything, but I must do this. I should have spoken sooner. . . ."

Her voice, like her hopes, trailed into the silence as she stared at him. He did not turn or acknowledge her in any way; she had not believed that his cold treatment could hurt her so much. She took a deep, quivering breath, remembering that he no longer trusted anyone with pale skin. He'd been hurt too deeply and too many times.

Sadly, she turned and walked back into the Sheriff's office. She did not see Eagle turning slowly to stare after her, his dark eyes filled with shock . . . and wonder.

The Sheriff was waiting to hear what she had to say. There was a tense expression about his eyes and mouth as she took a chair opposite him and repeated her story again. He listened quietly, his lips pursed, his eyes studying each feature when at last she revealed her identity.

He reached forward to withdraw a cigar from the box, then struck a match to its tip. Through a haze of smoke, he studied her again.

"Mrs. Christensen, you're mighty brave to tell me this," he finally replied.

"The truth is easier than pretending to be someone I'm not," she sighed. "I'm afraid this is a lesson I've learned the hard way. The important thing is, does my story help Wild Eagle?"

He frowned, turning the cigar in an ashtray to loosen an ash. "To a certain extent. But we still have the deputy and Slim Lewis's word that that guy"—he inclined his gray head toward the cell room—"is Mad Dog."

"He isn't." Sara shook her head, her eyes silently pleading with the Sheriff.

"How can you be so sure he's your brother?" he asked curiously.

She hesitated, considering his question. "Because he looks like me. Can't you see it? And because I feel something for him. I think we know our blood kin, Sheriff. If I weren't sure, I wouldn't have had the courage to tell you about myself. It's the first time I've ever acknowledged it. Somehow I didn't want to believe it myself, but now"—she shook her head, as a troubled frown marred her brow—"I know it's the only way I can ever have peace."

He nodded thoughtfully. "You're probably right. And I admire you for your honesty, Mrs. Christensen." He hesitated, studying the tip of his cigar. "This story is going to get out, you know. What if the townspeople are not so understanding? You know how feelings are running now toward—"

"I know," she interrupted him curtly. "And those feelings are unfair. It isn't right to condemn all Indians just because some have become outlaws." She sighed, thinking of how she herself had done just that. "I intend to take a stand now, Sheriff. Yes, everyone will know my story because no longer will I take the safe and easy way out. Some of my people are starving to death out on the edge of town, and no one will feed them. I intend to do that, Sheriff, though I have little to share. But perhaps by doing something, maybe I can influence others to help them, too."

The Sheriff shrugged. "Maybe."

"But you still haven't told me what will happen to my brother. What do you intend to do about that drunken mob outside the saloon? They're threatening to . . ." Her voice trailed away, as the fear of their threats returned to haunt her.

"They can make all the threats they want," the Sheriff snapped. "They'll have to come through me to get him. And they won't do that," he said, rising from his chair and crossing the room to the gun cabinet. He withdrew a rifle and checked the chamber. "Your brother claims Kit Carson can identify him. He'll be given protection until Carson gets here."

Sara nodded, pulling herself to her feet. "Thank you."

He nodded gravely. "I wish you good luck, Mrs. Christensen. I'm afraid you may be in for some unfair treatment, but unfortunately that's the way it is now. Maybe one of these days, things will change."

"Maybe," she repeated lamely, but she felt little hope about such a thing happening. If a change came, it would probably not be in Wild Eagle's lifetime, or in hers. But she'd done what she could to help him, and now she must go home to her child. "Good day, Sheriff."

As she stepped out of the Sheriff's office and walked back toward the gallery, she knew she must tell Andrew Hall immediately. News traveled fast in Colorado City, and it would be best if the story came from her lips.

Andrew Hall, however, was less tolerant than the Sheriff.

"Mrs. Christensen," he barked, "I'm shocked that you would try to pass yourself off as one of us if you're a Ute."

Sara stiffened. "I told you, Mr. Hall, I wasn't sure of my heritage until recently. There was always a question, but—"

"And the fact that this outlaw Mad Dog—"

"He's really Wild Eagle, Mr. Hall. My brother is Wild Eagle, not Mad Dog," she interrupted gently.

He sniffed, shuffling through a batch of photographs. "Well, whoever he is, his reputation is in question. And if you claim to be his sister, I'm afraid you've put your character on the line, as well."

Sara stiffened, trying to control the sudden flush of anger that stained her cheeks.

"I've done nothing to be ashamed of, Mr. Hall," she replied evenly. "It seems to me telling the truth should be appreciated, rather than condemned."

He was silent for a moment, as he continued to fumble with his camera and equipment.

PASSION'S PEAK

Then he cast a nervous glance at her.

"Unfortunately, this puts me in an awkward position, as I'm sure you can understand."

She swallowed, unable to believe that he was trying to find the words to dismiss her from her job. She raised her chin proudly and reached for her purse.

"What you mean is, you're no longer willing to have me as your employee just because I have Indian blood. Well, if that's the case, I don't think I want to work for someone so narrow-minded and unfair. Good day, Mr. Hall," she said, sweeping out of his office, ignoring his gasp of surprise.

It *doesn't matter*, she thought angrily, striking a path back to her apartment. I don't care if the entire town snubs me; I *don't care*. I did what I had to do.

With that knowledge, a faint smile touched her lips, and she suddenly felt better than she'd felt in a very long time.

Eagle lay on his cot watching the morning light filter down through his cell. He had not closed his eyes all night, for the memory of the woman who claimed to be his sister haunted him. He had tried to harden his heart to her and to the words she spoke, for his heart was overflowing with hate and bitterness.

If she had not first wanted to take his picture, he might have been more willing to believe her. But he had been tricked too many times by palefaces. He was prepared to ignore her completely; it was the most thorough insult he could deliver to the palefaces now. And yet . . . her words and the sad expression in her eyes had begun to haunt him.

It was possible that she really was his sister. If he let himself, he could see a resemblance; but he had no room in his heart for tenderness. He was going to hang if Kit Carson didn't arrive in time.

Still . . . she *had* come forth with this story, and the Sheriff seemed bothered by it. Eagle could tell the Sheriff was silently questioning the deputy's words. After she left, after it was too late, Eagle realized that he should have thanked her, but he was poor with words, even poorer with thanks. There had been so few occasions in his life when he had needed to speak thanks.

He closed his eyes and sighed, remembering that Bear Claw had said the sister was bad medicine. It was the thought he had kept uppermost in his mind when his conscience nagged. He had also said she was married to a white man, and for that reason alone, he wanted nothing to do with her. If by some miracle he got out of jail, he never intended to go near the palefaces again. Never!

Footsteps and loud voices roused him from the cot. The door was thrown open, and Rope Thrower came in, a dark scowl on his face as soon as his eyes lit on Eagle.

"You crazy fools!" he thundered as the Sheriff and deputy trailed him. "This man is Wild Eagle, nephew of Bear Claw. Whoever said he's Mad Dog is a damn liar!''

Eagle's dark eyes burned over the deputy's red face as he mumbled something and retreated.

"You're sure about that?" the Sheriff inquired.

Kit heaved a sigh and thrust his hands in his buckskin jacket. " 'Course I'm sure!" He turned to Eagle with a weary shake of his head. "Damn shame this had to happen to you. I'm just glad I got here in time, Wild Eagle!"

Eagle walked forward and extended his hand through the bars. "You are one paleface that can be trusted, Rope Thrower. I thank you with all my heart."

The Sheriff had returned for his ring of keys. "Deputy's gone for Slim Lewis. He'll have to retract his story before I can turn this man loose," he said, shaking his head, though he was already inserting the key in the lock. "Ever since his sister came in to back up his story, I knew he was telling the truth."

"His sister?" Kit glanced from the Sheriff back to Eagle.

"She lives here in Colorado City," the Sheriff continued, as the lock clicked and the door swung back. He looked at Eagle. "You might stop by and pay your respects to her. She's had a rough time, too. Town's snubbed her ever since she admitted she was your sister. Her husband went back South to fight in the war. Last year she had to shoot a man who'd robbed them."

Eagle averted his eyes, not wanting to hear

what the Sheriff was saying. He hadn't asked her to help him; she probably just did it to ease her own conscience if she'd been passing herself off as white.

A commotion brought Slim Lewis to join the group, and his glass eye was rolling wildly as he took in Eagle, then Kit Carson. His skin was deathly pale, and he seemed to be having difficulty swallowing.

"Still think this man is Mad Dog?" the Sheriff growled.

Slim's eyes made a dive to the floor. "Guess I was wrong," he mumbled, then turned and fled through the door.

The Sheriff glared at the deputy, who was shuffling nervously from one foot to the other. "Williams, this man nearly hung because of you and Lewis. You two were so damn sure—"

"Why's he wearin' that bracelet then?" the deputy argued crossly.

"If you don't have any better sense than to sentence a man to death because of a bracelet, I think you're in the wrong line of work, Williams. Leave your badge on the desk and get out!"

Eagle tensed, longing to dive into the man's lanky body and claim his revenge, but he felt Rope Thrower's eyes on him, issuing a silent warning.

Wordlessly, Eagle sauntered past the men as though they didn't exist and walked through the front door a free man. His pinto was saddled and waiting in front of the Sheriff's office.

"See you at the village in a week or so," Kit said, following him out.

Eagle nodded, swinging into the saddle. His dark eyes crept bitterly over the town, ignoring those palefaces who watched from windows and doorways. He kneed his pinto and cantered out of town, making a silent vow never to return. It was only at the last turn that he thought of Little Dove. His eyes swept the houses on the edge of town and he felt a sudden obligation to speak to her, but words came so hard for him. Perhaps another time . .

24

The night was dark and stormy on the plains, even though May was bringing the promise of spring to the Colorado Territory. While the stage jostled over the rutted road, three other passengers slept soundly, but Eric stared vacantly into the darkness. In a few more hours, he would be with Sara again. Sara . . . she was a sweet, dark presence in his mind, but he could not feel the rush of joy that he once knew when he thought of her. He wasn't even certain he loved her anymore. So much had happened to him, so much that had frozen his heart, until now he began to wonder if he'd ever feel anything beyond this strange numbness inside.

Ever since a neighbor at Pine Hill had found him lying in the grass, too weak to care about living, and had taken him home and nursed him back to good health, he had felt this way. Empty. Dead. Numb to everything. It was only out of a sense of duty that he was on this stage, heading back to Colorado, to see Sara. For a while, he had debated the wisdom of returning, certain that by now she assumed him dead. In many ways he was—in the ways that counted most.

* * *

It was a fine spring afternoon, and while there were still traces of snow on the Peak, the sun was warm in the small park in Colorado City where Sara passed out fresh-baked bread to hungry Utes. The townspeople were critical and aloof, though a few hearts were beginning to soften at the sight of the ragged, starving children.

"Alma, can't you donate a sack of flour?" she had inquired of her friend. Sara had sensed that Alma was one of the few people in town whose attitude toward her would not change, and she had been right. Alma had greeted her warmly, admitting that she admired her honesty and her dedication to helping the Indians.

"Honey, don't worry what some of these stuffed shirts say about you. Who needs people like that? I'm still your friend."

Alma's reassuring words, and the ten pounds of flour she donated, had lifted Sara's sagging spirits. Sara had stretched the flour and made a basketful of bread, then sent a message to those Indians loitering on the edge of town to come to the park.

As they shyly accepted the bread, Sara smiled into their grateful faces, remembering again her trip to Denver with Eric. She'd been haunted ever since by the hungry faces of the Indian children, and she was finally relieved to be doing something to help.

The afternoon stage rattled around the bend, drawing an eager welcome from those who waited for its passengers. Sara glanced at the stage too, always hopeful. Veterans from the war continued to pour into Colorado City, and each time she saw a couple joined in a happy embrace, her heart ached for Eric.

She was conscious of an outstretched hand, and she looked back at the thin, sick Indian woman standing before her. She was the last person in line. "Here, take an extra loaf," Sara said.

As the woman mumbled her thanks and departed, Sara glanced around her. They were all gone now, so she gathered up the loose newspapers she had used to wrap the bread, dropped them in the empty basket and turned for home.

She glanced back at the stage as the passengers stepped down, and suddenly she froze in her tracks. A tall man, dressed in worn pants and a faded shirt had just stepped out and was looking around. He stood with his back to her, but Sara's eyes moved curiously from the thick mass of blonde hair to the side of his face, catching a glimpse of his brown, spade-shaped beard. Her heart began to beat faster. She started walking toward him.

This man was at least thirty pounds lighter than Eric, and his shoulders were rounded in a weary stoop, which was unlike Eric; yet there was something about him that drew her, about the long legs and wide shoulders, the shape of his bare head, though Eric usually wore a hat.

He turned slowly, his eyes moving over the town as though he was not quite sure where he was. For a moment she stared in shock at the man whose body was now thin and gaunt, whose eyes held a bleak, dazed expression.

"Eric?" she called tentatively as she slowly approached him.

He turned and looked straight at her and she gasped before she could stop herself. The deep blue eyes, once so beautiful to her, were sunken and shadowed. Loss of weight had deepened the lines around his eyes and mouth, and his skin sagged against his bones. The mouth was drawn into a hard line, as though he had forgotten how to smile.

"Eric!" His name burst from her lips as tears filled her eyes. She laid down her basket and started running toward him.

"Hello, Sara." Even his voice sounded weak and hollow.

"Eric, I can't believe it's you," she cried, oblivious to the crowd as she threw her arms around his neck and kissed him.

Sara drew back when he seemed stiff and unresponsive, and she glanced self-consciously around her. This was not the time or place for a reunion.

"Come on," she said firmly, linking her arm through his. "Let's get your trunk and go home."

He hesitated. "I don't have a trunk."

"Did you lose it?" she asked as her eyes swept his plain, almost ragged, clothes.

"A long time ago," he sighed. "Until recently I wore a uniform."

"It doesn't matter." She smiled tenderly. "Nothing matters except that you're home! We have a baby girl, Eric," she said, her dark eyes glowing with pride.

"A girl," he echoed with a faint smile.

She felt a tug at her elbow and turned to see one of the Indian children she had fed earlier. He had a bright smile on his face and in his small hand was a pale turquoise rock. He extended it to her.

"For me?" she asked, smiling.

He nodded shyly, then dashed into the crowd.

She looked at the polished rock, touched by his gesture. Then, feeling Eric's questioning eyes, she dropped it in her pocket.

"I baked bread and gave it to some of the hungry Indians," she said as they started walking home.

"That's good," he responded vaguely, his glance sweeping over Colorado City.

"Eric, I found my brother last week," she began conversationally, sensing he would not want to talk about the war until they were alone.

His eyes returned to her. "Your brother?"

She nodded and began to explain what had happened. "I have finally admitted to myself, and to everyone else, that I am Ute," she finished proudly. "Now I'm trying to help the Utes, and all other Indians, as well. That's what I was doing this morning, passing out bread in the park. . . ." Her words trailed away as she searched his gaunt face, shaken by his strange behavior. She swallowed, trying to still the alarm rising within her. He was so different now; she couldn't imagine what had happened to him to change him so drastically.

"Arabella moved in with me after you left," she continued, trying to behave normally. "Rex joined up. . . ." Her voice dropped again at the look of pain on his face at the mention of war. "He came back last week and now they've moved to South Park."

Finally they reached the house and she squeezed his hand as they crossed the yard. "I'll get the baby. My landlady is watching her for me." She hurried inside, certain that the sight of his daughter would drive from his haunted eyes whatever nightmare still plagued him.

Marie gurgled and cooed as they approached Eric, whose eyes widened curiously. Sara followed his gaze, trying to see Marie through his eyes, and knowing he saw a child who looked more Indian than white. She waited, breath bated, as they walked around the side of the house to their apartment.

What could possibly have changed him so much? she wondered wildly.

She expected him to reach out and scoop the child into his arms, but he merely stared at her, saying nothing. Sara tried to push aside the swift hurt that rose within her, knowing she must give him time.

"What's her name?" he finally asked.

"I named her Elsie Marie after my mother, but I call her Marie. I hope you like the name."

He shrugged. "Of course." He reached out to open the door to the apartment and glanced back at the child. "She looks like you," he said, as they stepped inside.

"But she has some of your ways," she

pointed out.

He sank into a chair, as though he were too weary to stand.

"Want to hold her?" she asked.

"Not now," he said quietly.

Sara fought the tears rising to her eyes, knowing she must be calm; she must try to make him feel comfortable with her again.

"Eric, how is your family?" she asked.

He dropped his head and stared at his hands, folded in his lap. "There is no family."

"What?" she gasped. "Oh Eric, what's happened?"

She hurried to place Marie in her bed with a favorite toy then, quickly crossed the room and knelt beside him, her hand on his.

"Eric, tell me everything that's happened," she pleaded softly.

A haunted expression surfaced in his blue eyes as he looked over her head, staring for a moment in space. "I was shot from my horse in Kentucky one dark night. . . ."

"You were wounded?" she gasped.

He nodded. "A group of Confederates saved my life, then drafted me into their cavalry. I fought in Kentucky until we were taken prisoner." His jaw tensed as he stared into space. "We managed to escape from prison, and that's when I headed for Georgia. The war was almost over . . . the South was going down in defeat." His voice trailed away as he lost himself in thought. Sara squeezed his hand, saying nothing, waiting for him to continue. "When I reached Pine Hill, I learned that my brothers had been killed in battle, my mother had died. . . . And Pine Hill had been sold."

Sara was stunned by the horrible news, and for a minute she felt the numbness that seemed to envelope Eric.

"Eric," she rasped, looking into his sorrow-filled eyes and seeing the look of one who has seen such great pain that he is haunted by it.

"I should have been there," he said, his voice suddenly gruff. "I should have gone back sooner. My brothers died fighting while I—" He broke off, and when he looked back at her, there was more than pain in his eyes, there was anger.

She swallowed, wondering exactly what he was thinking. Then her eyes drifted to Marie, playing in her bed. Did he blame the baby, and her, for delaying him? If so, that was cruel and unfair. He simply wasn't thinking rationally.

"I'm so sorry," she said, trying to hold her tears. "It hasn't been easy for me, either."

"No, I'm sure it hasn't."

"But we'll put all this tragedy behind us. We've been through some bad times, but we have each other, and we have Marie!" She lifted his hand and pressed it to her lips. The tears she'd fought to control filled her eyes and streamed down her cheeks. "I've missed you so much, Eric."

"I've missed you, too," he said, and for a moment her hopes began to rise as she glimpsed a raw longing on his face as his eyes dropped to her breasts. Sara felt her heart beating faster as desire warmed her, and she waited for him to say or do something that would invite her back into his arms.

Instead, his eyes strayed from her to the small kitchen. "Is there any coffee?" he asked.

"What?" She blinked, wiping her tears away. "Oh. Yes, of course. Come to the table and I'll fix you something to eat," she said, still holding his hand. She stood, waiting for him to rise from the chair. He moved slowly, almost feebly, but Sara tried to remain optimistic.

He seated himself at the table while she heated the coffee and rumaged through the cabinet, pulling down a loaf of bread and some cheese. She poured a cup of strong coffee and placed it before him.

"Darling, I'm so glad you're home," she said.

A faint smile crossed his lips and he nodded. "So am I."

While he ate, she fed Marie, then put her nightgown on and prepared her for bed. As she smoothed Marie's silken curls, she remembered the sorrow she and Eric had felt when she lost their first baby. He had stood with tears in his eyes, telling her how much he wanted a baby.

Now he had one, and it didn't seem to matter. She looked into Marie's cherubic face and smiled sadly. *He will come to love you as much as I do*, she thought, pressing a kiss to the rosy cheek as she tucked her in bed.

Right now he seemed incapable of feeling anything. She turned from the baby and glanced back at Eric. He was wearily making his way across the room to the bed.

She was stabbed with pain at the sight of his gaunt body, his tortured eyes. How could she help him? What could she do?

Her instincts told her simply to let him heal, to help however she could but to make no demands of him.

Perhaps time would work things out.

He had unbuttoned his shirt and was peeling it from his thin chest. Her eyes fell on the deep scar at his side and she gasped.

"Eric"—she crossed the room and gently touched the scar—"it was a bad wound, wasn't it?"

He glanced down impassively. "Not bad enough to kill me."

Her fingers traced the six-inch scar. "Oh my darling," she said, and threw her arms around his neck, pressing her lips to his, aware more than ever before how close she had come to losing him.

His lips moved lightly against hers and his arm wrapped around her waist, but when she pressed her breasts against his bare chest, his hold slackened.

He drew back from her and smiled sadly. "I'm pretty tired. Maybe I'd better get some rest."

"Of course," she mumbled, reaching out to pull the covers back on the bed. "You're much too thin, Eric. Your body needs time to heal," she said, as he stepped out of his trousers and crawled into bed. Almost as soon as his head touched the pillow, he was asleep.

Later, after she'd eaten and cleaned up the kitchen, Sara undressed and crawled in bed beside Eric. Feeling the weight of his body on the other side of the bed that had been empty for so long brought a rush of joy to her heart. She closed her eyes and drifted off to sleep, thankful that Eric had come back to her.

She awoke the next morning to find him lying on his side, his chin propped in his hand, as he stared at her.

"Good morning." She smiled, reaching for him.

"Good morning," he said, returning her smile. His eyes looked rested, and the relaxed grin had returned to his face.

Sara's hopes soared as she wrapped her arms around his neck and pulled his mouth down to hers. The kiss quickly changed from one of tenderness to one of passion, but as Sara's mouth moved hungrily against his, she suddenly realized, with a start, that he was no longer responding. Sara leaned back and looked at him curiously.

He closed his eyes and sank against the pillow.

"Eric"—she touched his cheek and he opened his eyes again—"do you still love me . . . or have your feelings changed? Be honest with me."

His eyes held that strangely haunted look. "I still love you," he sighed.

"I'm glad. I was beginning to wonder if—"

"But I can't make love to you. I don't know why. . . ."

The words shocked her. If he loved her, why couldn't he respond? She swallowed, pressing her head against his shoulder. "You've been through a terrible ordeal," she reasoned. "It will take time for your body—and your mind—to heal. But we'll work it out. We've always been able to work things out."

But she was beginning to wonder as her body, starved for him, ached and throbbed and the blood ran hot in her veins. Eric, in contrast, lay cool and unresponsive.

She turned her head on the pillow and looked at him. A thick strand of blonde hair lay across his forehead. The deep lines around his eyes were like gashes, more pronounced by the loss of weight. And by so much pain. She sighed as her eyes moved down the slender nose, across the brown beard, and came to rest on the chiseled lips, slightly parted.

She pressed her lips together, fighting the urge to kiss him until he reached for her . . . whenever that was. Her eyes trailed down the bronze chest, lightly furred with golden hair, and ended on the deep scar at his side. Her heart twisted. She was lucky to have him back, even if he were scarred as deeply within as without. She'd help him heal, she silently vowed. She'd be loving and patient with him.

She closed her eyes, remembering the day he had come to Bear Claw's camp and traded a gold nugget for her. He had been kind and patient with her, through the trip back to the post, during the ordeal with Ernest Jackson and the loss of her mother.

She took a deep breath, remembering how tender and gentle he had been when first he made love to her, and the times he had held her in his arms after one of her nightmares.

Once before he'd helped her heal. Now she would do the same for him.

As the days passed, Eric seemed to grow stronger physically, but his vagueness and his reserve did not change. Nor did his inability to make love to her. Sara tried to be patient, but it was becoming more and more difficult when he refused to go to town with her or even to go out for a walk. All he could do was sit and stare out the window.

When, she wondered, would he snap out of this?

Sometimes Marie would crawl across the floor and tug and his leg, and Sara, watching covertly from the kitchen, kept hoping Eric would reach down and lift the baby into his arms, or show some kind of affection. He never did. It seemed as if Marie did not exist to him, for he managed to ignore her completely. That, more than anything else, tore at Sara's heart, and she began to wonder how much further her patience would stretch.

A week after Eric's arrival, there was a firm knock on their door, and Sara opened the door to a young Indian couple. She smiled.

"Good Morning."

They nodded. The man spoke in broken English, conveying an invitation to her and her family to visit Bear Claw's village when the sun rose again. It was the time of the Mamaqui Mowats, the spring celebration, and Bear

Claw and Wild Eagle wished her presence for this occasion.

Sara listened, her eyes widening in surprise, her heart leaping with joy.

"Yes, we'll come." She nodded, smiling at the couple. "Thank you."

After she closed the door and turned to Eric, her happy smile faded. A frown creased his brow and she could read the disapproval on his face.

"I don't want to go," he said flatly.

His stubborn attitude on an occasion that could be so special for her sparked her temper. She tossed down her apron, her patience snapping. "That's too bad," she said, "because Marie and I are going." She stormed across the room to lift Marie from her bed. "As a matter of fact, we're getting out of this house for some sunshine and fresh air. If you want to remain in here, sulking like a prisoner" —she saw the shock then pain her words brought but she couldn't stop—"just suit yourself. But I didn't die in the war, Eric, nor did Marie. We intend to be happy despite your gloom and pessimism."

With the baby in her arms, she crossed the room and threw the front door open.

"I'm going to the stable for Darkfire. If you don't want to come with us, then Marie and I will go alone."

With that announcement, she slammed the door, never once looking back as they headed for town.

Eric stumbled to the door and flung it open. Anger seared through his veins as he glared after the slim, proud figure in the worn calico dress as she hurried down the road. He could see Marie's little face bobbing at Sara's shoulder, her eyes fixed on the house.

He cursed and dropped his head. He hated the man he was now; he'd do anything to break through the frozen numbness that paralyzed him, but he didn't know how. He still loved Sara, even though he'd hoped his love, like his spirit, had died. It would have made everything easier for both of them.

But he did love her; he'd known that the moment he looked into her oval face and saw her love for him shining deep in her eyes. And yet he couldn't touch her the way he once had. His manhood would not respond. It was as though the bullet had struck him *there*, leaving him forever scarred. How could he live with this? H*ow*?

He slammed the door and leaned against it, a cold sweat breaking over his face. He couldn't let her go riding off alone to Bear Claw's village. There were too many dangerous men lurking along the road now, both Indians and whites. If she were determined to go, he'd have to go with her. And they'd need another horse. But he was poor now; he couldn't even afford to buy a horse! And he couldn't force himself to get out and look for a job.

Another wave of anger lashed through him. He knew Sara was struggling to keep food on the table; he had no idea how she continued to stretch the meager salary she'd saved. Their last two meals had been bread, jam and

water, yet she hadn't complained or nagged
him to get out of his sulks and find work!

He began to pace the room, feeling weak
and nauseated again. He fought the desire to
sink back into the chair and stare into space.
The only thing that stopped him was a vision
of Sara and Marie riding down a deserted
road on Darkfire, and some thief waiting in the
woods to capture them.

He headed for the door, his mind returning
for the first time to the memory of the days
he'd lived in Colorado City and made friends.
He'd find out if those friendships meant
anything. And he'd start with Bull at the
stable. Maybe he could get a horse on credit,
or maybe he could simply borrow one. . . .

25

The mellow notes of a flute trilled through the soft night breeze beyond Star and Eagle's lodge, and their breathing grew ragged as their nude bodies pressed together in need.

"Star," he moaned, dropping his lips to nip at the taut little nipple that swelled against his tongue. He suckled gently as his arms slipped under her body and her rounded belly pressed against his manhood.

He could feel the little life stirring inside her body, and it always ignited in him a feeling so gentle, yet so fierce, that he never ceased to be amazed. He stopped suckling her breast and looked at her soft brown skin stretched over the mound of the baby.

"The little one interferes," he chuckled, lowering his head to her belly. He nuzzled against her, waiting for another movement, and he felt it against his cheek. His heart leapt with joy as he turned his lips to the soft, warm flesh and kissed the spot where the baby had moved. He waited, but the movement ceased and his desire began to build again as Star wiggled against him, her hand lifting his face so that she could smile into his eyes.

"Mmmm . . ." He pressed kisses to her ribs,

her waist, her breasts, the hollow of her neck while she trembled beneath his fiery mouth. When his mouth settled over hers again, her legs spread for him, and he slipped inside of her and began to move gently. She moaned and lifted her legs to wrap around his waist as her arms encircled his back.

"Not so tight, little one," he moaned. "We'll crowd our papoose."

She relaxed her hold, though her breathing quickened as his thrusts became more persistent. Soon they were spiraling into the night, lost in the erotic wail of the flute and their own sweet, rapturous moans as they rediscovered the exquisite ecstasy that always bound their souls as one.

The next day the village was busy with preparations for the Mamaqui Mowats. The squaws were gathering six-foot tree limbs to make the enclosure for the dance. Eagle's thoughts lingered on the woman who claimed to be his sister, the woman who had come to the jail and told her story. He believed her now, for there was no reason for her to have lied. And the Sheriff said the palefaces had shunned her because of this admission.

"You are very quiet," Star observed as she led their son back into the lodge for his nap. Shane Shavano was growing more like his father each day, Star decided, in the way he held his head high, asserting his proud, independent nature. And the papoose growing inside her would be strong and proud as well. She glanced back at her husband.

"Are you anxious about meeting your sister?"

Eagle frowned, pulling himself up from the mat to stroll outside and see what was taking place. "Why should I be anxious?"

An amused smile lifted Star's mouth. "It's to be expected. You said she was married to a man who had gone back to the war, didn't you?"

He nodded. "He traded a nugget for her." His lips curled bitterly. "She was not happy here in this village; she preferred a life with the paleface!"

Star heard the anger rising in his voice and she tried to soothe him. "We don't know how she felt at the time. If she had been raised in the white world, maybe she was afraid of . . ."

"I was raised in the white world!" he snapped. "'Even if she is my sister, there can be no peace between us as long as she is married to the paleface. Never again will I try to be friends with the palefaces. If not for Kit Carson, I would be dead now!"

"Kit Carson is a paleface," Star pointed out softly.

He stormed from the lodge, never acknowledging her reply. Star watched him go, her dark eyes holding an expression of sadness. It was so hard for Eagle to trust anyone, or even be rational now where the palefaces were concerned. There was so much anger and bitterness inside him.

She smoothed little Shane's unruly dark hair back from his face as he dropped to his mat. Star knew that Eagle had thought of his sister often since his return; she sensed it in his brooding silences. Little Dove had come forward to help Eagle at her own risk, and Star was looking forward to meeting her. She just prayed that Eagle would be friendly to her.

By mid-afternoon the celebration was in full swing. Inside the circular enclosure, walled with tall limbs, couples danced the Bear Dance to the slow beat of the drum. Five musicians were repeating the bear chant, and as Eagle listened, the music seemed to fire his blood. He called to Star and motioned her to join him.

They walked inside and lined up opposite each other and began the simple dance—three steps forward, three steps backward. Drums and flutes swelled, and the voice of an Indian maiden rose above the other chanters in a high, tantalizing wail. Star and Eagle fell easily into the rhythm, and Eagle closed his eyes, letting the wild rhythm flow through him.

Their feet made swift, stamping sounds upon the ground, and at first they did not notice the approach of the two horses riding slowly into the village. But then one of the older squaws began to exclaim loudly. Star glanced toward the road, and her eyes widened in surprise.

"Eagle, she is here," she said, clutching his arm.

Eagle frowned, holding back. "I do not wish to greet her now."

Star glared at him. It was one of the rare occasions when she became angry at her husband. "Then I will!" she snapped. "And I expect you to be friendly to her!"

She whirled and flew out of the enclosure and hurried toward the couple who were glancing cautiously about the village as their horses stopped on the edge of the meadow.

Sara sat rigid on her mount as they turned their horses into the wide meadow that held the village of buckskin lodges. So much had changed since Eric traded for her and took her away. Her eyes swept the circle of lodges, and it seemed to her there were fewer. The hard freeze of winter had gripped the village when first she came here, adding to the somber feeling, but now it was summer. The mood was different. There was a festive air to the village, drums and flutes played cheerfully, and she could see people gathered in groups, laughing and talking.

She glanced down at her simple dark calico dress. She had plaited her hair in a single braid that fell down her back, and the sun had darkened her skin. She knew she looked more like a Ute woman on this day than she had on the occasion of her first arrival.

Marie wiggled in her arms and she glanced nervously at the child. Sara had dressed her in a white dress and bonnet, accenting her dark eyes and hair. The little girl tilted her head back and cooed happily and Sara bent down to kiss her cheek. These were Marie's relatives, the only ones she would know, now that . . .

Her eyes drifted to Eric. He sat tall in the saddle, wearing the plain clothes he had worn on his arrival. While he had agreed to come, he had stubbornly refused to buy any new clothes, even though Sara was willing to stretch the little money she had left. She hadn't argued with Eric, and the ride had been pleasant. He seemed to appreciate the beauty of the landscape, and she had tried to carry on a pleasant conversation. To her surprise, he had joined in, glancing often at Marie. This, too, was a departure from his usual behavior.

As they approached the lodges, a small Indian woman with long black hair and small features in a pointed face waved to them. She was wearing a white doeskin dress with pretty beading.

"Welcome," she called to them. "I am Star of the Morning, Wild Eagle's wife."

Sara smiled at Star. "I'm glad to meet you. I'm Sara Christensen. This is Marie, our daughter, and Eric, my husband."

"Welcome," Star repeated.

One of the braves had rushed up to take their horses, and as Sara looked around, she saw Bear Claw striding forward to meet them.

Sara tensed as the man approached, and she recalled how angry he had been with her that last day.

Eric had dropped from his horse and walked forward to greet him.

"How!" Eric said, lifting his arm.

"How!" Bear Claw repeated, jerking his head in a firm nod.

Sara stared at the bronzed chief—*her uncle*—unable to move or speak. She still saw no resemblance to herself or Eagle in his large blunt features, but that no longer mattered.

He took another step and his big lips slid into a cautious grin as his dark eyes rested on her. "How!" he said.

She smiled. "How."

Eric reached up for Marie as Sara dismounted. Bear Claw's deep-set eyes moved to the dark-haired baby girl dressed in white.

"How old is the papoose?" he asked.

"When the moon is round, she will be one winter," Sara responded, her eyes lingering on Eric as he held his daughter. It was the first time this had occurred, and she noticed that he was looking at her a little differently. She thought she saw a gleam of pride in his eyes.

"She is like Little Dove," Bear Claw said, his eyes slowly returning to Sara.

"And just as stubborn, I fear," Sara replied, meeting his gaze evenly.

A moment of silence hung between them as Bear Claw grinned again. The deep lines of his face crinkled, and Sara discovered that he no longer seemed such a terrifying warrior. Had he changed that much? She thought it was more likely that she was seeing him through the eyes of experience now. She was no longer a frightened young girl unwilling to accept anything beyond the limited world she had known.

She sensed someone walking up to join them, and her eyes moved to Wild Eagle. He looked from her to Eric to their baby and nodded.

"I am glad you could come," he finally spoke. Though the words were an attempt to be cordial, there was no warmth in his dark eyes, and his tone was stiff and formal.

"Thank you," she said. "This is my husband, Eric Christensen, and our daughter, Marie. Eric, this is my brother. . . ."

A strange expression flickered in Eagle's eyes as he heard her words. Even Bear Claw seemed to relax his formidable stance.

Eric extended his hand. "Glad to meet you."

Eagle hesitated, his dark eyes shooting to Star before he slowly extended his hand.

The handshake was firm, but there was a wariness in his face before he dropped Eric's hand and glanced at Sara. "I wish to thank you for speaking to the Sheriff. It helped," he added quietly.

"Come," Bear Claw's voice boomed over them. "We smoke the pipe of peace."

Eric handed Marie to Sara as he followed Eagle and Bear Claw back to the center lodge.

"We have a little brave," Star was saying. "His name is Shane Shavano, after my father, who was killed in battle, and after Eagle, who was called Shane by the people who adopted him."

"I see." Sara smiled at the friendly young Indian woman, grateful that she was trying so hard to make her feel welcome.

"And we expect another papoose when the leaves turn gold."

Sara smiled at her. "I am happy for you." For a moment, she thought of Eric's attitude toward Marie, and she couldn't help wondering if there would be more children, particularly since he was unable to make love to her. She suppressed a sigh and glanced toward the center of the village.

Star followed her eyes. "They are doing the Bear Dance. It is our best dance and is usually reserved for spring, or for special celebrations. Today is special," she added softly, "because you have come home."

A sad smile touched Sara's face as she turned to look at Star again. "You are very kind. I appreciate it."

Star touched her arm. "Please try to understand Eagle. He has been hurt so many times by the white people. It is hard for him to trust, but time will take care of everything. I am certain."

"I hope so," Sara sighed, thinking of Eric as well. She glanced back at the dancers. "There was a brave named White Buffalo who wanted me," she remembered. "Eric traded a gold nugget to Bear Claw in order to save me from White Buffalo."

"Do not worry," Star laughed softly. "White Buffalo now belongs to Bear Woman, the largest squaw in the village. He will not bother you, for Bear Woman will beat him if he misbehaves!"

Marie began to coo, and Star looked at her affectionately. "She is so pretty, and she looks like you!"

Sara's smiled faded. "I know. I wish she looked more like her father. Maybe then . . ."

Star saw the expression of sadness on Sara's face, and she longed to ask questions that would help her understand this sadness. She wanted to help if she could, but it was too soon to pry. Star knew she must not rush their friendship. In time Sara would trust her enough to share confidences with her.

"I hope to have a little girl like Marie," Star said, staring admiringly at the enchanting child.

"I hope you do," Sara said, hugging Marie. "She has been such a blessing to me."

They had walked slowly toward the center of the village as they talked, and now a small boy came bounding toward them, the mischief of play bright in his eyes.

"This is Shane," Star said, kneeling beside him. "Look Shane, you have a cousin. Her name is Marie."

Shane's dark eyes flew over Marie, widening as she gurgled and cooed and gave him a big smile.

"And this is your Aunt Sara. We will have him address you that way, as this is your custom."

"It doesn't matter," Sara began, but she was quickly interrupted by a group of older squaws who came rushing up with eager, friendly smiles. The only one she recognized was Owl Woman, who grinned and began to babble in her native tongue.

Star turned to Sara. "They want to take Shane and Marie with them to the first lodge. They are entertaining two little ones whose parents are dancing."

Automatically, Sara's hold tightened on Marie. She knew, however, that she must not appear distrustful; she was far too anxious to win their friendship.

"All right." Sara forced a smile and slowly handed Marie over to Owl Woman.

"Go with them, Shane," Star instructed. "Help take care of your little cousin."

Shane bounded off with the group and Sara had to force her attention toward the dance in order to conceal her reluctance to let go of Marie.

"This is the only dance that belongs to our people," Star explained. "The older squaws tell of a brave who dreamed he discovered a bear still in his winter sleep. It was spring and the brave knew the bear had slept long enough and would be needing food, so the brave awoke him. They became friends, and the bear took him deep into the woods, where all the bears were dancing to celebrate the end of their long sleep. The brave learned this special dance and brought it back to his people."

Suddenly a squaw appeared with a long stick, holding something in her hand that puzzled Sara.

"What is she carrying?" she whispered to Star.

"The jaw bone of an animal. It is supposed to symbolize the growl of the bear. She will drag the stick over the bone and provide another kind of rhythm. Do these things seem strange to you, Sara?"

"No. Not any stranger than some things I have witnessed in town."

Dusk was falling over the village as late afternoon gave way to evening. Sara glanced over her shoulder at the center lodge, where

Eric was smoking the peace pipe with Bear Claw and Eagle. She prayed things were going well. Turning back to the dancers, she crossed her arms and sighed with relief. So far, she felt comfortable here. Perhaps their visit would somehow close the gap widening between her and Eric. At least he had come with her to the village. He'd even gone to the stable and borrowed an extra horse.

The beat of the music reached out to her and she began to tap her feet, glancing at Star with a smile.

Meanwhile, Eric sat in Bear Claw's lodge inhaling the pungent tobacco smoke through the clay pipe. Bear Claw was telling the story of a brave who had been killed by a mountain lion the previous winter, and Eric listened intently, grateful to sit quietly rather than participate in the conversation. It gave him a chance to grow accustomed to the Ute ways again, and he was surprised at how easily he began to relax.

Eagle regarded him from time to time with darting glances. His hostility was as apparent as the smoke drifting over the lodge. Eric wondered if there was any hope of breaking through this hard shell of bitterness; it would take time and patience, he decided—or some kind of miracle.

He realized that Bear Claw had asked a question about the war, and Eric hesitated. It was the last thing he wanted to talk about, but he must make an effort to maintain their friendship.

"It was a hard fight," he finally replied.

Briefly he told of riding with Morgan's raiders, of the bloody fights and narrow escapes with death. He ended with a statement of his capture, then the escape from prison.

"How did you escape?" Eagle asked quietly. It was the first time he had spoken.

Eric looked at him through the haze of smoke from his pipe.

"We dug a tunnel underground with spoons stolen from the kitchen.

Eagle's eyes widened in surprise. "How long did that take?"

Eric stared at the low fire for a moment, remembering the many sleepless nights. He sighed. "About three months."

Eagle and Bear Claw exchanged glances, though neither replied. Eagle leaned back on the mat and sucked his pipe. The look in his eyes had changed from suspicion and distrust to a kind of begrudging respect.

Suddenly, hoarse cries and thundering hooves pierced the flute music and the drums. The men leapt to their feet. Under the cover of darkness, the Arapahoes had attacked. Gunfire from stolen muskets exploded into the shocked village; arrows sailed through the air. The attack stunned the Ute warriors momentarily, but then they were crawling on their bellies for weapons or leaping headlong to seize the feet of the riders circling the village and shouting war cries.

The terrified screams of the women rose above the thundering hooves and the boom of the guns. Eric quickly realized that the

Arapahoes were not good marksmen with their stolen weapons, but fear clutched his heart as his eyes raced over the chaotic scene in search of Sara and Marie. The women had already taken cover, but just as he felt a sense of relief, he saw Sara run from the first lodge with Marie in her arms.

For a moment, terror paralyzed him as he realized the danger she was in among the thundering riders. A cold sweat broke over his brow as he lifted his gun and aimed for the Arapaho riding toward her. The crack of the gun jerked the rider backward.

"Sara, get inside!" he shouted. Then he saw a small Indian boy tugging at her skirts, and she leaned down to lift him in her arms.

Eagle and Bear Claw had taken up firing positions behind a log used as a long seat before the fire.

The night was a cloud of smoke from fire and rifles and dust kicked up by the circling horses. Sara was running toward a lodge where other squaws had gathered, their faces frozen in shock and fear as they peered through the flap.

Dodging gunfire, Eric ran after her. He had almost reached her when a horse ran him down, and a tomahawk sailed past, missing his head by mere inches. Eric lunged for the tomahawk when it hit the ground, but as he grasped it a woman screamed and chills riveted down his spine, for he knew it was Sara. That pitiful scream pierced his heart, jarring him from the state of shock that had imprisoned him for the past weeks. He reacted now with the speed and accuracy of the good soldier he had been as he hurled the tomahawk into the neck of the rider just ahead of him. The Arapaho toppled from his horse and Eric sought Sara again, before he almost stumbled over her crumpled body.

He stared down in horror at her still form. In that split second the lifeless man he had been the past days rose in his memory, and as he fell at her side, he knew he would put a gun to his own heart if she were dead, if he never had a chance to make up to her for the pain he had caused.

Relief, like a strong gust of wind, shook him as she moved. Gently, he touched her. Dust covered her face, yet it scarcely obscured the bruise forming on her cheek.

"Sara! Are you all right?" he asked, lifting her into his arms.

Tears filled her eyes and flowed down her cheeks. "Eric, they took Marie and Shane!"

Eric looked through the haze of dust and gunfire to the horses thundering across the meadow.

Sara was trembling in his arms and he hugged her against his chest and glanced frantically around him. The Utes were racing through the village, firing after the disappearing Arapahoes.

"Don't worry." His eyes narrowed on the distant forms. "We'll get them back. I *promise you.*"

Later, as the warriors met to plan their counterattack, Eric knew he must dissuade them from their plan of striking the Arapahoe village at daybreak. The attack could mean certain death for Marie and Shane. For years the Arapahoes and Cheyenne and Utes had fought bitterly. One attack led to another. His eyes wandered over the group to Eagle, who looked heartsick. How could he convince Eagle, and the others, that there had to be a better way?

He took a deep breath, determined to speak his mind. "As the father of one of the children, I oppose a counterattack on the village," he said.

Some of the warriors understood his words; for those who did not, Eagle translated. Bear Claw's expression was grave as he laid down his pipe and looked at Eric.

"What would you do?" he asked.

Eric took a deep breath, choosing his words carefully. "The mountain men and trappers get along with the Indians by trading with them. That's how I claimed my wife from your village, Bear Claw," he reminded him with a grim smile. "If we offer the Arapahoes something they want, something more valuable to them than the children, I believe they will release Marie and Shane. Since there are no deaths to avenge, I think we should go to their village not to do battle but to trade."

Eagle walked around the campfire to stand beside Eric. "His words are true. Even if we sneak into their village, there will be someone to call a warning. I do not wish to risk my son's life. I say, when the sun is high we trade —and only the two of us will go!"

Eric nodded in agreement. "It is our fight."

"What will you trade?" Bear Claw asked.

Eric thought for a minute. "They need horses. I will trade my horse."

"And mine," Eagle quickly replied.

One of the warriors spoke in Ute; Eagle listened thoughtfully, then turned to Eric.

"He says the squaws will send beads and moccasins." The expression on Eagle's face changed from dismal gloom to radiant hope. "We will go when the sun is high." He looked at Eric. "We will trade, and we will have our children by sunset!" he said, determination animating his features.

Eagle and Eric went to the corral and began to groom their horses. The squaws gathered up trinkets and beads and moccasins to send along. Throughout the village, tension ran high, but everyone worked silently, their faces grim.

Later, Eric stepped inside Eagle's lodge, where Star sat beside Sara. Star had applied salve to Sara's bruised face, and now each woman sought comfort from the other.

"May I speak with Sara alone?" Eric asked.

"Of course," Star replied, smiling at Sara as she left.

Eric sat down beside the bed of animal skins where Sara lay. With the exception of the dark bruises on her cheek and temple, Sara looked deathly pale in the glow of the lantern. Fear mingled with pain in her dark eyes, swollen with tears, but she smiled at Eric.

"Star has told me that you've chosen a peaceful method of getting our children back, and you've persuaded the tribe to let you do it. Perhaps this will mean the end of the battles between the tribes."

Eagle sighed, turning her small hand over in his. "Probably not the end, but it could be a beginning."

They were quiet for a moment, then Eric's deep blue eyes filled with tears as he looked at his wife.

"I'm sorry," he began, but he could say no more as the emotion he had sought to bury began to surface.

Sara wrapped her arms around his neck.

"It's all right," she said, pressing her face against his wet cheek. "Maybe this will be a new beginning for *us*, too," she whispered, as the tears flowed down her face, mingling with his. "This time, when you return with Marie, we'll be a family."

He nodded. "She's a beautiful child and I do love her." He dropped his head to his hands as the agony of those he had loved and lost haunted him anew. But then he thought of Marie, and he knew he had to be strong.

"I've lost so many loved ones," he finally replied, his voice muffled behind his hands. "It seemed safer not to feel anything again." He removed his hands and looked down at her. Sara saw in the deep blue-green eyes, washed clean with tears, the old love surfacing again, the love that had shone so brightly before.

"When I saw you lying in the dust," he continued, "and I thought I'd lost you too . . . when I knew they had taken Marie . . .

there has never been any pain to equal that. . . ."

Sara nodded. "There is a high cost for loving, Eric. We risk heartbreak, but sometimes we have no choice . . . when we truly love."

She leaned forward and pressed her lips to his, and slowly the kiss deepened to a burning need that seared through both of them, and the blood ran hot in their veins.

"Oh Sara, Sara . . ." he moaned, stretching out beside her as his body throbbed with need.

"Eric?" Eagle's voice called from the flap.

For a moment, Eric was unable to respond, though his mind registered the voice and he knew it must be near daylight.

"Eric, we should be leaving soon," Eagle called.

"I'll be right out," he answered as he smoothed Sara's hair back from her face and kissed her forehead. "Don't worry. I'll bring Marie home safely."

"I know you will." She smiled bravely, trying to hide her fears as she watched him go.

Eric and Eagle were silent as they guided their horses down the narrow trail that led from the mountain of red rocks to the Arapaho valley.

The sun was warm on Eagle's face as he glanced up at the cloudless sky, thankful for pleasant weather; then his eyes shifted to the rocky trail before them. He'd been consumed with hate for the whites, but now he realized that the red man could be just as cruel. Stories of how tribes kidnapped children and squaws from other tribes had been common, and he knew these victims were often mistreated.

He sighed. Was there no justice in the world? No kindness among people? What had happened to make people so mean and bitter?

War.

The answer that came to him made him glance covertly at Eric. This man had had to fight against his own race. Sara had confessed to Star that his entire family was dead as a result of the war. He had been taken prisoner. At that thought Eagle's eyes narrowed. His own stay in jail had been the most terrible time of his life. How long had Eric been forced to remain behind bars? he wondered. It had taken him three months just to dig a tunnel!

A begrudging respect had taken root the night before. Now there was a common bond between them. Both had lost their children to the Arapahoes; both would give their lives, if necessary, to save the children. He suddenly realized that he liked the strong, silent man riding beside him, the man whose eyes held so much pain.

He glanced across at Eric. "The Arapahoe village is just over that next hill," he said. "We attacked them last year after they had sneaked into our village and killed three of our men. The last time we came here, Star's father was killed in battle." He sighed. "Let us hope we'll have better luck by trading."

"I think they'll be willing to trade," Eric said, staring into the distance.

"What if they refuse?" Eagle worried.

Eric's eyes traced the distant huddle of lodges. "Then we'll have to think of something else."

Eagle fought the impulse to draw his gun as they approached the village. The lodges were shabby and ill-kept, and some of the Indians still lived in brush huts.

Two warriors emerged, dressed only in loin skins, their guns and tomahawks raised threateningly at the sight of Eric and Eagle.

"Can you speak their language?" Eric asked, studying the men whose faces were filled with hate and vengeance.

"Enough to make them understand what we want," he replied and began to speak in strange, often broken words, pointing to the horses they rode and the goods loaded on the trailing horses.

The Indians fell into excited chatter. Most of the tribe had emerged from their lodges now, staring wide-eyed at Eagle and Eric. One of the men approached Darkfire cautiously, but Eric sat still and calm as the man reached out to stroke the horse's gleaming black neck. the man pointed proudly to the pure white blaze on Darkfire's leg.

Eric did not hesitate to give up his beloved horse for Marie; his only concern was that Darkfire would be treated well. He glanced at Eagle.

"Tell them they must take good care of the horses, or they will not be good mounts," Eric said.

Eagle repeated those words, and the men nodded thoughtfully, then moved to the pack

PASSION'S PEAK

horses to examine the items loaded there. Their faces beamed with approval as they returned to Eric and Eagle, and one of the Arapahoes began to speak to Eagle again.

"He says they will trade," Eagle looked at Eric.

"Are the children all right?" Eric asked.

"I don't know. I've asked to see them before we trade."

Eric took a deep sigh. It had occurred to him more than once that he and Eagle might simply be shot from the horses and the trading forgotten. He was counting on the Arapahoes' sense of honor.

His eyes searched the village, ending on a baby girl wrapped in a blanket in the arms of a squaw. When the little face turned toward Eric, a wide smile tilted her mouth.

Eric's heart leapt at the sight of Marie, and his heart swelled with pride at the knowledge that she recognized him. He dismounted and extended his arms to the child.

One of the warriors turned to the squaw and issued a command; with reluctance the squaw handed Marie over to Eric. He hugged her tightly, kissing her dimpled cheek.

"I love you," he whispered.

A small boy bounded from the end lodge, his face radiant at the sight of Eagle. Eagle swept him into his arms and whispered to him. The child nodded happily.

Behind them, the warriors stood admiring the horses while the squaws began to unload the pack of trinkets, moccasins and beads.

Eric and Eagle glanced at each other with

restrained smiles. It was amazing how easy it had been.

Eagle spoke again to the warriors, who exchanged glances, then nodded agreeably.

Eagle smiled and turned to Eric. "I told them trading was better than fighting, that we should meet to trade rather than to fight. They like the idea. But for now we'd better get the hell out of here!" he added under his breath.

Eric paused to rub Darkfire's neck one last time, then he quickly turned to the smaller horses that would take them home. "Your mother will be glad to see you," he said, smiling into Marie's happy face.

26

The soft summer night vibrated with excitement in Bear Claw's village. Torches flared across the valley, special food was prepared, and the drums and flutes were active again. Little Marie and Shane fell asleep early, however, missing most of the celebration in their honor.

To occupy Star's and Sara's anxious minds during the time Eagle and Eric were gone, the squaws had enlisted their help in a special project. They had built a lodge for Sara and Eric.

Sara and Eric sat together, contentedly watching the dancers, but their eyes kept drifting to each other with growing desire. Marie lay sleeping in Eric's arms and Sara looked down at her with deep gratitude.

"I am so thankful that you got her back," she said. She laid her hand on his arm. "Come. I want to show you the special lodge that was built today."

Eric stood, gently turning Marie in his arms, as his hand clasped Sara's and they walked away from the celebration to the new lodge at the far end of the village.

The paint was still drying on the front of the

lodge, but Eric could see the dove the squaws had lovingly painted on it.

"Little Dove," he said, smiling at his wife.

She nodded and opened the flap, lighting a small torch just inside the door. Eric followed her inside and looked around. The earthen floor was swept clean, and a new doeskin dress hung from a pole. An adjoining pole held a tiny dress and dainty moccasins for Marie.

"I was so touched by their kindness," Sara sighed. "If only it could have been this way the first time I came here."

"But it couldn't," he said. "If you hadn't been trying to escape, we might not have met."

With infinite tenderness, he placed Marie on her small bed of animal skins, then straightened and turned back to Sara.

"You're right!" Sara's eyes widened with the revelation of his words. "Life is strange isn't it Eric?" She thought of how terrified she'd been when she was abducted and brought here the first time, and how relieved when Eric took her away. Now something also had occurred that seemed horrible but had worked a miracle as well. The shock of Marie's abduction had shaken Eric free of the terrible grief that had frozen his emotions.

"Yes, life can be strange," he agreed huskily, "but it can also be wonderful."

He pulled her into his arms and lowered his mouth to her eager lips, tasting her sweetness and moaning with the pleasure of feeling her soft body in his arms.

Sara's heartbeat quickened as he pulled his lips from hers and his eyes dropped hungrily to the swell of her breasts. His hand began to work the buttons lose.

Sara's fingers slipped to his shirt, seeking to do the same.

With amazing speed, their clothing was shed and lay in a careless heap at their feet. Their eyes slipped down their bodies, and Sara reached out to gently touch the deep scar on his side.

"I love you," she whispered, looking into his passion-filled eyes.

"And I love you," he sighed. "We've been to hell and back, but it's over now." He pulled her tightly against him, enjoying the feel of her soft skin pressed against him. "We're free to begin again."

"And it will be a wonderful new life," she said, wrapping her arms around him and tilting her head back as his mouth covered hers again.

Passion too long denied seized them as the drums pounded and the notes of the flute danced on the evening breeze, delivering its erotic wail to their lodge. His tongue thrust into the silken depths of her mouth and she responded with equal passion. In the next instant they were stretched on their soft furry bed and in the mellow glow of the torch, their bodies entwined in burning desire.

Eric lifted her full breast, staring at the nipple tightening beneath his thumb. Then his eyes moved on, seeking the perfection of her creamy body, devouring the stomach less flat than before but even more pleasing now, for she had carried his child in it. He reached down to touch the silky V of her womanhood as his eyes traveled over the long, fine-toned legs.

As he touched and caressed her, his lips tugged gently at her nipple and Sara could not withhold a gasp of pleasure. She lowered her head to kiss his thick blonde hair while her fingers boldly explored his strong, firm body. Now they moved and breathed as one, giving as much pleasure as they were taking.

When Eric parted her legs and eased into the tightness of her body, Sara's face did not reflect the momentary pain she felt. It had been so long that it was almost like the first time again.

Then, as Eric began to move gently within her, her body relaxed and grew accustomed to the pleasure of his lovemaking. Her arms encircled his back, pulling him closer as their lips melded together in burning kisses while their bodies flamed with desire. They murmured love words as waves of pleasure began deep in their bellies and radiated outward. The waves grew stronger, deeper, cresting through them with a ferocity that wrenched them into a mindless explosion of passion.

They cried out in the intensity of this passion that was so strong it shook them to the core of their being. Then slowly the waves ebbed away, taking with them the tension that had gripped their bodies and leaving them with only a sweet, deep contentment. They lay on their sides, staring with wonder into each other's drowsy eyes. Neither spoke; neither wished to break this sacred spell.

Eric lifted a hand to cup Sara's face as he silently marveled at this soft and beautiful woman who had continued to love him through all the problems and pain.

"You and Marie are my family now, and you are all I need. I will never leave you again," he whispered, as his lips closed over hers again.

They made love again and again, and finally slept, their bodies entwined in total contentment.

The next morning Sara was the first to awake, and she slipped quietly from the bed. Marie was curled in a little ball and Sara smiled affectionately as she crept past the baby and pulled the doeskin dress from the pole. Today she would be Little Dove; she would enjoy and appreciate her Ute heritage.

She slipped the dress over her head and moulded it in place with her slim fingers. She glanced down at the dress, admiring the beaded design of a dove, then thrust her feet into the soft moccasins. When she glanced across at Eric, she saw that he had awakened and was lying there watching her.

"Good morning." She leaned down to press a kiss to his stubbly cheek. "How do I look in my new dress?"

His sleepy eyes focused on the dress and he woke fully as his gaze traced the curves and hollows of her body. He grinned. "You look like a woman I'd like to make love to."

She laughed softly as she dropped down beside him. "Oh Eric, I'm so happy," she said, her dark eyes dancing.

"Good morning," Eagle called from outside the flap. "Do you want to walk to the soda springs with Star and me?"

They glanced at each other and Eric nodded.

"Yes, we'll be out in a minute," Sara answered.

Later, while Owl Woman kept Marie, the two couples walked across the grassy meadow admiring the view of sweeping mountains, red rock foothills and silver puffs of clouds on an azure sky.

"What a perfect morning," Sara sighed, slipping her hand into the crook of Eric's arm. She leaned her head against his shoulder, suddenly remembering their passionate lovemaking, and the joy and beauty of being together again.

A few feet away, Eagle and Star seemed to be enveloped in their own special world as well.

"Will you make a wish for the little one?" Eagle whispered as they walked toward the bubbling fountain.

"Perhaps," Star said, smiling into his happy face.

The cooling mist from the springs drifted out to meet them as they approached. Eric stepped onto a large, smooth boulder, then extended his hand to Sara so they could look deep into the transparent water. The sun sparkled over them, highlighting their reflections there.

"You must leave something here," Star called to them as she dropped her beaded necklace into the water. "Then the Great Spirit will honor the wish you make today."

Sara smiled as she looked from Star to Eagle, who was dropping his elk-tooth necklace into the water.

Eric reached into his pocket and withdrew a coin. He tossed it through the air and the sunlight caught its silver gleam for a brief second before it rippled downward in the crystal water.

Sara reached into her pocket. "I knew we would come here, and so I brought something special from my trunk, something I have treasured over the years. She withdrew the cameo pin that had belonged to Elsie Jackson.

Eric's hand touched hers. "Are you sure?"

She nodded as Eagle and Star stood silently watching.

"This belonged to the woman who adopted me," she explained. She stared for a moment at the small pin. "It is the best gift I can leave, for Elsie Jackson was a wonderful woman. This is a symbol of strength and courage and love, the qualities that made her special."

She lifted the cameo pin and tossed it toward the fountain. The tiny ivory face spiraled downward and sliced the smooth water.

There was a moment of reverent silence as the four people watched the cameo drift through the water and finally come to rest on a tiny rock.

And that is my wish," Sara spoke softly, "that all people have the strength and courage and love that is needed to live life well."

"And I wish for our children that this strength and courage and love will fill their lives," Star said, "and that they will know great happiness and peace."

The men stood silent, not wanting to divulge their wishes, though both women turned questioning eyes to them.

"I've heard wishes don't come true if they're told," Eric said in reply to their inquisitive faces.

"Not today," Sara teased. "Today they come true only if they're voiced aloud, to be sure the Great Spirit hears."

Eric relented with a deep sigh. "All right, I'll tell. I wish to live in South Park and raise cattle as we do in the South. Mining is no longer a dependable means of livelihood. Most of the gold has been taken. I want to have some land, raise cattle, raise chldren. . . ."

Eagle and Star were whispering together, their faces reflecting surprise.

"What is it?" Sara asked.

Star looked from Sara to Eric with a bright smile. "This is what Eagle wished too. That we could return to the mountains and move farther west."

"I want to work the land," Eagle admitted quietly. "The time has come when we can no longer depend on hunting alone to provide our food."

"That would fill an important need for the families moving into South Park," Eric quickly assured him.

Sara nodded encouragingly. "That's a wonderful idea. Maybe we could all . . ." Her eyes moved from Star to Eric, meeting pleased smiles. She turned to Eagle, who was still measuring them cautiously. Then a slow grin began to break over his face, lighting his dark eyes with a radiant glow.

"Life will be good again. We will make it so," he said.

Eric nodded, extending his hand to Eagle. "We will be family," he said.

There was no longer any hesitation as Eagle gripped his hand firmly.

"Family." He nodded, glancing at Sara who stood with tears sparkling on her dark lashes.

"Family," she repeated softly, her eyes drifting back to the cameo resting on the rock far down in the bubbling waters. "And together we'll work hard to make life good for our families."

Eric hugged Sara to his side as Eagle and Star clasped hands and smiled. Eagle's eyes drifted toward the sky, and he suddenly thought of the person who had suffered to give them birth, whose spirit would now rejoice.

"I think," he said, looking at the three people beside him, "that Crying Wind would be pleased."

Make the Most of Your Leisure Time with
LEISURE BOOKS

Please send me the following titles:

Quantity	Book Number	Price
_____	_____	_____
_____	_____	_____
_____	_____	_____
_____	_____	_____
_____	_____	_____

If out of stock on any of the above titles, please send me the alternate title(s) listed below:

_____	_____	_____
_____	_____	_____
_____	_____	_____
_____	_____	_____

Postage & Handling _____

Total Enclosed $ _____

☐ Please send me a free catalog.

NAME _____
(please print)

ADDRESS _____

CITY _____ STATE _____ ZIP _____

Please include $1.00 shipping and handling for the first book ordered and 25¢ for each book thereafter in the same order. All orders are shipped within approximately 4 weeks via postal service book rate. PAYMENT MUST ACCOMPANY ALL ORDERS.*

*Canadian orders must be paid in US dollars payable through a New York banking facility.

Mail coupon to: **Dorchester Publishing Co., Inc.
6 East 39 Street, Suite 900
New York, NY 10016
Att: ORDER DEPT.**